LOLA KING

GIVING AWAY

STONEVIEW STORIES BOOK 2

First edition

Cover art by Outlined with Love Designs

This book was professionally typeset on Reedsy.
Find out more at reedsy.com

To my King. You are my inspiration, my love, my life. Without you, I'd only be Lola. Here's to forever together. 🥂

'Joseph,' lui cria-t-elle, 'il est des moments qui durent pour l'éternité.' Il aquiesça de la tête et lui offrit le plus beau des sourires.

Véronique Chouraqui

Contents

TRIGGER WARNING

This book is not recommended to readers under the age of 18. This is a dark bully romance and contains dubcon sexual scenes, bullying scenes, age difference, drug use, mention of child abuse, and other scenes that some readers may find triggering. Jake is not a hero and some characters in this series are unredeemable. If this is something you are not comfortable with, please do not go any further.

This book ends in a cliff-hanger! Jake and Jamie's story is *still* not quite over...

Enjoy!

Lots of love,
Lola ♥

PROLOGUE

Angels & Demons – jxdn

Jamie

When I was a little girl, I used to dream of an evil man taking me away to his cave. I never knew why me. What did I do to deserve this? He would keep me as his hostage, and I would desperately wait for prince charming to come and save me. My prince, he was tall, blond, and had a white horse. His laugh was a fountain of crystal and his eyes were like the sky.

When he did come, I would run away with him and we would have a beautiful wedding in his castle. My kind-hearted prince never killed my assailant, he was too good for such awful acts. But I never knew what happened to the evil man once I left.

I was fulfilled, happy, loved.

In my teenage years, the desperation for prince charming to come and get me slowly faded.

It was replaced by a tension in my stomach when the evil

man would get close to me. He was dark and mean. He was dangerous and scary. My whole body trembled around him. My heart would sink so low there was no way to dig it back up.

He would always take me away in the middle of the night, always dragging me kicking and screaming. I would put on a good show for him because I knew he liked it. He loved me vulnerable and afraid.

One day my prince came, and I refused to leave with him. The feeling of being surrounded by the evil man and his darkness was too consuming to leave for a boring wedding in a castle.

I was in love with my malicious man. He made me feel wanted, sensual, and wicked. Every night I'd go to sleep, hoping he would come for me. Longing for his touch in the dark.

Tell me, Jake, what made you so evil?

When did you stop saving the princess and turned to the darkness instead?

And why...

Why me?

CHAPTER 1

Heathens – Twenty One Pilots

Rose

The pounding in my head is what wakes me up. Where am I again? What happened? I take a few seconds to trace back my night before I even think of opening my eyes.

   -Getting ready for the ball
   -Sam's text
   -Paying a visit to his distributors on the North Shore of the Falls
   -Missing the ball for some sort of house party
   -Chris' incessant phone calls
   -Heading back to Sam's flat in Silver Falls
   -Jake's calls and–

"For fuck's sake, stop listing shit so early in the morning," I mumble to myself, finally opening my heavy eyelids.

There's an arm resting around my waist, and I know from the light weight of it that it's the girl that was in the car with Sam and I last night. I'm on my side, facing her way and when I can finally see clearly, I realize her head is nestled against my collarbone, her long blond hair tickling my chest. Emma. She was at the party in NSF. There's a heavier arm coming from behind me, one that definitely doesn't belong to a girl. The stranger's arm is right between my breasts, his hand tangled in Emma's hair.

Last night was a fucking mess. The number of lines I did with Carlo and Roy Diaz flash in my mind and I instinctively bring two fingers to my nose, grazing my nostrils before checking the tips. No blood.

"We'll take that as a win," I gratingly whisper to make myself feel slightly better.

I push away from the girl and move both arms away from me, getting up, not making the slightest effort to not wake them up. In fact, I'm doing the exact opposite. They both stir awake as I step out of the bed to find my clothes. I grab my sweater from the floor, then my pants to retrieve my phone, not bothering to put them on. I turn back to the two on the bed, now only wearing my grey sweater and panties.

"Morning, gorgeous," the guy says to me, stretching on the bed, smiling like the cat who got the cream when he sees both me and then Emma slowly waking up next to him. "And morning, gorgeous," he tells her.

"Ugh," I roll my eyes. This is fucking shit. I should have never let him join us. Straight guys desperate to finally have a threesome with gay girls are the worst.

What is his name? I don't know, meaning I didn't ask him. Otherwise, I would know. I don't forget, ever. A curse more than anything else.

"Time to wrap this up," I grumble at him. Emma is already getting dressed. Smart girl doesn't need me to tell her to leave, she already knows. The fucker on the bed is clearly a little slower to understand.

I try to check my phone, but it's dead. Shit. Jake is going to kill me. I can't believe I didn't make it back home to blow out our candles together. I really fucking hate myself right now. Chris is also going to kill me for disappearing on him and not giving a single sign that I'm alive.

I'll handle them later.

First, I need to get home.

I grab my pack of cigarettes in my jeans just to find it empty. I look around the room and see a pack of Newports on the bedside table. They're disgusting but it's better than no nicotine at all.

-*Menthol cigarettes*

-*Introduced in 1957*

-*Owned by*-

'Shut the fuck up. Seriously, shut the fuck up,' I think to myself.

I grab one and turn back to my special guests.

"See you soon, Emma," I tell her as I grab my glasses on the floor. At what point did I even take out my contacts? I give a look to the guy, who finally is getting the hint.

I walk to the bedroom door and as soon as I open it, I see the door across the hallway open as well. My traitorous heart skips a beat, like every time it senses Sam around, but I keep my face blank. He's standing tall, opening the door to his own one-night stand.

I lean against the door frame of the bedroom I'm in, try my phone again as if it would now turn on by some miracle and when it doesn't, I cross my arms. Sam imitates me, crossing his muscular, tattooed arms across his chest and looking at me with that seriousness of his. He's wearing black jeans and nothing else. Tattoos covering defined muscles, my tongue subconsciously wets my lips when my eyes fall on his pierced nipples. Having never slept with Sam, that's the worst fuckery life has ever thrown at me. A constant tease, always short of attainable.

Sam's eyes leave my face to watch as *anonymous guy* slides past me to leave. His gaze is dark. I want to say it's jealousy, but it really fucking isn't, sadly. That's just how his gaze is; his eyes are so black they constantly look like they're sucking at your soul.

I see a man squeezing past Sam to leave his bedroom. Looks like he had his own share of fun last night. I don't miss the dotted bruise around the stranger's neck. The British dickhead is quiet during the day and lets out steam at night. Preferably on men who welcome his brand of violence.

"Call me," the tall, skinny stranger whispers to Sam. I watch him walk down the hallway on his way out.

Lucky cunt, I think before mentally slapping myself for drooling over Sam.

Our gazes meet again, across the hallway from each other, leaning on our respective door frames.

Emma walks out of the room, squeezing my waist and going on her toes to drop a kiss on my cheek but doesn't say anything.

Sam looks at her, back at me and rolls his eyes. I want to laugh at his hypocrisy when a girl has to squeeze past him to leave his bedroom. Oh, this is just gold. I was wondering how far we could push each other.

Quite far apparently.

Once Emma and that last girl have left, he looks at me from head to toe and back up before addressing me. "Should I expect anyone else to come out of my guest bedroom?"

"I'm done if you are," I reply with a smile. I put the Newport between my lips and look down at it as I bring the lighter to the tip. I don't have to look up to know he's crossed the hallway, his scent is already sending butterflies into panic mode in my stomach.

He grabs the cigarette from me, slowly.

"Not inside," he orders in his low voice.

I roll my eyes before looking up at him. Fuck he's tall. He's so fucking tall compared to me and I'm five foot ten so I know what I'm talking about.

He tucks the cigarette in his back pocket and offers me what I know he considers a smile: a slight pull at the corner of his lips.

"Happy Birthday, Rose."

I look into the black pools that are his eyes, allowing myself to get lost for a few seconds.

"I need to charge my phone," I reply.

"You need to get home. Go get ready, I'm driving you back." He turns around and walks back into his room, shutting the door on me.

We're probably about ten minutes from my house when his phone pings, and his mood changes drastically. I mean, he's always a serious dick, but not as much with me. Granted he's usually in a mood when he has to drive me back – probably all that guilt for taking me away from a fairly normal life – but today he is especially moody, his eyes constantly checking his phone, careful that I don't see the screen.

After a second ping he brakes suddenly, muttering a 'shit'. He texts something back. Another ping, a mumbled 'fuck' and he turns the car around.

"What the fuck are you doing?"

He doesn't reply, focusing on not getting us crushed in-between two cars.

"Care to explain why you're being extra dickish today?" I insist.

"Care to explain why you have threesomes in my apartment?" he snaps back.

"You have threesomes in your apartment, no one complains about it." I turn slightly to show him the mocking smile that has settled on my lips.

"It's my place, I'm an adult, I can do whatever the fuck I want. I'm not some seventeen-year-old desperately trying to catch anyone's attention."

I bark out a laugh at his weak attempt to hurt me. "Some-one's sex must have been disappointing last night. Maybe try being a bottom?" I put my left hand on the small of his back and slide it to his back pocket. "A good dicking would help with all that frustration. It definitely helped me last night."

"Rose," he threatens in a low voice. He's about to grab my hand but I retreat, holding the cigarette he had put at the back of his black jeans.

He doesn't add anything, instead getting deeper in his broodiness. I roll my eyes and open the window on my side before lighting up the cigarette.

"Throw that fag away." He grabs the cigarette and throws it out of the window.

"Sam! What the fuck is wrong with you today?" He's starting to get on my nerves. He smokes like the fucking chimney of a nuclear plant and blackmails me into doing petty jobs for him, and now he wants to get on my back for threesomes and a cigarette?

He checks his phone again and runs a tattooed hand in his black hair. I decide to ignore him and plug my phone into the car. He eyes it suspiciously before focusing back on the road.

"Stop being weird," I order.

It only takes us a minute or so to park on a street I've never been to before.

"We need to stop here. It'll only be a minute."

"Really?" I know he sees the anger in my eyes when I turn to him. "Didn't I do enough fucking stops yesterday?"

"Yeah, well, it's urgent."

He goes silent again and I know there's something he's not telling me, but I let it slide.

I check the street; rows of rundown, small cottages and I have to do a double take.

"Are we in Stoneview?" I look outside his window and then the back window. Something isn't right. I saw the sign that says 'Welcome to Stoneview' but I've never been to this part of town. It's not North Shore of the Falls poor, but it's definitely not Stoneview rich. Our town is a sheer contrast to NSF, where trailer parks and rundown bungalows are the best one will find. This is...in the middle?

Sam ignores my question as he gets out of the car.

Shit. Something really is wrong. He's got his public personality on and I've got that terrible feeling in the pit of my stomach. The same that used to live in me rent free before we moved to Stoneview.

I swallow the lump in my throat and put my brave face on. I just have to.

One stop and home, I keep repeating to myself as I grab my phone and open the car door, jumping out of his jeep.

I finally manage to turn my phone on, but the piece of shit isn't showing anything on the screen yet, taking ages to catch up with notifications, so I slip it in my back pocket.

Sam has stopped just in front of four steps that lead to one of the cottages. I catch up with him and it takes him a beat before he looks at me.

"Do you trust me?" he asks. Images of the number of times he's asked me that flash in my mind.

When I was a child, it was always yes. 'Yes, I trust you'. Yes, I'll follow blindly like the fucking stupid, naïve kid I am. Since he's barged back into our lives like a loose cannon, that answer changed. He wouldn't know that though, because he hasn't asked. He's been here for a couple of months and hasn't had the need to ask me. So why now?

"What are you doing, Sam? You better not be fucking me over."

"Do you, Rose? Do you trust me?"

"What are you hiding?" My voice is low, vibrating at the bottom of my throat, giving it that huskiness everyone loves so much.

He gives up on getting an answer and takes the steps to the front porch. He waits until I'm right behind him to ring the bell.

I know I fucked up when, once he has rang, he takes a step back to stand behind me. He's making sure I don't turn around and leave, he's making sure I'm stuck between him and whatever is behind that door. I know something is wrong when the phone in my back pocket won't stop vibrating. Notifications after notifications make it go off non-stop.

I don't have time to grab it, the door is already open.

CHAPTER 2

Never Be Like You – Flume, kai

Jamie

I wake up to the smell of coffee and slowly open my eyes. I instantly feel the comfort of my own bed mixed with the reassuring scent of Nathan. I stretch and turn where I can feel him standing. I wasn't expecting the look of deep concern on his face.

"Morning," I yawn. I sit up and take the cup of coffee he's handing out. He sits on the edge of my bed, facing me. "Thanks for the coffee. Much needed."

He carefully puts a strand of chocolate hair behind my ear. "We need to talk about last night," he simply says, his voice smooth and reassuring.

That's what Nathan does; treat me like a porcelain doll he could break at any moment if he spoke too loudly or moved too fast. That's why he always treats me with care, and why he can't get himself to take my virginity. We've given each other orgasms, and lord knows they're amazing ones, but he just won't take that last step. He's just too scared to break

11

me, scared I'll regret it and he'll have to live with the guilt.

I don't want to talk about last night. I don't want to talk about Jake's state of fury, about Beth pouring a bowl of punch over me, and mainly...about that kiss. *The* kiss.

I stare at him. His glasses framing his beautiful face, his messy hair not yet in a sleek bun. My eyes run along his topless ripped body, his artistic tattoos, and his gorgeous eyes I want to drown in. I love him. I told Jake I loved Nathan. I'm sure I do.

Then why did I let this happen yesterday?

"There's nothing to talk about," I reply in a small voice.

I burn my tongue on the hot coffee to avoid having to say anything else. I need time to think before telling him what happened. I know I will tell him because I won't be able to live with the guilt. I just don't know how yet.

I don't even recognize myself. I've always been a rule follower, always tried to do right by people. I know I'm not perfect and I know I like to put up a goody-two-shoes persona because, up until now, I didn't really know who else I was, who else I could be.

Is this who I am? A girl who plays games and cheats? Saying I'm disappointed with myself is an understatement. And yet, I still wouldn't change what happened yesterday.

"'Me," he sighs. "I don't want to be that kind of boyfriend, asking what you've been up to and demanding explanations... but the state you were in last night...something happened to you and I want to know what. If you're in trouble I need to know."

His voice is soft and reassuring but I'm not ready to get into this.

"It's nothing," I reply.

"For fuck's sake, Jamie." He gets up annoyed and grabs his dirty blond hair between his fingers, bringing it all back as he combs through it. His biceps are bulging, and I sense he's trying to contain his anger.

He grabs my stained dress on the floor next to the bed and points at it, holding it with a white-knuckled hand.

"*This* is not nothing." He grabs the sticky, messy ends of my hair and points at the bits hardened by the dried punch. "*This* is not nothing. The state you were in...and don't think I didn't notice you'd been crying. Your face was a fucking mess."

He grabs the coffee cup from my hands and puts it down on the bedside table, hard enough to spill some of the liquid. He grabs my hands roughly. "*This*, Jamie, is not fucking nothing."

I look down at my arms. My wrists are dotted with light grey bruises. I knew Jake held me hard. I didn't realize how hard.

I'm trembling when Nathan lets go of my hands. "Oh my God," I whisper to myself.

Nathan gets up from the bed and looks at me with cold, hard eyes. "And I'm not even bringing up the guy that was running after you. I'll be in the living room for when you're ready to tell me what the fuck happened."

He leaves the room and I know it's because he doesn't want to take his anger out on me.

The guy that was running after me. I let the scene flash in my head, Jake running after me, Nathan coming out of his car to open the passenger door in the pouring rain. 'Was this guy bothering you?' he asked. I lied, of course I lied because I'm a liar. 'No, it's fine,' I said. 'I just want to go home.' Nathan's voice changed when he replied to me. It was tainted with that deep rage I know he can get in. With the promise of causing pain like he did when Dimitri attacked me at the coffee shop. 'You stay here. You don't move from this car, clear?' I don't know what he said to Jake. I'm just glad he didn't do to him the same he did to Dimitri.

I have to clear things up with Nathan. I have to tell him the truth. Put this all behind us. Accept the consequences. My stomach tightens at the idea of Nathan breaking up with me for what I did. He would be in the right...but I care for him. I don't want to be without him.

I take a deep shaky breath and pull off the covers. My top smells of Nathan's soapy scent and my insides twist in guilt.

When I walk into my living area, I see him sitting on the sofa, tapping on his phone and sending texts. I walk around the sofa and stand in front of him. He looks up and spreads his legs so I can come in-between them. His face is lined up with my neck and for once I'm the one who has to look down.

"I'm sorry," I say.

"Sorry for what?" he asks confused as he puts his phone away.

"For what I'm about to say and for not saying it to you before."

He frowns at me and I take a shallow breath, trying my best to stop the tears that threaten to fall anytime.

"Jamie, what's wrong?"

I don't know how to tell him.

I was bullied at school, but it turns out I actually kind of like it. It turns me on and I'm really into the guy who's doing it to me.

Or should I start with *I cheated on you with the guy who bullied me. We played a dangerous game and I lost. I like the bruises he left on me. I like when he possesses. He makes me feel alive.*

I can't. I can't do it. I'm a hypocrite. A liar. A cheat.

I'm facing a man who I know loves me, who saved my life, who is perfect. He is worried for me and in return all I have to offer him is lies and disappointment. And inevitably, heartbreak.

Just start from the beginning and be honest.

"At school," I start, and I've never felt like such a kid in front of him.

"Yes?" he insists.

"I think," I shift on my feet suddenly feeling uncomfortable. I'm not ready. I'm not ready to admit what Jake or Camila or Beth have been doing to me. I've never been so humiliated in my life. It's the part of my game with Jake that I hate.

"'Me," he grabs my hands in a reassuring gesture, "you know you can tell me anything."

"I think that maybe...maybe I'm being bullied," I finally blurt out and a single tear crosses the barrier that is my eyelid. I quickly wipe it away.

His face hardens and he pulls me closer to him. "How bad?"

I shake my head because there is no way in hell I will ever say in detail what happened.

"I don't know what bad is like, it had never happened to me before."

I'm sure some girls have had it worse. Some kids are bullied and don't fall for their tormentor. Isn't that how bullying works?

"Who? That guy from yesterday?" I can see his jaw clenching, his nostrils flaring and his sentences shortening with anger.

15

"Yes, and ultimately his ex."

"The bruises, is that him?"

I can barely nod yes. "But–"

"And the dress?"

"The typical mean girls poured punch on me. Listen–"

"How long has this been going on?"

"It started this year. Nathan–"

He suddenly gets up and looks down at me. "He's a dead man."

"No," I shake my head. "There is no way you're getting involved in this."

Especially with how he got with Dimitri. I might hate Jake but the deepest, darkest part of me also likes him and cares for him and I don't want to see him get hurt.

"No? Did I sound like you had a say in this?"

"You're not getting involved in this," I repeat with a voice of steel.

Why am I protecting Jake? After everything he's done, all the humiliation. He ripped panties off me, he brought Camila's wrath on me, they destroyed the café where I work. He threatened me, blackmailed me, he put a gun to my face, he's ruining my senior year completely. Worse, he made me feel good when I wanted so badly not to feel anything. He pushed pleasure on me I didn't want or expect, turned my body against my mind.

And I liked it.

"Don't worry, I don't need your help. I'll find him."

"Nathan," I scold.

He goes around me to leave the room and I grab his arm.

"You can't do that! I'm asking you to respect my choice. I don't want this to go any further."

16

He turns around suddenly and grabs my shoulders. "He hurt you, Jamie. Do you understand that? This is not some high school fun. You're bruised and hurt. Anyone who touches my girl faces the consequences. Period."

"What did you say to him yesterday? When you left the car?"

"Nothing!" he exclaims. "I was stupid, I asked why he was running after you and he said he wanted to check if you were okay." He starts pacing the room. "Why didn't you say anything there and then, I would have done something!"

"I kissed him," I admit.

There's a long, blood-freezing silence and I can't seem to be able to breathe.

"Last night?" he asks for confirmation.

I nod.

"Yeah, well looking at your state, forgive me if I still think it's all on him," he growls.

"I let him kiss me, Nathan, I-I pushed him away but only after I let him close," I say as a sob wrecks my chest. I can't describe it, it simply breaks my heart to break his heart.

Jake might have done his worst to me, but there are times I could have pushed him away and I didn't. I enjoyed it instead.

"I sent the wrong signals," I admit, wiping tears off my face.

"Guys like him will fuck with your head to get what they want, Jamie. But thanks for adding kissing my girl to the list of things I should fuck him up for."

"Don't do this. I'm the one who has to deal with him at school after you've nicely redone his face! I'm the one he's going to come to for revenge. You can't be with me at all times to stop that. Please, Nathan...you need to understand."

If Nathan hurts him, Jake will hate me. I don't want Jake to hate me. I don't want Jake's fury, I don't want the true scary side of him.

I'm confused, is he not mad at me? I let Jake kiss me.

"Fuck. You're scared of him," he huffs in disbelief.

"Of course I am!" I shout. "He's made my life a living hell since the beginning of the year!"

Jake scares me, that's the most exciting thing between us. The unpredictability of it all while knowing that he likes me too much to truly hurt me.

"Then let me deal with him," he hisses through gritted teeth.

I shake my head again. "No."

He lets out a grunt of rage and I grab his hands. I know this is driving him crazy, but he needs to understand my point. "Please. I told him I was seeing someone. I told him this couldn't keep going last night. He got angry but he left me alone. It's over," I conclude more to reassure myself than him.

Last night was a big mistake. I don't know if I thought I could be friends with Jake or if I was just too deep into our cat and mouse game to make rational decisions, but I should have never gone to the ball with him. I should have never followed him to the cafeteria. I should have never allowed him to get this close. For the first time I truly fought back. After months of letting him play with me, I finally told him my first 'no'. And Jake proved to be simply *dangerous.*

All those months he bullied me he was in control. When he loses that control, he's lethal and even I couldn't bring him back. I don't want this. I *shouldn't* want this. Last night was the end of whatever was going on between me and him.

"If anything else happens, *anything*, he's dead." Nathan's voice is a confirmation that he's the one I should be around. He's always there for me, he's my protector, he's my guardian angel.

"Nothing will happen. I promise."

"I trusted you, 'Me..."

"And I messed up. I did. I-I'm a fool for taking you for granted." The tears streaming down my face are warm, but they don't taste salty. They taste bitter. I let Jake get in the way of my relationship with Nathan. I let him play me...for what? To be another notch on his belt?

Nathan takes a step toward me and grabs my face with both his tattooed hands, his fingers threading the hair at the back of my head, his thumbs wiping my tear-streaked cheeks.

"I can't let you fuck this up," he admits. "I can't give up on us." A deep breath, his eyes darting away from me for a second, and I know what's coming next. "I'm in love with you, 'Me."

His words warm up my soul, spread a tingle of excitement and happiness through my whole body. He brings his face to mine and kisses my forehead, waiting for my consent to take this further.

"I love you too," I whisper back.

If Jake is set on destroying my entire being, Nathan is a promise to shield my soul.

I lean back and push on my toes to deposit a kiss on his lips. He licks the hem of my lips and I part them for him. Our tongues play with each other before everything gets hotter.

He grabs me by the waist and lifts me until I wrap my legs around his waist.

I deepen the kiss, exploring his mouth like I haven't seen

him in years. He carries me back to the bed and puts me down before coming on top of me. He pushes my top above my breasts and devours them like it's his last meal. I cry in pleasure and his hands pull down my leggings.

"Don't. Ever. Betray me. Again." He covers my body in bites and kisses after each word and slides his hand between my legs. My insides are already melting for him and I know he'll find me wet and willing.

He cups my pussy and brings his face above mine. "You got that?" he insists. He makes his point by sliding a finger in me easily.

"Yes," I moan. "Yes, got it."

He slides another finger and starts pumping. My cries come at his rhythm and the way he possesses me gets the best of me.

"I thought we were clear that I don't share. I thought you were a good girl, Jamie," he growls.

My hips follow his movement and my cries come louder.

"Will you be a good girl from now on? Will you be very good to me?"

I nod, incapable of forming any coherent word.

"Say it," he orders in a low voice. "Promise me, you won't talk to him again."

His hand retreats slightly, forcing my eyes to shoot open.

"Look me in the eyes and promise me, Jamie." Nathan's voice is dark, his fingers almost violent when he enters me again. I cry out in pleasure, but try to keep my eyes on him.

"I promise," I pant. "I'm so sorry for what I did. I promise you, Nathan."

He controls my body into an overwhelming orgasm and collapses next to me. I rise on my knees, undoing his pants. I pull everything down at the same time and lick my lips at the sight of his erect dick.

"Show me how sorry you are, beautiful," he whispers.

I lower my head and take him between my lips. I lick the precum that's already leaking. He tastes salty and my mouth waters at the thought of taking him, of finally taking everything further. I open my mouth and he slides in, but I quickly struggle with his length.

I gag and he puts a reassuring hand on my head, stroking my hair. Why am I struggling? It wouldn't be the first time I sucked his dick. He's big, but I usually manage.

"Breathe through your nose," he says in a husky voice.

I suddenly have a flash, imagining Jake's voice telling me this. His dark voice ordering me to take it like an angel. Pleasure pools between my legs as I see his face instead of Nathan's. I pull back in a rush, disgusted with myself.

"I-I can't," I whisper, guilt eating at my guts.

He sits up and puts his hand on my arms, warming me up. "Hey, hey that's fine. You don't have to." The hardness in his voice is completely gone, replaced by his reassuring tone that always makes me feel good.

I nod but I can't shake that awful feeling. I remember moments with Jake. That mix of fear and anticipation. I can't help recalling all the times he made me feel good and I was actually dying to have his dick in my mouth. I just could never admit it.

Why? Why am I like this?

Nathan puts his arms around me, lays back down on the bed, and takes me with him. "'Me, I'm serious. I don't care. As long as I have you next to me, I'm in no rush."

I smile in his arms, lying face down on him, my head in

the crook of his neck. I feel my eyes getting heavy from the post-orgasm haze and close them, thinking how lucky I am to have Nathan in my life and how I cannot mess this up again.

CHAPTER 3

Saints - Echos

Jamie

When I wake up again, Nathan is not in bed with me. His t-shirt is right next to my head and I put it on, loving the smell of him on me. I hear the shower running in the bathroom and relax instantly. Despite everything that happened, there's something I can't take away and that is that I feel so happy and safe when he's near, it's unbelievable. I just wish I didn't forget it so quickly when Jake is around.

I grab my phone to check the time and stare at the wallpaper with a stupidly contented smile on my face. It's the picture from Nathan's Instagram that I had asked Emily to screenshot and send me. He's lying topless on his sofa and I'm lying on top of him, my face to his chest, a drunk in love smile on my face. I look at the camera while Nathan looks at me, his eyes nothing but pure love.

I scroll through a few texts from Emily until my eyes fall on a notification from an unknown number. I open the text with furrowed brows.

Unknown: Nathan is dangerous. Have you not seen his tattoo?

There's a picture of a drawing. It's clearly been done in a rush with a pencil but I recognize it very well. *That* tattoo. I sit up in a hurry and reply straight away, but the message has been sent during the night.

Jamie: Who is this?

Nothing. I lock my phone and my eyes go back to that picture of me and Nathan.

I chuckle. Nathan doesn't have this tattoo. This is so stupid. Someone is pranking me.

But my heart skips a beat. Who could possibly prank me about this tattoo? I only know three people who have it and none of them would know of Nathan's tattoos.

Still, I decide to look intently at the picture. But his tattoos are hard to distinguish one from the other. I go to my gallery and decide to zoom in on the picture. Why am I doing this? I trust Nathan, I don't need to prove myself anything.

And yet, my heart stops and I can't quite believe my eyes when they fall on what I was looking for. I move the photo around with shaky fingers, not accepting what I'm seeing.

On Nathan's side, right below his armpit, is a tattoo of an X. Not any X. One with a crown on top of it and a W under it. A 19 on one side and 33 on the other side. My brain can barely process the news.

How have I never seen this before?

It's the exact same tattoo Samuel has on his neck. The exact same one Rose has on her arm and...Jake between his shoulder blades. *Jake.* This can't be a coincidence. It just can't.

I get up suddenly, my whole body shaking in confusion and fear. What the hell does that mean? He said he wasn't working for Mateo Bianco anymore. Does it mean he's working for Samuel? Is this possible? Did he lie to me?

The sound of my bedroom door opening and closing makes me bounce around in surprise.

Nathan is standing by the door, his hair still wet and a towel around his waist.

"What's up," he says as he must see the look on my face. He's casual though, using a second towel to dry his hair.

Reality dawns on me and I freeze in fear wondering who the hell I let inside my house, alone with me.

I slowly walk to him, panic screaming at me to stay away, and observe the tattoo from a closer angle. It's there. It's real.

"You lied to me," I whisper in shock.

"What?" he asks, confused. He throws the towel he was using for his hair on my bed. "What are you talking about?"

"I don't know if you're aware, but there's this guy in Stoneview. He's the head of a new gang," I say with certainty. I need to put up a brave face, show I'm in control. "Real scary guy. He has a tattoo on his neck. The exact same one as this one." I point at the tattoo on his upper ribs.

I know why I haven't seen it before. It's so well hidden within all the other ones, you don't notice it if you don't know where it is. It's like that with a lot of his tattoos. It takes time and attention to discern them.

"Jamie..." His voice is full of guilt. It's covered in it, dripping remorse all over his tongue. That's how I know I'm dead right.

25

He works for Samuel.

He starts babbling explanations, but I don't listen to him. I grab his clothes and throw them at him. I don't want to show how scared I suddenly am, and I cover it with anger. "You lied to me! Get out. Get out of my house!"

He starts putting them on, saying how he loves me and wouldn't hurt me, but my ears are ringing in fear and anger. I almost miss the moment he grabs his phone and shoots a quick text.

"Is that your partner in crime you're texting?" I bark out a hysterical laugh. Did he really just do that?

I'm not sure how long passes while I take our pictures, the gifts, the cute post-it notes he'd leave in my notebooks, his hoodies he had lent me...everything. I should talk it out with him, I should check if maybe I'm misunderstanding. But maybe this is exactly what I wanted. Maybe this is my reason to push him away.

"Jamie, you need to let me explain, please..."

"No! How can you let me apologize and beg you for forgiveness for the wrong I've done when you've actually been lying to me all this time! You're an impostor! You're a *criminal.* I should have known. I should have known the first time I confronted you about it that you were lying."

"I'm not an impostor, I was waiting for the right time—"

"Oh *please*," I rage. "There's no 'right time' for coming clean. The sooner the better."

"Like you cheating on me? Was that as soon as possible? Did you call me yesterday crying because you were *dying* to tell me you were being a slut for someone else?"

My mouth falls slack. Partly because he's right, mainly because his voice has turned a shade which until now had only been reserved for Dimitri, when he attacked me. Now that it's aimed at me, I can't help the terror from spreading through my veins.

He takes a step toward me, making me take one back. His body is hard, muscles tensing below the shirt he hasn't had time to button up.

Is he going to hit me? I don't even know who he is, if he's violent...dangerous.

"Do you know him? Jake."

"What?"

"Jake, the guy from yesterday, from school. You saw him, you talked to him outside the car. What did you say to him?"

"Oh," he smiles wickedly. "The guy you cheated on me with."

"Stop trying to change the topic, Nathan. You have the same tattoo as Samuel Thomas, you work for him. Jake has that tattoo too. Do. You. Know. Him?" I insist through gritted teeth.

I don't have time to find out. The bell rings loud in the house, cutting through the tension and making me jolt in surprise.

I jump on the occasion and go past him, moving toward the bedroom door.

"Just leave," I say in a shaky voice, looking at the door handle instead of him.

I go through the short hallway, and hurry to the front door. I can barely believe my eyes when I open the door.

"Jamie?" The look of shock on Rose's face tells me she had no idea whose door she was ringing.

"What..." I whisper confused as I see Sam close behind her.

She's about to turn around when she notices something

behind me. Her face completely falls, her eyes widen behind her thin, gold glasses, and I don't think I've ever seen such disbelief in anyone's eyes before.

"What the..." she begins but the words stay stuck in her throat.

"Happy birthday, Ozy."

I turn around, recognizing Nathan's voice. When my gaze lands on him, he's nothing like the sweet guy I know. His eyes are dark, and his face hardened, anger and hatred emanating from him.

I turn back to Rose, she's turned around, ready to leave. She can't though, because Samuel is right behind her and when he sees Nathan in the house, he puts an arm out, stopping her in her tracks.

"Fuck," he mumbles and catches Rose by the waist.

I take a step back trying to take in the scene as Samuel lifts her and brings her back into the house. He slams the door behind him.

"No, no, no," she panics but Samuel doesn't budge. "Put me down!"

I turn to Nathan who's looking at the scene with a mocking smile on his face. He crosses his arms across his button-down-clad chest as he watches Samuel putting Rose back down and spinning her around so she's facing us. He puts his hands hard on her shoulders, grounding her on the spot.

"What the hell," I say to Nathan. "What is happening?"

I've never been so confused in my life. Nathan ignores me and slowly walks to Rose. She's not even trying to escape anymore. She's just shaking like a leaf, incredulity like a shadow on her pupils.

"That's impossible," she keeps whispering on repeat. "Impossible, y-you're–"

"Dead?" he cuts her off. "I missed you too."

He reaches her, taller than her despite her height and she seems to shrink under his gaze. He looks above her at Samuel with a lopsided smile.

"You dating my little sister now or something? You think I'd let you do that?"

"Your what?" I choke as a wave of shock washes over me.

They both ignore me and Samuel chuckles at him. "Mate, let's not get ahead of ourselves here. I know how protective you Whites are."

"Fuck," Nathan curses. "I really didn't plan on seeing Jake yesterday," he says to Rose. "He caught me off guard. Now I can't make a dramatic entrance, I had to rush this before he spilled my little secret."

Rose doesn't reply. She's clearly too busy trying to breathe properly and failing miserably.

"Is anyone going to tell me what the hell is going on?" I question angrily.

I already know none of this is good, but I can't get my head around it all. Nathan turns to me as if just remembering I existed.

"'Me, I'm so sorry. This wasn't meant to happen. At least not here and not now. I was planning a big family reunion or something."

"Family reunion?" I ask, completely lost.

"Hey Ozy, you know my girlfriend Jamie, right? She goes to Stoneview Prep with you."

Ozy that's the nickname Jake usually uses for Rose. Still, my brain completely refuses to put two and two together.

"I'm sorry, beautiful," he says to me. "I was truly going to

29

explain everything. It just wasn't the right moment."

"Explain what?" I growl.

"Did she never mention me?" He turns to Rose again. "Do you not mention your older brother to anyone?" His gaze is back on me and I shake my head no.

"Right, she hasn't. That's probably because she thought I was dead." He turns back to her, his cold gaze staring daggers at her.

Rose is shaking her head, she still can't believe what she's seeing. I can see tears building in her eyes but not one falls.

"You did, didn't you? Because you *never* miss."

He suddenly grabs her jaw with a strong hand and I've never seen her look so small. She whimpers at his grasp, incapable of moving, frozen in place.

"Nathan," I shout. "What the hell are you doing? Calm down!"

He turns to me without letting go. "Jamie, I love you but when it comes to my siblings, you don't get a say."

"How? What? I don't get it..." I mumble, my fingers reaching my temples as I sense a headache coming. This makes no sense.

"You know what?" He lets go of Rose. "Let's all take a seat and catch up."

He moves towards the sofa and Samuel completely lets go of Rose. He leans down and whispers something in her ear that I can't hear but the color drains from her face before she nods.

Samuel walks around her to follow Nathan to the sofa. I can't take my eyes off her.

What. Is. Going. On?

I open my mouth to ask her something, but she just shakes

her head no.

"Today, Ozy," Nathan says as he sits on the coffee table in front of the sofa.

Samuel sits next to him leaving the two spaces on my small sofa free. She jumps out of whatever she was thinking of and reluctantly walks away to take a seat. I'm lost as to what to do, so I follow and sit down next to her.

"You explain," Nathan orders her.

"Don't do this to me," she whispers. She puts shaking hands beside her, holding the sofa, and he smiles at her discomfort.

"I *am* doing this to you. Go on."

"I don't know what to say," she says in a shaky voice, huskier than usual.

"Nathan, stop it," I hiss. "Why are you being like this?"

"Drop it, Jamie," Rose intervenes without even glancing at me.

Nathan throws me a dark look and gets up.

"You want to know why, baby?" he asks me. Baby? Since when is this a thing?

Who is he?

He walks behind the sofa and I try to follow him with my gaze as best as I can. He's slowly walking behind Rose and she flinches when he raises his hand to pull a strand of dirty blond hair away from his face. He notices and smiles down at her, adjusting his glasses.

"See, the twins and I grew up in foster care. We got lucky enough to never get separated. I took care of them for six years. Until one day," he slams his hands on Rose's shoulders and she winces at the gesture, "this little bitch here decided she was done with me and shot me."

"That's *not* what happened," she says, her teeth clenched so tightly her words come out in a whisper.

My thoughts are going a hundred miles an hour. I think back to the scar Nathan has below his chest, the rose tattoo around it, and look at Rose stunned.

"You shot him?" I ask, incredulous. This can't be. This... this is just unbelievable. Those kinds of things don't happen, not to normal people. We're *normal*.

"And she really, truly thought she got rid of me. Didn't you?"

"I–" she stops what she was about to say as if deciding it was not worth the risk. "It's not what happened."

Nathan lets go of her shoulders and she shoots up turning back to face both of us, courage finally back on her face.

"That's not what happened, and you know it," she hisses. "You made our lives a living hell. We were fucking fine until we got put at Bianco's house. And who wanted to stay, huh? Who joined a fucking gang and took us all down with him? Who got Jake in underground rings? Who made him beat up people for a fucking mafioso? *You.* It was all you. You who forced us to join, you who beat us up, you who built your life on crime. Whatever happened to you, you brought it on yourself. We tried to leave, and you wanted to stop us. You got shot? It wasn't my fault, I wasn't supposed to aim better than a sniper at fourteen years old. It was fucking karma, Nate. You reap what you sow."

A silence falls on the room as she pants, trying to catch her breath after her rant. I try to get my head around everything she just said but it barely makes any sense. Well, her words make sense, her sentences are formulated correctly, but I'm too shocked to process it.

Soon enough, Nathan comes around the sofa and puts a hand on her shoulder.

"You do reap what you sow, Ozy." He pauses, looking at her almost like he feels sorry for her. "And, boy, are you gonna reap." He punches her in the stomach, and she curls up in pain falling on the floor in a loud grunt.

"Nathan!" I shout as I get up, but Samuel is quicker than me. While he was silent until now, he suddenly shoots up from his seat and holds back Nathan.

"Mate, too far," he calmly says in his crisp British accent. He puts a hand on his shoulder and that's about enough for Nathan to take a step back.

"It'll be too far when she's got a fucking bullet in her head." Nathan is seething. His cheeks are red, his eyes are burning with hate. I never thought he could get this angry. I should have, because he beat one of Volkov's guys to a pulp for touching me.

If Rose really is his sister, what kind of brother would do this? Then again, what kind of sister would shoot her own brother?

"You don't want to do this," Samuel insists.

Nathan's phone rings in the back pocket of his jeans and he grabs it annoyed. "Saved by the fucking bell, aren't you?" he smiles down at Rose. He goes to the hallway to pick up and Samuel helps Rose back up.

"Are you okay?" he asks her. He's holding her arm as he pulls her back on her feet, but she pulls it back straight away.

"Are you for fucking real right now?" she chuckles sarcastically, holding her side. "Nate is alive. You knew. You fucking knew and you didn't tell me. You threatened me to go to the cops for killing someone that wasn't even dead, you fucking piece of shit. You two deserve each other."

"Rose, you have to try and understand—"

"I forgave a lot of things from you, Sam. But this...this I will never forgive." She turns to me as if his betrayal was nothing to her. "Come on, Jamie. We need to leave."

"You can't leave," Samuel warns. "I told him I was with you when he asked me to come. I said I'd drop you home before, he specifically said not to." He settles against the arm of the sofa and crosses his arm. Calmness emanates from him like this whole situation is nothing unusual to him. "You can't leave, Rose," he repeats.

This is anything but normal to me and I don't understand how Sam's keeping a clear head.

Probably because he runs a gang. Yes, that must be it.

"Watch me," Rose growls.

"He's going to hunt you and Jake down. He wants you guys back in, you know he does. He's not going to let this go. You don't want to go against him." This seems so logical to him. Even to Rose. She knows exactly what he's talking about and I'm dying to understand, even if I know it's something I should probably stay out of.

"I don't care. Stop me if you're so strong," she quips. "Jamie, let's go."

"But...it's my house. I can't leave." I can't but at the same time, I want to. I just want to be away from all of this and be able to process it all.

"I know it's your fucking house, let's go. *For now.*" She rolls her eyes as if I'm the most stupid person in this room and heads for the door. And me, well, I follow after her. What else?

"Where the fuck do you think you're going?" Nathan's

voice raises from behind us.

"Home," she replies but stops moving. I can see her hand trembling on the doorknob.

"Go on, Ozy. Leave and see what happens."

She hesitates for a few more seconds. Just when I think she's going to open the door, she lets go and turns around wincing 'fuck'.

"That's what I thought," he smirks.

I have no idea who I'm facing right now. This guy is nothing like the Nathan I know. He ignores Rose as she goes back to the sofa and sits back down, running her hands over her face and through her long black hair.

"I don't know what fucked up plan you got in mind, Nate," she sighs. "But it won't work."

"Really? And why's that?" he asks casually.

"Because you're a megalomaniac," she deadpans.

He stands right behind the sofa and looks down at her from behind. "At least I'm not a murderer. Hey, I like your new glasses. Do you like mine?"

"Don't talk to me like this is a family reunion," she huffs.

He shrugs and turns to Samuel while I stay planted by the door still trying to get my head around what I'm witnessing.

"Is Carlo waiting for you?" he asks Samuel.

Samuel simply nods, his attention is on Rose while she looks ready to kill him.

"They ran into some Wolves during their deliveries. Let's go meet them."

Samuel's gaze reluctantly leaves Rose for Nathan. "What? What are you going to do with the situation you've just put us in?"

Nathan shrugs. "You know what to do."

35

Samuel huffs, annoyed, but doesn't reply anything. He simply comes my way, walks around me like I don't exist, and leaves the house.

"'Me," Nathan says as he strides toward me. He goes to put his hands on my cheeks, but I instinctively take a step back. I used to feel so safe when he did this. How can it change so quickly?

"Please," he insists. I recognize his soft voice but not the man standing in front of me. "I didn't mean for any of this to happen this way."

"Is it true?" I ask. "Are you really related?"

He nods and any last hope I had that this was all a very well-rehearsed joke shatters in a thousand pieces.

"So you lied. Everything you said about leaving your house, about your inheritance."

"I didn't lie. Okay maybe about the inheritance bit but I did leave my house. Rose got rid of me, exactly like she wanted all along, and I had no choice but to stay away. Then they moved to the Murrays and I was able to go back to Mateo."

Mateo?

Mateo Bianco, the guy he promised he wasn't working for anymore.

"You said you worked for him, you didn't say he was your foster parent," I hiss. "You said you met him when you left your house, not that you grew up with him. You never mentioned being in the foster system."

I don't even sound like myself. I'm desperate for him to tell me none of this is true but it's not coming. My brain is finally forced to get over the shock and accept the situation. Bits of our relationship flash back to me and I grip my scalp, trying to ground myself.

"When I came to your apartment, and you had a friend over. Was it Samuel?"

He looks away for a second and huffs before replying. "Yeah."

"And when I asked you if you still worked for that man…"

"'Me, I was looking for the right time."

I can see from the corner of my eye, Rose watching us, dubious. She can't believe we're actually dating, just like I can't believe they're siblings. All this time we all were closer than we thought and never realized it. The world is such a strange place.

"I trusted you. You made me believe you lost your family like I had. You lied to me. You betrayed my trust."

I can feel the tears coming at the realization that our entire relationship was based on lies. That there was never any mutual trust but a one-way transaction where I opened up to him and he fed me lies in return.

I thought I was a horrible person for having feelings for another man, I couldn't comprehend how he was being so understanding of my mistakes. That's because his lies were rooted in our relationship, like a poison inked in the veins of our love.

I suddenly feel a wave of shame and regret overwhelming me. All the late-night conversations telling him all my secrets, my hopes, and fears. I told him how much I missed my dad when I couldn't tell my mom, I told him the pain I felt when my mom couldn't even pronounce my brother's name.

I feel sick to my stomach thinking of all the times I've let him explore my body and bring me pleasure. Thinking that I told him about Jake's bullying is the worst part.

Out of all the people I could have opened to about this, I

chose Nathan. Regret claws at me. I pushed Jake away to give a chance to my relationship with Nathan and he just threw it back in my face.

This is why deep down it never felt right to choose Nathan because it simply wasn't.

The sound of the door closing behind me drives me out of my thoughts and I stare at Nathan. He looks concerned but I know now that it's just a lie. Everything that comes out of him is a lie.

"We can talk about this later, 'Me. I have to run."

"Don't call me that," I retort. "Don't call me anything. Don't even consider me part of your life anymore." I go to walk around him and toward the sofa, but he grabs my arm tightly.

"Don't be like that. We'll fix this."

"We're over! There's nothing to fix! You're the one who needs to be fixed!"

I try to snatch my arm out of his grip, but he doesn't let go. I'm about to shout at him to leave my house when I see Rose looking behind me with wide eyes.

"Jamie, move!" she orders as she jumps off the back of the sofa to come help but it's too late.

I feel cold metal wrap around my wrist, the one Nathan isn't holding, and I snap around as Samuel locks a cuff around my wrist.

"What the hell," I shout. "What are you doing?!"

Samuel lets go of the cuff and the other half hangs from my wrist. I try to get away from Nathan's tight hold but he's not letting go.

"I promise you I'm not going to hurt you. It's just a precaution while we're out of the house."

"Let me go!" I shout in panic. I twist and turn, but there's nothing to do.

Nathan pulls me toward the kitchen, and I watch in fear as Samuel easily grabs and lifts Rose from where she's standing.

"Fuck you," she rages. "I swear to God, you cuff me here, I'll end your fucking life."

"Careful, she means it," Nathan laughs. How is this a funny situation to him?

Samuel doesn't reply to her even if he is clearly affected by her words. He easily carries her to the kitchen as Nathan pushes me to the floor, forcing me to sit down on the cold tiles.

I'm shocked speechless. There's clearly no point shouting at him. He's looking at the scene amused and slips the other cuff through the bar handle of the oven, forcing my left arm up as he pulls the other cuff.

"Stop. Sam, stop. I swear…" Rose's hoarse voice breaks as he puts her down and grabs her right arm. "You put my wrist in this fucking cuff you're dead to me," she says as he drags her by the arm across the kitchen. She grounds her heels to the floor but keeps slipping anyway.

Rose is a tall girl, yet she's so skinny and frail when I compare her to Samuel. She keeps fighting and it barely changes anything for him. He easily manages to lock her right wrist in the other cuff, but she doesn't sit down. Nathan takes a few steps back to admire the work.

We're now both locked in the cuffs and to the oven. Nothing to do, nowhere to go.

Rose is annihilating Samuel with her stare and I'm surprised he doesn't burn on the spot. He walks to her until their toes are practically touching and leans so his mouth is to her

39

ear.

"Don't look at me like that, it breaks my heart."

He said this low enough for Nathan not to hear but I'm close enough and my mouth goes slack. He sounds like he means it.

"Fuck you," she growls. She goes to hit him, but he takes a step back and she's held back by the cuffs. Ultimately my arm gets pulled harshly.

"Rose," I wince. She comes back closer and the pull eases on my arm.

Nathan comes up behind Samuel and looks at both Rose and me. She's still standing, refusing defeat, while I'm on the floor, too scared to do anything.

Nathan lowers to my level and grabs my jaw with one hand.

"Don't make this face please."

I don't reply. I'm too shocked and disappointed to even begin a conversation with him again. He chuckles to himself and probably sees the questioning look on my face.

"I can't believe you were worried that I was working for Sam. That new gang in town...I'm the fucking boss of it, beautiful."

My stomach twists with betrayal. I push his hand away with my free one. "Don't touch me," I spit at him.

He ignores my words and straightens back up before turning to Rose. "We won't be long. Be good." He gives her a patronizing slap on the cheek as a goodbye and I can almost feel it. Too light to hurt, hard enough to make her flinch in fear. She stays quiet but her eyes and clenched jaw say it all.

As soon as the door shuts, her back hits the kitchen counter and she slides to the floor to my left. She runs a hand through her hair and turns to me, anger rolling off of her.

"Nate." She takes a deep breath. "You have a boyfriend... and that boyfriend is *Nate*. Are you actually fucking kidding me," she hisses. "How could you...just *how*?" I hear the desperation in her voice, and I don't even know how to reply. How could I have known?

"I had no idea, Rose. I didn't even know you and Jake had an older brother...how could I have?" I reply in a small voice.

She stays silent.

"I'm sorry," I finally say. I don't even know why.

"You couldn't have known," she sighs. After a short pause, she keeps going. "Where did you meet him? When?"

"A little more than two months ago. At Church."

She breaks into a laugh. "Are you joking?"

I shake my head no and she slowly stops. "Fuck. What a motherfucker. He's been here for two months and we didn't know."

"Why is he here? What does he want with you?"

She shrugs. "Probably wants to make my life hell. Clearly taking over new territory for Bianco. Fuck if I know. Either way, it's not good news."

"Wh-what if he kills you?"

She lets out a sharp laugh. "Trust me, if he wanted me dead. I'd be dead. No, he's a psychopath, he loves torturing people too much to kill me."

She goes silent again. My brain is overheating as I think over all the information I've just learned. The twins have a brother. My boyfriend Nathan is their brother and none of us knew about it. Except Nathan. Nathan and Sam.

I remember the text where Sam threatened Rose, he said he'd go to the police about her brother. I thought he meant Jake had done something. Jake warned me though, he said not to play detective with him, he said I didn't have all the information.

That text was about Rose shooting her older brother. She thought he was going to send her to prison.

I think of Nathan's dodgy money, of his scar with a rose tattooed on it. How did I not realize it was a bullet wound when I've got one myself? His is a lot cleaner than mine and when he mentioned an abusive father, I thought it had to do with that.

Everything makes sense, everything is linked together and somehow, I missed it, somehow, I still can't believe it as if I heard something wrong or made up the conversation.

"Bianco, was he your foster dad before you moved to the Murrays?" I ask, cutting the heavy silence between Rose and me.

Rose just nods yes. Her eyes darken as she remembers. "Mine. Jake's. Nate's. He's a smart man. He runs his mafia family with a firm hand. Surrounds himself with people he can trust and uses orphan kids to do his dirty work. Jake and I tried to leave so many times, but he's got everyone in his pocket. And Nate...He wanted to stay and become part of his gang. So, we had to stay too." She doesn't say the rest, but I got that part.

"So, you shot him." I almost formulate it as a question, when I know she did. It might be unbelievable to me, but it happened.

"Look, you don't understand the situation we were in, okay? Nate became Mateo's favorite and with that so did we. We were fucking kids." She calms down before whispering, "We still are." I almost don't hear it.

"I'm not judging you, Rose. I-I'm shocked at what you've been through. That you even had access to a gun."

"Mateo taught me how to shoot. Apparently, I had a good

42

eye. Funny for someone nearsighted, isn't it? Every single day I had to spend hours at his shooting range while he was there watching, judging, grading." She huffs and her head falls on the oven door behind us. "When the Murrays tried to take us in, DCF insisted they had to take the three of us. It took me months to understand it wasn't normal. Bianco had bribed them into offering a three-kid-deal because he knew Nate would refuse to leave him. He got in the way as usual. He wanted us to stay there, and we wanted nothing else than to get out. Things got heated up at our house. Nate was being violent, Bianco was taking his side. It's not like I wanted to shoot my own brother. I was left with no choice. They would have never let us go. Bianco didn't want a death associated with him, so he pretended Nate just left, ran away. Then they finally put us with the Murrays."

"I'm so sorry—"

"It doesn't matter. What's done is done." Matter of fact. No feelings. She sounds so much like Jake right now.

I don't reply, simply nodding my head. I don't know what to say because I can't imagine what it was like. She sighs and runs her hand over her face again.

She reaches into her pocket with her left arm and I can't help but look at the X tattoo mixed with others on her forearm. For a second I'm hopeful she's pulling out her phone. It quickly dies down when she grabs a pack of cigarettes.

She opens it with one hand, her skilled fingers pulling a cigarette slightly out of the package before she grabs it with her lips. She pulls a lighter out of that same packet and lights it. My mom would kill me if she knew someone was smoking in the house and the smell makes me feel sick, but I don't say anything. It doesn't matter right now.

43

She finishes her cigarette in silence and puts it out against the sole of her shoe before putting the bud back in the pack.

"Right," she grunts while moving awkwardly. "Let's get out of here." She goes into her back pocket and takes out her phone.

"You had your phone with you all along?!"

"Yup," she says, making her 'p' pop.

"Why didn't you call the police?" I say, outraged. How could she leave us like this for so long?

She scoffs. "Dude, I'm not gonna call the police on my brother." I can almost hear the 'duh'.

"The brother that just threatened you...and hit you!"

"It's just how it is," she shrugs. "We don't get the police involved."

"Maybe if you *had* involved the police we wouldn't be here right now."

"Look, Goody, you involve the cops and it's gonna go to Bianco. For sure. He's got too many of them in his pocket. The last thing I want right now is to be on his radar, trust me." There is real fear in her eyes every time she talks about Mateo Bianco and I can't begin to imagine what she and Jake have been through when they were with him.

I shake my head as she dials.

"Where are you?" she asks. She pauses while she listens. "Yeah. I know. I know, Jake. My phone was dead." she sighs and bites her thumb, "I'm at Jamie's."

I stop listening as Rose explains that Nathan and Sam were both at my house.

Jake. He saw Nathan last night. That's why Nathan didn't want me to get out of the car, he didn't want me to see that Jake knew him. Well. We all know now.

So, what's going to happen?

CHAPTER 4

Riptide – grandson

Jamie

Less than fifteen minutes later the sound of the door bursting open makes me jump.

"In here," Rose says lazily.

Jake, Chris, and Luke appear in the kitchen, their faces a mix of concern and disbelief.

"What the fuck, Ozy! I was looking for you all night!" Jake barks.

"You missed all the fun," Rose mumbles as she gets up and I follow.

"Jamie, do you have any tools in here?" Chris asks.

"Uh, yeah. Hall closet."

Chris turns around and disappears in the hallway. I'm trying to get my thoughts straight, which turns out to be an impossible task with Jake's furious eyes piercing through me. He hasn't looked away since they stepped in the kitchen.

"What was *Sam* doing here?" Jake asks as his gaze finally

leaves mine.

Rose huffs. "Maybe I shouldn't have called you. Are you a detective now?"

"I swear don't piss me off, Ozy, because I'll leave you here, I don't fucking care."

"Man, calm down," Luke says as he puts a hand on Jake's shoulder.

Jake takes a deep breath and Rose just watches him with a mocking smile, not scared of him in the slightest. It's strange to hear Jake call her 'Ozy' after hearing it coming out of Nathan's mouth.

They're the same family. This couldn't feel more unnatural. It doesn't sound right.

Chris comes back with a heavy-duty cable cutter that I wasn't aware my mom owned. His biceps bulge right next to my face as he cuts the chain keeping me and Rose locked together. In a ping of metal breaking, both she and I are free, apart from each still having a cuff around one of our wrists.

"What are we meant to do with this?" I ask Chris.

I can't ask Jake because I'm too intimidated by his presence. The rage emanating from his body seems to be aimed at me only.

"You got a hairpin or something?" Rose questions.

I nod and we both walk to my bedroom in silence. As soon as she closes the door behind us, she turns to me.

"You can't tell them I showed up with Sam. I don't need a life lesson right now, you got that?"

I nod quickly, I wasn't going to say anything anyway.

She smiles at me as she grabs a bobby pin on my desk and starts working at my cuff. "You got yourself in quite a situation here, Goody. Jake and Nate...fucking hell, the guy is a psychopath how did you even end up with him."

"I don't know," I hesitate. "He is-*was* different?"

She doesn't reply, lost in her own thoughts. This situation has gone way past anything I could have imagined.

My cuff opens and she starts working on hers.

"You've got some strange skills," I admit.

"Funny enough, that's the least strange."

Her cuff opens and she looks back at me. "It's gonna be fine," she says. I'm not sure if she's trying to reassure herself or me.

"Enough chatting," Jake's harsh voice cuts through our moment. "He's obviously gonna come back. Let's go."

"I can't just leave my house like that," I say to Rose.

"Who said you're going anywhere. Let's go, Ozy," he repeats.

"Dude, you're being an asshole. Stop it," she tells him.

"I don't think you're really in a position to judge anyone right now." I watch as his hand tightens on the doorknob.

"You're really gonna leave her here alone when you know your psychopath of a brother is going to be back anytime?" She stands face to face with Jake, and I can see the battle for power in their gazes.

"Don't call him my brother. And she's not my problem. You're big enough of a problem, I don't need another one."

There's a slight frown on her face as her jaw clicks but she quickly regains composure. "You're starting to say things you're going to regret," she warns.

"And you've already done things I'll make you regret—"

He's cut off when Luke runs into the room. "Guys, there's a car parking in front of the house. I think it's them."

Rose and Jake are taken out of their stare-down.

"Are you packing?" she asks.

"Yeah."

"Give it to me." She extends her arm out, palm up, and expects him to hand out the gun.

"Fuck no."

"Jake!"

"Stay here," he says as he leaves the room with Luke. The first thing she does is follow him and so do I.

I see Jake's gun tucked in the back of his jeans and a chill runs down my spine at the well-known item.

As soon as I reach the living room, Chris strides toward me. "You should stay in your room, Jamie," he orders as politely as possible.

He looks at Rose but doesn't say anything, as if he already knows he won't be able to send her away. I should be more like this. More like her. Put my foot down and be strong and stubborn enough to stand my ground. Maybe that would have avoided me being stuck between Jake and Nathan. It would have avoided me Jake's wrath or dating a gang member without even knowing.

I don't have time to reply or walk back to my room because someone tries to open my front door. One of the guys must have locked it. There's a banging on the door and Nathan's voice leaks through.

"'Me! I know you're here, open the door!"

Jake's face instantly falls, and he turns to me. I know he spoke to Nathan yesterday, I know *he knows*, but the pain in his eyes... It still hurts to hear Nathan call me 'Me. That stupid nickname.

Nathan's voice is the only thing that breaks the heavy silence. "I don't know how you two got out, but you need to let me in. We need to talk. 'Me, please."

I squeeze my eyes shut, secretly hoping the whole situation will disappear. I'm like a kid thinking no one can see me if I can't see anything.

"Baby, please open the door."

This is not how this was supposed to go. Nothing was meant to fuck up this bad. I had made my choice; I chose Nathan no matter how much I wanted Jake. I chose simplicity and safety over the dangerous need my body and mind needed. Nathan was keeping me safe. He wasn't meant to suddenly become danger and lies.

Jake chuckles sarcastically and it slowly turns into a cold laugh. He still isn't looking anywhere but straight at me.

"I think your *boyfriend* wants to come in, Goody." His voice is lacerated with venom and poisoning me whole.

Chris runs a hand behind his neck and shakes his head. "Fuck," he huffs.

Jake makes a beeline for the front door. "You shouldn't have any problem dealing with him. I'm sure you were fine until now."

"Jake—" I try, but he's already opened the door.

On the other side, Nathan is surprised for a split second but quickly gives his brother a frozen smile. He crosses his arms on his chest as he leans against the doorframe.

"Here to the rescue, I see." Nathan's cold voice makes me shiver because, clearly, me and his siblings haven't faced the same person.

* * *

Jake

'*Go on, run to Ozy to let her know I'm alive. But tell Jamie who I am and the girl is dead.*'

That's what he told me yesterday. I couldn't warn Jamie that she was in bed with a psychopath, I couldn't risk her life like that. Nate's threats are anything but empty. So I did what he said, I spent my night trying to warn my sister. In vain.

I try to keep my head as blank as possible but seeing Nate alive and well in front of my eyes is making me dizzy. Second time in twenty-four hours and I still can't believe my eyes. In what world is this motherfucker alive? Because it sure as hell wasn't supposed to be this one. There was no way in hell my sister missed a shot.

She's been trained harder than in the army. Bianco wouldn't let her as much as eat or sleep if she missed her targets at training. Most kids had never held a gun at eleven and Ozy could already aim better than fully trained soldiers. Nate shouldn't be standing in front of me because Rose White *never* missed. Or so we thought.

I spent all night trying to contact Ozy, calling, texting. Chris, Luke and I drove around Stoneview looking for her. She always disappears, does her own thing, but never in our seventeen years has she missed blowing out our candles together.

After seeing Nate, I thought something had happened to her, I didn't sleep, I'm running on nerves and anger right now. Exactly like I used to as a kid. It helps to hide any other emotions, eventually it even makes them disappear.

"Cat got your tongue, brother?"

"Don't call me that," I hiss at him.

He shoulders past me and inside the house, Sam following him like the dog he is.

"I see you brought your pet along," I say purely to rile them up.

The two are best friends, but Sam has always been in his shadow. I've never really known what he does for Bianco, I just always assumed he would kill to be Bianco's right man, probably has, while that spot always belonged to Nate. And that's because Nate knows right from wrong perfectly and always chooses wrong. He is a master at pushing others to a life of crime and he has the charm that goes with it.

My chest tightens thinking that Jamie fell for that charm. I was fuming with jealousy when she chose another guy over me. I can't begin to describe what it feels like to learn that guy was my supposed-to-be-dead brother. Seeing him with her yesterday, her naïvely getting in his car like he was her savior...it broke something in me. I don't just hate my brother, I hate *her* for falling for him.

Years away from Nate and Bianco have slowly helped me find the humanity in me. The problem with feeling shit is that it's not always rainbows and unicorns. It's also hatred, jealousy, longing, painful love. I need something to calm me down. My fingers clench into fists and I release. I repeat the process multiple times before I turn around.

"You need to leave," I say as calmly as possible.

The simple fact that Nate is in the same room as me, as Rose, *as Jamie,* is driving me mad with anger. He's taking my control away and for that reason only I want to bury my fist in his jaw. I know better than to do so though. Not only is he a strong bastard and he's the one who taught me how to fight, but he also knows when to back away and is the king of revenge served cold. I might get a punch in now, but I'll regret it later...or Ozy will and that's the worst kind of revenge.

"Hey, Jake, you met my girlfriend Jamie, right?"

I risk a glance at Jamie as my blood starts to boil. She's looking at me with pity in her eyes and that's only making it worse. She has no fucking idea what she's done and who she got involved with, how bad it is.

Chris and Luke are looking at me like they know I'm about to snap.

I won't. I can't do this. Not here. Not now. It's okay, I just have to bring back old habits: stay calm, it doesn't affect you, don't feel anything. Rose is too focused on shooting daggers at Sam to stop me from doing anything stupid.

"You should go, Nathan," Jamie says in a shaky voice, her eyes to the floor.

She's settled her back against the breakfast bar and is rubbing her hands together. Anxiety is pouring out of her and I'm starting to feel bad for her. She's slowly realizing what a fucking mess she put herself in. She shouldn't have to go through the horrible situation of trying to escape Nate. No one should.

"You heard her," I insist.

Nate smiles coldly at me and slowly walks toward Jamie as Sam leans on the back of the sofa, folding his tattooed arms over his chest and watching my two best friends in case they try a move. He keeps quiet like he always does, but I know deep down he's waiting for it all to explode.

I can see Jamie squirming as Nathan gets closer to her.

"'Me," he huffs and grabs the back of her neck in a hard grip. His fingers tangle with her hair and she jumps at the harsh touch like it was the last thing she expected from him. "Why don't you try to understand?"

I thought Bianco had destroyed any sort of feeling inside me. That no matter how much effort I put in pretending to care, or to be happy, or to have fun it would never feel genuine inside me. Then how come, when Nate touches Jamie and she flinches, the beast inside me wakes up in a split second? I thought I was stuck in an infinity of emptiness, but Jamie...I can't even pretend I don't feel anything because right now... right now I see red. I tried to keep it together, I lasted about five minutes. Who fucking cares?

Rose is the first to notice the sudden change as I stride toward Nate and Jamie.

"Jake don't−" but I can't hear her. I grab Nate by the shoulder, pulling him away from Jamie, and my fist lands hard on his face.

"Don't. Fucking. Touch her!" I roar.

Jamie's loud gasp doesn't help. I wanted to not care about her or at worst hate her, and I wanted to stay away from her. I tried to respect the fact that she chose someone else, but that was before I realized the 'someone else' was Nate.

My obsessivity over her creeps back and drowns out my common sense. She's *mine*. She was always mine. The way her body responds to mine, the way she submits under my touch. She made the wrong choice, and I'm not about to let her forget that.

Nate staggers back but quickly straightens back up. The fucker can really take a punch and I can see Chris' surprise written all over his face. He knows how hard and technical my punches are. Both Chris and Luke knew *of* Nate, but they didn't know him. How could they? He was meant to be fucking dead. I think they're starting to get the kind of guy he is.

Chris and Luke are about to come for help, so I hold a hand up as Nate walks back to face me.

"I don't think I need to explain to you how bad you just fucked up, do I?" he taunts me.

"Get the fuck out of here. I don't give a shit about your threats."

"My threats? Oh, Jake, you're so cute."

"Leave. It's your last warning." I take another step toward him and our foreheads are practically touching.

I'm larger than him, but Nate's lean muscles and hidden strength is what has always fooled people into thinking he was an easy target. He's not. His strength comes from the psychopathic traits he hides and the lack of fear. It comes from the deep will of *actually* wanting to kill people.

He's slightly taller than me, but it's because he's instilled fear in me too deep and too long ago that I know it's not a good idea to fight him. Unfortunately, sometimes, anger drives one to do stupid things.

He chuckles, looks behind me, probably at Jamie, and back at me.

"What's up? You think if you play the hero you got a chance with her? You're no fucking hero, Jake."

He smirks at me and I instantly know where he's going. My heart is beating so hard in my chest, I'm surprised my shirt isn't moving to the rhythm.

"You couldn't save yourself," he lowers his voice, "and you definitely couldn't save Ozy–"

I punch him again and this time he falls to the floor.

"Fuck! Jake, stop!" Rose's husky voice pierces through my rage. It's drowned out as fast as it came.

She knows he's going to kick my ass. She knows what he's capable of and she's scared for me, but I don't care. My body is taking control and it wants blood.

I hurry on top of him to punch him again. He easily avoids it and flips us around. I feel the gun at the back of my jeans slip away before I can reach it.

"Really? You're packing? That's fucking weak," he laughs.

His fist lands just below my eye and the pain shoots all the way to my skull. It quickly disappears as adrenaline takes over.

"See, Jake, I don't need a fucking gun to beat you. You're so weak it's barely effort."

He punches me again and again. I think back to what he said. To the moments of my childhood where I couldn't save my own sister from Bianco. I hit back and, as I imagine the things he and Jamie have done together, my rage doubles.

I manage to punch him in the ribs making him slightly retreat in a wince. The break gives me a chance to land another punch to the side of his face and he gets off of me to avoid another blow. He gets up fast and I'm not quick enough to follow. I receive a kick to the ribs and groan in pain.

He's about to kick me again when the loud click of a gun makes everyone freeze in silence. I notice Jamie being held back by Luke, her face streaked with tears, while Chris and Sam are close to me and Nate, ready to jump in at any time.

In the middle of it all, Rose is pointing my gun at Nate and me. Sadly, she looks in her element and anyone who knows what she's capable of should fear her right now.

"You two need to fucking chill."

She looks so relaxed with a gun in her hands, it concerns me. I slowly get back up.

"Rose, put this down," Sam calmly says as he advances toward her with one hand in front of him.

Truly, if anyone can get her to do anything, it's him. Right now, though, she doesn't seem in the mood to listen to anyone but herself.

"Take another step and Nate will be picking cute coffins with Bianco," she smiles at Sam.

I can't help a small laugh from escaping my lips and it enhances the copper taste of blood in my mouth. I can feel it dribbling down my face.

She turns back to Nate and me. "You need to leave, Nate."

"You think you scare me because you're holding your favorite toy?" he taunts her. "You missed me once, you'll miss again. I wouldn't be surprised if you've lost your aim by now."

"Nate," Sam growls in warning.

She nods her head. "Your choice," she shrugs.

Without hesitation, she shoots in his direction. I flinch and my ears ring, but I can still hear Jamie's scream. The smell of burnt gunpowder fills the air and I instantly turn toward Nate. I know she hasn't killed him, but I want to check what she did.

"You *fucking* bitch," he hisses at her.

I notice the bullet lodged in the shelf right next to him, splitting the wood. A few centimeters away from his face. A warning from my twin.

"Get the fuck out of here," she spits at him.

Nate is about to jump her, and I'm ready to get in the way, but Sam seems to make the right decision for once in his life. He strides to Nate and grabs one of his arms.

"Let's go," he says in a voice that is almost a whisper. Nate

57

snaps his arm back and doesn't budge. "Mate," Sam insists, "Let's *go*."

Nate looks around the room and his gaze lingers on Jamie. I try my best not to move or say anything. If I do, he'll never leave.

"I'll see you very soon," he says to me. "Try to keep your hands off my girlfriend in the meantime."

I can't help the animalistic growl that bubbles in my throat. I still manage to keep my mouth shut as I watch him and Sam leave the house. They quietly close the door behind them as if not a worry in the world. My shoulders relax as soon as he's out of sight and I let out a breath.

I turn to Ozy who's wiping her brows with her wrist in an anxious gesture. She's still holding the gun.

"Put that shit down," I snap at her. She doesn't deserve it, but I have no other exit right now.

"You're welcome for not letting him kick your ass by the way."

"Ugh, fuck off, Rose. Give me my gun."

She reluctantly gives it back to me. I can see Chris and Luke talking to Jamie in the corner of my eye. I can't focus on her. I can't look at her. Not after everything I've learned. She's been dating my *dead* brother. Was there any other outcome than me losing my shit? Why did I even try to save her? I should know she doesn't need saving. She *chose* to be with him.

This is a nightmare I'm never going to wake up from.

CHAPTER 5

Don't Blame Me – Taylor Swift

Jamie

Rose has perfected the art of rhetoric. It's the only reason I'm at the Murrays with them right now. Jake didn't want me here, and she had to whip out her convincing skills. He wasn't even looking at me when they were discussing, talking about me like I wasn't in the room.

In the end, here I am sitting on their sofa in the pool house, my head in-between my hands and my elbows on my knees, because apparently, there is nothing Jake refuses his sister. Even when it comes to the girl that chose his brother over him.

I'm still trying to process everything. Nathan, Jake, Rose, their relationship. Samuel. They all know each other. They're all related to Bianco somehow. Mateo Bianco. I'd never heard of him and suddenly he's part of my life. Because I'm dating... *was* dating his right-hand man, apparently. I'm trying to swallow this while simultaneously learning that Nathan, my sweet, funny, lighthearted, and protective boyfriend, used to make the twins' lives hell. That everything dark in Jake, Nathan put it there. Him and Bianco.

I can't look at Jake, his cut lip and swelling cheek are just a reminder that this is all my fault.

Rose and Jake are having a heated discussion in the kitchen, but I'm not listening anymore. I'm just about realizing that this morning, Nathan was telling me he was in love with me. In the afternoon he cuffed me to my own kitchen and turned out to be a gang member. My heart aches at the unbelievable betrayal.

"Jamie, can you hear me?" Chris' voice leaks through my thoughts and I look up.

"I'm sorry, what?" I have no idea how long he's been trying to get my attention. He's sitting next to me on the sofa, I don't know when that happened either.

"Are you feeling okay?" he asks with genuine concern in his voice.

When everything has gone wrong, there's always a moment when someone will ask if you're okay. And it's usually at that moment that you realize how not okay you are.

I try to reply to Chris. Instead, I burst into tears. I do everything I can to hold them back, but it turns into shaking sobs and I bury my face in my hands in shame. I have no right to feel like this. Nathan betrayed my trust but it's not like my evil brother just came back from the dead. I feel horrible breaking down in front of Jake and Rose, who obviously have more reasons to be distressed than me and haven't shed a tear.

Chris places a hand behind my back, rubbing between my shoulder blades.

"I'm so sorry," I sob. I get up in a sudden movement and hurry out of the pool house. I'm so ashamed to break down in front of all of them.

A second later, I hear the door close behind me and Chris comes to a stand next to me.

"Jamie, you don't have to be sorry for anything," he assures me. I can't reply because my tears won't stop, and my voice isn't working anymore.

"This..." he waves a hand towards the pool house behind us. "This is complicated on levels you couldn't have possibly known. No one could have predicted this to happen."

"Except Nathan," I reply as another sob racks through me. "He knew. He knew and he lied to me."

He puts a hand on my shoulder. "That guy, Jamie, he's... he's−"

"A liar? A psychopath? Yes, I heard Rose say it all. But he was different to me, Chris, I swear to you. I would have never dated someone that would get anyone in trouble. You know me!"

He lets me try to catch my breath and gather for a minute before talking again.

"I know. It'll be alright, I promise you."

"So you knew, right? That the twins had an older brother?"

"I knew they had a brother that passed away, yes."

"And..." I hesitate. "About Rose?"

He nods at me. "She had a hard time dealing with what she did. She told me not too long after moving in here. I think she was trying to scare me away from her, so I wouldn't get attached. It only drew me closer."

"The twins...they're broken," I whisper.

"Yeah," he sighs. "But not irreparable. And when they let

you in, it's like nothing else you've ever experienced."

"Nathan is the one who broke them."

Chris shifts so we're facing each other a little more rather than both looking at the backyard in front of us. "He is."

The door of the pool house opens behind us and Rose walks out fuming.

"And here I was, thinking only one of my brothers was an asshole," she mumbles before putting a cigarette between her lips. "I'm going to Rachel's. I'm letting you know since, apparently, Jake now wants to keep tabs on my exact surroundings."

She walks past us and into the yard without a look back.

"How did you all end up at yours?" Chris asks me.

"Nathan was sleeping at mine. Rose just...showed up."

"With Sam," he sighs.

I shrug. This is not even my lie to tell so I keep quiet.

Chris runs a hand behind his neck, massaging the tension knotting above his shoulders.

"I know this is going to sound crazy but...he seemed protective over her," I admit.

He might not believe me, but I saw how Samuel was every time Nathan tried to hurt her. I saw the regret in his eyes when she said she would never forgive him. He cares for her.

"He is," Chris confirms. "Too much."

I can't help but wonder what kind of relationship Rose and Samual have. I guess it doesn't matter anymore anyway.

"Bet she won't be hanging out with him now," I say.

"If only," he murmurs to himself. "I'm going to go back to the house. You're welcome to tag along."

I look down at myself, realizing I'm still wearing Nathan's top and my leggings.

"I think I'm going to head home."

"You don't have to, Jamie. There's more than enough room here for you. I understand if you don't want to be alone at your house."

I shake my head. "It's okay." It's not but I can't be around them. I can't be around Jake. Not now, not like this.

"If you change your mind, you know where to find me."

He walks away to the main house and I turn back to the pool house. I need to get my phone in there, and I'm not sure how I feel about being alone with Jake.

I let out a shaky breath before opening the door and walking in. No one's in the living area.

"Jake?"

After a few seconds of silence, I get my phone on the kitchen bar and turn back around toward the entrance. I'm about to put my hand on the door handle when his deep voice startles me.

"How long?" he asks so calmly it freezes my blood.

I close my eyes and swallow before turning back around. When I open them, Jake is standing in the doorway leading to the hallway. He took off his bloody shirt and stands topless in his jeans only. He must have put ice on his face because it's not that swollen, just bruising. There's another deep purple bruise on his ribs.

"We shouldn't talk about this," I say.

"But we are. So, how long have you been seeing him?"

I try to swallow the lump in my throat again and ignore my heart hammering against my chest. "A couple of months."

He takes a step toward me and I try my hardest not to falter. "A couple of months? No. Not you, Goody. You wouldn't do that," he mocks me.

63

I know the state he's in. He's angry and he feels helpless. In a few months, I've come to understand there are two versions of Jake. The sweet one that allows himself to relax and not be on guard. The one that took me to the ball and danced with me. The guy that hugged me tight the morning after his party.

There's also the Jake that can't stand not being in control. That loses it when he feels his power slipping away. The one I couldn't bring to reason at the ball, who couldn't accept I was choosing someone else over him. The one who needs to blackmail me with something to keep me close. Sociopathic Jake. The one who doesn't understand right from wrong. Right now, I know exactly which one I'm facing.

Nothing could have been worse than the position we were in only a few hours ago. He lost control over the situation, over himself, and he wants to regain it somehow. I'm not sure I want to be the one he uses to claim back authority over his life.

I get it, really, I do. He's lived a life Bianco and Nate commanded. He did what he was told, paid the price if he didn't and he's fighting to heal from the trauma. But should I really be the one paying for that just because he decided so?

Chris is right. Jake is dark, darker than I could have possibly imagined. His past dictates his life, it makes him cruel and heartless, and I don't think I can handle that. I might get a rush from the way he's touched me but it's not sustainable. I know it's not. This is exactly why I had decided to stop whatever we had and focus on Nathan.

Fuck.

Everything always goes to shit and I'm the biggest hypocrite of them all.

"You're such a good little angel," Jake taunts as he closes

in on me like a predator on his prey.

I should move. I should turn around, leave, and slam the door in his face. But God, I am such a willing prey when it comes to Jake White and my insides clench in anticipation.

I can't bring myself to look at him when he reaches me, so I focus on a spot of dry blood on his jeans.

He puts his forefinger below my chin, forcing my head up to meet his gaze. He's got that lopsided smirk that mocks me. He's got that glint in his eyes he always gets when he's about to play with his favorite toy.

"A good girl like you, how could you do this to him, huh? Letting me touch you and make you feel so good when you were seeing him."

Guilt pulls at my chest because I know he's right. I've let Jake play his little games when Nathan thought I wasn't seeing anyone else. Jake is not going to let this go because this is the only thing he can hold onto right now. His perfect revenge.

His finger under my chin slowly turns into a tight hand on my jaw. He turns my head to the side in a precise movement. No violence, no rush, just control. He lowers his head to talk in my ear. His breath on my skin lights me up right away. There's no escaping how my body reacts to him.

"Did he wonder where you were when you were with me, Angel? Did you go back to him after I made you come?" I writhe at his words. Everything is making my skin long for his touch.

I let out a shaky breath when he puts his head in the crook of my neck. He inhales deeply and his hold tightens, making me wince.

He's going to bruise you again.

65

I know that voice in my head is trying to save me but maybe I don't want to be saved. Maybe I *want* Jake to bruise me. To make me his. To possess me. Maybe he's fucked me up that badly that I *need* this. Maybe I was already fucked up.

Jake lets out an angry growl and grips my hair with his other hand, finally letting go of my jaw. He pulls my head back so I'm looking right into his eyes and where there's lust like I expected, there's also something else. Anger. He is absolutely fuming.

"You stink of him," he hisses.

I can feel my brows furrow in confusion. How does he know? He suddenly pulls at my hair and drags me to the couch until the back of my legs hit the armrest. He lets go and I fall back on the sofa. My back bounces on the soft cushions and Jake climbs on top of me.

"Is that his shirt?"

I can't reply. I'm too focused on his body between my legs. His hand snakes around my neck and he squeezes. Hard enough to make me listen but not hard enough to hurt. The pleasure pooling between my legs makes me dizzy.

"Fuck, Jamie...you better fucking answer me, or I swear to God–"

"Yes."

He doesn't say anything. He just grabs the collar of the shirt and pulls down in one, hard gesture. His strong arm rips off the material and I whimper as it pulls at the back of my neck.

"Fuck you," he growls. "Fuck you for choosing him over me. That was the biggest mistake of your life. I hope you know that."

His free hand roams over my now bare chest. He pinches one of my nipples and I can't help the sudden moan from escaping my lips. The perfect mix of pleasure and pain. Only Jake knows how to control my body like that.

"I know," I whisper, my voice barely audible.

I know it was a mistake. Not because Nathan turned out to be a manipulative liar. I know because right here, right now, this is all I need. All I want. All I *crave.*

"Good. Because, trust me, you're going to regret it."

I shiver at his words and his mouth comes to my nipple. He bites hard on it and I can't refrain a scream of pain. He looks up at me with an evil smirk.

"Isn't this how you like it, Angel? Is that why you chose him? Because you like pain?"

His free hand slides down my stomach and inside my leggings and underwear. He pinches my clit hard, and I let out a strangled moan.

"Jake..." I breathe out. "Be careful."

"Why? Isn't that how Nate was giving it to you? Isn't that what makes you wet, Jamie?"

My name on his lips makes me squirm.

"Answer me," he growls, and his hand on my throat tightens.

"He-he wasn't like that. He was never rough." The surprise in his eyes quickly turns into anger.

His voice mimics mine, mocking me. "Was he sweet? Did he make love to you? Did he gently take that virgin pussy? Did you offer it to him on a silver platter thinking he was your prince charming?" He pauses and when he talks again, it's a few shades darker. "Did you *really* think he could save you from me?"

He pinches again before sliding a finger in me. My back arches under the unbearable pleasure.

"I didn't," I manage to say. "I never had sex with him."

Something in his touch changes. It's like he suddenly relaxes at the thought that I didn't let Nathan take my virginity. How stupid can a man get? Why does it even matter?

His hand slides from my throat to my jaw and he pins me in place before taking over my mouth. I don't hesitate to part my lips.

I can taste the blood on his cut lip. He's controlling every single cell in my body and I still want more. I want more of him, I want to be his. I want him inside me and even that, I'm not sure will be enough. Our tongues intertwine and I'm burning from the inside. He pulls away and his lips hover over mine.

"You didn't have sex with him because you belong to me. Do you understand that?" His finger is pumping in and out of me and I'm squirming under him. "Do you understand, Angel? You're mine to touch, to fuck, to play with whenever I want. You were never his because he doesn't know you. He doesn't know what you need."

I nod but I'm not sure what I'm nodding to anymore. I'm weak from the pleasure and all I can think is that I want him so bad to put his words into action.

He kisses me again and I wrap my arms around his neck and slide my hands through his silky jet-black hair. I buck my hips as he inserts another finger and curls them inside me. I'm so close to exploding, I freeze in place not wanting anything to change. The pleasure is perfect.

He senses I'm close because he instantly retreats his hand.

"Jake," I sigh. I know him, I know he wants me to beg but all I want is for him to understand I'm ready to give my all to him.

He gets up from me and stands in front of the sofa, his eyes roaming over my body. I push myself on my elbows as he looks down at me.

"How badly do you want to come?" he asks as he undoes his belt. He takes off his jeans and throws them to the side. His erection is straining his white Calvin Klein boxers and he doesn't hesitate to take them off too. "How bad do you want to please me?"

I lick my lips at the sight of his dick. I can't help it. It's the effect he has on me. Like a magnet. A big, strong magnet. Huge in fact.

"Come here. On your knees," he orders as he starts stroking his swollen length.

I get up in front of him and drop to my knees straight away. I'm dying to please him, for his approval, for his forgiveness. I grab him in my hands and they've never felt so small. I start rubbing him as he fists my hair. He grabs his dick from my hands, and I open wide because what Jake wants, Jake gets. That's the only way my body functions.

I lick the tip before taking him in and his head falls back. As soon as it reaches the back of my throat I choke and gag but his fist tightening in my hair warns me not to move away.

"Fuck, Jamie...you feel too good."

For some reason, his approval wills me to take more of him. I bob my head up and down as he fucks my mouth and my thighs clench to try and find some release.

"Look at you. So willing," he smiles.

I accelerate as he pushes down on my head one last time before he finally pulls out. He gives himself a few pumps and pushes back in my mouth straight away. To the back of my throat it goes, and I clamp my lips around it. It doesn't take him long before I feel him tense.

"Fuck," he hisses as I feel the thick, warm liquid hitting the back of my throat.

The inside of my thighs is damp from arousal and I tingle in a teasing sensation as I do my best to swallow his cum. He pulls out of my mouth and I can't help the whimper. I need him. I need more.

He traces cum on my lips with his tip. "Beautiful," he whispers. He grabs my jaw, helping me back up before pushing me back on the sofa.

"Now let me show you what regret feels like." He gets on his knees in front of the sofa and pulls at my leggings and underwear until I'm free of them.

He hooks one of my legs on his shoulder and his head disappears between my thighs. I have a flashback to being on Nathan's sofa, in the exact same position with him, but I'm taken back to reality when Jake puts my clit between his lips. My body tries to jerk away and he grabs my hips to keep me in place.

"Stay still."

I try not to squirm as he licks me, his tongue running from my entrance to my clit and back. He nibbles and bites. He laps like a starved man and the pleasure is too much. I can't refrain the moans from leaving my mouth. My voice quickly gets higher as I shamelessly explode and scream his name. He gets up and kisses me, letting me taste myself. He picks me up in a sudden movement and my legs wrap around his waist.

He carries me to his bedroom, both naked, throws me on the bed, and quickly settles over me, his hands on both sides of my head. I'm reminded of that same position we were in, only a few weeks ago. I was scared of him, scared to give in, scared of the pleasure he could have given me. Now I'm ready to beg for this pleasure. Beg him to take me. To do to me what Nathan never did.

He straightens up, looking down on me with the power he knows he holds. He places a knee between my legs and presses against my pussy.

"You are so wet, Angel. Always for me, aren't you?"

I simply nod and he presses harder. I slowly start rubbing against him brazenly. When Jake pushes my buttons, I become the little toy he so desperately wants me to be. Worse...I love it.

"Ah. Ah. I see you trying to pleasure yourself. That's my job."

He slightly pulls his knee away and I whine a wordless complaint.

"Tell me who you belong to, Angel," he says, slowly bringing his knee back.

"You," I reply without hesitation. Him, him, him. It's always been him. I was just too scared to accept it.

"And who does this pussy belong to?" He presses his knee so hard I let out another shameless moan.

"You. Please, Jake..."

"Yes?"

"Make love to me," I whisper.

He comes down right above me again and grabs something in the drawer above us. I understand what it is when I hear the wrapper of the condom tearing. I watch as he slowly rolls it over his dick. It's steel hard again, despite coming in my mouth only minutes ago. He brings his lips to my ear.

"I can't do that, Angel," he presses his dick against my

entrance and I almost recoil in fear, only the anticipation stops me, "but I promise I'll fuck you real good."

I suddenly push his chest. "Jake, please...please be gentle."

He looks at me and confusion is clear in his eyes. His lashes are so long, it's the only thing that softens his face. Beautiful, long, black lashes that will be my downfall. They make him look sweet and caring. A trick to attract his victims so he can trap them in the addiction of his touch.

"Please," I beg. "It's all I'm asking for."

His jaw ticks and his whole body tenses over mine. He doesn't get it. I can see it in his eyes, he simply can't grasp my emotions, my fears. He doesn't empathize with people. Sometimes I think I see glimpses of empathy in him, but it's always crushed by his selfishness.

"Just this one time..." I try one last time. I know he'll do whatever he wants in the end. And I know I'll let him because that's just how my body is wired, but I don't want it to hurt. I bring one hand up to cup his cheek and look at him straight in his beautiful eyes.

"I'm not him, Jamie," he smiles wickedly. "I don't do gentle..."

His sentence hangs in the air and I squeeze my eyes tight, bracing for the invasion.

Nothing happens.

Jake sucks at my nipples slowly. So slowly it's torture. He brings a hand down to my clit and circles it with his thumb, so gradually I can count the circles. One, two, three, four—

A moan escapes my lips.

"...but just for you, I'll do slow. Until you can't take it anymore."

I feel his hips starting to move as he penetrates me. Oh.

So. Slowly. I barely wince when he passes my body's barrier, eager for him to be inside and pleasure me. Every inch, I feel myself stretch further and the initial sting is quickly replaced by warmth and the warmth by torturous pleasure. I let out a long moan, the pleasure too much and not enough. Never enough.

"I'm barely halfway through, Angel."

"More," I breathe.

"As you wish."

He pushes all the way inside and I can't help a loud gasp. He stops for a second, his strong body tightening as he squeezes his eyes shut. I feel so stretched I need a second to breathe.

"Wait..." I whisper.

"Fuck..." he brings his head down, kissing my neck and jaw. "Fuck, Jamie, you feel so fucking good."

To my surprise, he pauses as I adjust to having him inside me. He's watching me, waiting for any sign to keep going. It takes me a few seconds to nod slightly and he starts moving his hips, bringing me more pleasure. My mouth falls slack as he moves inside me, painfully slow. I try to move my hips with his to pick up the rhythm, but he pins me down with both hands on my hips.

"Tsk. Tsk. You wanted slow. Now you take it."

I let out a frustrated whimper when he pauses again. I can see his face tightening as if he's struggling.

"Stop squirming, you're gonna make me come," he growls.

He finally accelerates and I feel my eyes roll to the back of my head. Heat builds in my lower belly, inside me, creeping up everywhere. I'm melting and my skin is on fire. Every touch, every caress brings out another moan. I whisper his name between panting breaths and Jake starts pounding harder and faster. Every time he seems close to finishing, he pauses and plays with my clit instead, bringing me to the edge and back.

"Don't stop," I beg as he slows down again.

I'm so close to exploding I bring one hand on his shoulder and one on his steel abs to keep him in place. They stiffen below my hand.

"Please," I insist.

"Anything for you, Angel."

He picks up again with more strength than he's ever shown, and it takes me all of ten seconds to melt for him. My nails scratch at his back as his thumb finds my clit again. My body finds release on a high like never before. In one last hard stroke, his whole body tightens and freezes over mine. He lets out a loud grunt and drops on me, his head in the crook of my neck.

"Fuck, Jamie. What are you doing to me?" he breathes.

I can't reply, still too high. My eyelids are too heavy to keep open and my mouth feels like cotton. I'm flying on a cloud, surrounded by Jake's scent and Jake's warmth and I never want to come down.

I keep dozing off and I don't know how long it takes but I know at some point I feel his weight lift off of me and cold overtakes me. I doze off again until I feel a warm cloth against my pussy. As soon as this is gone, I'm out again, incapable of thinking straight or push myself out of my drug-induced state.

Just before I fall completely into darkness, I feel the bed dip beside me and two strong arms pulling me until my back hits a warm chest.

"See, Angel," Jake's deep voice reaches all the way to my cloud. "You might want Nate, but you *need* me. Make sure you don't forget that."

These are the last words I hear before sleep overtakes me as I think; *I couldn't agree more.*

* * *

Jake

"*No, no, no, Jake, please. I don't want you to go.* Please."

"*I know, I know.*" *I bring a shaking hand up to grab my sister's shoulder, but she slips out of my grasp.*

"*Please. You're gonna come back all bruised or knocked out o-or worse.*"

I don't know what to reply. She's right. Last time I went, I got knocked out, and fuck I thought Mateo was the one who was going to kill me.

"*I'll be fine,*" *is the only thing I manage out of my tight throat. Seeing her like this makes me want to grab our stuff and run away with her. Unfortunately, we both know Mateo's reach goes much further than Washington D.C. He will always find us.*

"*Just go to bed and when you wake up tomorrow, I'll be back.*"

She shakes her head and squeezes her eyes, desperately trying to hold back tears. She runs a hand through her long ponytail, pulling at it as if trying to check this is reality.

"*I can't. I can't just go to bed.*"

"*Everything will be fine. I promise.*"

I'm so fucking naïve. How can I be so naïve?

"Jake, when you're not here," she takes a shaky breath and looks away before looking back at me. "The nights you and Nate are out fighting..."

I try to catch her gaze as she avoids mine but I'm not sure I get what she's getting at. Or I'm not sure I want to understand.

I hear a door open and close behind me. Her gaze locks with someone else over my shoulder.

She scratches her throat and quickly dries the only tear that slipped from her eyelid with the palm of her hand. She readjusts her glasses and smiles at the person behind.

I try to read her. I try to get the truth out of her eyes, out of the features on her face or the way her jaw ticks. And I understand it. I understand it too well to ever forget the look in her eyes when Mateo comes into view from behind me. Nate follows quickly as his boss grabs me by the shoulders.

"Ready?" he asks me. "Nate is going to drive you and get you warmed up. He's your coach tonight, not your brother, remember that. Now listen real close. I want you to knock him out in the sixth round. Got it?"

"Yes, Sir," I reply, my jaw clenching instantly. Only 'yes, sir' when it comes to Mateo. Never refuse him anything, that's the first lesson we learned here. Refusal is not in his vocabulary. He doesn't insist, he doesn't convince you, he just punishes you.

"And I don't want none of this 'I don't want to hurt people' complaint, yeah? Ignore the guilt, son. It will never do you any good. In this world, eat or be eaten."

I nod, not being able to say anything else. Six rounds. I gotta hold six rounds.

"Don't be late, and make me proud, son." He walks away and speaks to us one last time without even looking back. "Rose, come see me in my office before you head to bed."

76

"Yes, Sir," she replies automatically but as soon as he's out of view her pleading gaze meets mine. "Please don't go," she whispers.

Nate takes a few steps back as he mumbles a quiet 'fuck' to himself then speaks louder to both of us. "Ozy, com'here."

She looks up at him in surprise and walks to him. He pulls both his sleeves up to his elbows and that's the only warning before his fist crashes against her cheekbone and she goes down in a screech.

"What the fuck!" I shout as I hurry to her. Nate pushes me back violently.

"Let's go," he orders when I try to fight him back. "Keep your energy for the ring, Jake, let's go."

"I'm not just gonna leave her here you sick fuck! What did you do that for?!"

Ozy slowly comes to a sitting position holding the side of her face in a groan. I try to go to her again, but Nate has managed to slowly push me all the way to the door. "Trust me," he seethes, "I'm doing this for her."

"What?" I choke.

"There's nothing he hates more than seeing a fuck up on her stupid perfect face. Let's go."

"What?" I ask again, too focused on checking if my sister manages to get up.

"You wouldn't get it," he growls. "Now let's go." I try to look at her again, but Nate slams the door and I'm outside.

Then in the ring, beating up a guy that's probably just as forced as I am to be here. Probably risks just as much as me if he doesn't deliver what he's been asked. Yet, there's no mercy in the ring and in the sixth round, I knock him out with a merciless punch right in the jaw. I try to check if he's still alive, but I'm suddenly *at another fight, knocking someone else out, and another one.*

Another one until I'm the one who gets knocked out cold. I feel blood dripping down my face, but I can't open my eyes. I want to. I want to get back up and give Mateo what he wants. I want to go back to his fucking mansion, put a bullet between his eyes, grab my sister, and leave forever. I can't, though, because I'm knocked out and so tired. So. Fucking. Exhausted.

My eyes snap open and I wipe the sweat rolling down my temples. These nightmares make sleeping completely useless. There's no way to get rest when I go down memory lane.

Everything from the day before hits me. Nate is alive. He threatened Ozy. Jamie was dating him. She chose *him* over me. She didn't just choose anyone, she chose Nate. If that fucker is back, Bianco isn't far, and I can't let Bianco back into our lives. We can't get sucked back in. Rose couldn't take it. *I* couldn't take it.

Thoughts go round and round in my head and I can't do anything about it. Anxiety creeps in and I check the time. 4:21 am.

Anxiety. Shit, it had been too long I hadn't felt that.

Don't feel. Numb it down.

I look down at Jamie, asleep on my chest, one leg hooked around mine. The only thing that chases all the other thoughts away is thinking about last night. The way she gave herself to me so willingly. The way she was begging me to take her. My cock wakes at the thought. Everything that happened has put me in a shit, messed-up state and I only feel back in control when I control her. She might not get it now, but I'm not letting that go.

I run my hand up and down her back. Her petite body weighs

nothing against mine and I want to pick her up and sit her back down on my dick. I look at my phone again. Between texts from Cam and some random girl from the North Shore of the Falls I fucked at some point in my life, there's a text from Luke sent at 3 am.

Luke: Your brother showed up at Em's house. Said he wanted to see Jamie. We can't have that bro. It's not safe for Em.

My hand tightens on my phone at Luke calling him my brother. Nate isn't my brother. He might be genetically, but he lost the title long ago.

He showed up at Emily's house. He wanted to see Jamie. He probably showed up at her house first.

Does she want to see him?

My hand on her back creeps all the way to her head and I close my fist around her hair. She's not going back to him, I don't fucking care what she wants. The beast in me slowly wakes up at the thought of her with him and my grip tightens. She stirs awake and looks at me with sleepy eyes, confused.

"Jake?" her voice is husky from sleep.

As soon as she leaves, she's going to go back to him.

I try to shut up the devil on my shoulder, hopelessly.

Control. Control. Control.

It goes in my head on repeat, flashing a bright red light of warning. Everything else might be slipping from my grasp, Jamie won't. I'll make sure of that.

She puts a hand on mine in her hair, but I don't let go.

"What are you doing? That hurts."

I pull hard enough for her head to rear back. She pushes away from me and goes on her back to avoid the pain.

79

You're not getting away from the pain, my little Angel.

I climb on top of her and let go of her hair to grab her wrists. She's so fucking tiny it's no effort for me to keep them both above her head with one hand.

"He's looking for you." I barely recognize my own voice. It's low, dark, and angry.

She's still struggling to wake up fully and she looks at me confused. "What? Who?" She tries to pull her wrists away. "Jake, what are you doing?"

"Guess who, Angel. The guy whose dick you sucked before mine."

Her eyes widen at my crude words, but she doesn't deny it. My anger doubles and I slip a hand all the way down her naked body and grab her pussy.

Fuck. She's wet. She's so fucking wet.

"Always so ready for me." I slip a finger inside her warm pussy and I feel her clenching. I take it out and add another one. She lets out a deep moan as her eyes flutter shut.

"He went to Emily's house—"

"What?" Her eyes snap back open. "Is she okay?"

I dig my fingers deeper in her and she mewls. "I think you should worry about yourself. Because you're in a shit lot of trouble and you're not finished paying for trying to escape me."

Her eyes grow with concern, not without a glint of antici-pation in them. I know what it looks like because I've seen it in Camila. My ex worked hard to get used to how I liked it and to please me. I've seen this look in one-night stands who naturally liked my ways. But in Jamie...in Jamie it's priceless. She thinks she doesn't like it and she thinks it's wrong even if she feels so right. The fight between her body and her mind is something I'll never get tired of.

I tighten my grip on her wrists as I grab a condom from my nightstand. I pause for one second, hesitating. Will she freak out if I tie her wrists to the bed? It's annoying to put a condom on with one hand, but I don't want to let go of her.

She pulls at them again. "Jake," she whimpers, bucking her hips up, trying to find the release she needs.

"Stay still," I growl.

"Let go of my wrists," she snaps back. Does she think she's being brave?

She will definitely freak out if I tie her up. Better not. I need to take it slow with her or she'll shy away.

I manage to roll the condom on with one hand and place my cock at her entrance.

"We did it your way yesterday, Angel. Today we're doing it my way." I slam hard into her and she lets out a loud gasp.

"Oh Gosh..." She takes a deep breath. I slide out slowly then back in hard and she lets out a moan. I feel her getting wetter around my dick and I'm scared I won't be able to reign myself back.

"You're so fucking tight," I growl under my breath.

I stay buried deep inside her for a few seconds as she catches her breath and I feel her squirm under me. My balls already feel tight as fuck and if she keeps moving, I'm going to come. I've got a problem when it comes to this girl, I turn back to being a virgin who tries pussy for the first time.

I accelerate my rhythm and her cries of pleasure follow my strokes. She pulls at her wrists and I know she wants to touch herself, which is exactly why I don't let go.

"Please..." she pants.

I graze the tip of my fingers over her clit and she writhes.

"You beg so well, you know that?"

She nods as she bites her lower lip and I slam hard into her. She lets out another cry and I can't hold back. I keep going harder and faster with my cock and my fingers. I feel her inner walls tighten as her nails dig in my hand when she comes. Her mouth opens but no sound comes out. The pressure in my dick gets too much and I explode as she comes down from her high. She clenches around my dick and I empty myself, falling back on her. I grab her jaw and kiss her. She willingly parts her lips and I eat her mouth like I'm starving and she's my one and only meal. I bite at her lip and she lets out another moan.

I can already feel my dick stirring back to life. I need to calm down, she needs a break, a few hours ago she was a virgin.

That's something Nate didn't take from her.

Fuck. I need to calm down.

"Can you let go of my wrists now?"

I can't help a smile before letting go.

"How sweet," she deadpans.

"That attitude needs to go away, baby, or your ass is going to pay the consequences."

She scoffs in indignation. A second later, I can see her biting her lip to avoid a smile as I roll back to my side.

My phone pings and I grab it from the nightstand.

Chris: Have you seen Beth's story?

God, this guy always wakes up at 5 am. Even on Sunday mornings.

I roll my eyes and go on Instagram. If Chris texted me about it, it's got to do with Rose. I click on Beth's story at the top of my screen and look through a picture of her and Camila getting ready for a house party. The next one is the two of them taking shots with Jason. The one after is a picture of Ozy and Rachel kissing with the caption 'The cutest couple'. I can't help another eye roll. What a fake bitch.

I skip other videos of the party. People need to stop posting five-hour-long stories. There's a video of a guy taking body shots on Cam and I can't even pretend to care because I really don't. Is that what Chris wants me to see? The next video answers my question.

Rose is threatening a guy about twice her size. She looks high off her face and keeps rubbing her nose with her index finger. Coke really makes one brave because that guy doesn't look like he's joking around. I can't help but chuckle hearing her shout 'put a hand on my girl again and I'll make you swallow your own balls, asshole'. Fuck, she was so far gone. I check when it was posted. Two hours ago. *Great.*

I leave Instagram and call my sister right away. She better be alive, she's gonna give Chris a heart attack one day.

"*The fuck you calling me for?*"

"Chris is worried," I reply.

"*I don't think he wants to know what Rach and I have been doing.*"

I try to refrain from laughing. "There's a video of you threatening some big guy on Beth's story. So, Rachel's *your* girl now?"

She laughs. "*We have a new agreement. You should have seen Carlo trying to talk me out of punching that dude's face.*"

I hear her sniff and I know she's probably still high.

"Where are you?"

"*That door across the hall from yours, that's my room.*"

83

I hear Rachel complaining in the background and I know it's my cue.

"Have fun coming down tomorrow," I conclude.

"*Make sure Jamie grabs her clothes back from the living room before I get out of bed. We share that sofa, Jake. That's nasty.*"

When I hang up and turn back to Jamie, she's fallen back asleep. In two years of seeing Camila on and off, she has never slept in my bed. I always walked her out after sex. I would never really sleep at hers either, I like sleeping on my own. I usually don't want anyone to be next to me when I wake up from a nightmare that reminded me of the fucked-up years at Bianco's.

I'm forced to realize that in two months, Jamie's slept in my bed twice and for some reason, it doesn't bother me. She could stay all day if she wanted.

I don't get how I feel about her. I'm not stupid, I know how my body reacts; her lavender scent is hypnotizing and the touch of her skin addictive. Her moans are the most sensual sound, playing with her has become more than my favorite pastime.

But I don't get my feelings. I don't get feelings in general. That's not how I function because it has been beaten out of me. All I know is some people I like, some people I don't care about. Chris and Luke have adapted to me, I can laugh and be myself around them. To me, that means I love them, even if I don't feel that strongly about them. I've associated the fact that they know and accept me with love. The same way I've associated protecting my sister with love. I know it angers me when she isn't well or when I miss her. That's love, right?

Something goes further with Jamie. It's more than anger

when she's not around, it's something lacking in me. I used to carelessly play with her, I did my thing and it didn't really matter if it hurt her body or her feelings. Except I'm getting slightly addicted to it. And it's not just that, something pinches inside me if anyone other than me hurts her. Something, somehow drives me insane when she dares live through everyday life without me. So surely, if I feel something for her that is stronger than for the people I love... then I must be in love.

I chuckle to myself, running a hand through my hair. Good fucking luck with that, Angel. Because I'm not about to let go of the only person who makes me feel something after years of being ingrained it was forbidden to do so.

I lay down next to her and spoon her from the back. She feels so small next to me, I want to keep her like this forever and protect her from the big bad world outside. The problem is, who's going to protect her from me?

CHAPTER 6

F U till I F U – Call Me Karizma, Cass

Jamie

Jake parks on the street by my house and we walk together to my front door.

"You didn't have to walk me to my door," I say, even if I love that he did and can't stop the smile that warmly spreads across my face.

"I'm coming in, making sure there's no bad surprise in there."

I can't believe I had sex with Jake. *Three times.* He woke me up in the middle of the night *and* made sure to have another round before I left his house. I have this feeling of being utterly fulfilled and happy, yet, as soon as he walks past my front door his demeanor changes and I fear the bliss isn't going to last.

It might be because I know it's not like him to get in touch after sleeping with a girl. Jake's reputation has always preceded him. A couple of months ago he didn't even know who I was, whereas I've always known *of* Jake White before knowing him. And what I knew was that he was the king of our school, he had Camila and many other subjects to keep him company. What I knew was that if he wanted a girl, he could have her and he never went back for seconds. Only Camila ever had that chance.

I'm not Camila. I don't have her beauty, I don't have her curves. I don't take care of myself like she does, not of my hair or my skin. I don't hide my pimples when they come out, I don't whip out a pocket mirror after eating bolognese and I buy my clothes at the charity shop. I don't have her money or her status. I don't have her naïve, superficial happiness that so many privileged people get to live with.

Maybe that's why I've got this anxious feeling deep down. I know I'm not special. I'm not ugly and there are many things I like about myself – my brains, my skin complexion, my gorgeous eyes thanks to my mom, my thick hair – but I'm petite, shapeless, almost kid-like. I skipped the glow up and went straight to bags under my eyes from nights worrying about our financial situation or having nightmares about my dad and my brother. Camila has the confidence that puts her above other girls. She's got that blue blood running through her veins; she and Jake are royalty. I'm not her and I have nothing that could keep Jake. Nothing.

I don't regret my first time being with him, it was the best I could have hoped for. He's experienced and knows how to drive my body to pure bliss. I just wish...maybe I just wish we had gotten to know each other more outside of our cat and mouse game. Maybe that way he would know I'm worth keeping, I'm worth coming back to.

Gosh, can you hear yourself? You need space from this guy, you sound like a pathetic fangirl. Get a grip.

He walks in after me and we go around my house together. It's insane, I remember doing this on my own when I would be scared he was following me. After all, he *did* break into my house while I was inside.

I'm feeling dizzy from all this back and forth thinking, from everything that happened yesterday and the angst making me feel like I'm stuck in quicksand. I feel dirty and sticky from last night and I'm uncomfortable in my clothes, a bit too hot from the stress.

We walk back into the living area and I settle against the kitchen bar, letting him go around my tiny living room one more time. He comes to a stop in front of me, eyebrows furrowed, and lips pinched together, but he says nothing. So I fill in the blank.

"I should probably call my mom and all that. Do my homework for tomorrow. We've got a paper to hand in for English. I haven't even started."

He drags the heavy silence I leave after my slightly panicked pace of words. I can't get myself to look at him, my gaze hopping between imaginary points behind him. I still feel like this scaredy-cat around him. We had sex, what now? He got what he wanted. Why do I still feel like a trapped mouse? I still feel at his mercy. It might not be the fear of bullying anymore, it might not be the fear of giving in, but it's been replaced with that anxiety of having been taken for a fool. Have I? Did I lose our game?

A Cheshire grin spreads on his lips. That same smile that shows he loves watching me squirm, that he's about to play with his little mouse.

"Why so fidgety, Angel? What's on your mind?" he gloats,

proud of how he's making me feel.

"I'm not fidgety."

"You're like a lamb waiting to be slaughtered."

I'm about to debate but my mouth clamps shut when he raises an eyebrow. I take a deep breath before throwing myself into the difficult topic.

"So, what now?" I spill. "Wh-what's going to happen next?"

The smile turns into a slight pull at the corner of his lips as he pretends to take a serious thinking face. He cocks his head to the side. "What do you mean?"

"Come on," I sigh. "Don't make me say it."

"Say what?"

I pinch my lips and make sure I glare at him before continuing. "What are we?" I huff.

He chuckles, satisfied from getting me to ask the clingy question.

"You're mine. That's what we are," he replies in all seriousness.

My heart skips a beat when he says that, but the giddiness is quickly replaced by annoyance. It makes no sense to say that. It means nothing except that he's a possessive fuck and I hate myself for wanting to be his.

"What does that even mean, Jake," I sigh. "Maybe I don't want to be yours, maybe I want us on an equal foot where we're both each other's."

"Fine," he shrugs.

"Fine? Just fine? Don't you think we should...I don't know, do things normal couples do. Like, get to know each other or something? Date?"

He chuckles at me, mocking my innocence. "Sure, I'll take

you on a date, Jamie."

And that's Jake for you. He likes me. I know he likes me or he wouldn't just agree to everything I'm saying. But he's incapable of expressing it in the right way.

"Please don't sound so enthusiastic about it," I growl. I feel stupid. He's *making me* feel stupid. I hate that, that's not what I want. I don't want to become the girlfriend who begs for attention and dates. If he's going to treat me the same way he treated Camila, I don't want to be his girlfriend at all.

"God, Jamie," he sighs. "What do you want from me?"

"I just want to get to know you," I argue. "Why do you have to be such a prick about it?"

His silence forces my tongue to uncontrollably push words out of my mouth in panic. "Shouldn't we talk about yesterday at least? Aren't you going to tell me about Nathan? About your childhood?"

Nothing. A block of stone. Blank, frozen.

"Something? Anything?" I insist, my brain giving up way too slowly for my dignity to stay intact.

Dejection washes coldly over me.

"I-I guess I just wanted to make sure I wasn't just another notch on your belt. But don't worry, your reaction says it all," I conclude.

He takes the one and only step that was separating us and runs his knuckles down my cheek, as if soothing the heat from the sting of rejection.

"You're not. In fact, I'm pretty sure I couldn't be with another girl if I tried to, and I don't even want to try." My heart accelerates at his words and I gasp slightly when his thumb starts tracing my lips. "But..." He pushes the tip of his thumb ever so slightly against my top lip, just enough to then drag my bottom lip down. My body tingles from the gesture, yet my brain knows that 'but' isn't announcing anything good. "I'm not going to open up to you, I will *never* talk about my childhood and I'm not going to be the perfect boyfriend to you, Jamie. I don't really feel like being a boyfriend at all to be honest. This isn't who I am. I'm possessive, I'm an asshole, and I want you. Your opinion doesn't matter much to me. You like me, and you can't resist me so, really, what are you gonna do about it?"

My body starts trembling with anger and humiliation.

"What do you think of me?" I slap his hand away from my face. "That I'm some sort of…of object or something?! Some girl… some *toy* you can use at your will? That you can just take and take and give nothing in return?"

"I'm not taking," he explains in his sociopathic way. That way he has of being entirely unempathetic. "You're offering willingly."

"I…" I want to defend myself, but nothing comes out, the shock too great.

"I didn't force you yesterday, I didn't put you on your knees in front of me. You went willingly, you sucked and swallowed like a good girl and no one forced you."

"Shut up," I whisper.

"You knew what I'm like, Angel and you still offered me that sweet little pussy. All I did was help myself to the silver platter."

The tears that threaten to fall feel like acid in my eyes. My fists are so tight I feel like my knuckles are going to pop.

"Just accept that you're happy to be mine, Jamie. Why you're even fighting anymore is beyond me. You had all the information from the beginning, and you still played with me.

You've fallen too deep to go back now."

"This is not what I want, Jake. It's not who I am. I still have some self-respect."

He lets out a short, mocking bark and pushes his body tighter against mine. "Self-respect? Aren't you that same girl who cheated on her boyfriend for me? You were with two different men in less than twenty-four hours, Jamie. The good girl act isn't as believable as it used to be."

"Why are you being like this? All I wanted was to not make the same mistake I did with Nathan. I wanted us to get to know each other and our pasts before we went into something deeper than sex."

His hands intertwine behind my head, tangling in my hair and he lowers his forehead to mine. "And I don't want to get deep. I just want you. All of you. I want you to let me use you, to give me everything and—"

"And give nothing in return," I finish for him. Confirming the words I said a minute ago.

"I can't," he sighs as if slightly lowering his guard. "I can't because there's nothing to give, Jamie. You can peel and peel away at it, you'll just find the same heartless asshole I am on the surface. I'm pretty sure, actually, that you'll find something crueler. The best I can do is put my Stoneview Prep cover on. Under that, it only gets worse."

"You're a horrible man," I rasp, my throat tight and vocal cords tangled from pain and regret. What did I do? How could I think he would suddenly become sweet because we had sex?

"I never pretended otherwise." He straightens up, takes a few steps back, and fishes his car keys out of his gray sweatpants. "I'll give you some time to think about it, but don't make me chase you again. I enjoyed the hunt, I want to savor my treat now."

He doesn't wait for my answer and turns toward the front door. He's about to leave, his hand on the handle, his muscular shoulders defined under his black sweatshirt, when I speak again.

"It was a mistake." My voice trembles, but it's not with pain this time, it's determination. He hurt me and I want to hurt him back. Because that's the only way he'll understand he hurt me. That's the only way he functions. Anger and revenge.

He slowly turns around, an eyebrow raised. "You wouldn't be the first girl who regrets losing her virginity to the wrong guy, Angel."

My nostrils flare. "I don't care about having my first time with you. Only guys like you make a big thing out of virginity.

"What is it then?" he huffs, running a hand through his messy hair.

"Breaking Nathan's trust for you. It was a mistake."

His ocean eyes darken like a winter night as he strides back to me. I'm too late to move away, too slow. His arms are on either side of me, palms gripping the kitchen bar as he lowers his furious face to mine.

"What did you just say?" His voice is a raspy hiss, fury like fire on his tongue.

"I said–"

"You didn't break his trust, Jamie. You didn't leave him for me, he gave you away. He gave you away the moment he started lying to you. He played you all along, don't you fucking get that? Are you really that stupid to think he cared for you? Nate doesn't *care* for people, he uses them. He took the first naïve girl he could use to spy on Rose and me and he *utilized* you."

My chest is rising and falling so far, my breasts touch just below his chest, reminding me of how much my body likes Jake being close to it.

"You just had to ruin everything, didn't you?" he spits at me, disgust contorting his beautiful face. "You just had to remind me that you were Nate's little bitch before coming to me. You're right. This was all a big mistake. I don't want Nate's sloppy seconds. I don't want *you.*"

My heart breaks and I have to use inhuman force to not show it. It would have worked if the look on his face hadn't been utter betrayal, disgust, *regret.* The tears I was trying so hard to keep at bay start overflowing and I bring a hand up to try and wipe them, but he seizes my fist.

"Don't," he orders. "Nobody cries like you do, Angel. Your pain is the biggest turn-on. I want this image imprinted on my brain when I go around fucking other girls."

"You're heartless," I cry out as I push at his chest, desperately trying to get him away from me.

"At least I'm true to myself." He lets go of me so suddenly, I almost fall on my ass. "Whatever we had...it's over. I won't waste any more time on you, Jamie."

I watch him leave, tears free-falling down my face. How did everything get so bad?

* * *

Monday, Jake didn't show up to school and the rest of the week he completely ignored me.

Now two weeks after the Halloween ball incident, he and Camila are stuck together like glue, even if Emily tells me they're not back together. I didn't explain why I don't want to hang out anymore when she's with them and she didn't insist but I can feel us slowly drifting apart. Her relationship with Luke is strong and she admitted to me that she's falling in love with him. Who am I to get in the way of love?

School has never felt so lonely, but it's also never felt so calm. My grades are going back up and my focus on everything is sharper. Lacrosse training is hard and rewarding. Life is peaceful, life is...boring.

In some wicked way, I miss Jake's insistent techniques. I miss his hands on me, his dark voice ordering me around. I'm finding out ignorance really *is* the best revenge. He hurt me when he admitted he wouldn't change for me, he would never be a sweet loving boyfriend, and I hurt him by mentioning Nathan. Our love/hate relationship is all over for good. There is nothing left of us.

I don't know if there's any way to fix this, I just know I hurt from being invisible to him.

"Miss Williams, is that clear?" Mr. Ashton's voice drives me out of my daydreaming, and I widen my eyes, lost.

Everyone is looking at me with mocking smiles on their faces.

"I'm so sorry, Sir, I zoned out."

"Make sure you pay attention please." He turns back to the class. "So, I was saying the homework is due on Monday. They're short poems and there are two of you working on it, so I expect no struggle."

I look around in confusion and my gaze lands on Jake, writing something in his notebook.

The bell rings, he gets up and drops a piece of paper on my desk.

"The poems." His voice is ice cold, and my chest constricts at the resentment in it.

"What do we have to do?" I ask.

"We're supposed to answer all the questions together by Monday. I don't want to work with you so write half of it, I'll pick it up from your house tomorrow and write the rest."

"Are you sure you don't want to just do this together? We can do it in the library at lunchtime."

He scoffs. "I'm not wasting my time with you, Goody. You're not worth any of it, not even for English homework."

His words hit me hard, but I try not to let it show. "I'll be done by tomorrow," I nod.

He doesn't reply and just leaves the class without looking back. My heart aches at the silence, coldness, and hatred he leaves behind.

By the end of classes, I've spent another lonely day at school. I find Emily by our lockers.

"Can I hop in for a ride?" I ask. The weather outside doesn't exactly appeal to a bike ride.

"Are you not going to the café?"

"No, I moved my shifts this week, I'm going home, and I don't really want to bike in that rain. Unless you're riding with Luke?"

I can sense her hesitation and my stomach aches when she replies, "Sorry, I'm going to the Murrays. We're all working on our English homework together since I'm with Rose, Luke with Rachel, and Chris with Cam..."

"Cam? You call her Cam? Are you part of her clique now?"

I can't help the bitterness in my voice. This is riling me up, how can she do this to me? Befriend the she-devil that runs this school.

"I'm not. It just came out like that, don't be so rude," she cringes.

"It can't just come out like that unless you hang out with her, Em."

"Look. I hang out with Luke, Luke hangs out with Jake and she sticks to Jake so here we are."

"How can you do this to me," I rage. "You know what she's done to me. You know how she is! You're supposed to be my friend."

"She was hurt, Jamie! Jake cheated on her with you. And then, you guys had sex and you didn't even tell me about it... you're supposed to be my friend."

I freeze at her words. "How do you know?" I ask.

"Because she told me. Because real friends share secrets."

"How would she even know?" I ask in shock. I think I know how, I just don't want to believe it.

"Because Jake told her, obviously, did you really think he's the kind of guy to take a girl's virginity and then not go around bragging to his friends? They're in the same group. Everyone knows." She pauses to take a breath and sighs. "I thought you were different from all these girls that just fall for Jake's shit, 'Me."

"I *didn't* fall for Jake's shit," I hiss. "You have no idea what happened! And you're the one who was trying to set us up!"

"Only after they broke up! I didn't know anything was happening before that because you stopped opening up to me a long time ago!" She readjusts the bag on her shoulder. She's louder than I am because she's part of the popular kids and she doesn't care if people hear her arguing. I do. I hate bringing attention to myself.

"Have you ever wondered if maybe I stopped opening up to you because you were too busy fucking your new boyfriend? You thought I was better than other girls, Em? I thought you said you'd never get over Aaron. We all change, I guess."

She gasps in shock and I instantly regret my words.

"Em, I–"

"Stay the fuck away from me," she spits as she takes steps back. "I'm serious, Jamie. Don't talk to me. Ever again."

"Emily..." I insist, but she's gone, disappeared in the wave of students exiting the building.

Fuck.

I leave school fuming and hating myself. Outside, the rain hits hard and feels like needles against my cheeks.

I spot Emily by her car and I hurry to her. She's about to close her door but I hold it with a hand.

"Em, I'm so sorry, I didn't mean that. It was out of anger. I don't know why I said it."

"Leave me the fuck alone. Did you not register what I said? *Don't* talk to me. Not today, not ever. Go back to the shed you call a house, Goody."

My heart shatters into a million pieces. Never has she called me that stupid nickname before. Never has she made fun of my financial situation.

I hear laughter behind her and realize Camila and Jake are sitting at the back while Luke is next to her. Only Camila is laughing at me but it's enough to force me to let go of the door.

Emily doesn't look back at me when she pulls out of her parking spot.

I let out a raging grunt that quickly turns into full-on sobs while the rain mixes with my tears.

The parking lot is practically empty but even if it wasn't, I don't give a shit anymore.

When I get home, the lonely house hits me hard. I check my phone. No text from Emily. I guess she is officially done with me.

I try to call my mom and sigh as I reach the voicemail for the second time today. I feel so lonely, and that feeling that I brought it on myself is exhausting.

I shower and open a book in bed. Before I realize it, it's 9 pm so I check my phone again. Nothing. I feel so empty, so miserable. No friends, no boyfriend, no family.

I don't really control my body when my hands grab my phone and go to Nathan's conversation. I cringe at what I'm doing and yet I still type my thoughts.

Jamie: You hurt me.

I don't know why I'm opening myself up to him that way. Especially now that I know what he's really like. I also can't help my mind going back to all the times he was sweet to me.

It takes less than a minute for my phone to ring and his name to show up on my screen. My heart galloping in my chest, I don't know what to do. I hover a shaking thumb over the screen, take a deep breath, and swipe.

But I don't say anything.

"'*Me...*'" I recognize his voice, but I can't help thinking it's a few shades darker now that I know who he is. The background is noisy, some bass music and voices.

I can't get myself to talk.

Think, Jamie. Use your brain rather than your heart or pussy for once. None of the White brothers are right for you.

"'*Me, talk to me. Please.*"

Tears build up in my eyes and I sniffle to try and keep everything at bay.

"*Please, please don't cry. Not for me. I fucked up, 'Me, I really did.*"

Some voices get clearer in the background and I recognize Samuel's British accent.

"*I have to go*," he sighs. "*Just say something...*"

"You're a liar," I rasp. "I hate you."

"*At least you still feel something for me.*"

I hang up.

Because maybe I do.

My heart is broken. It's not all Nathan. It's a mix of him, Jake, my own decisions, my friendship with Emily that we've both let fade to nothing. And missing my mom. I miss her so deeply right now.

I put my phone and book to the side and choose sleep over everything else. Anxiety fights me on this decision, but I eventually fade to darkness.

My phone ringing wakes me up. My heart skips a beat, fear gripping me, and my brain goes to the worst scenario: it has to be about my mom. Something terrible happened.

"Hello?" I answer in a groggy voice.

"*Open the door.*"

"Nathan?"

"*Now, before I break your window.*"

Wide awake, I jump out of bed and run to the front door, my heart beating frantically against my ribcage. My brain is shouting that he is more than capable of breaking my window.

I open the door in one rushed movement and my eyes widen on their own accord before the image in front of me actually hits my brain; Nathan is standing tall, his dark blond hair completely disheveled, his lean muscles tensing with anger. But the main two things that petrify me are his blood-covered shirt, and his right hand casually holding a gun.

"You stupid girl," he growls. He bumps into me as he gets in, grabs my upper arm tightly, and drags me along with him. He slams the door shut as fear grips my insides.

"Wh-wh-what are you doing? What happened to you?" I stammer.

"Why don't you tell me what the hell *you* think you're doing?" he asks, his voice cold as ice.

He knows. He knows I slept with Jake. He knows my heart always wanted his brother. He's dangerous, he's going to hurt me...

"I was ecstatic when you called, 'Me. There it was, my chance to make it up to you. I rushed over here like the fucking fool I am. Now imagine my surprise when I get to your house in the middle of the night and find a *fucking* Wolf watching your house. Watching *you.*"

Fear seizes me tighter than his hold on me.

"You're still looking for your brother, aren't you? Are you out of your fucking mind?" he insists after my silence. The ache emanating from his strong hand disappears as my blood runs cold. Of course I am still looking for my brother, but he never knew I was looking for him in the first place.

"I never told you I was looking for him," I gulp.

"I did." Sam's British accent resonates behind me.

I snap my head toward the kitchen, where he stands leaning

against the counter, hands in his pockets, big, tattooed arms bulging under his tight black tee.

I don't wonder how he got in, the open kitchen door that leads to our small patio tells me everything.

"How did you kn—"

"Rose told him about the stolen phone. Don't mind Sam, he only came to help me get rid of a dead Wolf. Now focus on me."

I know it doesn't take a genius to guess why I would have stolen Rose's burner phone. Jake had guessed it, why wouldn't they? But the fact that they all know I'm still looking for Aaron makes me uneasy.

"I thought you were a smart girl," Nathan seethes. "Didn't the night at the café teach you anything? Volkov and his men are dangerous. They're not *funny* sort of dangerous, they're not Jake's childish bullying sort of dangerous. They're *deadly*. I know you're dying to put your nose in everything that is remotely interesting to you but how about you try to live past your eighteenth birthday?"

How did I ever think Nathan was one of the good ones? Watching him right now, bloody, holding a gun, and using my weaknesses as a way to make fun of me after I opened up to him about how much I missed my brother...I want to scream, to cry, to throw myself at him and scratch his face bloody. I would if I were brave. I'm not, so I fume on the inside and grit my teeth when I reply.

"Looking for Aaron is more than 'remotely interesting' to me."

He laughs – he *fucking laughs* at me – as he lets go of my arm. "Stay here," he orders before heading toward the hallway.

I don't. I follow him even if he's not looking back. I don't make it one step. Sam is already in front of me, his huge form completely blocking me. I step to the side and he follows silently, making sure I can't go around him.

"You are *so* tough, Samuel. Such strong men, you and your *boss.* Two big, brave men against one dangerous five-foot girl."

I hear things being moved around in my room. I try to slide left and he blocks me again. It makes him chuckle.

"Hilarious," I fume.

But he doesn't say anything.

"What are you doing?" I feel myself paling as I see Nathan walk back into the living area with a shoe box.

Not any shoe box.

The one I keep hidden under my bed, the one that contains the very limited bits of information I have about Volkov. He is an impossible man to find, but his men on the ground aren't ghosts like him. They're discreet, but I'm *very* nosy.

"Nathan," I panic as he heads to the kitchen with the box. He puts it on the counter next to the empty sink. I follow after him, but before I can reach him, Samuel grabs both my shoulders and pulls my back to his chest. He slips an arm around my neck and I feel like I'm being suffocated by a boa constrictor. His arm is huge enough to completely stop me from moving any further. He's not squeezing hard at all, but my airways constrict at the size of his biceps against my neck.

"Let go of me," I rage, hitting his arm with both my hands. It's like a mouse fighting a lion. I stand no chance whatsoever.

Nathan puts the gun on the counter and opens the box. He takes out the pair of old sneakers I had left in there to hide my secret and takes out the small notepad. He opens it and chuckles.

"Volkov's club in Silver Falls is Vue. Private sex club," he mimics my voice. "Samuel Thomas equals against Wolves. Diaz brothers not selling for Volkov anymore. Man from the café is Dimitri." He laughs so hard I wince. "Fuck, 'Me, you're a real detective, aren't you? You even wrote that Garcia-Diaz is Volkov's bribed attorney here in Stoneview. How did you figure that one out?"

"We tried to get her help after I was shot. She refused, advised us to 'not go against powerful men like him'." Why am I telling him the truth?

"Interesting," he nods. "Your information is outdated, she's *my* bribed attorney now." His eyes move as they read along the lines of my notes. I don't have much, it's little things I have picked up with time. Little notes I made when I would lie to everyone that I was not looking into it. This is all I have. I keep it hidden so my mom doesn't find it.

"There are a lot of notes in here, Jamie." His voice has turned darker, lower, and I tremble. His eyes widen slightly when he reads a new page and I wriggle in Samuel's hold. I found something. Something real. Something he knows about Volkov and that I got right.

"What is it?" I struggle some more, desperately trying to get an answer. My heart picks up, I need to know. "Nathan, what is it?"

He throws the notepad to the side and reaches in his back pocket, pulling out a cigarette pack. "Tell me, beautiful. What's the big plan? You gather all these shit notes. Then what? You find Volkov?" He lights up a cigarette and takes a drag before going back to his little speech. "Let's say you find him. What do you do then? You go to him and force him to tell you what happened to your brother? You seduce him into telling you his darkest secrets?"

He takes another drag and smiles at me. Not the warm kind he used to give me, the freezing kind that makes me shiver again. "Stealing Ozy's phone so you could talk to Sam." He laughs again. "Sam doesn't fucking know where Volkov is. *I* don't know. No one does. That's the whole point of his business tactics. You think curious Jamie Williams from Stoneview Prep is going to find him? You stupid, naïve girl."

He takes his lighter again and grabs the notepad.

"Nathan!" I panic. "Don't. Don't do this, please." He looks at me with no emotions in his eyes. Nothing, not even the slightest regret. "Nathan...this is the only thing I have left, the only thing linking me to Aaron."

He doesn't even react. He simply lights up the paper and watches it burn with a sadistic smirk, then lets it fall in the sink when the flame reaches his fingers.

The sob that wrecks my chest is so loud I feel Sam shifting behind me. Tears spring in my eyes and I let them fall freely. I don't even fight back against Sam's arm anymore. There's nothing to do.

Nathan takes long strides toward me and grabs my jaw tightly, making me wince in the process.

"To say I'm pissed at you would be the understatement of the century. It's a big bad world out there, Jamie. Careless girls who look into the Wolves get killed. And guess what? I have other shit to do than to look out for you. I have other shit to do than kill a fucking Wolf who thought it was a good idea to keep a close eye on you. In your own home."

Another sob passes tightly through my throat, but he doesn't care. "Are you *listening* to me?" He insists by tightening his grip. "Stay away from the Wolves. You think

your brother is the first man Volkov had killed? Get over it."
The coldness in his voice breaks my heart all over again.

I watch helplessly as the flames die in the sink, the last notes I had regarding Volkov and the Wolves gone.

"You were meant to love me," I rasp.

He lets go of my face and takes a step back, finally showing emotions. It's rage, it's...sadness? "Go wait in the car, Sam."

It only takes him about three seconds to execute. Now free to move, I try to stand tall in front of Nathan. I never noticed how intimidating he could be. As soon as the front door is closed his hand flies to the back of my neck, and he grips me hard enough to make me scream in surprise. He pulls me toward him, steps to the side and I land face first against the counter. He keeps me bent over, his hand a warning not to move.

"I'm just really fucking sick of all this blame you put on me. You were meant to love me back," he growls. "I guess all this fooling around with my brother changed your mind. It's a really believable cover you put on, isn't it? That untouched, goody-two-shoes persona." His knee pushes my legs apart and I gasp when his thigh settles against my leggings-clad pussy. It feels good, that's undeniable. But it's not what I want, not after what he just did. I've never hated someone more than I do him now.

"I—"

"*You* are nothing but a little slut, so desperate for cock you had to go get it somewhere else."

He presses harder and I cry out. A mix of pain, pleasure, and deep angst coming to the surface. His hand close to my face smells of that particular copper tang of blood.

"Stop," I whimper.

"What's wrong? You wanted my dick in that cunt for so long, beautiful. God, it must have been so horrible for you, begging like a bitch in need to two different guys."

"I get it, Nathan. You're mad," I rage. "You're mad because I put myself in danger, you're mad because I was attracted to Jake while I was with you. Now imagine how I feel that our relationship was based on nothing but lies. Every single day you lied to my face." I brace my hands against the counter and try to push myself up, harder this time, but he pushes me back down harshly enough that I whimper when my cheek hits the counter again.

"Let me go!" I cry out. "We weren't good for each other. You made your point."

For a second, I think he's going to do something violent again. Nothing happens until I feel his breath on my cheek. His grip loosens slightly, and his voice has gone back to a leveled vibration. "You know what's great, 'Me?" he chuckles in my ear, like preparing himself for a sick joke. "You are so infatuated with Jake..." I can hear the smile in his voice when he talks again. "...and he will inevitably break your heart."

I groan a wordless complaint and he tightens his grip on me. "Can I tell you a secret, beautiful?" He doesn't wait for me to reply. "I still haven't decided if I still love you, or if I want to hurt you real, *real* bad for betraying me."

"If you want to hurt me so bad, why did you just kill someone for me?"

He grunts in anger as he suddenly lets me go and pulls away from me. Yeah, I thought he wouldn't have a reply to that.

"You're done looking for your brother, Jamie. Because next time a Wolf comes after you, I won't fucking save you."

I push up and my eyes land on the ashes in the sink. "You

burnt it all," I whisper in unbelievable sadness.

He stays silent for a few seconds, his breathing going from angry panting to slow, calm breaths. Now that he's calmed down, I can almost hear him gulping as I turn around to him, tears streaking my cheeks.

We look at each other in silence, ashamed of what we've become. I think he's probably thinking the same as me, how could we have been so horrible to the other? We've shown our nastiest sides unapologetically and now we pay the consequences.

"It had to be done." His last words are barely audible. "I'm sorry."

There is nothing left to be said, and so he slowly turns around and leaves my house, walking around the kitchen bar and through the door in no particular rush.

CHAPTER 7

Monster – Willyecho

Jake

"Happy birthday"

"Which one's older?"

"Happy birthday, bro."

"You get more handsome every year, Jake."

"I've got a surprise for you, meet me in the bathroom in fifteen."

A hand on my chest, a pat on the back, hugs, kisses peppered on my cheeks. Full hugs from my best friends, tons of pictures of Ozy and me.

And tequila. A *lot* of tequila.

Only Luke Baker would insist on celebrating Ozy and I's birthday *again*. Well, the first time didn't really happen. It did for everyone, just not for me and my friends. Everyone showed up at Luke's, but we weren't there, too busy looking for Rose all over town, too busy worrying over Nate being alive, over Jamie...

I can't help the sigh that leaves me.

"It's your birthday, bro. Lighten up," Luke shouts in my ear over the loud music in his gigantic living room. He shakes a small packet of pills in front of my eyes. I grab it but put it in my back pocket.

"Later. And it's not even my birthday," I mumble. My mouth feels like cotton and I'm struggling to articulate. I'm really fucking drunk.

I wonder if the people partying tonight even truly realize it's not my birthday. It was two weeks ago, this is really fucking stupid. Whatever, it's just another Stoneview party. Too much alcohol, too many drugs, too many kids living like adults and throwing away their parents' money.

"Jakey, just tell me what's wrong." My friend flutters his long, blond eyelashes at me, pretending to be one of the girls that have tried to help with my mood tonight. Now that they know Camila is out for good, I feel like a goddamn open bar.

She's been sticking to me like a bee on honey since I told everyone I had fucked Jamie and that I was over her. But at the beginning of the night, when she tried to kiss me in front of everyone, I pushed her away. I told her in private that we were done. I told her a month ago that we were done. Me not being involved with Jamie anymore doesn't change that. Now, it's like all the other girls were waiting for the Queen Bee to be kicked off her throne.

That's because none of them understand Jamie is the real deal.

Was.

Was the real deal. Until it turned out she was the one playing me.

Our night together was like being in heaven. Everything was perfect, she was perfect. But walking into her house the next day...the weight of everything fell on my shoulders and I panicked. I really panicked. Jamie wasn't made for my world, she's been through enough herself. Here I was going around her house making sure my supposed-to-be-dead brother wasn't coming after her.

And that's the worst part. Her not being part of my world? Meh, I can deal with that, I'm selfish enough. But she was with Nate. I can't get over *that*. I want to, I really want to, but every time I think of it, every time she reminds me, I want to kill him. I want to hurt her so bad she will never dare think of him again.

It doesn't matter that she didn't know he was my brother, she chose him over me. Finding out he is a manipulative psycho and sleeping with me doesn't mean she's over him. It doesn't erase the fact that she chose *him*.

"Jake," Luke insists.

"Nothing's wrong," I snap back.

He runs a hand through his bright blond hair, a smile spreading on his face. He takes a long sip, letting me simmer in my own thoughts before speaking again.

"It wouldn't have anything to do with a teeny-tiny, green-eyed girl by any chance? The one you keep bragging about taking her virginity just so you can have an excuse to talk about her."

"That obvious?" I ask.

"It's been two weeks, bro. We're all a bit tired of hearing about it." He pulls out the joint that was placed behind his ear and puts it between his lips. "Let's go outside," he kindly suggests.

Luke Baker is one of the gentlest souls that inhabits this planet.

His soul is kind and caring. He means no harm, ever. He is a great listener, and he likes making people feel better, helping them out. He truly is my best friend, always cracking a joke when everyone is down. He's got his flaws, like everyone. Mainly, he can't keep a relationship going for more than a week or so. People call him fuckboy-Luke, but in reality, he never promises anything to any of them. He tries his shot, scores, and happens to not fall in love. I wonder if he loves Emily. He's never been with a girl for this long.

He's not a fuckboy, he's just desperately trying to find the one. Unlike me, number one asshole who dated Camila for two years and spent most of them cheating on her with NSF girls. North Shore of the Falls, where the girls are wild and don't give a shit about Stoneview politics. Maybe that's where I should be right now to forget about Jamie. Except I won't, because people *expect* me to be here. They expect me to give them a wild party, to be Stoneview's golden boy and smile and be the life of the party.

The guys expect me to play beer pong with them and down solo cups, shouting about how we're going to destroy everyone in the upcoming lacrosse season now that I'm their captain. And the girls, they expect me to take one or two up to one of Luke's guest rooms. They probably also expect Chris to join but the fucker is way over this now. Him and his secret girlfriend who's just too good for us.

But what they don't understand is I don't *feel* anything when I'm around them. All those people who want things from me, they don't get that I don't give a shit about them. I play the part well because that's what it is to have a normal life. That's the whole point of being with the Murrays. But inside, there's nothing. Absolute blackhole. I stopped caring for people, stopped differentiating good from bad a long fucking time ago. Bianco made sure of that.

The only time I feel is when I'm around Jamie. The girl made her way through my heart without even trying and now look at me, an idiot in love with a girl who played him. I tried to show her I cared. I agreed to take her on a date, didn't I? I told her she was mine, I told her I didn't want to sleep with other girls. What is it she didn't get? I basically poured my heart out when I asked what she wanted from me. She didn't take it that way, instead she threw Nate in my face desperately trying to hurt me.

I follow Luke out in the cold. There are way too many people chilling in his backyard for this temperature. Mid-November, fuck off inside.

Ozy is on a rattan egg chair, pretending to listen to her friend Ciara scolding her for ditching her in their physics class today. I'm not even asking my twin where she was. She stank of Sam's cologne when she showed up here, five minutes before midnight. Right on time to blow out our candles together. I can't believe she almost missed out on this for the second time.

I recognized his smell because it's the kind that brings me back to my childhood. The kind that could send me into a panic attack. I'm still trying to understand if she's doing jobs for him or...more. I'm not sure which one would be worse but she's not about to tell me anyway. He's got nothing to blackmail her with anymore, why does she keep going back?

"Jake!" some girl shouts after us.

I turn around slightly – showing I'm not actually stopping for a conversation but still hearing her out – and recognize one of Ella's best friends. Anna? Anita?

"Hey, I don't know if you remember me, I'm Ania, Ella's friend. Um, so she kind of ditched me and I was wondering what you're doing now? Like, do you want to hang out or something?"

The girl is a hot mess. A mix of alcohol-induced braveness and intimidation when she realizes she took the bold step to come and talk to me.

"Where's Ella?" Luke cuts off before I can answer anything.

Ania's eyes widen. "She's...uh...she went...to...the bathroom?" She says the whole sentence with her eyes on her solo cup.

Her hands are perfectly manicured and the jewelry on her wrists adorned with diamonds. I take my eyes from her hands to look at the rest of her. She's cute, small with great curves. Her black dress fits her flawlessly, her hair is a perfect blond that's been worked on by an expensive hairdresser. She is typical Stoneview. Perfect on the outside – polished to the point that she could be the cover of a magazine right now – and no doubt as empty inside as Camila is. Beautiful shells they are, the girls who grew up in Stoneview.

Except Jamie.

"You're at a party full of drunk people and you left my sister on her own? How about you find your drunk friend before you chase after dick?" Luke scolds.

I chortle so loud I can see the girl's heart breaking through her eyes.

"You should go back, Ania. Nothing for you here," I conclude. As soon as she's far enough, I turn to my friend. "Do you want to check on Ella?" I ask. God knows I get the feeling of looking for a sneaky sister.

Luke shakes his head no. "And find my sister doing god

knows what with god knows who? No thanks. She always invites Ania to parties just to leave her on her own."

Luke and I walk around his swimming pool and past the last people hanging around. The Bakers' grounds go far into the forest. They own a good chunk of it. Stoneview lake is part of the forest they don't own, it's not too far from here. The bit they don't own is where I tried to scare Jamie out of my life. Whereas now I'm pretty desperate to be in hers.

We pass a few trees before we settle in our favorite spot to smoke. As soon as Luke turned eighteen, his wonderful, typical Stoneview parents fucked off to their New York penthouse and left him with Ella and their au pair. Au pair that Luke used to fuck occasionally and now pays double to stay out of the house most of the time. But when we were younger, his dad, Gerald, would be on Luke like a fucking hawk, trying to find the smallest flaw in his behavior and use it as an excuse to belittle him. Because his son couldn't give Bakers & Son a bad image. That's why we would go that far into the forest to smoke. We wouldn't get caught.

I recognized Luke was being abused about a week after meeting him. It wasn't physical, well sometimes it was but nothing that would show. Mainly, it was emotional. It still is. That's the thing about emotional abuse, you can do it from New York when your kid is in Stoneview. Smart.

It was obvious Ozy and I were abused when we arrived in Stoneview. We were covered in bruises. The Murrays had to wait three weeks before putting us in school, some were still fading. Anyone who tried to say anything, I shut them up with a fist to the face. Luke helped and we became friends. He was already friends with Chris, it was just meant to be.

It wasn't that obvious for Luke, but his behavior screamed

mistreated. In his mind, he wasn't good enough, or he'd say he retook eighth grade because he wasn't smart enough. It was in the way he would apologize for the smallest things and try to change the topic when I'd ask about his parents. He was always happy, that was the main thing. He spent his time trying to make others better when he was broken inside. This is where our closeness grew. This is why I felt comfortable opening up to him about my past.

We both settle against a huge tree trunk, leaning our backs on it. We stand in silence for a minute or so. I know he's waiting for me to talk, I'm just not sure where to start. He offers me the lit-up joint and I take a few puffs before handing it back.

"Did Emily ever say anything about a boyfriend?" I blurt out.

"Nah, bro. I would have told you."

"I don't get it, how could she ever fall for Nate. He's…" I get lost in my own thoughts looking for a word to describe the devil that is my brother. How could Jamie be attracted to him?

I guess the girl has a dark side. Not in a way that she would ever hurt someone, but she is attracted to darkness. Or she would have never been attracted to *me*. In her eyes, I am darkness personified, for good reasons as well. She's not wrong, it's who I am, and I took great pleasure in letting the golden boy mask down to show Jamie who I really was.

But now…

Well, now I regret it. Because when I thought we were starting to share something beyond our stupid games, I was actually pushing her into someone else's arms.

"I don't get it, man, I had her in the palm of my hands. I

had her," I insist.

Somewhere between playing with her and making her go in circles, I started to believe Jamie Williams was mine. Isn't she? Am I the only one who felt more? Am I the only one who fell in love? I keep trying to find out exactly when it happened.

Jamie played too well into my game, she was the perfect victim. She was feisty but still fell down to her knees when the time came. So when did I stop seeing her as a little toy and start feeling shit for her?

"Are you sure she never mentioned a boyfriend?" Luke asks.

"We weren't exactly besties, we didn't share much, but I would know if she had mentioned my own brother."

"You weren't besties, but you were definitely doing things that would have pushed her to let you know if she was seeing someone."

"I'm so confused," I admit. "All along I thought I was in control. Turns out she's the one who played me. She's the one who was in charge."

"Really, Jake? Don't you get it?"

I grab the joint from my friend and take a long drag, shaking my head to show I don't know what he means.

"If she had told you she had a boyfriend, you would have stopped. You would have stopped seeing her, you would have stopped running after her."

Debatable, but that's not the point.

"Yeah, and?" I exhale the smoke and let the THC take over my mind.

"And she *didn't* want it to stop." A smile pulls at the corner of his mouth. "You weren't in charge. She wasn't in charge. You both fell for each other and are in way over your heads.

117

It's up to you now, do you want to chase after her? Or do you want to get over her? Because if you want to be with her, you're going to have to get over the fact that Nate and her probably had something strong."

I let my head fall back and hit the trunk of the tree. I'm so fucking dejected, how could she hide this from me?

"I think you should chase after her," my best friend says, ever the endless romantic. "Because however strong it was with Nate, what you have with her is obviously stronger."

"Can we talk to Emily about it?"

"Bro..." he hesitates.

"Please. It's my birthday," I pout.

"Not even your birthday," he murmurs back.

It takes a few more shots to convince Luke to let me talk to Emily about Jamie and Nate. Surely she knew something.

"In your dreams, White. She's entitled to her privacy," Emily says as calmly as a girl that has ingested three shots in a row can.

"Em, I thought we were friends, you and me." I offer her my most charming smile, but she rolls her eyes at me.

I wonder if Emily ever had a thing for me. Most girls did or currently do. Emily has average features, her hair is a dark blond, her brown eyes don't stand out in any way and her skin is porcelain that gets tainted pink when she's embarrassed, angry or, in this case, drunk.

But it's her body everyone is after. Despite her mom trying to erase her curves, Emily's sporty figure never disappears. Every guy in Stoneview Prep spends a good part of their day drooling over her. She has tits most girls would kill for. My professional opinion tells me they're a D but Luke just won't confirm nor deny. Her legs are strong, and my best friend has told me before that being between them is the best place he's ever been. Don't even get me started on her ass. I know I've stared longer than I should many times.

She's hot, there's no denying it. She's a lot sexier in the way she uses her body than Jamie. And yet...she doesn't compare. Jamie is *everything*. I know most guys' gazes don't linger on her. She's small, she's fucking miniature really. She's not too skinny but her body is proportionate to her size, meaning I can wrap my hand around her thigh and make her feel like the size of a doll. Meaning her head can land perfectly on my heart when we're both standing. Meaning when I hug her, I could break her. She is so *breakable* and walking that line between breaking her and making her feel good gives my life purpose.

Emily's voice drags me out of my thoughts. "Jamie is my best friend, Jake. I'm not going to spill out her private life to anyone who asks for it."

I let out an exaggerated gruff. "Didn't you just have a massive fight with her? You're on my side now. If you asked me *any* of Luke's secrets I would spill right away. You don't even have to ask, did you know until he was six he wouldn't even *look* at Ella because he was so jealous of her?"

"Bro!" My friend exclaims. "This isn't about me."

"Jake, have you ever thought that if Jamie never told you about her boyfriend maybe, just *maybe*, she didn't want you to know?"

"Exactly. Because she didn't want me to stop pursuing her."

"Or maybe, for once, she just wanted you out of her business?"

She wanted you out of her business.

Maybe she really did. Maybe I really was the only one falling for her. Otherwise, why would Emily, the girl who knows her better than anyone, tell me to just drop it.

My tone is low when I speak again. I'm almost ashamed to ask. "Does she love him?"

"Do you mean, is she in love with him?" Emily is pushing my buttons. I don't know why but she's not with me tonight, she's completely on her friend's side.

"You know what I mean."

She doesn't reply and that's when it hits me. Emily has been my little informant for the past two months. She is an extrovert, she loves going out, chatting, and making friends. That's just her personality. And since I broke up with Camila, she has been trying to set Jamie up with me.

When she saw I was showing more than a little interest, we got closer. More often than not, she accidentally spills more than she should. But not about Jamie's boyfriend, she never said anything, not a hint, *nothing.* And I can see it in her eyes right now that she doesn't know if her best friend is in love with my brother or not.

"You just found out," I think out loud. "You didn't know until the ball, did you?"

"I'm not going to entertain you anymore tonight, Jake," she sing-songs.

"Just tell me," I say in one last attempt. "Do you think...do you think she loves him enough to get back with him?"

"Honestly?"

I nod.

"Honestly, I think she was falling in love with him. But I couldn't tell you if she could get over the lies. Or the fact that you guys are related. What the fuck, how did no one know

120

you and Rose had an older brother?" She shakes her head like trying to put it all together in her drunken mind. "She has more than enough reasons to not get back with Nathan. She also has more than enough reasons to not become your girlfriend, including you going around and talking about deflowering her. That's low, Jake." She grabs her drink and turns around, grabbing Luke's hand before heading out of the kitchen.

In case my heart hadn't taken enough tonight, Emily's words are like a knife in it. It's deep, it hurts, it makes me bleed.

Jamie Williams played me. For weeks I thought I had the girl in the palm of my hand when she was the puppet master all along. Playing me, playing her boyfriend.

This isn't even the worst. The worst is how I lost control around her. I can't be trusted when I'm with her, I become a danger to her and to myself. I become a shadow of myself, a monster from the past. This isn't something I should have let happen. She loves Nate? Good, I can go back to my usual act. The normal Jake White, the one who is friends with everyone, who fulfills the expectations.

My twin walks into the kitchen, holding a bottle of whiskey in one hand and Rachel Harris with the other. Are they together right now? I've lost track of their on and off relationship. My sister is smarter than me, she never lied to Rachel about not being able to commit to one person like I did to Camila. The girl knew exactly what she was getting herself into.

"Why do you look like a lost puppy?" Rose asks as she offers me the bottle of whiskey. Her raspy voice that usually gives her an uninterested tone is tenfold worse when she's drunk.

"You're not getting that back," I announce before taking a mouthful of the burning alcohol.

She shrugs and lets Rachel wrap both her arms around her.

"You guys look disgustingly in love," I grumble.

Ozy lets out a loud cackle, neither confirming nor denying if she is in love with Rachel. She never does. Not to us. "Hater."

"Is Jamie not coming to the party?" Rachel asks in her crystal voice. This girl is the incarnation of innocence. How she ended up with the immoral soul my sister is will forever be a mystery.

I take another swig of whiskey before answering, "No." My voice doesn't really allow questions.

I leave them to be the happy fucking couple they deserve to be and walk around the house, as I drink the rest of the bottle.

Fuck Jamie Williams, fuck her and any cunty boyfriend she ever gets. I bet she's gonna find Prince Charming like she had always dreamt of. I bet he fucks her all vanilla, missionary, once a week and no foreplay. Slow and gentle exactly how she hates it. Good, she'll never know how much pleasure I could have given her, all the dark places I could have taken her, how I would have made her scream in pleasure.

I go for another sip just to realize I finished the bottle. Ugh, fuck this shit. Looking around the living room is a slightly more difficult task than it was an hour ago. Things are a little blurrier and the walls are not exactly staying still. Thinking of fucking Jamie made me rock hard and I'm now a drunk, horny bastard. Good, exactly what everyone expects of me. Just the lacrosse captain, Stoneview Prep jock I should be acting like.

A small blond makes her way to me and it takes me a few seconds to recognize Ella's friend.

"Ania," I smile as she reaches me. "Did you find your

friend?"

"I don't think she wanted to be found. But I found you."

"Again."

"Again," she repeats in a breathy voice. "You didn't keep any for me?" she pouts, pointing at the empty bottle in my hand.

"You're not going to need any for what we're about to do, trust me." I offer her my 'I'm about to fuck you good' smile and I can see her breath catching in her throat. Her cheeks blush and her eyes dart to the floor as she pushes a strand of hair behind her ear.

"Should we find somewhere quieter?" I offer her my hand and she takes it without hesitation.

"Yeah," she whispers.

"I can't believe this is actually happening," Ania says as I lead her up the stairs. My drunk ass misses a step or two and I realize she's the one who has to hold me up more than anything else.

I push open one of the many doors on the first floor, surprising Ewan McKee from the lacrosse team, and Jessika Drew from the cheer team.

"Out," I drunkenly mumble.

Ewan jumps from the bed, where he was on top of Jessika. They're still dressed, and I can't help myself when I talk to my teammate. "You gotta take your clothes off if you want to lose that virginity, bro," I chuckle.

"Fuck off," Ewan complains as he helps Jessika off the bed before walking to the door.

"Feel free to stay, Jess," I throw at her. She stills by the door and I feel Ania's hand squeeze mine.

"Are you sure?" she whispers to me.

"Whatever," I shrug as I let myself fall on the bed, forcing Ania to let go of my hand.

I hear Ewan whispering insults at Jessika and realize my eyes have closed. I open them to find both girls staring at me from the side of the bed.

"Are you gonna stare all night or are you gonna start sucking my cock?"

Jess is the first one on the bed, her tight dress is restricting her movements and that's the only thing that brings my cock to life right now, knowing that she's not in full control. I am.

She's on me in a split second, unbuckling my belt while Ania is looking at me with wide eyes. Jess is used to sucking my dick and asking nothing in return, she's used to doing it on her own or with company. Ania isn't. I don't know what she expected out of tonight, but I sincerely hope she wasn't hoping for a good guy to take her virginity.

I let my head fall back on the pillow and it makes me feel dizzy as fuck. I drank way too much. I can't remember the last time I was in such a shit state.

Jamie played me, but at least she tried to fix things. She wanted to get to know me, she wanted us to open up to each other. And I pushed her away. I put up the steady walls that hold everyone at bay. Because what if I tell her what I've done, and she finally understands I'm not deserving of happiness, of her? Letting her in, it would just be opening myself for pain again. I thought everything I did to her gave me away, showed her my true identity. But I don't think she quite grasps how bad it is.

"You don't have to do anything you don't want, Ania," I reassure her.

Fuck, I feel like such an asshole when I see the glint of jealousy in her eyes as Jess lowers her head. I never used to feel this way, never questioned if what I was doing was wrong or right. That's Jamie's work right there. Making me feel shit and all.

My thoughts disappear for a millisecond as Jess' mouth wraps around the tip of my dick, but they're quickly brought back to Jamie. If I don't think of her, I'm not going to be able to stay hard. I need to stay hard because I need to come. I need to release some tension.

I look up to see Ania finally deciding to join the fun. She puts her solo cup on the bedside table before crawling onto the bed. Her eyes widen slightly when Jess takes me all the way to the back of her throat, gags, and lets my dick out in a loud pop.

Jess moves to my right to let Ania settle on my left and grabs my dick in her hand again.

"Ania, right?" Jess asks for confirmation.

"Yeah," she lets out in a breathy voice, her eyes never leaving my dick.

"Have you ever given a blowjob before?"

"This isn't fucking teatime, Jess, get to it," I order, but my voice isn't as tough as it usually is in bed, I'm just too drunk. Jess tightens her grip and I groan.

"Um...uh, no I haven't actually." Ania's voice forces my eyes to open again.

"That's okay, I can show you," Jess' drunken voice replies excitingly.

"Fucking...shit," I growl as I slap Jess' hand away.

I zip up my jeans and sit up. Struggling against the pillows and mattress, I finally manage to stumble out of bed.

"Where are you going?" Jess whines.

"I-I-" Ania tries to say.

"You need to find a guy who cares if you suck his dick or not. And I don't. I'm an asshole, Ania, your first time should be with a great guy."

"But-"

I don't really listen to her answer, my ears are buzzing anyway, and I just stroll out of the bedroom.

I know the two girls are after me, but they stay silent. The music from downstairs grips me again and the bass from Dillon Francis' 'Look At That Butt' makes my head pound. I know Camila has talked to the DJ for this song to come on. Jarina De Marco is her favorite Hispanic artist.

Speak of the devil and he doth appear.

As soon as I step back into the grand foyer, Camila's eyes are shooting daggers at the two girls behind me.

"You two sluts need to remember who rules here," she spits at them. Her venom is lethal, her obsessivity over me dangerous.

"Not now, Cam," I growl as I push her to the side to make my way back to the living room.

I know she's following me because every strike of her heels against the floor angers me a little more. I'm back with the living room crowd when she grabs my arm.

"Jake, wait!"

I spin around, forcing her hand to release my bicep and grip both her arms so tightly she jumps in surprise.

"That's enough! How many times do we need to fucking break up for you to get we're not meant to be a thing, Camila?"

A smirk tugs at her lips, lust glints in her green eyes and that's when I understand she's got me exactly where she wants.

"Are you mad at me?" she pouts. "Am I being a bad girl?"

"No, we're not getting into this. Absolutely fucking not."

"You've lost your fun since you've started deflowering good girls. How's that coming along for you?"

I want to let her go and I want to show her she doesn't affect me. But my body refuses to relax when she mentions Jamie.

"Why did you help her at the ball if you were going to humiliate her right after?"

"I didn't, Beth did," she lies as if I was born yesterday.

"Beth doesn't have two brain cells to rub together, don't tell me you didn't order her to pour that bowl of punch on Jamie."

She lets out an exaggerated innocent sigh and looks up right into my eyes. "I was just trying to help the girl. If she keeps getting involved with you, she's going to have everyone hating on her. I just cut it short. Did her a favor, really."

"That's not your fucking decision to make, you might think you're the queen of this school but don't forget who truly rules it. I will destroy your reputation, Camila."

"What are you going to do?" she mocks. "Tell everyone I like to be cuffed and spanked? Don't forget who administers those spanks, baby."

The growl that comes out of my chest when I push her against the nearest wall shows that I have completely lost control. We never get into these sorts of fights in front of people. But why should I fucking care? I pushed away the girl I really like and the one who's obsessed with me won't let me go. What do I have to lose anymore?

One of my hands slides to her throat and the other under her dress. Images of Jamie against the cafeteria wall flash to my mind and my cock is back in business.

"No underwear. That is very naughty, Cam," I whisper in her ear.

'Sex money feelings die' by Lukke Li resonates in the room as the atmosphere calms down. Everyone is too far gone to dance to bumpy music anymore.

I run a finger down Camila's slit. She tries to readjust herself and I tighten my grip on her throat.

"Don't you fucking move," I growl, my lips rubbing against her earlobe. I feel her getting wetter straight away. She's so fucked up. So am I. That is the only thing that's ever linked us.

I slide a finger inside her wet pussy, making her shudder in pleasure.

"You love being fingered in front of a crowd. It makes you wet, doesn't it?"

She tries to reply but my hand tightens again. I can sense her need to cough, her chest is heaving with need for air, but I don't really care.

I'm drunk, the girl I truly want doesn't fucking want me back.

Jamie. Doesn't. Want. Me.

I add another finger and pump in and out of my ex with anger. "You know what your problem is?"

She shakes her head, and my nails dig in her neck.

"You're not her."

The pleasure in her eyes mixes with fear and I feel her pussy tighten around my fingers. Her face reddens, her shoulders fall, and I don't realize it's because she's running out of air until a strong hand presses on my shoulder.

"What the fuck are you doing?" Chris' voice seethes as he

drags me back with force.

I let go of Camila, stumble a few steps back and bump into my best friend.

"Are you out of your fucking mind?" My friend rages in a whisper. "Are you trying to kill her?"

I turn back to Camila, who's still against the wall, a hand on her chest, taking huge gulps of hair.

"I—"

"*You* are way too drunk and need to get to bed. This party is over."

I don't really know how I got to bed. I wouldn't be surprised if Chris had to carry me up to the bedroom next to Luke's. All I know is there's only one girl on my mind as I fall asleep, and I don't know how to get over her.

CHAPTER 8

Fetish – Selena Gomez

Jamie

What the hell is this noise? My heart picks up at the surprise of the drill in my ears. I sit up in a sudden movement, my eyes slowly adapting to the light in my room. I forgot to draw the curtains last night. My face feels sticky and my eyes swollen, I cried myself to sleep last night. The sound comes again and I finally realize it's the doorbell. It's not a nice 'ding-dong' or some classical music like other Stoneview houses. It's a horrible 'brrring' that makes me want to hit my head against the wall. I push the covers away and hurry to the door. I hate that we don't have a peephole, especially now that I know it could be Nathan knocking with yet someone else's blood on him.

I open the door slightly, hiding my half-naked body behind it and only popping my head out.

That's pretty much the last person I expected to see here. He must see the surprise on my face because he feels the need to explain himself.

"English homework," he simply says.

Jake is wearing a pair of black sweatpants and the same black sweater as the last time he was here. How hot can someone get wearing such simple clothes? Really damn hot according to the God in front of my eyes.

"You're drooling, Angel," he smiles.

I have to scratch my throat before talking again. "I-I forgot. I completely forgot, but if you give me this morning, I'll bring it to you this afternoon."

He puts a strong hand on the door and pushes, walking in at the same time.

"You can't come in," I panic, taking a step back as the door opens. I'm in just a crop top and panties. It's just how I fell asleep. What is it with the Whites and inviting themselves in?

"We can work on it to−" he pauses as soon as he notices my state of undress. His eyes drag from my face to my panties and a gorgeous smile spreads on his cheeks, "−gether."

I cross my legs, putting my hands in front of my intimate area, only covered by a little bit of cotton. "What?" My brain didn't process what he just said, I was too focused on his gorgeous dimples.

"We can work on it together, Angel. What are you trying to hide exactly? Nothing I haven't seen there."

"I don't want you here, Jake," I defend. "I know what you've been doing, going around telling everyone about 'taking my virginity' like we're in some 18th Century novel. That's low, even from you."

"I *didn't* want to be here, Jamie," he hits back. "You're the one who hasn't done your part of the deal so let's just get this over with."

I take a deep breath, trying my best to be the bigger person.

At the end of the day, better his company than Nathan's. Or better than being completely alone. I can't stand the one on one sessions with my thoughts at the moment.

"I'll be back," I huff as I disappear down the hall.

"I'm happy for you to stay like that," I hear him shout and I can't help the tiny smile tugging at my lips.

No. This is homework, Jamie.

I speed-brush my teeth, put on some leggings and grab my backpack. I look at the bottle of perfume on my desk and can't help myself; I spray a little on my neck. It's a cheap lavender and citrus body spray my mom always gets me, it's not much, but it's what I wear.

When I walk back into the living room, Jake has made himself comfortable on the sofa.

"I didn't bring anything with me," he says. "I was just gonna pick up your half."

I take a moment to reply. It's weird having him here, acting almost normal when the last time we spoke he did his best to make me cry and I did my best to make him hurt.

I don't know how to act around him, I'm mad at him for what he did. Virginity is a concept I was never really big on. To me every sexual experience should be special, no matter if you've done it before or not. Should I really have expected anything different from Jake though? He openly spoke about doing anal with Camila in front of all his friends and me. Their whole group talks about sex and their conquests like a little game they have between them. After all, Rose openly taunts Beth about sleeping with her boyfriend. Luke and Rose talk about their first time together like it was just a little bit of fun in their friendship. Only Chris stays quiet and humble about it. I don't get it, it's just not my world, and I wish Jake had kept our intimate moment to ourselves, but I can't say I'm surprised.

"Uh...it's alright. Do you...do you want a drink or something?" I have to scratch my throat again. How can he pretend like nothing happened?

"Any soda you have, please. I'm curing a mean hangover."

It stings slightly to think that he was partying last night, without me. I'm not big on parties, but if he was still chasing after me, he would have invited me. He would probably have ordered me to come. It's wrong...but I miss that. And if I had been with Jake, I wouldn't have been with Nathan, he wouldn't have burned my one and only source of hope to look after Aaron. My heart sinks in my stomach at the thought.

I grab us two sodas and walk back to the sofa. I put them down, set up notepads and our English homework on the table before sitting down next to him. This is awkward. Too awkward for me to focus on homework.

"I thought you said you didn't want to waste your time on me," I drawl with sarcasm.

I expect him to mock me or do something to humiliate me, but instead he just shrugs his shoulders and gives me a small smile. "Maybe I regret saying that."

That is probably as close as Jake will get to an apology.

My heart hammers in my chest, desperately knocking on my ribs. "You do?"

"Let's get to work, Angel." He ignores my need for reassurance in such a soft voice I feel compelled to drop it.

We get started on our homework, reading the poems we've been given and looking at the questions together. It takes only about ten minutes before I feel Jake shift next to me.

I'm answering the first question about the context of the

first poem when I feel his hand on my thigh. I startle and look up at him. He's not looking back, just reading the second poem, his eyes following the words in a boring dance.

"What are you doing?" I whisper. I don't know why, there's no one else in this house, but knowing I was secretly wishing for his hand on me makes me feel like he read my thoughts.

"I'm reading," he replies casually without lifting his gaze.

"I meant–" the tightening of his grip makes me clamp my mouth shut.

"Just keep working, Angel."

It's easy to say for him, he doesn't have a firm hand just a few inches away from his sensitive area.

I'm answering the second question when his hand moves higher, his pinky finger is a light touch against my clit, but it instantly sets me on fire.

"Jake," I sigh. I want to make it an annoyed sigh, but it comes out needy.

He doesn't respond, just keeps rubbing his hand up and down my thigh, not touching me *there* anymore. His eyes stay on the poem and his fingers tap on my leg like playing his favorite song on a grand piano.

I'm on question four when he reaches my pussy again, this time not moving away. He adjusts his hand and I jump in surprise when the tips of his fingers purposely rub against my core.

"Fuck homework. I want to feel you, Angel." His raspy, lust filled voice reaches my ear like music notes, it enchants me and lulls me into submission. As usual, all I now care about is what Jake orders.

"I..." I try to formulate a coherent sentence but his fingers rubbing against me turn my thoughts into nothingness.

"May I?" he asks as he puts his fingertips just under the waistband of my leggings. He's not even holding the poem anymore, he's put it to the side and is now fully turned toward me, his enthralling gaze captivating my whole being.

Since when does Jake care if he can or cannot do something?

I nod anyway, because of course he can. He can take me, he can play with me. He can fuck me and break my heart as many times as he desires, my body and my heart will always welcome him back. Only my brain fights, but my brain has no power when Jake is nearby.

Before he puts his hand below my leggings, he grabs my left leg, dragging it onto the sofa and positioning himself between my thighs. He doesn't just slide his hand below my clothes, he fully grips my leggings and panties and pulls them down my legs, as far as they can go, just below my knees.

"We shouldn't," I breathe out. "We've got homework to do...and...and we're supposed to–"

"I want to apologize," he cuts me off.

"Apologize?" I pant as he runs his knuckles between my folds.

"For hurting you, last time I was here." He lowers himself and starts kissing my neck, leaving light kisses and moving down to my collarbone. He pushes my crop top above my breasts and leaves a trail with his tongue between my boobs. When he takes a nipple in his mouth, my hands shoot to his hair, entangling themselves as a warning to never leave this position.

He moves to the other one, pulling, nibbling, licking. My breathing is so ragged, butterflies in my stomach dancing to the rhythm of his tongue on me.

I can feel the tightness in my lower stomach begging to snap, my insides clenching in need for him. I'm so close to orgasm... is it...is it even possible? To orgasm from Jake feasting on my breasts? It feels just short of attainable and when I let out a long, almost frustrated moan, and start rubbing myself against him, he leaves my chest to carry his trail south. He leaves kisses on my stomach, my hips.

I scream when he suddenly bites the skin of my right hip, he soothes me by licking before going back to sucking. I feel blood rushing to the area, and when I try to move left, his hand grips my left hip, keeping me in place. I don't know how long he spends there, but long enough to have me desperately wanting his mouth to be somewhere else.

He keeps going down, and starts kissing my inner thighs, never quite reaching the place I'm desperate for. I'm squirming, moaning under his torture. When he finally settles his head right between my legs, his very breath makes me shudder.

"I'm sorry for talking about our sex to everyone, Angel. It was a special moment to me, and I'll never take it for granted again. Let me redeem myself."

I don't get to reply, his tongue on my core only draws a loud moan out of me. He doesn't give me a second to take a breath or get used to it. He keeps going, licking with a flat tongue before entering me. When he comes back to my clit, he circles around it before taking it between his lips and tapping with his tongue. There's not a single break, the intensity only building without a chance for it to dip back down.

"Fuck, fuck, fuck..." I pant just as he makes out with my pussy, using my clit as he would usually my tongue, lips against lips.

"Fuck!" I scream in release. The tension in my body that

has been begging to explode for what feels like hours is now like a medley of emotions in my lungs, in my heart. Like a drug I can feel coursing through my veins, soothing me and awakening me at the same time, setting me on fire while the cool sheen of sweat on my skin barely manages to stop me from combusting.

Jake's lips are on my mouth the next second. I moan again when I taste myself on him, the sweet and salty tang awakening a new need.

He breaks away just long enough to whisper to me in a raw voice, "Swearing sounds awful coming from that beautiful mouth, Angel. I prefer when you scream my name." He kisses me again, robbing me of air and reason.

I have no time to talk, to respond, to even *think.* Jake pulls away, grabs my hips and flips me around before ridding me of my leggings and panties completely. His hands are back on my hips and he pulls me so I'm almost resting on my heels, my cheek still against the softness of the cushion.

"Tell me, *fuck*, tell me why this pussy is always so wet for me? How do you even expect me to stay away when I know this is the effect I have on you?"

He slides a finger in, the sensation feels entirely different from the times he's done it before. I recoil slightly, trying to lift up, but his palm between my shoulder blades pushes me back down.

"What—"

"Ssh," he cuts me off. "Trust me." He inserts his finger in my pussy again, it's not that deep but the sensation is overwhelming. His mouth is next to my ear when he talks again. "It's my thumb," he whispers reassuringly. "I just want to make you sing a new tune."

There's a hint of teasing in his voice and I don't understand what he means until his thumb starts rubbing the front wall of my pussy. He presses slightly and I don't control my voice when a high moan escapes my lips. It's loud, almost like an uncontrollable squeal. He slides out. I barely have time to take a deep breath before he slides back in, slowly, and rubs again, a little longer. My whole body contracts and I let out another delicious scream, my head buries into the cushion and it absorbs my shameless sounds.

"What do you think you're doing?" The pull at my hair brings my head up as he slides his thumb back out. "These moans are mine, Angel. Don't you fucking dare hide them from me."

His voice is always so dark, so authoritative when he's drowning in lust. He wants control, he craves it. He might get high on commanding me, but he is utterly out of control over himself when we're together.

He presses the inside of my pussy again, rubs and I scream his name shamelessly, panting like I just ran a marathon. When he presses again, I get the sudden urge to pee, and I recoil with more force than I tried earlier.

"Wait," I gasp. "I-I-"

"Just trust me, will you?" He tries to make his voice softer but the order in it is still clear.

I feel more than wet, I feel like I'm leaking. It's the strangest sensation, and yet the pleasure is so intense I can't get my body to move.

My orgasm comes slowly, building warmly in my guts, exploding like a never-ending firework in my heart.

He pulls slightly away from me and I hear him pull down his sweatpants.

"You're well on your way to squirting for me. You know that, Angel?"

I want to reply, I want to turn around and face him, but the lethargic state from the orgasm and embarrassing heat that is spreading from my chest to my cheeks are making it impossible. I make this so easy for him. I'm malleable for Jake, easy to manipulate and play with.

The feeling of his cock sliding against my pussy lips makes me tremble with pleasure. It's almost too much, how could I do this again? I can't come anymore, but I can let him use me like I know he wants to. I don't mind, in fact, I *want* it. Need it like my next breath. Jake's satisfaction is the ultimate road to my happiness.

I feel the tip of his erection against my entrance and that's when it comes to me.

"Condom!" I gasp loudly as he begins to penetrate me.

I hear his frustrated growl before he freezes and lays back. "Come on, beautiful. Don't do this to me."

My whole being freezes in aversion. "Don't call me that," I say as I grit my teeth.

"Why?"

Beautiful.

That is what Nathan calls me. That's sweet Nathan, the one who didn't lie, the one who didn't manipulate me. But the hate that springs in my body when I hear that word now is lethal. I'll never forgive him for what he did yesterday. He said he saved me from one of Volkov's men. I think I would have rather died than watch my notebook disappear in flames.

I try to turn around, but Jake's hands are on my hips, keeping me in place. His thumbs start kneading my ass cheeks. "Why?" he asks again, his voice a little rougher, a little more demanding, edging toward anger as his brain slowly makes the connection.

"Let me turn around," I try to say in a resolved voice.

He ignores my demand. Instead, his grip tightens, possessive, too close to painful. "Is that what he called you?"

It's not even a real question, it's rhetorical. His thumbs are pressing so hard on my ass cheeks, his fingertips anchored on the front of my hips, marking me with toxic greed.

"Why do you do this to me, Jamie?" I can't see him, but I can practically hear how tight his jaw is. "Why do you remind me of you and him? Do you *want* me to hurt you? You're practically begging for it."

"I'm not I–"

"Shut your fucking mouth," he seethes as he flips me around. He rises over me, straddling my waist. I put both my hands on his chest to keep some distance between him and me. Angry Jake is a danger to life, to health, to sanity. He slaps my hands away, like they're nothing but a pestering fly, and moves further up, dragging himself along my body until he's straddling my chest.

"What are you doing?" My heart picks up as he grabs my wrists, pinning them against the sofa above my head with one hand.

"You seem to forget who's in charge." His voice is lethal, poisonous. "You're a disobedient little bitch. Every time I leave a bit of slack on your leash, you run wild. And I can't have that."

I try. I promise I try my best to feel rage, disgust or even slight repulsion. I don't want a misogynistic bastard as a boyfriend. I don't want an asshole who thinks he can own me, who thinks he can call me a bitch, treat me as his pet.

Except I do. I do if it's Jake. It's liberating, it's magical. The tightness coiling like a dangerous snake in my stomach, the violence of my heartbeat, the madness coursing through my veins. The insanity of our relationship gives me life.

I pull at my wrists, but it's like my body just wants to test that I *truly* can't get away. And I can't. He's got me exactly where he wants and I'm ready to be used all over again.

"Goody doesn't want to be fucked without a condom. Such a safe little angel," he taunts me.

He takes his dick back out of his boxers and his free hand pries my jaw open.

"Well then, I'm gonna have to use one of your other holes, aren't I? Fix that filthy mouth, make you choke on my dick to make sure you watch what you say when you're around me."

I try to reply something, try to at least pretend to defend myself, but he slips two fingers in my mouth, sliding them against my tongue, going so deep that I gag around them.

"That's it, Angel. Choke on your words." He takes his fingers out just to replace them with his thumb, that same thumb that was inside me a few minutes ago. I taste myself on his skin, vibrate to the scent of my arousal. He pulls down until my mouth is slack for him and shoves himself inside my mouth. His cock hits the back of my mouth, attempting to breach down my throat and my body automatically tries to bring my hands to his hips to push him away. He holds tightly, a bruising touch that lights my skin on fire. I gag, saliva pooling at my lips, slowly dribbling and dragging along my chin as he pulls out and back in.

"I'm not playing no game anymore, Angel. Mention him again and I'll choke you unconscious, you got that?"

He called me beautiful, and I asked him not to. I'm the

141

one asking not to be reminded of him. But if there is truly something that brings Jake to the brink of sanity, something that brings out the demons in him, the darkness that's eating him up from the inside out, it's the mention of Nathan.

I instinctively rub my thighs together as he goes deep again, a moan forming in my mouth and pulsating around his dick. He fists my hair, pushing even deeper. I choke on him, spluttering.

Shit.

This is scary.

My eyes open, expecting to see him lost in a lustful craze. No. He's watching me struggle, his spine straight, his gaze looking down on me with all the smugness in the world. The evil in his soul is reflecting in his eyes and an arrogant smile pulls at his lips before he licks his bottom lip. He watches the fear on my face with such satisfaction that my heart picks up at the terrifying thought that he might actually be trying to choke me.

I attempt to move my head, but he pulls slightly out, barely enough to feel oxygen slither into my lungs before pushing back in. He repeats at a quicker pace, his jaw falls slack, pleasure relaxing his features. I'm still struggling to breathe and for some reason it makes my thighs tighten, my awakened clit seeking release from them.

Just when I'm about to fight back again, desperate to take a gulp of air, he pulls out completely, pulling away from his position, releasing my hands and going further back. I'm so worried about bringing air in, gasping for it, that I don't realize what he's doing until I feel spurts of thick cum on my breasts, my collarbone, my neck.

I freeze in shock, my heart galloping, my eyes widening in

disbelief. But that's not the worst. The worst is when I see his hand coming back from his pocket, his phone rising in front of me and the sudden flash.

I bring my hands to my front, pulling down the top he had pushed up.

"Jake," I shout. "What the hell?!" I push him off me – he's a lot more compliant now that he released his anger on me – and I jump off the sofa, running to the bathroom, locking myself in.

I re-run the whole thing in the shower as I thoroughly wash his cum off my body. How does he do it? How does he poison my mind so I let him do whatever he wants to me? It's not just because he's hotter than anyone I've ever seen, it's not because he's more beautiful and enchanting than any mythological God. There's something about his broken pieces, they fit right into mine. Maybe I'm more broken than I thought.

Obviously, there are events in my life that have affected me, have broken small pieces of my soul that will never be the same. I was fifteen when Volkov's men took me and my brother. When they held us for hours, waiting for my dad to come just so they could shoot him. Just so I could watch him die. *I* got shot that day. I lost my brother. For months, certain sounds, certain smells would send me spiraling down into panic attacks. I felt lucky at how quickly I worked on PTSD with my therapist. It shouldn't have been that *easy*. Only now do I realize I shouldn't have gotten over it that quickly. At some point, somehow, I buried the fact that I lost a figure of healthy authority in my life, a figure of healthy protection. A father, a brother. People who laid their lives to save mine.

My mother is a wonderful woman, a superheroine. She

supports the both of us, she works hard, she is strong-minded. But she is no protection when it comes to the dangers of the outside world. We're both scared of it, we're both traumatized.

When I thought Nathan was just a normal guy, I had found safety in him. Normality. But it wasn't enough. I found possession in Jake. He doesn't just make me feel safe, he picks up the broken pieces and crushes them in his hands until they are cut and bleeding from the shards of my trauma. He accepted his own demons, embraced them so tightly that he's not afraid of mine.

He doesn't protect me, he *owns* me. And there is nothing that can surpass that. It comes with the thrill of his control, the tension of his hold on me, the metaphorical collar around my neck that constantly reminds me I'm his but that *he* is impossible to domesticate. And my body, my heart, my soul, that's all they want. That's their deepest, darkest desire. My brain is only starting to catch up now, and that's okay. I'll give time for my consciousness to understand there is nothing else. Just Jake.

In my room, I look at myself in my full-length mirror as I dry myself. There are already bruises forming on my hips, and a dark hickey from when he bit and sucked at the skin covering my right hip. There's another hickey at the curve where my neck meets my shoulder. I sigh, knowing I won't be able to hide it at school and knowing perfectly well that he did it on purpose. He is so selfish. He uses and abuses me, and he didn't even run after me after I left the living room.

I don't even know if he's still there.

I put on another pair of leggings and this time a large sweater that won't leave me so vulnerable around him.

When I walk into the living room, he's still right there, on the sofa, lying down. His feet are far off the right end and his head resting on the left armrest. He's got an arm folded behind his head, looking at something on his phone, fully dressed. I post myself by his feet, crossing my arms across my chest, and his gaze meets mine.

"I could look at this picture all day long, Angel."

Discomfort feels heavy in my stomach as I understand what picture he means straight away. I don't want to see it, I don't want to know what I look like; flushed from two orgasms, saliva dripping from my lips from him fucking my mouth, and covered in his cum.

"Just delete it," I order quietly. My voice is a little raw from how far he went down my throat and I feel myself getting tingly again at the thought. Surely it isn't *normal* that I enjoyed it so much.

"Watch my lips," he says as he sits up and gets closer to me. I roll my eyes and it makes him chuckle, one of those rare chuckles that he can't help and sounds genuine.

He grabs my arms, softly, forcing me to uncross them and he holds my hands in his, threading his fingers through mine. "I will *never* delete it. I might even print and frame it." The humor in his tone forces a laugh to cross my lips. "Unless you promise I'll get to take another one? Another hundred? We can settle on that, if I can take another hundred, I won't frame it."

His soft side gets to me, especially after the violence of our sex, after the rawness and exhaustion of strong orgasms. He pulls at my arms and his back hits the sofa before I fall gently on him.

"Why are you so addictive, Angel?" He wonders aloud as

his hand mindlessly strokes my hair.

I giggle into his neck, nestling myself closer to him, inhaling his wooden scent, as his other arm wraps around my waist to keep me on top of him.

"Let's order some food," he suggests as his lips hover over my ear. He kisses the soft skin under my earlobe, then drags his lips across my jaw, stopping at the corner of my mouth.

"We haven't even finished our homework," I answer. "We need to finish that."

"But I'm starving, you sucked the life out of me. I'm hungover. We'll finish after food."

I don't reply for long seconds because I'm hungry and I know he'll order if he wants to, anyway.

"Sushi?" I ask in the quietest voice I can. I feel him chuckle, his mouth against my temple.

"That sounds like a wonderful idea."

The sun is setting down and the night creeping in on us when another episode of the Real Housewives of Atlanta finishes.

"How often do you watch these things?" Jake queries. "I thought you were meant to be a bookworm or something."

I laugh, but it's a little quiet, I'm exhausted and can barely keep my eyes open anymore. Probably because I was teased and deliciously tortured into another orgasm as I was trying to rest and watch my show, followed by my boobs being used for Jake's pleasure. This guy can get pretty creative when we don't have condoms.

I ate my own weight in sushi and I'm now lying on the sofa while Jake is behind me, holding me tight against him and drawing calming circles with the tip of his fingers on my arm, my shoulder, my collarbone. He keeps going back and forth, lulling me into a state of total relaxation.

"I'm not a bookworm." I yawn and rub my eyes. "I enjoy studying, homework. I like organization and discipline in what I do. But I'm no bookworm, I read the same as everyone else."

"Mm, discipline," he murmurs in my ear, not realizing the kind of pleasure it brings to my body. The kind of electricity it sends through my veins. "I can think of a lot of ways to discipline you, my sweet Angel."

I giggle, but it's only to hide my anticipation. "I meant as in rigorous work."

"Sure, you did." He keeps going with the caresses on my body and I don't realize when I fall asleep. All I understand is when my body hits my bed and covers are being drawn on me.

* * *

On Monday I bike to school earlier than usual. I don't want to bump into Emily at our lockers. I still haven't talked to her and I know I should apologize, but I'm still hurt by her words. I bet she's still hurt by mine. It's not just about my best friend though. My head hurts from the back and forth of all the problems I'm dealing with. Nathan has been texting me all weekend, apologizing for scaring me, apologizing for the things he said to me. I don't get it. I don't get *him*. The state of rage he was in on Friday night was beyond anything I thought he was capable of. He *killed* a man. A Wolf that was lurking outside of my house, ready to pounce anytime. Add that to my list of problems to think about. Volkov. I should be more scared than I am that one of his men was after me but I'm not. I've felt Volkov's presence weighing on my life for years. In truth, I believe he was there because the Wolves think I'm important to Nathan, their current biggest enemy.

I park my bike and hurry inside to my locker to grab some books. The halls are empty, and I enjoy some peace and quiet.

Jake left after I fell asleep on Saturday. All our stuff was gone from the living room when I woke up, apart from a note. I think of it again, his words and how vague they were about us.

I've got an early Sunday practice and I didn't want to wake you.
I'll be spending the rest of the weekend thinking of ways to
discipline you.

That doesn't really help now, does it? I still don't know what is truly going on between us. Are we just a weekend thing? Is it just sex? Does he want more? I'm not sure myself that I want more. After our first time together, I did, I wanted us to date and be in a serious relationship with him. But after what he said that day, I have to keep my distance. I have to drill in my mind that his favorite thing is playing with me, possessing me, not loving me.

As soon as I shut my locker, a strong figure is right next to me. I almost jump in surprise, but quickly calm down when I recognize Cole.

My student body co-president offers me a sweet smile, his light blue eyes looking down into mine. I'm surprised he even wants to talk to me after the Halloween ball fiasco. I was meant to go with him, but Jake made sure to threaten him into cancelling so I would accept his offer instead. Just Jake being...well, Jake.

"So," he says with a big smile. "I have a great idea for the new cheer uniforms, and I thought we could use your brains."

"Good morning to you too, Cole," I smile as I start walking toward our first class. He wouldn't usually go to class so early, but I think his uniform idea is very urgent, so he follows me. I can bet my house that he wants the tops to be cropped. He has complained many times that other schools' cheerleaders had sexier outfits than ours. I don't think he gets that I truly don't care, now less than ever. When you learn that your ex is part of a gang and that your...whatever Jake is...is your ex's brother, cheer uniforms start using a lot less space in your brain.

Cole has been talking, but I haven't been listening. Not one bit. So, I stop and turn to him. He's a handsome guy, the typical high school jock, with his wide shoulders, his letterman jacket sporting our lacrosse team logo even though the season hasn't started, and his dark blond hair brushed back. I could fall for someone like Cole, I'm sure I could, physically. Wouldn't life be so much simpler if I did? No gang, no secrets, no darkness. How simple, how boring.

"I'm sorry, I zoned out."

He's about to start talking again when his eyes zero in on my neck. He lets out a low whistle, his teeth grazing his bottom lip.

"Damn, Jamie. Did you have sex with a vampire?"

My hand shoots to my neck, drawing my shirt tighter. The heat spreading on my cheeks, itching my skin, forces my eyes to look at the floor.

"I'm only messing with you," he laughs, putting a hand on my other shoulder. "You should enjoy yourself. I'm very open for you to enjoy yourself with me, by the way."

My eyes shoot up to watch a beautiful smile spreading across Cole's lips.

"Um..." I scratch my throat.

He laughs and lets go of my shoulder. "So, cheer uniforms," he goes back to the initial topic, not phased one bit by my hesitation in sleeping with him.

"Yeah, cheer uniforms. Did you..." My words die in my throat when I notice who just stopped a few feet away from us. Jake is standing tall, looking at us with his usual golden-boy smile on his gorgeous face. His features look calm, his mask well in place, but it's the way his knuckles turn white around his bag's handle that kicks my heart into a frenzy.

He walks to us, settling behind me, and I just *know* he's looking straight into Cole's eyes when his free hand grabs the back of my neck.

"Cooper, I'm so glad your nose is better. That is why you should always keep your helmet on on the field." Jake's voice is warm, but the undertones of threats remind us all that he's the one who had broken Cole's nose for inviting me to the ball. A shiver runs down my spine at yet another realization that our relationship is just as toxic as magical.

Cole's lips thin into an angry line, his jaw clicking. "Yeah. I'll make sure to remember that."

"You better." The words come out a little colder, a tad more threatening.

"Whatever," Cole mumbles. "I'll see you later, Jamie." He turns around, but Jake's voice stops him in his tracks.

"You know something else you better remember?" This time, he's mocking him, going straight for humiliation. Cole looks back and raises an eyebrow at him. "That there's a lot more than your nose that might get broken if you keep hitting on my girlfriend."

The lump that gets stuck in my throat stops me from defending Cole, from defending myself.

I'm sorry, Cole, I love it too much when he takes control. I can't do anything about it.

Cole shakes his head. "Fuck you, White." He leaves us behind, carrying on his way to English class. Leaving me at Jake's mercy.

Jake's grip tightens on the back of my neck, and his mouth grazes my ear when he talks again. "My my, Angel, I'm glad I've been thinking of creative ways to discipline you. You just love stepping out of line, don't you?"

I shrug his hand off with force, stepping away from him and making sure that, while on the inside my body is thrumming to the rhythm of his words, I have to make sure to keep a strong face on the outside.

"Girlfriend?" I ask in a strong voice, changing the topic from discipline back to him announcing a relationship I wasn't aware I was part of.

"What?" he asks in genuine surprise. "I apologized this weekend, I thought we had moved past that."

"Moved past *what* exactly? I don't remember me agreeing to be anyone's girlfriend."

"I don't remember me ever asking your opinion for any-thing," he beams.

"Get that stupid self-satisfied smile off your face, White," I grumble, but there is warmth in my chest begging to take over. A cheerfulness making my bones vibrate.

"Oh, she called me by my last name. She's mad. My woman is mad. What to do?"

151

I chuckle and shove his shoulder playfully. "I am not agreeing to be your girlfriend, Jake. Stick that in that beautiful head of yours."

"Huh," he puts an arm around my shoulders, steering us toward English class as he pretends to be thinking over my words. "I *am* very beautiful. Very duly noted."

It's strange to walk into English class with Jake's arm around my shoulders. I feel awkward, especially since only Chris and Cole are in the class. Chris' brows furrow in disapproval but he doesn't say anything. Jake and I probably look like a casual couple right now, but my heart is hammering in my chest. We both sit in our neighboring seats and he pushes his chair closer to mine straight away.

"Here," he says as he puts a piece of paper on my desk. "Our homework."

"Crap," I let out a sigh. "I completely forgot."

"Don't worry," he shoots me a gorgeous smile, "I did it all." My eyes lock with his before he sits back in his seat. "Don't stress, Angel, I'm a grade-A student. I won't jeopardize your chance of a scholarship."

I let out a chuckle. "Thanks. I really appreciate it."

He bends towards me, his lips close to my ear. "Anything for my girl."

This sounds good and it feels good but it's too quick. Until a few days ago I was basically dead to him. He wouldn't talk to me, he wouldn't even look at me. It wasn't too long ago that Nathan was calling me his girl. My emotions are all over the place and this feels too much like Jake's revenge on his brother, it's not genuine.

"Jake, I'm not—"

I'm cut off when someone kicks my bag at the foot of my

desk and my stuff spills everywhere. I look up to see Beth and Camila walking by, Emily following close.

I huff and get up to face them. "Are you done with your childish behavior yet? My patience has its limit."

"Ooh, Goody, you bite!" Beth exclaims, attracting the attention of every student that had started to settle in their seats. Camila stands next to her, popping a hip out as she crosses her arms over her chest. She emanates power but I'm done taking her shit.

"Getting brave I see. Just pick up your shit and bow your head. It's better for you this way, Goody," Camila says in her calm, silky voice.

My blood is boiling. I've taken enough of this in the past month, and I'm done. None of this was my fault. I didn't go after her boyfriend, I didn't ask for any of this.

"You kicked it, you pick it up," I snarl.

There's a round of 'ooh' from the people in the class and I realize I might be in way over my head. Beth laughs and I notice Emily behind her, shifting uncomfortably on her feet.

Camila takes a dangerous step toward me, affirming her height over mine and it takes all my strength not to take a step back.

"Aren't you used to being on your knees? Don't you scrub floors at Luke's dad's café? Don't you suck Jake's dick on a daily basis?"

I can't help my mouth falling slack as heat creeps up my cheeks. Everyone around is laughing mockingly at me and I want to retort something but I'm too embarrassed and she doesn't give me time. My vision narrows as she gets in my face.

"I don't know in what other ways to tell you you're not

fucking welcome here. You can't afford anything in this town. You couldn't even afford the trailer park if we had one. You're like a nasty STD, sticking around when everyone is desperately trying to get rid of you. Your only friend can't stand you anymore. The only reason you're still in this school is because the city pities you because your daddy died. But let's be honest, he wasn't even that good of a sheriff."

Tears burn my eyes at her cruel words but as soon as she mentions my dad, rage takes over.

"You *fucking* bitch," I hiss as I rear my arm back to punch her. I'm stopped dead in my tracks by a hand on my arm and an arm slipping around my waist. I desperately try to fight back, screaming to let me go so I can finish the bitch.

Before I realize who's grabbing me, I see Camila flinch as a hand takes a strong hold of the back of her neck. She's snatched to the side and I watch Jake tightening his hold as he bends his head to talk to her.

"You and I need to have a chat," he hisses. I watch her face fall in fear. Jake is fuming and I can see him almost trembling trying to hold back, the nice act he puts on at school crumbling down.

He walks past me without as much as a glance toward me and drags Camila with him. The hands holding me let me go and I turn around to face Chris.

"You would have regretted it. You know this would have turned against you," he explains in a soft, reassuring voice.

"Thank you," I breathe out. It would have turned against me. Who am I? A nobody. Everyone would take her defense. She practically begged me to punch her so she could get me kicked out of school.

"I need the restroom," I say, trying to hold back my tears.

I run out of the room and hurry to the bathroom, but before I can reach my destination, I find Jake cornering Camila against a row of lockers. Neither one of them can see me but I can hear them very well. Jealousy pinches my guts until I hear what he's saying to her.

"I swear to God, Camila, if her name so much as crosses your lips one more time you're going to regret it so, so bad."

"I know," she whimpers. "It won't."

"How many times did I warn you, huh? You know me, you should know my threats don't go empty."

A heavy silence falls in the hallway as she squirms under his touch.

"Touch me," she finally says. Surely, she can't be serious. "I'm sorry. I'm sorry, I did this to piss you off. I wanted to bring out our games again. Please, baby, touch me." She grabs his hand and tries to put it under her skirt, but he pulls it away.

"Stop with this shit, you hear me? It's over. I don't want anything to do with you or your pussy. Imprint this on your brain because I'm not going to repeat myself. Next time there'll be no warning."

"You can't leave me," she starts crying. "After what you did on Friday? You practically killed me while fingering me and I took it, *for you.*"

My heart breaks at her words. He had sex with her on Friday. How? How could I be so stupid? How could I think he would actually be different with me?

"I did everything for you," Camila insists. "Everything you asked. I changed who I was, I became what *you* wanted to please *you.* You can't just throw me away."

"But I can, Cam. You're not interesting to me anymore. You

155

bore me to death, and you couldn't get me hard even if you choked on my dick."

I retreat slightly at his words. He's so horrible to her. Camila has made my life hell, but she said it herself: she's a hurt woman. And Jake did this to her.

I feel bad for her. She is in love with him. He toyed with her for two years, pushing and pulling at her and she let him. Five days of the week he pretended to love her and every weekend he cheated on her. She took him back every time because that's what love does to you.

And now I'm his new toy. It excites him. He wants to break me and build me back up exactly how he likes. The same way he did with her. And it's already working, I'm already falling into the addiction, I'm already feeling jealous, I've started craving him long before today.

I keep taking steps back as Camila cries genuine tears.

"You're being pathetic," I hear Jake say. His words warn me of what my near future could possibly be. And if not in a few months, then maybe in a year. Or two, like Camila. I'll fall desperately in love with him, and he'll throw me away the second he gets bored, for someone more exciting. Someone who initially wanted nothing to do with him and made him work for it.

I feel sick thinking of what we did on Saturday. Of what I let him do to me because deep down, I wanted him to fall for me. I wanted him to treat me differently from all the girls before. From Camila. But really, Emily was right. All I did was fall for his tricks. He's good. He's very good at this.

I'm just like all of them.

"Jake. Jake! Come back! You can't leave me, you turned me into this. It's your fault," I hear Camila shout but I'm not looking anymore. I'm hurrying away from them and to the bathroom.

I hear his steps behind me, but I don't stop.

"Jamie," Jake says calmly in his deep voice.

I accelerate my walk until I'm practically running. He needs to leave me alone. I'm not strong enough, I'll fall back and I can't. I just can't. Him, Nathan...it's just too much.

I feel tears prickling at the corner of my eyes. How could I be so stupid?

"Jamie!" he shouts after me and this time I run. I sprint out of the doors and into the lawn at the front of the school. Where am I going? I don't have my bag or my phone. I don't have the key for my bike. Why do I even lock my bike? No one in this stupid school would ever want to steal it.

I don't know where to go and I can hear Jake catching up so, just like the stupid girl I am, I stop dead in my tracks. He's going to catch me anyway.

What Jake wants, Jake gets. I should know this by now.

"What's wrong with you," he breathes as he catches up. "Why are you running?"

I snap around to face him. "Is this what you want from me? To turn me into an addicted girl who can't refuse you anything? Who begs for you to stay? Who willingly lets you play with her in your twisted ways? For what?" I take a deep breath as confusion and regret settle on his face. "So you can throw me away like a rag doll just like you did with Camila?"

"Jamie–"

"I can't do this, Jake. I can't be your plaything. It's not who I am, and I won't stoop down to this. I want respect. I want love and honesty. And that's not something you can give me."

He snickers coldly. "But is that something Nate could give

you?"

My blood turns boiling hot at him bringing this up again. "So what if he did?!" I bring both my hands flat against his chest and push him hard, but he doesn't move. Instead, it forces me to step back slightly. "I made my mistakes, but I will not be a pawn in the games you and your brother play. I won't be the revenge you take on him. Sort yourself out, Jake. Take time to do it yourself because no girl, no one nightstand, and no plaything will ever fix you. No matter how much you take control over them."

I see that I've hit the right spot when he takes a step back. "You've made up your mind and you won't even let me prove you wrong," he says in frustration.

"I'm no different from Camila. Just new and shiny. Just giving you a hard time. But I'm human. I'll fall for you, hard and deep and you'll get bored. You'll grow bored when I don't turn out the way you want me to or worse...when I do and there's no more fun for you."

"You are the opposite of Camila, Jamie. She's no fucking angel, trust me! You're so far from being like her you wouldn't even understand."

"And maybe that's what is attracting you to me, but you don't know me! I know we're physically attracted to each other, but these things are ephemerals. I don't know you, Jake."

I see him thinking about it for a long minute. He's clearly conflicted but I'm not going to wait for him to decide I'm not worth it. I'm making that decision for both of us.

"I'm going back to class. Hopefully, it's not too late to hand in our work. Thanks for writing it."

I go around him to walk back to the building, but he grabs

my elbow gently.

"Wait."

I stop and turn my head to look at him. "Jake..." I sigh.

"Come with me." He pulls me and starts walking.

And I follow.

My brain is screaming at me to go back to class, to go back to my life, try my best to forget about him but my body gives in. It always does.

CHAPTER 9

Love No one – Christian Gates

Jake

It pains me to admit but Jamie is right. The girl is too smart for her own good. She thinks things over and over again and always finds what could go wrong. It stops her from enjoying a lot of things in life but mainly, it stops her from enjoying what we could have. It also makes me realize that she truly believes I don't know her. And while that's a good enough excuse for her to let go of what we shared, it only motivates me to work harder for our relationship because I want her. I want her so bad my chest ached when she suggested stopping now. I can't let her go, not until she's given this a chance and makes a decision with all the information.

We pass the sign that says, 'Thank You for Visiting Stoneview - See you soon!' as I drive us out of our suffocating town.

"This is looking a lot like kidnapping," she says for maybe the third time. She doesn't know where I'm taking her, but it doesn't matter. We just need to get away from everyone, from our expectations. From Camila and Nate. From everyone seeing her as a good girl who's only allowed to care about the rules and the same people thinking I'm Stoneview's player. We need to meet on neutral grounds.

"What's your plan exactly?" she asks after another twenty minutes of silence.

I shrug. "I want to get to know you. I'm hoping you want to get to know me too."

She gives me a shy smile and shakes her head. "We're cutting."

"Wouldn't be the first time. For either of us." I give her a look to show that I remember that time she cut after our moment in the bathroom. Now that I know she was dating Nate, I don't want to imagine where she went that day. Was it to his house? Did they cuddle and spend the day together? Where does he even live? I'm sure I'll know soon enough.

I exit the motorway and pass the Silver Falls sign. We park at the bottom of the trail that leads all the way up the fall. I hop out and go around to open her door as well. She needs to see what it's like when I'm on my best behavior.

"You don't mind a short walk, do you?" I say as I help her out of the car. She shakes her head but keeps quiet.

"What are we going to do about the stuff we left in class?" she asks.

I can't help a small laugh. "Relax, Angel. Someone will pick them up. Chris would never leave your stuff when he takes mine."

She nods and I grab her hand, threading my fingers with hers.

"Have you ever been up there?" I question and she quickly

nods again, making some strands of hair fall in her eyes.

"My parents and I used to go every weekend," she says as she puts the strands back behind her ears.

"Damn. You probably know the quickest way up then, don't you?"

"Yeah you have to–" I cut her off with a quick kiss on her soft lips.

"Let's make sure we avoid it. We want to take our time." I pull at her hand and we start the gentle hike to the falls.

We're the only people walking the long path and probably any path right now. No one really makes it a point to hike to the silver falls at 10:30 am on a Monday.

"Is Camila going to be okay?" she asks. And isn't that typical of her? I'm trying to get us away from everyone so we can get to know each other, and she worries about the girl who has made her life hell in the past few weeks.

"She's a strong girl," I reply. "She's in love with me. Deeply. And I know it's my fault. I should have ended things a long time ago. It had to be done at some point and I can't keep this going."

She looks at me in surprise as if she didn't think I'd have the rationality in me to end a one-sided relationship. And I really didn't. Until I met her.

She doesn't say anything, and I feel obliged to go into more detail, especially after what she heard in the hallway.

"It's true," I say while I try to gather the right way to explain my complicated, toxic relationship with Camila.

"What's true?"

"What she said. Look, I'm not trying to use this as an excuse but know that Camila is not exactly the purest either. She cheated on me too. Long before I started cheating on her. Our relationship was never right, she did it again, so did I. We kept hurting each other just as much as we made each other happy. We were a whole new breed of toxic for each other." I can see her eyes growing wide at the revelation that Camila isn't the victim in this relationship like she loves everyone to think.

"That said," I continue. "I did change her. Not for the best. I let her fall for me. The deeper things went, the more I was learning who I was, what I liked…and she followed along. She never complained, she always adjusted. Then she learned to love it too. I know now it wasn't right. I should have left her when I realized she was changing to please me. But I was too selfish."

"What's *it,* Jake? What did she learn to love to please you?"

My jaw ticks because I know she sees what I mean but she wants to hear me say it. "You know it, Jamie. I like…" I hate saying it out loud. "I like being in control."

"That you do," she huffs. Her hand grips mine harder in a reassuring gesture, "And that's fine Jake. You're allowed to."

She doesn't say anything else. Doesn't say if she thinks she can take it. Doesn't ask why I'm this way and doesn't say if she would change for me.

"I think I like it," she finally drops, and my heart somersaults in my chest. Shit, I hadn't felt that in a very long time.

Deep down, I knew it but hearing her say it is different. This sounds nothing like the girl everyone knows from school and I feel special to her. I stop and turn to her, cupping both her cheeks in my hands. She has to go on the tip of her toes as I lean down and kiss her lips softly. It quickly heats up and our tongues intertwine.

"Good," I wink at her as I take a step back. "The last thing I would want is you changing for me."

"I don't want to," she admits. "But I do want to understand you."

We start walking again and she's the one who grabs my hand this time.

"Ask away," I say in a light voice. "But I'm warning you, it gets fucked up."

She chuckles and goes silent for a moment.

"Do you know your real parents?" she asks shamelessly after a minute of silence.

"Oh wow, we're starting strong I see. I thought you were gonna ease into it, ask my favorite color."

She blushes at my comment, whispers a 'sorry' and I can't stop a laugh. "I'm fucking with you, Jamie. I don't care. No, I don't know them. My first memory only goes as far as being at the orphanage."

Her face scrunches up in pity. "I'm sorry."

I shrug at her response. "Can't miss what you never had, can you?"

She gives me a shy smile in response. She opens her mouth to ask another question, but I cut her off. "Ah ah. My turn. It's one for one."

"What? That's not what we agreed," she complains, her brows furrowing.

"You should know by now I don't play by the rules, my little Angel."

She blushes again and I tighten my grip on her hand. I want to kiss her so bad, but I have to refrain myself. This is about her, about making her comfortable around me.

"Fine," she huffs.

"Why did your mom go to Tennessee?"

"Her sister is ill. She went to tend to her. How did you find out she was gone?"

I smile at her mistake. "Luke's dad told him, he told me."

"You guys really share everything? You, Chris, Luke?"

"It's my turn," I smirk. She rolls her eyes at me and for some reason, my dick stirs to life. It's everything she does, the tones in her voice, the blushing colors on her skin, the way she always embraces what she feels. It does shit to me.

"Do you regret having your first time with me?" I ask the itching question. Everything is leading me to think she does, and I don't think I could take it if it was the truth. I try not to ask about virginity because I know it's not a term she likes that much, or at least the stereotypes around it.

"If I could, I would do it all over again," she smiles. Her green eyes sparkle with gold and I see the mischief on her beautiful face.

"I'd be happy to oblige."

"Answer my previous question," she almost orders.

"Yes. On my side definitely. They know everything about me. I guess Ozy is a little more secretive at times," I shrug. Rose has got more to hide, and she hates being told what to do. She'll keep something to herself as long as she can if it means no one will bother her about it. Unfortunately, with Chris, Luke, and I on her back at all times, it's not always easy for her sneaky ass.

"What's with the nickname?" I see her wanting to know more about me by the minute but I'm burning with the need to know every detail about her life.

"It's my turn."

"Please! Just this once," she pouts as she looks up at me through her long lashes.

"Oh, you're good at this, aren't you?" I mess up her hair

with a hand and she giggles. It's the most beautiful sound I've ever heard. That and her moans should be a whole playlist on my Spotify.

"When we were kids, everyone used to call her Rosie. My stupid ass couldn't pronounce 'R's so Rosie sounded like Ozy when I was calling her. I guess it stuck with time."

She nods at my answer and we walk in silence for a few minutes, appreciating each other's presence.

"Do you want ice-cream?" I ask as we walk past the ice cream stand.

"For sure," she smiles but it quickly dies. "Crap, my purse is with my stuff."

This time, I'm the one who can't help an eye roll. I grab my wallet from my pocket as we stand closer to the stand. "Which flavor?" I ask.

"I'll pay you back, you got the sushi on Saturday."

"This is a date, I'm paying."

"I'll get the next one then," she teases, and my heart skips a beat again. I thought she was going to snap back that this isn't a date, but she looks fine with it.

Fuck. I actually want another date.

"Chocolate, please," her gentle voice brings me back to reality.

I pay for both our ice creams and her nose crinkles in disgust when she looks at mine.

"Pistachio? What are you, fifty?"

"You're gonna get yourself in trouble, young lady."

"I'm older than you," she chuckles.

I smile down at her as she licks her ice cream, and my brain goes to dirty places.

Dammit, she could be taking the trash out, I still think my cock would enjoy the view.

"Whatever your age, nothing justifies pistachio ice-cream."

"I hate chocolate," I reply, looking at her cone.

"That's impossible. What's wrong with you?"

I put an arm around her shoulders. The height difference makes it that she's supporting the whole weight of my arm. She stiffens for a second but quickly relaxes.

"Is this okay?" I ask.

"What's your favorite color?" she asks, ignoring my question.

"Gray," I reply knowing it's pretty basic and expecting another comment from her.

It doesn't come though, she's too busy licking some more of her ice cream and I have the urge to readjust myself in my pants. It's fucking hard being a decent guy, I'm dying to push her behind a tree, bend her over and fuck her brains out while she scratches her cheek on the rough bark.

Just think of something else.

"I need to ask you something personal, Jamie." She looks up confused but I carry on walking with my arm over her shoulders.

"Why did you take Rose's phone?"

She freezes and I'm scared I pushed it too far. I squeeze her shoulder in a reassuring gesture, but I feel her tensing even more. *Shit.*

"You know why. I'm sorry I did," she says in a barely audible voice.

Fuck, that's not what I meant. I just want to understand. It's so unlike her to do this that I didn't get it at the time. I was just mad. I just wanted the whole Sam thing to go away.

After Chris told me what happened with her brother, I started figuring out she would want to try and get in contact with Volkov. She thought Sam would be a good way for her. She had no idea he's just a middleman.

There's nothing I can do about Sam or Nate being back in our lives, but I can try to understand in detail why Jamie so desperately wanted to get involved with this. Starting with hearing her side of the story.

"I'm just trying to understand," I admit.

She turns to me as she takes a deep breath. "I wish I hadn't, it wasn't worth it, and it didn't help me."

"But why did you do it? Please, I'm trying to get to know you."

"You know I was trying to get in contact with Volkov through Sam. We don't need to get into more details, do we?"

I chuckle sarcastically because she's the most curious person I've ever met, and she doesn't mind asking me about my parents, but she keeps quiet when I'm trying to know about her life.

"What happened that day? It has to do with your scar, doesn't it?"

She nods. "My brother took a bullet for me."

* * *

Jamie

It's always surprising that not everyone in town is aware of what happened. People loved gossiping about it, and for a while, it was the topic on everybody's lips. But Jake wasn't there at the time. He and Rose weren't with the Murrays yet.

I'm sure Chris has mentioned what happened to Aaron. Otherwise, he wouldn't have known why I wanted to get in contact with Sam or why I wanted to get to Volkov. He wouldn't have cornered me in the janitor's closet to tell me to drop it. But I can see he doesn't know the whole story. I guess no one does except my therapist and me.

I could never have described to Emily exactly what happened. Even Nathan knows the outline only. No one knows how it felt to have to see my dad on his knees, begging the guy with the scar – that I now know is named Alek – to not hurt his kids. I never told anyone that it is impossible to squeeze your eyes hard enough, that the noise of my dad's head exploding and his brains splashing out on the floor next to him is something I will never forget. I never said what the weight of my brother's unconscious body felt like on my chest, crushing me and stopping me from breathing.

"Jamie," Jake finally breaks the silence he had gone into after I told him that my brother took a bullet for me. "You must miss them so much."

My brows shoot up in surprise. I'm used to people telling me that they don't know what to say. Or that they're sorry or they can't imagine what I've been through. Never has someone so bluntly said that I must miss them so much.

"I do," I admit.

"And you're holding on to the hope that you'll find Aaron," he carries on.

"I was." I finish the last bite of my ice cream cone and lift my right hand to hold his left one on top of my shoulder. "Then Nathan destroyed that."

169

I can already see his rage rising but I cut him off before he can say anything. I explain to him what happened at my house and his fists tighten and release multiple times.

"It's not just that," I add. "I had started giving up anyway. That day in the janitor's closet you...you opened my eyes. It's been three years. Either he's dead or he doesn't want to be found. I don't know which would hurt the most, but I have to accept that he's not coming back."

"Do you remember how it went down? That day?"

I ignore the fact that he sounds exactly like my therapist. I don't know if it's because he struggles with emotions and empathy or the complete opposite.

I repeat that day automatically. Like I always do. With time, it's become almost robotic. "They took Aaron and me on the way back from school. They told my dad to come on his own and he did. They offered him protection if he dropped the case he was building against them and turned a blind eye to their business."

I take a deep breath as I try to not let myself flashback to the worst day of my life. "He was a good guy, you know. Rebellious, but with such a kind heart." I try to keep my voice steady, but he doesn't miss when it falters.

"Jamie..." He holds me tight in his arms and my throat tightens. His scent reassures me, and his strong arms bring me warmth.

Then, I go into what I never told anyone. The part no one is interested to know and never ask about. The part that feels too real for me but doesn't feed people's need for gore.

"Sometimes I wish he had just accepted their offer. His job was everything. He wanted to protect the whole town so badly that he refused to protect himself when it came down to it and he took my brother down with him. Volkov's guy shot my dad, then he aimed at me, but Aaron got in the way. It went right through his chest and into my shoulder. I was so sure I had watched both of them die. But Aaron's body disappeared. It just completely vanished."

Tears flow freely by the time I'm finished explaining.

I never admitted this to anyone, not even Emily. Sometimes, I do feel like my dad made a selfish decision that day when he refused to accept their offer. They threatened to kill Aaron and me and he chose to protect the town over his own children. In the end, he saved neither. Volkov still runs Stoneview, and I lost the two most important men in my life. My sobs are muffled by Jake's chest as he runs his hand up and down my back. I can hear his heart beating fast, or maybe it's mine. It seems right now, we're in complete sync.

CHAPTER 10

Dancing With Our Hands Tied – Taylor Swift

Jamie

When we get to the top of the falls, Jake has already made me feel better. I had no idea this was a possibility, but his rare goofiness makes me crack a laugh even when I don't want to. The unlimited kisses might help too. He insisted I shouldn't seek revenge on my brother and dad, just like Emily did.

I'm really starting to see we are much alike. He is angry at the world too. Despite what he said, he is affected by not knowing his birth parents. It's only natural. He told me he looked for them when he moved to the Murrays. He was always told that he wasn't allowed to be given any information until he turned eighteen, but even after that, he doesn't know if there is actual information to be given. He's come to accept that he shouldn't look for them, especially if they didn't want to be found, and he promised me that doing the same with Aaron would help me heal.

I told him what happened at the Bakers' shop helped me

realize that I would put myself in danger looking for him, but closure doesn't come overnight. I wonder if it will ever come as long as Volkov isn't dead or in prison.

We get to the barrier at the edge of the falls and we both hold onto it to look down. It's beautiful and the sound of the water crashing all the way down is therapeutic.

"When we moved to Stoneview, Hannah and Thomas used to take us here all the time. Ozy got sick of the hike up after like, two times. I hated the walk but was so thrilled by the view that I knew it was always worth it."

Still looking at the drop in front of me, I smile imagining Rose and Jake being unbearable until they reached the gorgeous view. I turn to look up at him, but he doesn't notice. He's clearly lost in the memory, a nostalgic smile on his lips.

I rest my head on his arm and he puts it around me to bring me closer until I'm nestled against his side.

"I owe the Murrays so much, you know," he whispers.

I let a moment pass before asking the question burning my lips. "How bad was it at Bianco's?"

I sense his body tightening and I look up to see his jaw ticking. Way to ruin the moment.

He runs a hand up my back and all the way to my hair. "Bad." His grip slightly tightens as he pulls my hair to make me look up at him. "It was so fucking bad, Jamie."

"You can talk to me about it. You can let it out, Jake. You don't have to hold onto the anger."

"I'm thankful you opened to me, Angel. I really am, but I can't talk about that. My childhood with Bianco...the words simply don't cross my lips. It's physically impossible."

His other hand grabs my jaw, and he bends down to take over my mouth. I melt at the touch of his lips on mine.

The kiss becomes savage and possessive, and I whimper when he bites hard on my lip. He pulls away from my mouth and rests his forehead on mine.

He keeps a hand on my jaw but the other leaves my hair to wrap gently around my throat. He rubs his thumb up and down and I feel my whole body tingling. Right here, right now I just want to be his. I just want to chase his demons away and free him from the past that's holding his happiness back.

"I don't want to hurt you, Jamie. I promise you, I don't. But I think I need to."

I don't understand his statement. Yes, he's rough and yes, he's got his demons, but I know he would never truly hurt me. I can feel it in my bones.

"I know you won't hurt me," I whisper, our mouths so close I'm tempted to close the gap.

"You don't know what I used to do. Who I've hurt. The violence."

I'm brought back to when Rose shouted her truths at Nathan. When she accused him and Bianco of getting Jake into underground fights.

"I know about the fights," I reveal.

He chuckles, but it's as sarcastic as it can get. It's sad and desperate.

"Those were only the last year we were with him. I think they were the easiest part." He takes a step back. "Nate and Sam being back in my life...fuck, Jamie, I'm scared. I'm scared because I know they're starting a war with the Wolves for Bianco. And I know they want me in. If not now, when things start heating up, they'll need me and who knows what they'll use against me to do their bidding. Who knows *who* they'll use."

I'm shocked. The fear in his eyes is real. He's scared of them. He's scared of me being caught up in this. Images of Nathan beating Volkov's guy to a pulp for touching me flash in my head like a nightmare. For some reason, I trust Jake will do everything in his power for me to stay safe. For some reason, knowing, unlike Nathan, he *doesn't* want this life is reassuring me. I close the space he's put between us and go on my toes, putting a hand on each side of his face.

"I trust you, Jake." I don't know how or why. I don't know when it came to this, but I do trust him. Maybe not with my heart, but with my safety I do.

He puts his hands over mine and lets out a long sigh. "Fuck, what are you doing to me?"

He lowers his face to take my lips with his again and this time, it's nothing but pure softness. He kisses me like it's the last time he ever will, like he's loved me for years and will love me forever.

"Give us a chance," he whispers as I pull away to fall back flat on my feet.

This should be so simple. To just let go and give in. The only thing holding me back is the fear of getting hurt. Jake has such a hold on my heart, he could crush me. He could break me into a million pieces, and I would never be the same again.

He can sense the hesitation because he palms my cheeks again. "I know you, Jamie. Maybe not as much as your mom or Emily but I feel close to you. I might not know everything, but I know your favorite food is sushi, I know your favorite color is green. I know you enjoy going to church on Sundays because you used to go with your family. I know you and Chris were close friends before Rose and I showed up." He shifts, drops a kiss to the corner of my mouth before he carries on.

"I know you're the most curious person in this town. I know you're aiming for UPenn because they have one of the best medical schools and you want to become a surgeon." He drops another kiss on the other side of my mouth, the softness making me shiver.

"I know it's because you owe your life to the surgeon that saved you after that horrible day. I don't know you by heart, but I feel like I've known you forever and it feels right. I-shit I'm not even sure what I feel, it just feels good. I know you hate taking risks that could get you hurt but...you feel the same as I do, Jamie. I know it. You just need to take that leap of faith, just this *once*. I-just–" he runs a hand through his hair before putting it back on my cheek and the honesty in his eyes goes straight to my heart. "Just give us a chance," he sighs.

His words turn my brain off, and I simply nod but it's enough for him. He sweeps me off my feet and into his arms making me squeak in the process. I giggle once he starts kissing my neck a million times.

"I don't even want to know how you know all of this," I tell him.

"Why do you think I befriended Emily? That girl chats so much I'm pretty sure she spilled out the pin to your credit card at some point."

I laugh again and he gives me another kiss then he buries his nose in my neck and inhales deeply. His whole body relaxes, and he puts me back down.

I dust off my uniform to put it back in place and smile at him. "I do have one condition."

His brows knit yet he doesn't talk, like biting his tongue so he doesn't say anything he'll regret.

"I need time before being...open about it in front of every-one. At school and all. I don't know how I feel about PDA right now. I want this to stay between us. I understand you'll tell your close friends, I mean *everyone* else."

He looks like he's thinking for a minute. I need him to accept this, I don't want girls on my back at school. I don't want to take the risk of being humiliated if he changes his mind, if this doesn't go as planned. After rushing into a relationship with Nathan and making the biggest mistake of my life choosing him over Jake, I want to take this slowly. No screwing up this time.

"But then how are all the other guys gonna know you're mine?" His voice snaps me out of my thoughts, and I look at him unimpressed. He's clearly joking but deep down, I know what he's like.

"The caveman behavior needs to stop as well."

He pretends to not understand what I'm saying and bends over, putting his shoulder to my hip. I shriek when he picks me up, true caveman-style, and starts walking back down to the trail.

"Oh my Gosh, put me down!" I giggle out of control.

"Me no share. Woman mine. All mine," he growls exces-sively. He proceeds to tickle my side with his free hand, and I can't stop the loud laughter from escaping my mouth. It's pure and light. The kind of laugh I hadn't heard myself having in years.

He puts me down when we start seeing people going up as we go down. I'm out of breath and we both can't stop laughing. He leans toward me to put a strand of hair behind my ear, and he kisses my mouth in the process, then my cheek, my jaw, and stops at my ear.

"Your laugh is making me hard."

I can feel the heat rushing to my cheeks and wetness pooling between my legs. This is just the effect Jake has on me and I don't think I'll ever get used to it.

After almost running down to the parking lot, Jake starts his car and drives to a remote road, parking deeper in the woods than allowed. At least no one can see us. He barely puts the car in park when he grabs both my hips and pulls me on his lap like I weigh nothing. My knees on either side of him, he kisses me without ever taking a breath and growls as he struggles with my uniform slacks.

"Skirts. Always. I want access," he complains.

I giggle as I lift myself on my knees and take a minute to get rid of my pants, or at least get one leg free. He looks at my underwear that is still on and then at me deadpan.

"And tell me, what do you think is going to happen now that you've left these on?"

"Oh, I-"

He doesn't even let me finish as he suddenly rips my panties in one violent gesture.

"Jake!"

He captures my lips before I can say anything else, and I feel his fingers slipping in my wet pussy. I let out a loud moan that he swallows. I undo his pants and free his cock before stroking it. He grabs a condom from his glove box, unwraps it with lightning speed, and rolls it on his hard length before capturing my mouth again.

"I want you so bad," he whispers in my mouth.

"I *need* you so bad," I reply, my lips kissing his hard jaw.

A growl resonates from deep in his chest and my pussy

tightens around his fingers. The fire leaving from my lower belly and spreading to my whole body makes me shiver in pleasure. He grabs my ass with one hand to lift me up slightly and positions his tip at my entrance before slamming me back down. He buries himself deep inside me and my mouth falls slack, but no sound comes out for a second, just a hitched breath. He starts moving slowly and I put both my hands on his shoulders to follow the movement.

"This is mine," he breathes as he grabs both my breasts. He rips open my uniform shirt and buttons fly everywhere in the car but right now I couldn't care less. I keep the rhythm going as he sucks at my breasts and my head falls back.

The moans coming out of my mouth are uncontrollable. I realize the music is still playing on the car radio and Best Years from 5 Seconds of Summer fills the car, barely audible behind our breaths and me screaming Jake's name as I come undone at the same time as him.

After a few minutes of just listening to each other breathe, I lift up and awkwardly sit back in my seat trying to put my pants back on without any underwear.

Jake gets rid of the condom and starts the car after zipping up his pants. He puts his right hand on my thigh as he drives us back to Stoneview. I let 5 Seconds of Summer lull me to sleep, deciding that Best Years is officially my favorite song.

"Wake up, Angel." Jake's soft voice brings me out of my heavy sleep.

"Are we there already?"

He nods, "I drove you back home. There's not much point showing up for last period only, is there?"

"What about our stuff?"

He smiles and points at the back seat. "Got them back from Chris."

"Do you want to come in?" I ask as I grab my bag.

He shakes his head, "Chris's parents are in town this week. I'm gonna have dinner with them. Are you okay being on your own here?"

"Of course I am," I smile. I don't really know but there's only one way to find out and I'm not about to keep Jake away from his family dinner. My phone beeps in my pocket but I ignore it.

"It's been going off the whole drive back. You should probably check what it is," he suggests.

I give him a shy smile because I'm not sure what to say. I won't check because there's only one person that has been texting me non-stop since yesterday and the last thing I want is for Jake to find out Nathan hasn't given me a break since I had called him.

My phone beeps again and I can't help a short huff.

"Is anyone bothering you?" he asks, concerned.

"No, don't worry."

I should have known he'd read right through me. Nothing escapes him, especially not if it has to do with his brother. It's like he can sense it.

"Is he texting you, Jamie?"

I hesitate before replying. I don't want to fuel the fire, but I don't want to lie to him either. Unfortunately, my hesitation lasts too long for his liking.

"Let me see," he orders, holding his hand out.

"Jake," I sigh. "Didn't we just agree you'd drop the caveman behavior?"

I just know how he gets when Nathan is mentioned, and

I don't want the peaceful afternoon we had to be ruined so quickly.

"Don't fucking drop this on me. I want to see what he's saying to you."

"Nothing! He just wants to apologize for lying, but I don't care. I don't want his apology anyway. I don't want anything from him."

"Give me the fucking phone, Jamie!" he shouts in rage and I jump at the violence in his voice. He loses all sense of control when it comes to Nathan.

"Don't be like this," I beg in disbelief. "I need you to trust me."

He huffs and runs a hand in his hair, slightly pulling at it. I can see him grinding his teeth and I've come to know the bad habit he gets when he's stressed.

"I trust you," he finally says. "But I sure as fuck don't trust him. Promise me you'll tell me if he gets out of line."

Hasn't Nathan been out of line from the beginning? The whole time he lied to me about his identity? All the times he let me open myself to him while feeding me lies in return? The whole thing still makes my chest tighten but I can't admit this to anyone, especially not Jake.

"I will," I conclude as I open the door. Jake grabs my wrist and pulls me back close to him.

"I think you're forgetting something," he growls as he pushes his lips onto mine.

My phone beeps again and he freezes mid-kiss. "Just let me see," he insists in a huff. He hovers his lips over mine. "Please, Jamie."

I pull away and grab my phone from my pocket. I overlook the countless texts, scrolling through my locked screen to check there's nothing I wouldn't want him to see.

"I don't think this is a good idea," I rasp, my throat suddenly dry at the sight of the messages.

One of them makes my heart skip.

Nathan: We're in love with each other, don't let this ruin us. I'm begging you.

"Jamie?" Jake's voice makes me jump.

"I –" I don't know what to say or what to think.

I can't deny what I'm feeling at seeing this text. It's not love, but I can't just flush Nathan out of my system when he's been in my veins for the last few months. While Jake was occupying my every thought, Nathan was keeping me safe and worshipping me.

I scroll to another text where he apologizes for losing his control on Rose and I struggle to swallow the lump in my throat. It reminds me of all the reasons I can't feel anything for him anymore. It's like a cold shower and hatred for him overtakes anything else.

Jake's spellbinding scent becomes more intense before I realize I've zoned out again and he's looking at my screen. He's reading the text and when he looks up his eyes are burning with an animosity I've never seen before. He sits back in his seat and grips the steering wheel so hard it's bound to break.

"Did he hit her?" he asks through gritted teeth. He's not even looking at me. Just looking ahead at the road in front of us. He's calm. Too calm to be genuine.

"What did she say to you?" For some reason, I know Rose wouldn't want me to repeat anything that happened without her prior approval and I don't want to be on her wrong side. She should be able to trust me.

"It doesn't fucking matter!" he explodes as he brings a hard fist on the steering wheel. He stops, takes a deep breath, and clearly tries to calm himself. "Look, Jamie, it doesn't matter what Rose says because half of what comes out of her mouth is a fucking lie anyway. She's so fucking used to the abuse she doesn't realize when it smacks her across the face. Do you understand that?"

I don't think either of the twins will ever tell me everything that truly happened at Bianco's but seeing him so worried over her is making it hard to keep what Nathan did to myself.

"So you need to tell me. Did he hit her?" He turns to face me and grabs both my hands gently. "It's important. I need to know."

I nod, incapable of explaining in detail the moment he punched her in the stomach for standing up to him. He nods back, clearly thankful for my honesty.

"Thank you," he says as he cups both my cheeks. He kisses my lips one last time and turns on the car. "So, am I allowed to drive you to school tomorrow or is that on the no-no list?"

I chuckle as I open the door. "No-no. But we can hang out after school."

"And in empty classrooms, empty locker rooms, my car at lunch..."

"You're incorrigible," I laugh as I close the door. He winks at me and revs the engine before leaving at a speed that's certainly not allowed in the neighborhood.

I find it strange that he suddenly dropped the Rose and Nathan topic and I'm scared his sudden disinterest was only pretend. All I can do is hope he's not about to do something incredibly stupid.

CHAPTER 11

Boys Like You – Anna Clendening

Jamie

The rest of the week goes at different paces. Classes are too slow because I have to keep my hands off Jake, or I don't share them with him. Evenings go too quickly, and it seems Jake sleeping at mine every night is not enough time together. I thought giving in would mean I would get satiated from the craving to constantly feel his body, be overwhelmed by his scent, and hear his deep voice, but it seems it's only making it worse. Nothing is enough. We can't touch each other enough, we can't laugh enough, can't talk enough. We simply can't get enough of each other.

On Tuesday we waited until everyone had left lacrosse practice so we could hang out before both heading our own ways. Well, at least that was the plan. We ended up having sex in the girls' locker room. In that same shower Camila and Beth had kicked me in. How ironic.

I lasted four days, refusing him to drive me to school. This morning I let him drive me here and as I'm getting into his car after class, I can hardly ignore the hate stares from some of the girls. One in particular.

"Don't mind her," Jake says as he opens the passenger door for me. Who would have thought he could be such a gentleman? Not me. He puts a hand on the small of my back to incite me to get in the car. Once the door is closed, I let out a long breath. I glance at Camila who's still shooting daggers at me and I look away in a split second. This girl gives me chills. Especially because I've been finding notes in my locker telling me to stay away from Jake.

Jake sits next to me and starts the car.

"She scares me," I say only half-jokingly.

He chuckles as he reverses out of his parking spot. "She can only make assumptions since you won't let me anywhere near you in public."

"You're near me now," I smile.

"I meant in a boyfriend sort of way," he growls. Why do I find it so cute?

"Surely you can understand why," I insist. "I don't think it'll only be dark looks and threatening notes if she and her friends learn we're actually together."

His hand on my thigh reassures me as he squeezes.

"I hate to say it...but she knows I cheated on her with you. It can't get much worse than that."

I almost choke on air at his statement. "Jake!" I scoff. "Don't...That's not what happened. I never wanted you to cheat on her!"

"I definitely did," he chuckles. "You're coming to mine tonight by the way."

I roll my eyes because he's been trying this every night of

the week and every night he's ended up at my house. I give him a knowing look and he huffs.

"It's Friday, aren't you gonna go to some party somewhere?" I know he missed a lot of get-togethers with his friends this week, and not only his close ones. He missed one of the many lacrosse pre-season parties on Wednesday to stay home with me.

"No. It's the last night the Murrays are here, I can't sleep at yours. Please come," he insists.

"I'd rather stay at my house, Jake. We have all weekend to hang out. It's fine."

He pouts and I can't help a giggle. "Stop it," I say as I slap his arm.

My phone beeps in my bag and he looks at me, eyes filled with questions. "It's been going off all day, Angel. You gotta tell me if it's him."

I only nod because it's not something I want to talk about.

"Let me talk to him," he grits.

"Absolutely not. If I'm not answering, neither are you. He'll get the message eventually."

His only response is a low growl and I shake my head at him. Caveman.

After dropping me off, Jake leaves me promising to spend the day with me tomorrow.

It's strange having gone from a hate relationship to being so openly adoring each other, yet somehow it feels the most natural I've ever felt in years. This game of cat and mouse we've been playing for months got us attached to the other. As if we already needed to be part of each other's lives but couldn't find the right way to do so. It's like our bodies and

187

minds were meant to fit perfectly together.

What I had with Nathan doesn't even compare. It's strange to realize that I truly thought I was in love with him when really...it wasn't a quarter of what I feel for Jake. Only, I know that's not something I could tell Jake. It's too early.

It's late when I'm making food on FaceTime with mom, finally catching up on some of what's going on in Tennessee and telling her about the worst customers at the café.

"Anyway," I wave the wooden spoon in the air after explaining that Mr. Baker stopped by last week before going back to New York. "Wanna see my latest grade?"

"*Is that a real question? Of course I want to.*"

I leave for a second to go grab my backpack. I could tell her I got an A+ in Calculus, but I love showing her the red mark on my papers. It makes me proud to see her eyes light up every time. I unzip my backpack and throw my hand inside to fish my calculus notebook. I go back to the kitchen and open my notebook to find the sheet I had folded and put in there but the only thing that falls off is a note.

Another damn note.

How many times do you need to be warned? Stay away from him.

This is getting ridiculous. I scrunch it up and throw it in the recycling. What a bitch. I grab my grade and show it to my mom.

"*Sweetie, I'm so proud of you,*" she smiles as her green eyes light up on the screen. Her face is suddenly replaced by Jake's trying to call me.

"Oh, mom, let me give you a call back."

"Is that your boyfriend," she winks.

"Oh Gosh, I should have never mentioned him. We've been seeing each other for like a week. Please don't be like this."

"Well as long as he's keeping his hands to himself."

"Right. Bye, mom. Love you."

By the time I hang up with her I've missed Jake's call and I've got a text from him.

Jake: Dinner with the Murrays was shorter than planned. I'm heading to Jason's party with the guys. Let me pick you up?

I smile at his attempt to bring me to a party, but my previous ones haven't exactly been a great experience.

Jamie: I'm going to have an early night but thanks for the invite xoxo

I try to ignore the voice inside me that is scared of him being at a party where Camila will be, and focus on the fact that he knows he cannot mess things up with me.

But it's not only Camila. He's got a reputation at parties.

I shake my head to chase the bad thoughts away. This is exactly why I don't want everyone to know about us yet. I'm basically giving us time to fuck things up. I keep my distance emotionally while I see if we can do this.

A small laugh escapes my lips. Who am I kidding? I've been emotionally involved with this guy since his eyes landed on mine in English class on our first day of senior year. Jake White has had my heart in the palm of his hand before he even wanted it. The chemical reactions in my brain when he's around is something neither of us can control. I'll just have to pray he doesn't throw what we have away at a stupid party.

Dinner in front of reality TV on my own is not the most exciting part of my day but I'm glad to get some rest and quiet. For a girl who is used to having homework as company, the last few weeks have been rather eventful.

My mind drifts back to my first time with Jake and all the other times since. This guy plays my body like an instrument he knows inside out, and I instantly feel pleasure pooling between my legs at the memories. I slip a hand under my leggings and press my index on my entrance, spreading some of my wetness and bringing it to my clit. A low moan escapes my lips as I circle my bundle of nerves. It feels good but it feels nothing like Jake touching me. I keep rubbing, using more fingers for more friction and I'm on the edge of climax when a loud knock on my front door makes me jump. I instantly pull my hand out of my leggings and check the time. No one should be knocking on my door at eleven at night.

Excited at the prospect that Jake changed his mind and decided to spend the evening here rather than at Jason's party, I walk to the door.

I open the door full of hope, but my heart stops when I see who is standing in front of me. The same ocean eyes as Jake, the same malice in his traits, but it's not him.

I go to slam the door, but Nathan puts his hand on it, holding it open.

"Please, I just want to talk."

"No," I say firmly. "You're not coming in here again."

He pushes his way in and slams the door behind him, making me jump.

I want to ask him to leave. I want to shout for help or run to my phone and call Jake, but I'm too preoccupied with the cut on his lip, the dry blood under his slightly swollen nose, and the bruise forming on his red cheek.

"What happened to you?" I whisper, almost too ashamed to voice my worry out loud. Was there a Wolf outside *again?* That's impossible, it's not like them to take too much risk.

"Aah...that, beautiful. That's just my sweet little brother and his two besties jumping me out of nowhere because he's too fucking weak to take me on his own." I can hardly believe what he's saying but I know how Jake can get.

I need to tell him to leave. Now.

"Are you okay?" That is not what I should have asked.

"I don't know. You tell me." He stumbles forward as he tries to take a step and that's when it hits me. The slur in his words, the smell of whiskey. He's completely drunk.

In our almost three months relationship, I haven't seen him drink once. Then again, it wouldn't be the only thing he hid from me.

"You're drunk," I say as if he didn't already know. He walks past me and heads for the kitchen.

"You got any whiskey in here?" He opens cupboards in the kitchen, holding onto the handles so he doesn't fall and growls when he realizes all we have is snacks and sodas.

"Nathan, you need to-"

"You know, 'Me, I can understand Jake being pissed that I hit Ozy. Fuck, I get pissed at myself when I do that." He turns back and walks towards me, meeting me in the middle of my small living room.

"You shouldn't have hit her," I agree.

"Yeah, I fucking know that. And Jake has every right to want to beat me up for it. But number one," he holds a finger up too close to my face, "fucking Christopher fucking Murray doesn't get to tell me shit. Who the fuck does he think he is, telling me how to treat *my* little sister? She ain't his to fucking defend. I can defend her just fine." He has no idea he barely makes sense but I'm not sure how to stop him. "What? Is he in love with her or something?"

"I really don't think he—"

"He doesn't get to be in love with her. He's not good enough. Sam ain't good enough. No one is. You know? She's just…" he lets out a long huff and brings his sleeves up to his elbows. "She needs to be taken care of. She's too precious for her own good. She needs protection…she…I couldn't…" He takes a few steps in a circle until he's back in front of me, using his palm to rub his forehead. "I didn't protect her. I was too fucking scared, 'Me. I was a coward and Jake…he was too young."

I have no idea what he's going on about anymore but the pain in his voice and the tears glistening in his eyes tell me this is about much more than Chris being protective over Rose. His head drops to his chest in shame and sadness.

"Nathan, she's fine. With the Murrays, with Chris and Jake. She's fine."

I put a reassuring hand on his shoulder, but he suddenly grabs my wrist violently.

He looks up and the look in his eyes has gone from guilty to predatory. I try to take a step back, but he follows, holding me tight.

"Number two," he growls. "Jake might be right in warning me not to lose my shit against our sister, but in what fucking world does he think he can order me to stay away from you?"

The lump of panic forming in my throat and the fear gripping my stomach stop me from breathing correctly. "He's just trying to help–" His other hand wraps my jaw so tightly that I can't finish my sentence.

"I swear to god, 'Me, if you let him touch you the way I touched you. If you fall for him...I'll fucking raise hell."

"Nathan, you're hurting me. Let go." I try to keep a voice of steel, but he can perfectly read me.

"I take full responsibility for the lies, but I won't let you throw away what we had. I won't let you choose him."

"We're not together anymore. It doesn't matter what I do now. It's none of your business."

"You said you loved me." His head falls in the crook of my neck and I have to take further steps back. Surely we can't be back to this conversation? Our relationship has gone past anything reparable. I'm forced to stop when my back hits the wall. His face doesn't leave my skin and I can smell the whiskey on him, on his breath. His hair smells of cigarettes and his body feels heavy on mine as if he can't hold himself properly.

"You're drunk," I whisper. I'm scared if I raise my voice he'll flip.

"Not too long ago, I was making you come in this house, on this sofa, in your bed. You told me you were in love with me. A few weeks? Is that what it takes for you to get over me?"

No. It took a few hours because I was always involved with Jake. Because Jake was always on my mind. Because it was always him.

For a second I think I'm going to tell him but I'm too much of a coward to say the truth, so I tell him part of why we were doomed.

"You lied to me. Our relationship was based on nothing but lies and that is *your* fault."

"Who gave me away? That morning you were fine, then I

get out of the shower and you suddenly see a tattoo you had missed hundreds of times before. Who was it? Who told you?" he seethes. "Was it, Jake?"

I hadn't even thought about this again. That unknown number...it must have been Jake, who else?

"I don't know," I shake my head. "It was an unknown number."

I push at his chest and thankfully he's drunk enough to stagger back. He lets go of my jaw but not my wrist. I pull at it and try to snatch it back but there's nothing to do.

"I won't let you go, 'Me," he slurs, and I know he's not talking about my wrist. "I fucked up. I fucked up so bad. Please, I'll tell you anything you want to know. The whole truth. Fuck, I'll do anything."

The anger boiling in me threatens to overflow and I stand stronger, feeling a sort of courage I had never felt before. It's about time I tell at least one of the White brothers they can't play with people like toys.

"I want you to leave. That's what you can do," I say in a voice cold enough to make his eyebrows rise in surprise. The fact that I got to him refills my cup of courage. "If you think after *burning* my notebook, after all the lies and deceptions we still have a chance...You must think I really am a stupid girl. We're over, Nathan. Now just leave before this goes too far." The threat in my voice makes it sound like he's the one in danger if it goes too far when we both know it isn't true.

I expect him to retaliate. Instead, he takes a few deep breaths and lets go of my wrist. "I'm only leaving because it's not the right moment to talk. I'm fucking drunk and beaten up but this conversation is not over."

I don't reply because this *is* over. To me, there is nothing more to say but I need him to leave my house. He heads towards the door and looks at me one last time. His dirty blond hair is messy and not in its usual bun, his button-up shirt is undone from his suit pants and he's looking at me like he's carrying the pain of the whole world on his shoulders.

"You're making a huge mistake, 'Me. You two simply can't work. He'll break your heart."

It's too hard to stay calm. I've lost that naïve innocence I had only a few weeks ago. Who does he think he is telling me what to do or not to do? He's been lying for months. It's like I don't know him, and I feel stupid and dirtied having let someone I didn't truly know touch me the way I've let him.

"You want to talk about breaking my heart?!" I snap. "I was attacked by Volkov's guy for fuck's sake. At my workplace. Just because you're *oh* so important to Bianco and I was important to you. You put me in danger by hiding the truth."

I was surprised when a Wolf came to the café. To attack me? Finish the job after so long? No, it wasn't possible. When I understood how involved Nathan was with them, it made more sense. But he let me believe it, let me fear for my life thinking they were coming after me. They weren't, they were after him.

"You came here last time, threatened me, and destroyed my work under the pretense of protecting me. You're either stupid or naïve, the only person the Wolves are after is you. You want to protect me? Stay away. You're only a danger to me."

The flash of pain on his face only lasts a second but it's enough to know I've hit hard. He lets out a desperate chuckle and his chin falls to his chest. He shakes his head as he brings it back up and looks at me with a mocking grin. Like he knows secrets I don't, like he understands things I would never.

"And you think Jake isn't? You think he's such a good guy, don't you?"

Good guy is not the first thing that would come to my mind when I think of Jake. But the more I get to know him, the more I think it's possible for him to be good to me at least.

"Fuck," he huffs. "If you knew the things he's done. You might not choose me, but you definitely wouldn't choose him either."

He exits without looking back. I thought I had won this round, but his last words leave me with a thousand questions and a hint of regret at the back of my mouth.

If you knew the things he's done...

* * *

I'm looking at my silky dark green dress in the mirror of Jake's room and shrug. This isn't exactly the dress I wanted to wear but it's not like I could have afforded the other one. Jake offered to pay but I refused. I worked hard to buy myself a dress for the winter ball and I'll go with what I can afford.

The three weeks coming to the Christmas break have been emotionally confusing. Jake and I are spending every single minute outside of school together and he is slowly making his way into my heart for a whole new reason than he already had.

Before we decided to give each other a chance, he was my drug because of the physical reactions he was getting out of me. He was my dirty secret that I wouldn't allow myself to fall for. He was in my every thought because he was forbidden.

Now...now it's a whole different story. The cravings are heightened, the drug-induced states he puts me in are addictive, but the way my heart reacts around him is indescribable. The drunken feeling I get when he opens up to me, when he takes care of me, when he deposits butterfly kisses on my cheeks out of nowhere or when his dimples pop out as he laughs, is an experience out of this world. It has become almost impossible to keep away from him in front of others and Luke and Rose have been begging us to stop hiding because everyone knows something is going on.

Of course, I haven't forgotten Nathan's words, but I don't believe them. The Jake I'm in love with is the one I want to believe in, not the poisonous lies his brother spreads. I am well aware of Jake's dark side, of the things he's done, to me especially. But I'm also witnessing the way he blooms when he's with me.

I didn't tell him Nathan came to my house. The day after, when I saw his and Chris' grazed knuckles, I didn't say anything. I know there are things Jake doesn't want to talk about, and I reserve the right to keep this for myself too. There is no point discussing Nathan anymore, it's in the past. All I'm focusing on is the way Jake is slowly letting go of his old demons and turning into a truly happy person. Knowing I'm the one doing this to him erases any other mistakes we've both made to get where we are now. I might be fucked up thinking this way, but I don't care, we'll be fucked up together.

I accepted going to the Winter ball with him, and tonight we're not going to hide anymore. I don't care what Camila thinks. I don't care about the jealous stares and the guys who think he's settling down while I'm punching above my weight.

I'm in love with him and the only thing that does scare me is that he might not love me back.

"You look like...an angel." Two arms slither around my waist as I look up to see Jake standing behind me in the mirror. "*My* angel," he continues before dropping a kiss on the top of my head.

For this ball, I opted for a short satin dress that embraces my body flawlessly, like a cascade of water following my small curves. My tan skin goes perfectly with the dark green and my eyes pop out like two gold spots on my face.

Jake slides a finger under the slim strap and hovers above my scar. "You're beautiful, I like when you show yourself like that."

It's true that since Jake has been loving my body in the way he does so well, I've been feeling more comfortable to show myself, especially the scar I used to be so adamant on hiding.

"Do we have to go?" he asks. "I'd be fine keeping you here all to myself."

I giggle as his mouth kisses my neck and my body contorts under the soft tickling of his lips on my skin.

"We'll have fun, I promise," I reply as I turn around to face him. I go on the tip of my toes and put my arms around his neck.

"Wow, what happened to us? Since when do I want to stay in and *you* have to convince me to go out?" he chuckles.

I laugh and leave a quick kiss on his lips before going to put my shoes on. "I don't know, you're changing me, Jake White."

He lets out a small laugh and grabs me from behind pushing both of us onto the bed. He spoons me as one of his hands comes around my throat and the other between my thighs.

My breath hitches as he dips below my dress and cups my pussy.

"Mm, so warm," he murmurs in my ear.

I can only nod as he pushes my underwear to the side and slides a finger inside me, the heel of his hand resting on my clit.

"I forgot to mention the after-party is at Cal's, Jason's brother. He's got a huge ass mansion in Silver Falls."

"Right," I breathe as pleasure spreads in my whole body. Who cares? It could be on the moon right now, I would still agree to go.

He puts another finger in and my eyes roll to the back of my head as my mouth falls slack.

"And so, we offered to pregame here since we're the closest to school." I nod again and try to ask if that's why he already smells of weed but the only thing that comes out of my mouth is a loud moan.

He laughs a little before his hand on my throat slides to my mouth.

"All this to say, a lot of our friends are in the living room right now."

I try to push his hand away from my mouth, but he doesn't move.

"Did you just hear the part where I said people are in the living room? You're loud, baby, and I should be the only one who gets to hear your moans."

I'm about to protest doing this when there are so many people so close, but his fingers accelerate, picking up the pace of the friction of his hand on my clit. The lack of oxygen from his hand on my face makes me slightly dizzy and I squirm, bringing myself closer to unbearable pleasure. He drops kisses on my neck, going up, licking my earlobe.

"How does it feel, Angel? Knowing our friends are waiting on the other side of the wall while I turn you into my little slut in here?"

I clench around him and as soon as he curls his fingers, the tips hitting the magic spot. My cries of climax are drowned out by his hand. I shake against his body behind mine and my thighs clamp around his hand.

"You're such a good girl," he whispers in my ear and another shiver of pleasure runs down my spine. As I'm coming down from my high, he retreats and re-arranges his beautiful charcoal suit.

"Angel?"

"Mmm," I hum, still enjoying the aftermath of my orgasm.

"When I say a lot of our friends are here, I just want to warn you that it includes Camila."

My heart drops in my stomach and I sit up straight on the bed in a split second. "What?" I choke.

"I don't want her here, but she's part of the group. It's not like I can say much about it."

I get up and rearrange my dress. "Jake...this girl is horrible to me! It's one thing to see her at school but at your house? Tonight was meant to be about us."

I hate how I sound right now but the truth is, I know Camila will try to ruin my night. No matter how much I try to tell myself that he played her, that I was part of what hurt her too, I just can't bring myself to feel bad for her. The second she gets the chance, she'll stab me. It doesn't even have to be in the back, the bitch would be happy to let me watch as she approaches with the knife.

He takes me in his arms and runs his hand through my

hair. I can hear his heart beating fast against his chest and somehow it reassures me to know he gets like this when he's close to me as well.

"She's not going to say anything to you because I'll be by your side at all times. It's only while we all drink up before going to the ball."

"And at the ball and at the after-party in Silver Falls. Do we even have to go?"

He pulls away and holds me at arm's length to look at me.

"You didn't seem to mind the after-party a minute ago."

I roll my eyes but can't help my lips spreading into a smile. "That wasn't even fair," I fake pout.

"I don't play fair, Angel, you know that." He bops my nose and I giggle at his touch.

Why is it that everything he does always makes me feel like a kid who just got their favorite ice-cream? Not just my favorite ice-cream. It's like I walked into the parlor, they told the kid in front of me the best flavor had run out and when I get to them, they had saved the last scoop for me. I re-adjust the bow around his neck as he pushes my hair away from my face and behind my ears.

"You smell like heaven. Can someone become addicted to a smell?" he whispers.

"You smell like weed," I joke back.

He messes my hair again, making me gasp. "Jake!"

"I pre-pre gamed with Luke and Ozy. I needed something to relax before telling you Camila is coming over."

"I'm the one who needs something to relax now. Is she here already?"

"I think pretty much everyone has started without us."

Only now do I realize the music coming from the living

room. "Right."

"I'm more than happy to provide you with something to relax," he says as he starts putting his shoes on.

"I think I'm alright."

He straightens back up, gives me a deep kiss that awakens a hundred butterflies in my stomach, and takes my hand tightly in his.

"Let's enjoy tonight. I promise it's going to be *you* and *me*."

I smile at him as we start walking out of the room.

Jake and Rose's small living room is full of their friends. I spotted Camila and Beth straight away when we came out of the hallway. She hasn't said anything to me in the last hour and I'm actually starting to believe she won't dare since Jake isn't leaving my side.

Luke and Emily have been whisper-arguing in a corner of the room since probably before I arrived. I want to know what is going on and bring her support, especially as I see her blushing from frustration and the attention it might bring to them, but we still haven't spoken since our argument. It's been a month now and I'm starting to worry that we really went too far.

Rose, Chris, Rachel, and Jason are on the sofa, drinking from solo cups and chatting away. Rose has her head on Rachel's lap while the latter is stroking her hair and the former smoking a joint, passing it around to everyone on the sofa.

"Jas', for the love of God, Rachel isn't interested in a threesome with you. Stop asking before I bury your head into this table." I hear Chris' half-joke to his friend.

"Rachel hasn't exactly said no," Jason insists. "And I know Rose wouldn't mind."

Rose's loud, raspy laugh resonates in the room. "I think what Rach is too shy to say to you is that she only sleeps with people that can make her come. I'm afraid you don't meet that requirement."

The whole group laughs and a smile tugs at my lips. She has no filter.

There are a lot of other people I don't know but I recognize Ella, Luke's younger sister, and I'm guessing some of the guys and girls with her are her friends. Everyone is dressed to the nines and I can't help but feel underdressed.

I'm sitting on one of the high chairs and Jake settles in front of me, offering me a third drink but I shake my head. "I won't make it to the ball if I keep drinking."

"I'm sorry, it's just I can feel how tense you are and it's making me tense."

I chuckle and glance at Camila and Beth but they're not looking my way. I don't think they have so much as given me a look for the whole evening so far.

"Why has everyone gathered here before the ball when you have all the space in the world inside the house?" I ask.

"Ugh, because it's too long to clean the big house. And I like how cozy it is here. Not much space," he gets closer to me and wraps his arms around me. "forced to stay close to the guests."

I giggle and jump off my seat. "I need the bathroom, too much alcohol already."

I go to leave but he grabs my face in the palm of his hands, his thumbs in front of my ears, and his fingers threading in my hair. He kisses me long and hard, making my insides tighten and my cheeks flush.

I hear some people whisper around us. This was our first

kiss in front of everyone. All his friends, other school kids. My heart is hammering in my chest and I feel patches of red spreading across my chest and my cheeks as some conversations drop silent and 'no fucking way's are murmured here and there.

"Be quick," he winks.

I hurry out of the room, my body on fire from Jake and the attention we got in the living room. I do my business quickly and double-check my make-up in the mirror, silently giving myself a pep talk. 'You are good enough', 'who are they to judge', 'who cares when you're with someone you love', 'they're just jealous'. I take one last deep breath and grab the door handle but as soon as I open the bathroom to step out, I'm pushed back inside.

"What the–"

"I just need to talk to you, Goody." Camila closes the door behind her and locks it.

"Really, Camila? You're cornering me in bathrooms now?"

She chuckles wickedly but doesn't move. "You're so scared of me, aren't you?"

"I'm not scared of you," I growl back. "But I know how obsessed you are over your *ex*-boyfriend."

"I don't know what's making you so brave, but you need to calm down. I just want to warn you."

"Warn me?" I know I shouldn't listen to her and I should just get out of the room, but she's got my attention even though I don't want to admit it.

"Listen, Jamie." It's the first time I think she's ever said my name. "You might think you can handle him, but you can't."

"Oh God, not this again." I walk around her, but she grabs my wrist in a tight grip. "Are you for real right now?" I snap but she stays perfectly calm.

"You couldn't handle him the night of the Halloween ball and you surely can't handle him now. I had to save you from him, never forget that." She lets go of my arm, but she's not done. "You find it exciting now, the way he makes you feel. You think this is all just a bit of fun, but I can promise you he gets worse. As soon as you find comfort in the way he is he'll push your limits further. Then further again...and again."

"You need to let it go, Camila."

"You think you know him, but you don't. I was his girlfriend for *two* years, Jamie. He's got this ability to make anyone feel special but we're all the same. Do you know how often he goes to the North Shore of the Falls? How often he fucks NSF girls because he knows none of them will come to brag about it in Stoneview? He thinks I won't know if he goes there. *You*, naïve little thing that you are, wouldn't even know if he's been to NSF parties in the last few weeks that you've been together and pathetically been trying to hide it."

I swallow the lump forming in my throat. Rumors of Jake going to parties on the wrong side of the Falls is not news to my ears. But thinking he could have gone while we were together is something I hadn't really thought of.

"I'm not saying this because I'm against you," she insists. "I'm saying this because I'm against him. You're in way over your head. You just don't realize it yet, and when you will, it'll be too late."

I shake my head at her and hurry out because I don't need to hear her lies and excuses to incite me to push Jake away just so he can run back to her.

As soon as I open the door, I fall face to face with Emily. Her red eyes and the way she's biting the inside of her cheek tell me she's about to cry but I stay frozen in place. I have no idea what has been going on in the past month. I don't know how her relationship with Luke is; if it's going well or not, if he's treating her right. Nothing. I'm about to ask if she's okay when she looks above my shoulder and snorts.

"Fucking hell Camila, let it fucking go," Emily almost shouts. "I've spent enough time with you in the last few weeks to tell you: you're seriously obsessed."

I barely hold back a laugh as Camila's jaw drops to the floor.

"I was the one who supported you when your little friend here turned against you," Camila snarls. "I was the one who advised you on your shitty relationship with fuckboy-Luke. This is how you thank me?"

Emily pops a hip and rests a hand on it, rolling her eyes. I feel like she's putting her cheerleader hat on, her bitchy popular girl personality that she always uses to defend me if other girls at school try to put me down. A smile pulls at my lips knowing she'd do anything to support me right now.

"Yeah, well look where your advice got me. Fuckboy-Luke stayed true to his reputation and we're over. I should have dumped his ass when I said so instead of listening to your desperate girl advice. Now if you don't mind, I'd like to piss. Thanks."

Camila shakes her head and walks past both me and Emily before joining the party at the other end of the hall.

I look anywhere but at Emily, not feeling the courage to face her yet. "Thank you," I whisper.

"God, 'Me, stop being so awkward," she starts laughing and I can't help but follow.

It might be the alcohol, but it feels good to laugh with her, to have her by my side after this long.

"I'm sorry," she says once she's stopped laughing. "I started seeing Luke and all of a sudden the rest of the world didn't matter. I was the worst friend possible. And I've been dying to talk to you but...it just always looks like you don't want to open up about what's going on."

"I'm sorry too." I take her hand in both of mine and lock my gaze with hers. "I *have* been reluctant to share what's going on...and I think part of me was just too ashamed to. Em, what I said to you about Aaron...it was not only out of line but unjust. I can't begin to imagine how much it hurt to hear it."

"I shouldn't have said anything about your house, and I surely shouldn't have used Camila to get back at you. I love you, 'Me. I'm sorry."

She pulls me into a tight hug, and I almost cry from happiness. "I missed you."

"I missed you too. So much," she replies.

When we pull away, I look at her from head to toe. "Luke... what happened?"

She snorts and rolls her eyes. "I need more alcohol to talk about Luke and to hear about you and Jake because I don't think what Luke told me was the whole story."

"What did he say?" I chuckle.

"Bullshit. That's all he says. That's all this group says anyway." She says it in such a light tone that I wonder if she means it, but an uneasy feeling settles in my stomach.

Between Camila's words and Emily's, it's not simple to think Jake is as honest as he pretends. Add Nathan's warning and a heaviness takes a seat on my shoulders.

"Come, let's drink." Emily grabs my hand, and we walk back to the party. As we pass both doors of Rose's and Jake's rooms opposite each other, Emily stops.

"I need to ask you something," she says, excitement filling her voice.

"Go ahead."

"Which one is Jake's room?"

I can't help but laugh at her. "This one," I say pointing to the door on my right.

"'Me, do you know how many girls would die to be in this room?"

My laugh heightens and I try to push her toward the entrance of the hallway. "Stop it, would you?" Trust Emily to force any worry out of my system with her silliness.

Before either of us can move we hear Rose's voice spill from her room. We can hear her perfectly well because her door is ajar. I've noticed her door is never fully closed if she's on her own.

"You're not selling me anything? Since when?"

Em and I both look at each other and agree in silence to keep listening. Curiosity, curiosity, my worst flaw.

"Don't give me your 'you're too young' bullshit you've been selling to me since we fucking met. That's how we met, Carlo. Just...just let me talk to Roy."

Emily shrugs and looks at me. "She's just trying to score," she whispers. "Let's go."

"Fuck, Roy, I thought you were the smart one out of you two. Is it Sam? Did he say that? Tell him to go fuck himself. You three can suck each other's dicks. It's only a tiny step further from kissing his ass."

Em and I both look at each other barely able to hold out our laughs at her words. We hear her move behind the door, and both hurry out of the hallway.

As soon as we reach the living room, Jake snatches me away

from Emily, pulling me into a tight hug.

"Mm," he says smelling the top of my head. "Which shampoo do you use? Or does it smell amazing just because it's on you?"

"It's yours, idiot," I giggle. "I showered here".

"Oh, that might be why it smells so good then." He messes my hair, slides his hand until it's at the base of my hair, and grips me tight until I look up at him. His lips crash on mine and the smell of vodka has replaced the weed.

"Boy, you're going hard tonight, aren't you?" I ask.

He shrugs as he pulls away, giving me his most innocent smile. "It's the last day of the semester. I'm celebrating the start of the holiday!"

I smile back at him because I love him like this, careless and happy.

"Tonight's gonna be a big night." He gives me a long, hard kiss and I happily kiss him back.

Tonight is going to be a big night.

CHAPTER 12

superstars – Christian French

Jake

Jamie turns around, her green dress swinging and showing more of her legs. I want to grab her right here and now and fuck her against the car, but I guess it's not okay to do that in front of all our friends as we embark limos to get to the ball. My dick twitches, thinking of making her come in front of everyone. Just to show she's mine. Just to show I'm the only one who gets to do that.

"I forgot my purse!" As she finishes her spin, I catch her. She's flushed from the two drinks she shared with me and I find it cute that she's such a lightweight. When Camila would get drunk, I'd find it annoying. It took my ex a lot and she would be the kind to hit on other guys to make sure I knew she could do better. That was her thing. Then we would argue and she'd cry or throw up or both. Jamie becomes this relaxed, giggly girl that I can't get enough of.

"I'll go get it," I say, holding her hips tight and spinning her back the other way. "Just get in the car."

She giggles and Emily grabs her hand. "She's coming with me. Our limo is leaving now. You can have Luke." She starts walking away, dragging Jamie with her before I can say anything, and I can't help a growl.

Luke and Emily have been arguing on and off in the past days because my best friend has finally found a girl that won't take any of his attitude and he's struggling with it.

I look at the car Jamie just got in and check who's in it. Chris, Emily, Rachel, and some of Ella's friends. That'll do.

"Dude, tonight we're getting *fucked.* And I mean I don't want to remember anything tomorrow," my best friend exclaims.

I laugh as Luke slaps my shoulder and agree with him. We're leaving for the break legendary style.

I run back inside to grab Jamie's purse but it's nowhere to be found in the living room. I hurry to my bedroom and find the door ajar and the light on. That's weird, I always close my door.

As I push the door, I see Camila is sitting on my bed, drinking from a bottle of champagne. Her long white dress has a slit on the side and one of her legs is completely uncovered. Her dress is a look-alike to the dress Jamie was wearing at the last ball, but she could buy the most expensive dress in the world, she just doesn't compare.

Her deep brown hair is displayed around her shoulders and she's looking up at me, blinking her full lashes in a seducing way but I can't seem to react to it. My body completely refuses to be excited about anything or anyone other than Jamie. Camila is smoking hot but she's not for me. She's the only girl I know that can look classy while desperate. That's a trick only the truly rich and powerful like her know.

"Fuck, Cam. Get out of here," I huff.

"How many times did you fuck her on this bed, Jake?" Her words are slurred, and I know that the bottle in her hand must be near empty. "Does she get to sleep over? Cause we both know I never got that chance."

"This isn't cute anymore. You're just making a fool of yourself."

"She's got condoms in her purse," she says as she lifts her hand that's not holding the bottle. She's holding Jamie's golden purse upside down, the contents displayed on the bed. "That purse is the same one she took to the Halloween ball and it was bought on Asos by the way. It's not even a brand. You've stooped down pretty low."

I can't help the growl that escapes my mouth. I want to fucking smash her head in for talking shit about Jamie, but I know I have to rear myself back.

She knows me, she knows I've got tons and tons of built-up anger in me and she wants me to snap. She wants me to get angry and out of control and then she wants to offer herself as a means for me to grasp back that control. That's her thing, she knows me really well and that's the power she always used to have on me; knowing what makes me snap, knowing how to get what she wants out of me. Fuck, she really thinks I'm that fucked up that I wouldn't realize what's she's doing right now.

"Beth is waiting for you outside. You should really go."

"I think she was planning on fucking you at the ball. Look at that." She picks up two condoms that have fallen out of Jamie's purse and my cock wakes up at the thought of fucking Jamie at the hotel where the winter ball is held.

A lot of students book rooms at that hotel for post-ball fun but I doubt Jamie would have done that. I shake the thought away and try to focus back on the bitch that's now laying down on my bed.

"I miss this bed. Remember when you'd text me at crazy hours because you needed me?" She lays on her side, facing me, and rests her head on her hand. "You needed me to get the anger out. A good spanking, that's what you'd give me when you made me come here in the middle of the night. I'd sneak out of my house and come to you just so you could spank me and call me a bad girl. Have you done it to her yet? Does Jamie know all your kinks, Jake? Or are you scared she would judge you? Are you scared she'd leave?"

I can feel the heat of anger boiling in my chest. I need to remember she's just trying to get a reaction out of me. Think of Jamie, think of her golden-green eyes. Think of her soft skin. Of the sound she makes when she giggles.

But she's right, Jamie doesn't know any of your kinks.

"I'd never judge you, Jake," Camila says as she drops the empty bottle to the floor and grabs her dress to open up the slit a little more.

She goes on her front and uncovers her backside completely, revealing black lace panties covered by suspenders that are tightly holding her stockings.

"Stop it," I growl.

"Do you still have your handcuffs? The rope? I want to play, baby. Please."

She starts grinding against the sheets and her hand drops between her legs. "Will you be mad if I touch myself?"

I slowly approach her, and I know she can see the rage on my face because she starts touching herself harder and a soft moan escapes her lips.

During our time together, I would have pinned her to the bed. I probably would have tied her hands as a punishment for touching herself without my authorization. I would have teased her until she begged and couldn't take it anymore and jerked myself off over her, come on her tits just to show her who is in control. And then, maybe then, I would have allowed her to orgasm. I lose myself in those memories for a second as I approach her.

I put a hand on the bed next to her shoulder and my knee next to her hip. She automatically raises her backside to grind against my crotch but before she can touch me, I grab her by the nape of her neck and drag her out of the bed as she shrieks. I keep pulling her until we're by my bedroom door.

"Don't *ever* come in this room again, you hear me? Fuck, you think you're so great because you've got money and a great ass? Take both to someone who fucking cares." I stop for a split second. "Oh and if I find one more of your threatening notes in Jamie's stuff, I'll send some of those nice pictures we took to your dad. You know, the ones where you're all tied up and covered in my cum?" I don't wait for her answer. I push her out of the room, a little too hard, and slam the door in her face, way too hard.

I let out a groan as soon as I'm alone. I fucking hate this girl, but what pisses me off the most is she's got money and power. If she truly wants to make Jamie's life hell, she's perfectly capable of it. And I wouldn't be able to do shit about it. I don't even have those pictures anymore. I might have access to the Murrays' money, but true power only belongs to Stoneview's finest, and Camila is one of them. All I have is my fists, my anger, and a fucked up past that drives me. I can keep threatening Camila, but if she wants Jamie out, she'll get what she wants.

I try to calm myself down as I pick up Jamie's stuff and put them back in her purse. I try but I can't. I can feel my teeth clashing, grinding, and cracking against the other and my jaw straining as I think of how this all started. Me. I'm the one who was too stubborn to take no for an answer when Jamie was avoiding me. I blackmailed her, I bullied her into being interested in me.

It all hits me at once and my legs give up, forcing me to sit on the bed.

Is Jamie with me because she wants to?

Or because she's scared that I'm going to bully her if she says no? She's scared I'm going to call the cops on her and her mom. I'd never do that, but she doesn't know that.

My heart is beating too fast for me to control it. I'm in a genuine state of panic because Jamie is slowly teaching me to feel again, and I'm realizing I care for her so much more than I thought. I was most certainly not in love with Camila and I've never taken the time to get to know any other girl other than to stick my cock in them. But Jamie? If she's not into this as much as me it's going to break my heart.

I'm going to show her I'm serious about this, that it's not about the games we played at the beginning of the year, this isn't about Nate. This is about us. I won't let anything else get in the way. And I'm going to start by deleting everything I had on file regarding her work at the Bakers. Luke's dad is going to go ape shit if he learns what they did, and he won't hesitate to call the cops. He's the kind of fucker that doesn't care if he's underpaying his employees and gives them no benefits whatsoever. He probably has no idea what kind of situation Jamie and her mom are in.

I move over to my desk and hover my mouse to wake my computer. For some reason, the screen is already on. I don't think too much of it. I'm full of weed and vodka right now, I might have moved the mouse while I was talking to Camila. What I'm truly focused on is deleting a certain document, so Jamie can never get in trouble. I find the document I had made of everything missing at the Bakers' café, and my notes on the potential employees who could have stolen from the shop depending on their shifts.

I delete it. And once I've double-checked I've emptied the trash properly, I grab Jamie's purse and head out. A weight falls off my shoulders, and I can't wait to tell her it's all gone.

Actually, I can't wait to tell her I love her.

As soon as our limo gets to the hotel, I hurry to Jamie. She's still waiting outside with everyone that left before us.

Luke heads to talk to Ella's date and I can't help but chuckle. This girl's dating life is so fucked with all of us looking after her. Ozy seems to be trying to cheer up Chris who's been in a foul mood all evening, God only knows why. I suspect it's got to do with his secret girlfriend he still hasn't introduced to any of us and thus can't bring to the ball with us.

"What took so long?" Jamie smiles at me and my world suddenly lights up.

How I managed to live my whole life without her in it until this year is a fucking enigma.

"Here," I say as I hand her her purse.

"Thanks," she takes it and looks for her student ID then looks back up at me. "Everything okay? Did you drink too much already?" I must have been staring at her.

I grab her hand tightly in mine and drop a kiss on the top of her head. "Everything's perfect," I reply.

We take time having our pictures taken just the two of us before we join the others inside. I straight up go to Emily. I've come to know she always manages to sneak in flasks wherever she goes.

"Aaah, here they are. Can I borrow my best friend for a minute if you don't mind?" she tells me.

"Mm, I don't know. I like to keep her close." I squeeze her between my arms, her face buried just below my chest.

"I'm right here you know," Jamie groans, her words drowned against my shirt.

"Where's *my* best friend," I ask back.

Emily rolls her eyes in a huff before grabbing Jamie's hand. "Who knows what the fucker gets up to behind my back."

She drags her away and I watch as they both head to the hall, probably to the bathroom. This hotel is huge, and I don't want to lose them, but I also can't really follow them to the girls' room.

I decide to join my friends instead, as I spot Chris and Ozy man-talking Luke. They've complained so much lately that I don't spend time with them anymore. I love them, they're my family, but they don't understand that I'm *addicted* to Jamie.

I don't call her Angel as a mockery anymore. I think she's fallen from heaven and was meant to be in my life. The way she keeps me happy and in check is forcing me into believing someone up there sent her for me. Not once since we've been together have I lost my shit over some unimportant stuff that makes me feel out of control. Or maybe once, which I have failed to mention to her, but it was anything but unimportant.

Beating the shit out of Nate was long overdue not only because he's been harassing Jamie but for all the things we never solved in the past.

That won't happen again because I have Jamie now and she teaches me to let go of what I can't change. She reassures me when Rose comes back home stinking of Sam's cologne. She takes all the horrible thoughts away and replaces them with pure bliss. She even chased the nightmares away. I used to get Camila over to my house in the middle of the night to take the anger out, now Jamie wakes up to calm me down with her soft lips. That's how I know she's the best thing that's ever happened to me.

"...she's a great girl, Luke, why do you always want to fuck things up?" Chris finishes as I approach.

"You're fine, she'll come back," Ozy says lazily, typing a text on her phone at the same time.

"I don't think you're in a great place to give girlfriend advice," I taunt my sister.

"Oh, look at that. He remembers we exist," she replies with a lopsided smile. She puts her phone in her purse and I look up and down at her.

"Yeah, you're seeing right. She's wearing a dress," Luke cuts in before I can say anything. Her long black silk dress touches her ankles, and I can't help but smile when I notice the white Nike sneakers she's sporting proudly.

"So you *are* a girl after all." The tone in my voice makes her chuckle but she doesn't let me walk all over her.

"Not as much as you but yeah." She nudges Luke in the shoulder. "Nice change of topic by the way."

"What's wrong with you and Em?" I ask as my friend runs his hand through his pale blond hair.

218

Luke has always had any girl he wanted but it was mainly them who wanted him. He doesn't often go out of his way to hit on girls and it happens for him to just take whoever falls on his lap – literally sometimes. But with Emily? Boy, has she made him work for it. He's acting like he can move onto someone else anytime but if he really could, he would have by now. No, he's too into the stubborn hellraiser to let her go.

"They've entered an unofficial competition as to who can make the other the most jealous. I think Emily is winning," Chris mocks.

"No, she's not," Luke growls. "I am, which is why she's mad as fuck. Shouldn't have let Jason hit on her after practice if she didn't want me to talk to her cheer teammate."

"Jason?" I ask. "He hit on her? I swear he's never mentioned her before."

"Oh, he has," Rose says before taking a sip from a flask. Where did that come from?

She rolls her eyes when we all look at her with disgusted eyes. None of us want to hear of her sexual adventures with Jason. "I won't go into more details but just know it includes a time where he told me his ideal threesome. And it did *not* include Beth."

We all laugh as she passes the flask around. I take a sip after Chris and almost choke on pure vodka.

"Hey, pass me your phone," she nudges Luke. He does it without asking any questions and I roll my eyes at him, letting my head fall back in a groan.

"Luke." I snap the phone from Ozy's hands. "Times like this are when I wonder if you know her at all."

"You're a dick," she huffs before I can even ask her why she needs his phone.

219

"You own a very nice phone, why do you need Luke's?" I smile but she perfectly knows she's angering me. Does she think I like checking out everything she does?

"Why do you act like a big brother when you're the exact same age as me? You're not wiser. If anything, we both know I'm smarter. Give it back."

I give the phone to Chris, offering her my most innocent smile and he takes it gladly.

"Here. He's older, wiser, *and* smarter," I taunt.

She looks daggers at the both of us. "You two are shit."

"Why do you need Luke's phone?" Chris repeats my question as Luke looks at her with a sorry face that says, 'I tried'.

"Because Roy and Carlo won't sell to me and we all want to have fun tonight," she replies casually. "What are we gonna do, score from Volkov? Can you imagine if he knows we're related to Nate? I don't want to die, do you?" She completely ignores Chris' disapproving look and speaks only to me. "Come on, Jake, as if you wouldn't drop on the last day of school."

It pisses me off that she's right. I do wish we could all take pills together tonight. I wouldn't be against doing it with Jamie and having the best sex of our lives.

"Only in Stoneview do you hear seniors complaining they can't score ecstasy for their winter ball. This is rich people problems, Rose," Chris scolds her, cutting my thoughts short.

"You *are* rich people Chris, my friend," she replies. "And thanks to your angelic parents, so am I. That's the kind of problem I'm happy to have."

"It's not your only problem though, is it? They won't sell to you because Sam told them not to, and having Sam's attention is a *real* problem," he bites back and, sadly, he's right.

She doesn't say anything for a few long seconds. I love when Chris deals with her because he always knows how to outsmart her, and she rarely finds a way out of it.

Chris gives Luke his phone back. "If you want to score with Luke's phone, fine. But I don't want to hear you complain about Sam making your life hard after that, especially when you should be focusing on people like Rachel."

"Oooh..." Luke and I release at the same time. He hit home.

Ozy opens her mouth to say something but closes it straight away. "Whatever, let's get drunk," she snatches the flask from my hands and drinks a few sips at a time.

"Alright soldier," I grab the flask back and put my arm around her shoulders before messing up her hair. "One sip at a time, shall we?"

As I start walking with her in my hold, I spot Jamie and Emily coming back to the ballroom. I let go of my sister to give a kiss to Jamie as soon as she reaches me.

"You're so beautiful," I whisper.

"I took drugs," she replies straight away. I practically choke on air as Emily explodes laughing.

"You smoked three puffs of a joint, Jamie, chill out," Emily manages to squeak past her throat. Jamie follows her friend in an uncontrollable laugh.

I can't help but smile at her reaction, who wouldn't? She's so fucking cute.

"She's too good for you," Ozy throws my way before going hers.

She really is.

"You're the cutest," I say as I cup both her cheeks before giving her another kiss.

* * *

I open the taxi door for Jamie and help her in before following. After giving Cal's address to the driver, I turn back to the beautiful girl next to me and grab her hand.

"How are you feeling?"

"I'm feeling fine, Jake. I can't even feel it anymore."

I don't know why I started worrying about her smoking weed. She seemed fine during the whole ball, but I know she barely ever drinks, let alone smoke. I know I'm in no place to judge seeing what Luke, Ozy, and I usually take on nights out, but Jamie is different. I don't want anything to happen to her.

"Why did you want to take a taxi? Everyone's left in the limo." She slides closer to her side of the car just to lay down, her head on my lap. My heart is beating hard against my ribs and I have to take a deep breath before I raise a shaky hand to stroke her hair. I've never felt anxious around a girl and fuck do I feel anxious around her.

"Because I wanted to tell you something," I almost whisper. She sits back up at my words and I can read the fear on her face.

Does she think I'm going to break up?

"Is everything okay?" she panics.

"Yeah, no, everything's fine. I just thought you'd want to know that I..." Why can't I get myself to say it? Am I that scared she's gonna realize she's way too good for me?

"Want to know what? You're freaking me out." She lets out a chuckle, but I can see she's getting scared. She shouldn't be, I'm the one who's terrified.

"I know it's not a big deal, but I wanted to let you know

I've deleted everything about, you know, your mom and you... regarding the Bakers."

Her brows narrow in confusion, but I know she knows what I'm talking about.

"Why would you do this," she whispers.

"Because I—"

"I wasn't mad at you, Jake. It wasn't holding me back." She cuts me off before I can say the end of my sentence.

Love you.

Because I love you.

Why would she cut me off? Did she know what I was going to say? Does she not want to hear it? Is it too soon? Or worse, is she still in love with Nate? Shit, how does this fucking thing work? I thought loving someone was meant to be simple, why does it come with all that stress?

I scratch my throat and try to put up a brave face. "I didn't want you to think I had something on you."

She chuckles and puts a hand on my cheek. "I know you'd never do that. You're good. Deep down I know you're good."

My heart stops at her words before exploding completely in my chest. She believes in me. She believes I'm a good person. I don't remember the last time someone has truly believed this deep down.

My friends are like my family and I know they love me, but I also know Chris keeps an eye on me like I might flip any minute. The same way he does with Ozy.

Jamie drops her soft lips on mine and murmurs on my mouth, "I appreciate what you did. It means a lot."

I grab her hips and drag her on my lap. She rests her knees on either side of me and I capture her lips in a loving kiss.

"My angel," I whisper.

223

Her warm core against my pants is making my dick hard but I don't do anything. Not only because we're in a taxi, but mainly because this is not what it's about right now. I'm dying to tell her that I'm in love with her, but I don't want to ruin the moment. If she can't reciprocate my feelings, I don't think I'd get over it.

"I want to go home," she whispers sensually in my ear and my cock strains against my pants painfully. She grinds a couple of times on my hard dick.

"Jamie," I warn. "If you keep doing this, there's gonna be no time to get home. I'll just rip your clothes off in this taxi."

She giggles and gets off me to sit back in her seat.

"We're here," the driver says in a hurry.

I wouldn't be surprised if he sped to our destination to avoid two horny teenagers having sex in the back of his cab.

CHAPTER 13

Him & I – G-Eazy, Halsey

Jamie

As soon as we enter Cal's mansion, the heat submerges us, making my breath shallow. The music is loud and over-whelming, and I squeeze Jake's hand tighter. The house is completely packed, and I don't even know how we're going to find our friends through all these people.

I reach for my phone in my purse and shoot a text to Emily. I doubt she's going to see it at this point of the night. It was impossible to stop her from drinking her whole flask at the ball. She's upset over Luke flirting with Jessika, another cheerleader, and I can't blame her. These two have been playing a dangerous game. She keeps saying she's breaking up with him and they'll be over by the end of the night but if she really wanted to break up, wouldn't she have done so by now?

As we make our way through a crowd of unknown faces, the heat becomes unbearable in my winter coat.

"Who are all these people?" I ask Jake.

"Cal's friends. College guys."

I feel slightly uncomfortable being at an after-party with college people. I heard what happens at these parties and I'm not really into being roofied or peer pressured into drinking. Jake puts an arm around my waist to keep me close as we look for a space in the crowd and we end up in the kitchen. I notice Camila's brothers, Carlo and Roy, going around laughing with people as they exchange small bags for money in handshakes.

"Are you hot? I'm boiling, let me take your coat," he says as he starts taking my coat off my shoulders.

I'm glad that my dress wasn't enough for the ball because here, it's borderline too much. Jake fits perfectly now that he's shrugged his suit jacket and bow. His hair looks like he's just gotten out of bed, as usual, giving him that sexy look that only he can rock. He's popped open the top buttons of his shirt and taken it out of the suit pants.

I look around and can't help but notice that he is the sexiest man in this room, probably in this city and it's clear that he doesn't even try. Beauty simply runs in his blood. I see girls looking our way and I know it's not me they're looking at. He attracts all the female attention and, as I finish scanning the room, my gaze falls on his. He hasn't looked anywhere else but straight at me.

"I hope you know you're the most beautiful girl at this party." I blush at his words but don't say anything because I know it's not true.

There are so many girls here tonight, older, hotter. Some haven't made the effort I have tonight, and they still outshine me by far, but it seems Jake doesn't see it.

"Are you sure you're wearing your contacts?"

He laughs and his dimples show on his cheeks, making my insides melt. God, I would die if I couldn't see these every day.

In the last few weeks, I have seen all sorts of versions of Jake. The hot guy everyone knows from school, the brother who can't sleep when his twin doesn't come home, the ruthless lacrosse captain, the geeky coder wearing glasses spending sleepless nights in his boxers building apps and websites. I've seen the romantic who brings me dinner to work when I'm closing the café, the sex beast who takes me in his car and empty classrooms, who makes me go to the diner without panties on just so he can play with me in public.

I love every single one of them. I'm addicted to his sweet-ness and roughness equally and I'm in so deep, I don't know how much longer I can hold off from telling him how much he means to me.

"Angel, if you really feel like shit being here, we don't have to stay."

"I mean, how often do you go to these kinds of pa–"

I'm cut off by a big guy, about twice my size, hurrying toward Jake with a huge smile plastered on his face. "Jake! My man!"

As he hugs Jake tightly, his deep brown eyes land on me. His white and dark green football jersey pops out on his dark skin and it contrasts with Jake's golden tone. When they part, he turns around for a second to grab a drink and I read the surname on his jersey: Simmons. Jason's brother.

"How have you been, bro? You've disappeared from the party scene man. Jas' came with your sister and her girl last Friday. I thought I'd see you."

"Dude, I missed like two parties and you get all clingy?"

The guy whom I think is Cal, laughs and gives him a friendly punch to the shoulder. "What can I say? You were the best I've ever had."

Jake chuckles and puts an arm around my shoulder. "Cal, this is Jamie, my girlfriend. Jamie, this is Cal. He's like Jason but older and not talented enough to play lacrosse."

Cal chokes on his drink and nudges Jake. He gives me a hug but pulls away quickly when Jake tightens his arm around my shoulders.

"Nice to meet you, gorgeous. And don't listen to him, unlike your boyfriend, I don't enjoy playing with sticks. I prefer real men's sports."

"You prefer real men, period," Jake chuckles.

Cal laughs heartily, "That I do."

"Where's the drink at here?" Jake asks.

Cal shakes his red cup. "Bro, this is water. I'm not drinking tonight. I'm waiting for Carlo to give me his new good shit."

Jake's body tenses slightly but his face stays exactly the same and I have to give him credit for that. He's too good at pretending everything's fine when not much is.

"They're selling new shit?"

"Yup," Cal pops the 'p' like he can hardly wait to get what he's waiting for. "Rose brought it with her last week. You missed a good night." Cal lowers his voice and gets slightly closer to us. "I think they got a new supplier if you ask me because all their products have changed. In a good way."

"Cool," Jake replies casually. "I'll have to try."

"For sure, man. I'll come get you, we'll celebrate you showing up at a party. Anyway, help yourself to anything you want, yeah? I'll be finding myself some nice guy in the meantime. Or girl. Your sister here?"

From the smile tugging at Cal's lips, he's clearly joking to rile him up, but Jake pushes him a little harder than playfully.

"How about go fuck your mom, huh? Mayor Simmons is a MILF."

Cal explodes laughing and leaves shaking his head.

"He's a j—" I start.

"Jerk?"

"I was gonna go for jock, but I guess that works as well."

"I think all the Simmons brothers are. But they got the biggest houses and unlimited supply of alcohol."

"Right," I roll my eyes, "because that's so important in life, isn't it?"

"Nope. What's most important is my beautiful girl and her happiness. So, are you okay?"

It warms my heart that he goes back to where we left the conversation before being interrupted. It's not much but anyone else would have forgotten or gotten into the party mood after seeing their friends. Jake still wants to make sure I'm okay being here and that counts.

"I'm fine. Your friends haven't seen you in, like, two parties, bro." I mock. "You've left the party scene, dude."

He laughs at my imitation of Cal and takes my hand. "Let's put our jackets in the limo."

As soon as we're outside I shiver from the cold. I'm still a little tense from the party, I have a bad feeling about it. Which is stupid because Jake is here, nothing can go wrong when he's next to me. I see Emily getting out of one of the limos and relax. I'm going to have one friend here and it's better than nothing. Emily excitedly jumps into my arms and I laugh at her drunkenness. Luke and Rose follow out of the car in a laughing fit.

"Your boyfriend is officially drunk," Rose says to Emily.

"He's not my boyfriend," she snarls back, making everyone's eyes roll.

Ella is the last one coming out and I turn to Em. "Where's Chris?"

"Oh, he left his seat to Ella because her dickhead drunk date kept feeling her up," she replies casually.

"What?" I choke, turning to Luke. "Didn't you say anything?"

"Chris had a chat with the dude. We thought he'd have more of a chance of survival than if he was having a chat with Luke," Emily keeps going. My eyes cross with Ella's, she looks incredibly uncomfortable.

"I'm going in," she mumbles and pushes past Luke.

"Hey, I'm keeping an eye on you," he shouts as she walks away.

The second limo arrives and a random guy I recognize from Jake's house comes out with a black eye, looking like he would rather be anywhere but here.

What the hell?

I look at everyone coming out of the limo one by one.

Jason, Rose's casual fuck.

Beth, his fiancée.

Camila, my boyfriend's ex.

And Rachel, Camila's best friend and Rose's on and off love of her life.

Could this group get any more wrong?

Chris is the last coming out, sporting a deep scowl. All of us already here look at him in shock.

"Did you do that?" Rose asks, pointing at the guy walking up the driveway.

The only response he graces us with is a low growl before he heads for the house himself.

"Right," Emily claps her hand then shakes her now empty flask. "Shall we go fill up, my friends?"

Everyone starts walking toward the house except Jake and me. He opens the door of the limo to put our jackets away and I see him looking for something with his hand under the seats. He finally pulls out an item I barely see but recognize straight away. He tucks it quickly under his button-up shirt, between his lower back and the waist of his pants.

"Jake," I whisper. "What the hell are you doing with this?!"

He turns around as he shuts the door and grabs the back of my neck to kiss me, but I put up resistance and he frowns at me.

"Jamie, I practically live with this on me. I just don't take it to school."

"Why? You don't need it. It's dangerous, what if someone grabs it from you? People could get seriously hurt."

"We live in America, Angel, I'm probably not the only one in there with a gun."

"But you're seventeen, Jake. That makes a difference." My words make his grip on my neck tighten and he pulls me closer.

"This is not a fight to have, Jamie. Because I'll do what I want anyway. You know that, right?"

I love him. I really do. But he had made such great effort on his behavior that I almost forgot he was this way.

The anger heats my cheeks as I struggle to get out of his hold.

"Do you think you can tone down the alpha act for a minute to listen to rational thoughts or are you too deep into your male chauvinist world to hear what I'm saying?"

Jake chuckles coldly as he lets go of me but only for a beat. It takes him a split second to grab my jaw and push me until my back hits the car.

"I can't drop the alpha *act,* Jamie. It's not a fucking act, don't you get that?"

I try to huff mockingly at him, but his fingers press into my cheeks until my lips are pouting for him.

His breath smells of alcohol and mint. He's so close to me that it's all mixed with his deep wooden cologne and everything together makes my knees weak. I hate my body even more when I feel my underwear dampen.

Why? Why does it have this effect on me?

This is a serious conversation, I'm more than honest when I say I hate that he carries this around to make himself feel more powerful.

"Listen real close; If Carlo and Roy are selling here, I have not a single doubt that Sam is not too far, and there is no way in hell I'm not always ready to put a bullet in the fucker's head. Do you understand that? This is no fucking act. I'm never letting anyone affiliated with Bianco hurt the ones I love. Ever. Again." His grip turns so hard that my eyes start to water.

"Jake..." I try to say but my lips can barely form the word.

The burning hate in his eyes is mixed with guilt that I can't begin to understand. He leans down towards me, his forearm above my head on the car, and his forehead rests on mine as his hand drops back to his side.

"Talk to me. What happened there? At Bianco's." I try to keep my voice as unthreatening as possible but I'm dying to understand him.

"There are things better left unsaid. What's important is that no one gets hurt anymore," he whispers. "Not under my watch."

I don't know what to say, so I do the only thing I know I want for sure. I let the moment pass until I grab the hand that was holding my jaw a minute ago, slide it against my thigh until it reaches my wet underwear.

An animalistic growl rumbles in his chest.

"Jamie," he breathes. "You're a bad girl deep down, you know that?"

I bite my lower lip and nod in response. He cups me through my panties, hard enough to make me gasp. I go on my toes to kiss him, but he pulls away.

"Get in the car," he orders.

I don't think, I execute.

He follows me in the limo but doesn't let me sit down. He grabs my hips straight away, spinning me around and lying me down on the back seat, he grabs my wrists and pushes them above my head.

"Don't move," he grumbles.

I keep my arms exactly how he left them while he gets off me and looks around.

"What are you doing?" I whisper like I'm too scared someone will hear us in the house up the driveway that's blasting music loud enough to make you deaf.

He ignores me and suddenly grabs a trench coat that I believe belongs to Rachel. He slips the soft belt out of the loops and turns to me, his eyes burning with a carnal need.

I prop up on my elbows, not sure if it's anticipation or fear sending electricity down my lower belly. "What are you d–"

"Tsk tsk, I said not to move. Didn't I?" He's back on top

233

of me in a split second, putting a hand on my chest to push me back down. He drags his hand down my breasts, pinching one nipple at a time through my dress, making them perk for him, and then lower again until he rips my lace thong away and throws it on the other side of the limo.

"Jake! I-I need this."

He doesn't bother replying before his knuckles graze my wet entrance, then my swollen clit. I don't even try to refrain my moans. I know he's going to get them out of me either way. I start to buck my hips to meet his teasing hand and as I'm about to grab his wrist he grabs both of mine again.

"Do you trust me?" he whispers in my ear.

I can only nod. My breath hitches when he puts a finger in me, and I start moving to the rhythm of his hand. Another follows, driving me crazy with lust. He curls them, sending a jolt of electricity through my entire body, and the pad of his thumb presses hard on my clit.

"Yes," I pant. "Oh my Gosh, Jake..."

He slowly pulls his hand away and my eyes fly open. I'm about to say something but his lips crash on mine in a kiss so feral I almost come from this alone.

"More," I pant as he pulls away. "I need to come."

He smiles down at me and wraps the trench coat belt around my wrists. I hadn't even realized that he was still holding it.

"Jake," I panic but he thrusts his hips forward and the bulge in his pants rip out another moan from me. A moment later my wrists are tied together above my head.

"Be a good girl, keep them above your head."

His head dips between my legs and at the first lick my hands come down to grab his hair. He brings his head back above mine.

"Jamie," he warns, and I bring my hands back above my head straight away.

He grabs the belt and pulls, stretching my arms far above. I can feel he's hooking it to something but when I try to look, he's in the way.

"What are you doing?" I ask.

His only response is to kiss me again. He trails kisses down until he's at my thighs and my legs quiver with need.

"I wouldn't try to put your arms down if I were you. I've locked the car from the outside but if you pull the handle the door will definitely open."

I can feel my eyes widen. I look up at the door just to confirm my fear. He's hooked the belt tightly to the door handle. One pull and the door will open.

"This...someone's going to see us. It's not a good idea."

"But it's my idea and I'm the one who decides." Another wave of pleasure pools between my legs at his words.

"If you comply, I'll let you come, Angel." He accompanies his words by pushing his fingers in my pussy, making me jump with pleasure.

My arms automatically pull slightly, thankfully not enough to open the door. My heart races as I push my hands against the door to avoid the reflex of bringing my hands down.

My breath hitches as he plays with my clit and I can feel myself starting to lose it. His hand pulls away again and he doesn't fail to notice the cry that escapes my lips.

"You need to trust me, baby. When I decide it's safer for me to carry, you just go with it because I can't have you forgetting who's in charge."

He strokes my pussy again, making everything inside me tighten, and it takes all my strength to push the words out of my mouth. "I worry for you. Not only is it illegal but you put yourself at risk by carrying a gun. It scares me."

"I scare you?" he asks, surprised.

"Guns scare me."

He pulls away from me for a second to reach behind his back and pulls out his gun in front of him.

"This scares you baby?" he asks in his evil voice. My heart picks up and cold panic runs through every cell of my body.

"Jake, this isn't funny." I want to pull at my binds, but I'm quickly reminded that I'm half-naked in a limo with hundreds of students not far. I can't help Camila's words coming back to my mind.

You think this is all just a bit of fun, but I can promise you he gets worse. As soon as you find comfort in the way he is, he'll push your limits further. Then further again...and again.

He runs the tip of the gun against my cheek, and I fail to jerk my head away.

Why? Why don't I try to stop him? Why can't I stop the wetness from running down my thighs?

He traces my lips with it and runs it down my belly, sending chills down my spine.

There's nothing that can stop my moan when he settles it between my legs. I'm scared. I'm scared and excited. So much that the anticipation of what he's going to do next makes my thighs clamp around his hand. The initial coldness quickly passes as my burning core and juices warm the weapon.

"You're dripping Angel," he growls in his low, animalistic voice.

He starts rubbing the barrel against my pussy and clit. The pleasure zapping through my body forces me to cry out. His eyes shine with lust as mine start closing with heaviness. He shifts slightly, moving the gun a little slower and circling my swollen clit with it.

"Jake," I moan. "Faster."

He chuckles and slows down even more, making me whine a wordless complaint. I move my hips, desperate for a quicker pace.

"Such a greedy Angel."

The pleasure is too slow and overwhelming. I can feel sweat rolling down my temples from the need to come. My moans turn into desperate cries exploding from my chest. I try everything; I squirm to get more pleasure, I buck my hips at a quicker rhythm. He just keeps his torturously slow pace. I don't know how long I fight him, practically sobbing from the frustration, but when I finally decide to calm down, stop moving and wait for him to decide, he smiles at me.

"That's a good girl. There's no point in trying to go against my decisions. You know I always get my way."

He finally accelerates. Harder, faster and it takes less than a minute for me to break apart. To forget everything around me, the car, the belt, the fact that he's making me come with a gun between my legs. Every cell in my body is electrified by the sensation and any fear I had is overcome by pure, intense, blissful, and *shameless* pleasure.

He muffles my scream with his mouth before putting the gun right beside my head on the seat. I'm struggling to keep my eyes open from the pleasure but his voice in my ear brings me back to life.

"I'm going to fuck you so hard, everyone in that house will know you're mine."

The sound of his zipper, the rip of the condom package, and an instant later he's slamming into me, my wetness allowing him to slide home easily.

He fucks me relentlessly and each stroke holds no mercy on my body. When he slows down, it's only to grab the gun and put it to my lips.

"Clean," he orders in a barely controlled groan.

I stick my tongue out and let him rub the barrel of the gun against my tongue. I take the initiative to take it slightly deeper in my mouth and roll my tongue around it before he pulls it back out, a satisfied growl rumbling from his chest. His movements grow harsher, his hips hitting against my pelvis quicker. He pulls away slightly, taking a shaking breath to control himself. He's still partly inside me and he now moves in shorter movements, rubbing the perfect spot rather than slamming inside me.

"Aah..." I cry out as he rolls his hips to the rhythm of mine. He stops for a couple of seconds before going all the way in again, it's not fast but it's hard. Hard enough to make me scream.

"You ready to come for me, Angel?"

I nod, my breathing too ragged to form any word. God, I was ready to come long ago.

"Good. Don't."

The pleas that go past my lips are incomprehensible. There are no actual words, only breathless moans that beg for release.

"You come when I say so."

I nod again, hoping following his lead will grant me mercy. I can feel the beginning of uncontrollable electricity shooting from my lower belly and he must see it on my face because his dexterous fingers slip between us. I expect a flick, some rubbing, anything to help me. Instead, I get a harsh pinch on my clit. I cry out in pain. There was no pleasure in the gesture whatsoever and he knows it.

"I...I can't hold it," I breathe out.

His devilish grin doesn't give me much hope. "But you *are* going to hold it a little longer. Unless you want me to stop right now?" A slow, languid roll of his hips warns me to listen.

"No, no. Please, don't stop."

He slams hard and my head hits the door. He lays over me, his forehead against mine, his lips close enough to be a delicious temptation. I lick my lips, begging him to take my mouth and he only smiles in return. I feel his hand on top of my head and realize he's stopping me from repeatedly banging my head against the door. He pushes hard another time, and another. A pause, another...I have to bite my lip hard to bring some pain into the mix, anything to balance the pleasure that is attempting to force an orgasm out of me. I feel his breath against my ear and the words I was waiting for finally land.

"You can come."

When I cry out his name, he pulls up and smiles down at me like he's won a trophy. Like he knows something I don't. A secret so well guarded, only he knows that it even exists. But when he curses as he comes, I smile back. Oh, we are both so deep into our insanity.

As soon as we're back inside, I run to the bathroom. I spend long enough there to rinse between my legs but not long enough to get over the fact that I'm not wearing any underwear anymore.

I take another few minutes to rearrange my hair, my makeup, and send a text to Emily to ask where she is. She never replied to the previous one, I doubt she'll reply to this one. I'm about to put my phone back in my purse when a text from Jake pops up.

Jake: Everything okay? You've been gone for ages.

I quickly type that I'm still freshening up but before I can hit send, another message pops up.

Jake: Did I go too far? The safety was on, I promise.

It's scary to think that he doesn't know in the heat of the moment if he is going too far or not. I know the need to control everything takes over him sometimes, and I know I'm the one he takes it out on. That's how our relationship started after all.

The thing is, I liked it then and I still like it now. Technically, it's wrong. But physically and emotionally it feels so damn right that I would be a liar if I replied that he went too far. To anyone else, he probably did. But to my fucked-up self? I loved every second of it. The fear, the anticipation, the panic that gets overtaken by sheer pleasure. I've never felt like that before and there's only one person that can bring this to me. Only Jake.

Jamie: Honestly? ... no.

I can almost hear his sigh of relief. I know he doesn't want to repeat the same mistake he did with Camila. He doesn't want to mold me into someone who likes it the way he does just to keep him. But he doesn't have to mold me, our broken pieces already fit together perfectly.

Jamie: I'll only be another minute.

I look at myself another time to make sure everything is fine and leave the bathroom. I'm about to walk the long hallway back to the living area when Emily replies to me, saying she's in the backyard but leaving soon. I turn around and make my way to the Orangery leading to the backyard.

I'll find Emily and let Jake know where we are exactly. As I pass two loungers, I notice two girls arguing in hushed voices. It doesn't take me long to recognize Rose's husky whisper and Rachel's sweet voice.

"...but I won't stop seeing him, Rach', you gotta understand that," Rose says.

I stop a second in the dark because my curiosity is stronger than anything else and I'm sure Emily will love to hear about it.

"It's different to see him and to not want to tell me where you are or what you do with him. You go completely M.I.A. on me when you're with him, Rose, that's not okay. Surely even you can comprehend that?" Rachel's voice is calm and composed and it contrasts with Rose's unpredictable personality.

They're sitting in complete darkness and I have to squint my eyes to see that they're sitting opposite each other and Rose is holding both of Rachel's hands in hers like she's afraid she's going to fly away like those helium balloons you get at the fair. Rose throws her head back in a groan.

"You know I hate when you talk to me like I'm some sort of fuckboy or something. Yes, Rachel, I can *comprehend* that you don't like it when I don't reply to you when I'm with Sam. I get busy, that's it."

"Can you hear yourself right now, Rose?" Rachel's voice rises and I don't think I've ever heard it above a calm tone. "You get *busy*, is that your explanation? Is that why you disappear for whole nights and days? How do you think I feel when Jake calls me because he thinks you're with me and you're with *him* instead? Where do you guys go? What do you do with him?"

Rose runs her hand through her hair, and I can't see, but I can imagine her jaw ticking like Jake's does.

"Why does it matter? We chill, he's my friend."

"Fine," Rachel almost shouts. She pulls her hands away from Rose's and gets up. "Since you want me to spell it out because you're such a shady bitch: Do you cheat on me with him? Have you ever? Just tell me the fucking truth, I swear don't make me feel like I'm crazy for asking this."

Rose doesn't raise her voice. She stays calm. "No. I would never cheat on you, you know that. Why you even ask is beyond me."

"Beyond you? I ask because you don't share shit. I ask because you're a liar and you know you are. You would rather lie than get in trouble. To me, to your brother, to everyone."

"I lie when it's necessary. When I don't want to chat about pointless shit. You know me better than anyone Rach', you know if I think a conversation will lead nowhere then there's no point having it."

Rose slowly gets up and puts a hand on each side of Rachel's face.

"I love you. I'd never cheat on you. I've known Sam since I was a little girl. He's a constant in my life. But he lives in a world that's so different from ours, I just have to adapt. I have to because I don't want to not see him. I don't want to lose him again."

"His world is not that different. You spent half of your night tonight with him. He's at the same party as us. In fact, he's never really far."

"Yeah, I spent half the night *arguing* with him," Rose scoffs.

"Stop finding excuses!"

There's a long silence and I'm about to leave when Rachel's words make my curiosity take over my common sense.

"Do you love him?" Rachel's voice is barely audible anymore like she's ashamed of asking it.

"Baby, no one compares to you."

"Answer the question, Rose."

"I," Rose gets closer to Rachel. They're so close I think they're kissing for a second but when I hear Rose's voice again, it's clear they're not. "Yes. But not like I love you. I don't think so."

"You don't think so?" Rachel rips herself away from Rose. "You don't *think* so?"

"Rach, please–"

"No. I gave you everything. My energy, my tears...my heart. Do you know what love is? It's putting up with your girlfriend's lies. With the missing info. It's putting up with the breaks so you can go *fuck* some other girls out of your system. It's seeing Jason every day when I know he fucks you behind Beth's back whenever you grant him the chance. It's soothing you from nightmares every night when you won't even tell me why it scares you to close your fucking door." Rachel takes a ragged breath, her voice broken by soft sobs.

"It's seeing past the fact that you escape all your fucking

problems with drugs and meaningless sex. That's love, Rose. And I gave you all I had of it. All of it. But you wouldn't know because you're broken. I'm so sorry because I don't know what made you this way, but you're so fucking broken and I'm done trying to fix you."

Rachel's words are so strong they hit *me* hard. I can't see Rose's reaction. I can only see her taking a step back like she's just been stabbed in the chest.

With a voice lower than usual she keeps her reply simple. "You're right. And it's not fair to you."

Rachel lets out a cold chuckle. "Why am I even surprised you're not fighting to save us? You just accept it. It's that easy."

There's a short silence before Rachel speaks again. As if she was giving Rose a chance to correct herself. "We had a nice ride. But I think we're over for good this time. No more breaks, Rose. No more us."

"I don't want that."

"But I do and, for once, I'm going to put myself first."

"You're breaking my heart. I hope you know that."

Rachel lets out a small genuine laugh. "No. I'm really not. You don't know what it's like to get your heart broken. And even if you do, you're Rose White. Someone will come fix it in no time."

Rachel leaves before Rose can say another word. When she walks past me, she pauses from surprise for a second but doesn't say anything. She just wipes the tears that are falling from her eyes and keeps walking.

I shouldn't have stayed. I've intruded on an important moment in their lives and relationship. Guilt gnaws at me, but I feel like now that I know, Rose could probably use a friend. I take a step toward her as I see her sit back down on the lounger, put her arms on her knees, and her head on her arms.

"Rose," I say as I approach.

She doesn't lift her head, but I can hear her loud and clear. "Fuck off, Jamie. And, by the way, eavesdropping is rude as fuck." Her voice is threatening enough for me to get the message.

I take a few steps back and hurry to the backyard.

As soon as I'm outside I take a deep breath. That was intense and the cold air can only do me good.

The patio is made of dark blue hard tiles until the floor turns into lawn. They even have outside warmers like those fancy restaurants on Stoneview main street. The only lights are the countless fairy lights that surround the yard. Not everyone's face is clear, but it's lit enough to continue the party outside.

I try to relax a little. Rose won't be mad at me. She has bigger things to worry about. How long has she been with Rachel? Their on and off relationship has been going on forever. And she loves her, that much is clear. Yet, she still doesn't open herself up to her. It's like Rachel knows nothing of Rose's life prior to Stoneview. Like me with Jake. I know he loves me. We haven't said it to each other but it's there, it's real. Then when will he open up about his past? He avoids the topic like the plague. He always has an excuse not to talk about it. He will change the topic in any way he can, more often than not he will push me to my knees and fuck my mouth as a punishment for asking things I shouldn't. I know Stoneview Jake and I know what hides behind the mask, but I don't know what made him this way. And right now I'm scared I never will.

"You look like you just got told off, beautiful."

I jump at the voice that I recognize too easily. My heartbeat doubles as I turn to my right, towards the familiar face.

Beautiful ashy blond hair in a small bun, a jaw so hard it could cut concrete, dark glasses surrounding deep, dark, blue eyes.

"Nathan," I breathe out. I can't even hide my surprise and swallow thickly to try and ground myself.

CHAPTER 14

Love and War - Fleurie

Jamie

He's wearing a crisp white button-down, as usual, and the sleeves are rolled up to his elbow showing his strong forearms covered with countless tattoos. Like Jake, he's popped out the first couple of buttons but on him, it shows the tattoos that creep up to the bottom of his neck. Sitting on a wide wooden garden chair, he's resting his arm on the armrests, his strong hand hanging on the side, holding a beer.

I can't help but examine his face. He's completely healed from weeks ago when Jake, Chris, and Luke beat him up. And he definitely looks more composed than the drunken state he was in.

"Who was it?" His voice makes me jump. I was so lost in him that I forgot what he said.

"Wh-what?" Why am I stuttering? He never had this effect on me. He shouldn't.

A few different mocking laughs rise up and, only now, do I

realize we're not alone.

Roy and Carlo are sitting on a bench to his left and Sam is sitting to his right in the exact same kind of chair. Roy and Carlo are looking at me with sardonic smiles on their faces. They've clearly just laughed at me. Sam is barely paying me attention, his gaze looking for someone in the crowd.

But Nathan... Nathan is looking right through me. His piercing gaze is calling my name like a terrible curse. Like an enchantment promising nothing but chaos. His hard face softens and a cocky smile tugs at his lips.

"Who was it that told you off, 'Me?'" he repeats.

That nickname on his lips makes me shiver. It brings back all the memories. It makes me miss the good times, the pleasure, the love. It also reminds me why he's not allowed to call me that anymore. He betrayed me. He cheated me. Only my friends and family get to call me this.

Jake doesn't call me 'Me.

No, Jake calls me Angel and Baby because he's special. More special than anyone else.

"It doesn't matter. No one." I wave a hand in the air to show the unimportance of the topic.

Why am I even talking to him? I shouldn't be near him. It gives him the wrong idea. It makes him think he's got a hold on me, which he doesn't.

Doesn't he? He used to.

He didn't. He did...does. I don't know.

The fight going on inside me is making me feel dizzy.

Or is it Nathan?

I don't know. And I don't want to.

I take a step back. We don't have anything to say to each other. At least I don't.

"Enjoy your night," I say coldly as I'm about to turn away.

But he's too quick. He's always too quick. He could sense I wasn't going to stay while I was still debating myself.

His free hand is on my wrist in a split second. He didn't even have to get up. When did I get so close to him? I could swear I was a few steps away when he called me.

"Wait," he orders with a low voice. He's not sweet or begging, he's expecting me to simply obey.

I look at the men around him again. He's the boss here. He's the head of their little organization and it shows.

He's Bianco's right-hand man, I remind myself. I wonder how many people work for him. How big is their organization? How many of them are here tonight?

"Do *not* touch me," I fume. I snatch my hand away but can't seem to get myself to walk away.

"What are you doing here?" he asks. "Parties aren't your scene."

I scoff at his audacity. "You don't know what my scene is. You don't know me."

Way to sound like a teen Jamie, keep going.

He chuckles mockingly at me. "I think I know you. Enough to know you shouldn't be at a Frat party."

I'm about to retort that *he* shouldn't be at a frat party. That he's too old, that his business is so damn wrong, but I freeze when a strong hand clamps the back of my neck. I'd recognize this possessive gesture anywhere, anytime.

"I've been looking for you," Jake's low voice resonates in my ears.

Jake.

I told him I was going to be a minute. Then I went to the backyard, then I eavesdropped on Rose and Rachel and then...

249

Nathan happened.

I should have ignored him. I should have kept walking and found my best friend, text Jake, and forget he was even here. But I didn't. I fell into the trap. I kept the conversation going and now the worst that could have occurred is happening. Jake and Nathan, face to face.

What were the chances Nathan was going to be at this party? What were the chances of them bumping into each other at a party with hundreds of people?

"Don't worry Jake, she was just with me," Nathan taunts.

"I-I was looking for Emily, I was about to text you," I justify. "Let's find her." I try to move but Jake's hold tightens as he settles beside me.

He looks at the guys and back at his brother.

"I'm glad you healed fine," Jake taunts. "Would be a shame for that pretty face to scar. Don't you think?"

My heart picks up and sweat rolls down my back, like sensing the imminent danger. Jake is trying to undermine Nathan in front of his subordinates and he's not going to take it. He simply won't and I can't stand and wait for it all to break out.

"You wanna know what I think, brother?" Nathan says as he slowly rises.

Jake tenses at the word and I can feel the anger vibrating off of him. Nathan takes a sip of his beer and casually puts it on the edge of his seat. He walks to us until he's about arm-length away from Jake.

"Please, let's go," I beg Jake, trying to take a step back. I try to grab his hand but the one that's not on my neck is already balled into a tight fist.

"I think," Nathan continues, ignoring me as he wipes his

nose. "I *think* you should take your hand off my girl."

A loud laugh escapes Jake's mouth as if it was the last thing he expected to hear.

"But see, Nate–"

"Jake, I want to leave," I try again but none of them can hear me.

They're too deep into their mutual hatred. They're too far gone already. Jake doesn't even pause to listen, he keeps going.

"–what you're saying only works if your girl was around. I see your three bitches but I sure as fuck don't see your girl around here."

A disapproving scoff escapes Roy and both he and Carlo start the momentum of getting up, but Nathan puts a hand up to stop them and they both stay put.

Sam finally pays attention to us. He runs a hand behind his tattooed neck, and I notice his strong biceps and shoulders flexing with apprehension.

"Nate," he warns. "If you get in a pointless fight, you're going to give us a shit reputation. None of these rich kids will buy from us because they'll be too scared and you're most definitely not going to have a good time explaining to Bianco why we can't sell in Stoneview anymore. Just because you got territorial over a bitch."

I'm pretty sure that's the most I've ever heard Sam talk since I've been made aware of his existence. I have to bite my tongue not to insult him for calling me a bitch – in his crisp British accent – because, technically, he's on my side right now. The side that doesn't want it all to explode.

The tension is such that I feel like Nathan is holding a tank of gas and Jake a match.

Nathan looks like he's thinking over what Sam just said. He won't retreat but I see in his eyes that he's trying to calm himself down. Bianco gave him a whole town to run. He also sent him straight to war with Volkov. He must trust him.

As Nathan's shoulders relax slightly, I actually think this is going to be over. But Jake consciously lights up the flame that will make everything explode when he drags his hand from my neck, down my back, along my hip, and grabs my ass tightly. Nathan's eyes don't leave his brother's hand and the eruption of fury in them makes me wish I hadn't ever met any of them. For a second, it makes me wish I didn't even exist.

"Let's make shit clear, *brother,*" Jake says, leaving me and taking the final step that separated them.

"Jake," I panic.

"Jamie's not your girl anymore." His hand lands on Nathan's shoulder in a grip so tight I'm surprised it doesn't show on either of their expressions.

Their gazes don't leave the other. "In fact," Jake drawls, "I don't think she ever was, you know?"

I know exactly where he is going, and I can't stop my body when I join Jake and put a hand on his arm. Nathan doesn't deserve me, but he doesn't deserve what Jake is about to say.

"Please don't," I try to stop him even though deep down I know there's no point.

"She was never your girl because every time you turned your back. Every time you dropped her at school. Every single time she wasn't with you. She was with me. She was with me at parties when you thought she was at home. She was in my room when you thought she was in her bed. Whatever you did to her, I was doing it better in our school bathroom, in classrooms, in my car…fuck the list is too long to waste my

252

breath on it. Just know you didn't count. You never did."

I can feel the satisfaction rolling off Jake's tongue. He needed his revenge like the air he breathes. He needed to use something against his brother and he purposely decided that it would be me.

The disappointment I feel is too deep to even understand it myself. I thought he was getting better. I thought he was letting go of his past and resentment but that never happened. I lied to myself because I wanted to make a good person out of him. It was pointless.

It was all trivial.

There's a long silence, Nathan looks at me as if seeking the truth in my eyes. I know he can see the flash of guilt just like I see the flash of pain in his. When he clicks that everything is true, and not just Jake trying to rile him up, he lets out a short chuckle.

"Huh." Is the only sound that comes out of him.

All the men around me are looking at me like I'm some kind of witch that just cursed all of them. Them, their family, and their next three generations.

"You're fucking dead, Jake," Nathan says in the lightest tone possible.

Those are the last words before his behavior shifts completely.

Next thing I know, his fist is crashing against Jake's temple, violently pushing him a few steps back. I can't help a shriek.

"Don't!" I scream but Jake is already walking back to Nathan.

I don't think, I just follow my body. I put my adrenaline-controlled self in between them, my back to Jake, and facing Nathan.

"Jamie, get out of the way," Jake growls.

"You heard him," Nathan confirms.

"Please, please stop. Nathan, leave it, I'm begging you." My voice is strangled by the sobs constricting my throat and pleading to be let out.

I can't let this happen. It's my fault. It's all my fault because I was too fucking stupid and selfish to make a choice.

I know Nathan is going to kill him if I get out of the way. I saw what he did to Dimitri for touching me.

A few people are looking at us from afar, not too sure if this is going to turn into a full-on fight. The music is too loud to confirm our words, they're too drunk to fully comprehend our situation. But I know.

I know if I step out of the way they won't stop until one of them isn't standing anymore. Roy and Carlo have stood up behind Nathan, and Sam is eyeing every single one of us as if he is calculating the chances of this going to shit. It's too late, Sam. This went to shit months ago when I made the biggest mistake of my life getting involved with the Whites.

"Get out of the way. It's your last warning." Nathan is looking right in my eyes, but I don't recognize him.

I used to drown myself in these eyes. Now they're burning with rage. He's insane, bestial, *possessed.*

I shake my head no at him. Desperate to protect Jake, myself, *him.*

I don't realize what's happening until it's too late.

Nathan grabs my jaw with one mighty hand. He's not hurting me, but I can't go anywhere. "Get out of the way or I swear I'll hurt you," he barks.

The last shreds of his control are slipping away, and I think he saved them for me. He could seriously hurt me. Instead, it takes him a total of two seconds to take a sidestep and push me hard enough to make me take a few steps back without shoving me. My heels make me slip on the tiles and my ass hits the floor.

I don't hear what Jake says in the seconds it takes me to grasp what just happened and when I look up, they're already beating each other up.

I hear Sam utter a 'bloody hell, Nate', and next thing I know two arms are helping me up. I end up face to face with a slightly alarmed Sam.

"Get Rose, hurry the fuck up." He turns around and tries to grab Nate but it's about as possible as catching plankton in a fisherman's net. He's too quick on his feet, jumping there and back, fighting like he is in a boxing ring.

I run back inside like my life depends on it. Mine might not be but Jake's surely is. Thankfully Rose is still in the Orangery, this time on the phone. She must see my face straight away because she straightens up and her hand holding the phone falls by her side.

"What's wrong?" she asks.

"J-jake and Nathan they're…" I pant.

She doesn't need any more explanation. In a split second she's sprinting outside, and I follow closely. "Should I call the cops?"

She turns to me suddenly and grabs my shoulders. "No. Never, you hear me? No matter what, you don't call the cops."

I nod quickly and she's back on her way.

A crowd has already formed around them, and Rose and I have to push our way through. When we get to the front, it's worse than I thought.

I feel like my worst nightmare is unfolding right in front of my eyes. Chris is in a heated argument with Roy and Carlo, about one second away from getting in a fistfight themselves. Some people are shouting encouragement, some shouting to stop but Jake and Nathan don't hear anyone. They haven't tired one bit and are relentlessly going at each other. Their skills make them look like professionals.

"Nate. Nate, stop," Rose says as she hurries towards the both of them. Of course, he doesn't hear her.

As soon as they both take a step back from the other, she gets in front of Nathan. "You tryna go to prison or something? Calm the fuck down."

"Why don't you tell *him* to stop, huh?" Nathan replies as he wipes a bloody lip.

"I will!" She runs her hand through her hair, pointing at Jake with the other to show she's about to go to him too.

The two brothers are using this break to catch their breaths, but they look far from over.

"No, you won't. You won't tell him to stop because you always side with him!" The jealousy burning in Nathan's eyes runs deep.

Is this as far as the competition goes between them? Putting Rose in the middle of their feud?

"Nate, don't be like this—"

"Leave, Ozy," he cuts her off.

A sudden commotion starts next to them as Roy, Chris and Carlo go at it themselves.

"Fucking...shit," she mumbles to herself like all of this is just a small inconvenience.

She doesn't seem too fazed. Like this has happened too many times before.

Nathan goes around her while she's distracted, and I suddenly feel a surge of uncontrollable panic. My whole body shakes and I have to hold my hair at my roots to try and stop it.

"Please, please, please stop," I whisper to myself perfectly knowing none of them can hear me.

Everything is too loud, I'm too hot, everyone is too close. Everything becomes blurry and all I can focus on is Rose's voice and her skinny form as she tries to calm down her brothers. Two arms suddenly wrap around my shoulders.

"Jamie, calm down it's going to be okay." Luke's voice barely pierces through the noise of the crowd and the ringing in my ears.

I can't take it anymore. My knees give up and I would have hit the floor had Luke not been holding me tight against him. He pulls me to the side and helps me sit down on the floor.

"You're fine, I promise. Just panicking–"

"Jake, shit, stop!" Rose's yelling cuts Luke short.

She's slowly losing her composure and it makes me panic even more. Has it not gone that far before?

"Stop it or I'm calling the police," Beth's whiny voice reaches my ears and Rose's dead stare turns to her.

She's pissed. Murderous even. She's on Beth in two strides and slaps her phone out of her hands and into the floor before stepping on it.

"No cops," she growls, her voice a warning to everyone.

She's back on Jake in a split second. "Jake...Jake people are gonna call the cops. You hear me? You need to stop this *now*."

He hears her but it clearly doesn't register. She pulls at her hair and turns to Sam. "Fucking *do* something," she shouts at him her arm pointing toward the two brutal fights going on next to her.

"You want me to do something? Fine!" he replies. "Remember you asked."

Sam is big, tall, and clearly strong. He could probably snap Rose in two with one hand. But I've come to learn being big doesn't necessarily mean powerful. Jake is bigger than Nathan but he's certainly not in a dominant position right now.

My attempt at a rational reflection is cut short when Sam gets in-between them. In one swift, violent punch he knocks Nathan out cold. He then proceeds to knee Jake in the guts, hard enough to make him fall to his knees.

I try to get up, I want to get to him, but my legs give up straight away.

"Why?" I look at Luke, dread filling my whole body.

"You're just having a small panic attack. Just breathe, Jamie."

"Jake," I cry. "It's all my fault."

"He's fine. I promise you he's been through worse." It should help but it doesn't.

Why? Why has he been through worse? Why is life so unjust?

Sam walks over to Chris, who was holding his stance so far against Roy and Carlo, and grabs his shoulder to turn him around.

"Enough! Enough you made your fucking point," Rose shouts at him.

"Ah, but I've been waiting so fucking long to knock out your overprotective rich mate."

"Enough, Sam," she seethes.

Chris's attention turns to Sam and Rose completely and in

that split second, Carlo's punch catches him in the jaw. He staggers back and falls to the floor. Roy is about to kick him when police sirens are heard outside. Everyone starts to panic, and the crowd of underage drinkers disperses.

Sam grabs Rose straight away, she fights him back but isn't left with much of a choice when he lifts her up and leaves with her.

Luke helps me up and I walk to Jake as he runs to Chris.

Nathan is slowly coming back to reality next to us.

"Are you okay?" I ask him.

He doesn't say anything for a few seconds. One of his eyebrows is bleeding and he spits blood on the floor.

"I'm fine."

Heavy boots can be overheard coming our way and I'm almost relieved that it means it's officially over, but Jake obviously thinks the opposite.

"Fuck," he whispers. "Fuck, fuck, *fuck.*"

As soon as the police appear in the backyard and a few officers call toward us it hits me: he's still carrying his gun.

CHAPTER 15

Miss Americana and The Heartbreak Prince – Taylor Swift

Jamie

Two hours. That's how long I've been waiting at the police station with Luke by my side. He finally got through to Emily, waking her from her drunken sleep, so she could bring me some clothes. She must be on her way now. We still haven't heard from Jake or Nathan, both in custody.

"How's Chris?" I ask. My voice is so quiet and raw from the lack of sleep and from screaming.

Luke sends him a quick text and the response comes straight away.

"Still at the ER, still waiting to be seen. Don't worry, he's tough. It wouldn't be the first time he loses a tooth in a fight. In fact, I'm pretty sure it's the same one every time."

I appreciate his attempt at a joke, but I can't get myself to even smile. Not when Jake is in there. Not after they found his gun on him.

"Look," he puts a hand on my knee in a friendly gesture.

"It's not my place to tell you all of Jake's life but I can sure as hell tell you about all the stupid shit we did together. He fires up at the slightest spark, so do I. We got in fights countless times over meaningless shit. Chris is always there to support our dumb choices even when we're in the wrong. The three of us have lost teeth, got concussed, and know that shitty cell they put you into to sober up like it's our vacation home. And don't get me started on the times we got Rose out of shit she put herself in. The number of times *we* waited for her to be let out. It's going to be fine, Jamie."

"Was he carrying a gun all those times?" My cold statement forces him to retreat as he runs his hand through his bright blond hair, over his face, and rubs his eyes.

"No. No, he didn't." He pauses while thinking of all the outcomes possible.

I'm guessing this is what he does because he looks like how I feel, and I've been running through every possibility on how this could end.

Most of them lead me to Jake being in juvie. How is that fair? How can he live a fair life when it started with his parents leaving him behind? When he grew up in the foster system. When he got taken in by organized crime and was forced to follow their lifestyle. When he got a chance at a better life only for his shitty past to catch up with him. None of this is fair. None of this should have happened, even less because of me.

"This is Stoneview. It's all about reputation. Everyone loves Jake. Mayor Simmons secretly wishes she could adopt him. And you know who loves him above all? Judge Joly. Emily's mom. You know her, I know her, Jake knows her. There is no way in hell Jake is going away for carrying a stupid gun."

I don't know if I agree but his words do give me a glimmer of hope.

The glass door to the police station opens and Rose enters. She's still wearing her long black silk dress from the ball. Only it's creased, her white sneakers are now dirty from the party and she's wearing a dark grey sweater on top of the dress. I don't even wonder who it belongs to, especially when Sam enters right after her.

"Fuck," Luke whispers. "Good thing Chris isn't here. See? It all works out," he jokes.

I wonder where he finds this optimism. I guess it's just who he is. When Rose and Sam reach us, he stays slightly behind her, not willing to participate in any conversation with us.

"None of them are out?" she asks, surprised.

She puts her purse on a seat next to Luke and puts her hands in the pocket of the sweater.

"Nope. It's only been like what–"

"Two hours and twenty minutes," I cut off Luke.

"We've spent entire nights in there," Luke insists, and I know he's trying to get Rose on board to reassure me.

Rose runs her hands through her hair and she and Sam share a look. She's worried. Rose White is concerned and there is nothing that scares me more.

"Yeah, but we were drunk or coked up. Neither of them is." Her naturally hoarse voice hits me. Her statement is like an ocean wave: You don't expect it to hit hard but the force always surprises you.

There's a long silence. Even Luke can't find anything to comfort us because she's right; Jake didn't have time to drink more at Cal's and he wasn't even tipsy in the car. Nathan was clearly sober.

"Rose," a voice calls out. We all turn to a young police officer. I've never seen him before. He never worked under my dad. He and Rose seem to know each other though.

"Hey, Craig," she says as she walks to him.

I'm the only one noticing Sam shifting from his phone to shooting daggers at Craig, but this is the least of my concerns right now.

It's hard to hear their conversation, Rose is leaning against the reception counter and exchanging whatever secrets she has with 'Craig'.

It becomes impossible to hear when the door opens again to Emily. She hurries to me and takes me in her arms straight away.

"Oh my God, I'm so sorry. I was so drunk I just took a taxi and crashed as soon as I got home. Are you okay?" She pulls away, holding me at arm's length, and checks me out from head to toe.

"I'm fine," I reply. "We're still waiting to hear anything."

I'm fine. What a lie. I'm so far from fine. I'm on a speedboat towards the end of the world and *fine* is the land getting further and further out of view, and Emily can see it clearly.

"Right. Here, I brought you some clothes, you should go get changed."

She's wearing leggings and a long sweater under her expensive coat and I hope she brought me leggings too because I feel awfully naked under this dress. Probably because I am. I grab the backpack and make my way to the bathroom.

When I come back in one of Emily's fluffy cashmere sweaters and her Lululemon leggings, Sam and Craig are in a heated conversation and Rose is next to them. Her eyes go from one to the other like she's following a tennis game, but her face has paled.

I only catch a glimpse of their conversation but I'm too tired to try and comprehend why Sam is fuming at him.

"I don't give a shit, Miller. Get him out of there."

I haven't often heard him speak but his accent somewhat makes everything he says harsher like you don't have a choice but to listen.

"I get what you're saying. But you can't give me what I need, the only way I can do that is by calling—"

"Find another way, you twat."

By the time I've reached my friends, Sam is talking in hush voices with Rose only. They seem to agree on something. He squeezes her shoulders reassuringly and drops a peck on her forehead as a goodbye before heading out. She walks back to all of us and crosses her arms across her chest.

"You guys should go," she says to Luke. "Chris is still at Silver Falls' ER. He's going to be there all night. You should stay with him."

I'm not sure if she's talking to the three of us or just Luke and Emily but she's crazy if she thinks I'll leave before Jake gets out.

"You're right. Come on, Em, I'll drop you home."

Luke gets up from his seat at the same time as Emily. She gives me a tight hug and promises to call tomorrow. Luke gives Rose a hug. "Call me when you hear anything."

An hour later, the clock keeps ticking and Rose and I are still sitting in our exact same seats. While I keep my eyes on the clock, she keeps fidgeting, squirming on her seat, her foot tapping the floor. Every time I glance at her, she's looking at the officer she called Craig and biting her thumb.

"What is happening? We've been waiting for hours," I finally say.

Rose doesn't reply. She keeps eyeing the only police officer at the counter. Further behind him, there are other officers on night duty.

"Rose," I push. "What's happening? What did you talk about with that officer?"

I know she's not one to share but this is a different situation. *Jake is going to jail.* That's all my brain says on repeat.

"Nothing," she mumbles, her foot still tapping.

Why does she have to be so secretive when people talk to her? Like she holds the world's biggest secrets.

"Do you know him? Can he help us?" I ask.

I hate when people make you beg for information. They're usually seeking attention, withholding information in the hope of themselves being the topic of the conversation and it usually turns out that their information is useless. Rose isn't like that though, she's *always* the center of attention. She just wants to be left alone. And I have a feeling the information she's withholding isn't exactly useless.

"Help us get Jake out of being caught with a gun? I don't think so."

I roll my eyes at her sarcasm.

"No. Help us know what's going on in there?"

"They're being questioned," she replies as if that was the most obvious thing.

It seems like there are only two kinds of conversations with Rose when you're not her inner circle. Either she's hitting on you or you're bothering her by addressing yourself to her.

We fall back into a heavy silence until I can't take the anxiety emanating from her anymore.

"Fuck, just tell me what you guys talked about," I whisper-shout.

"Shit, Goody, you just swore."

Really? That's the only thing she notices? I swear all the time in my head, I just try to refrain myself in public. My dad was always so adamant about it.

"Because I'm so anxious and your stress is making me even more anxious."

She stays silent for a few more seconds as if hesitating to tell me the truth.

"I don't think Jake's gonna get out. Nate will because no one is going to fucking sue him for beating the shit out of Jake. But gun possession, Jamie...They won't let him out until he's tried unless someone pays for his bail and I doubt anyone's going to do that."

"W-what does that mean? What about after he's tried?"

I already know the answer because I'm not stupid, but my brain refuses to accept the truth.

She looks at me with a hard face and takes her time to look around before her gaze falls back on mine again. When she finally says something. It's factual as if she's a lawyer going over a problem with her client. She's detached from what she tells me because her brain works faster than anyone else's.

The first thing I did when I became president of the student council was to check Rose's GPA. It's wrong but I'm a curious girl and I needed to know if she was that genius everyone believes she is. 4.8, that's how much of a genius she is. She doesn't even try. She didn't even *want* to take AP classes, the school insisted so they could bring up their average GPA.

For every minute she spends on her work, I have to spend an

hour, and right now, her brain has already worked everything out.

"You're a smart girl, Jamie. You know what happens. He's tried, goes to juvie and they spit him back into the system if he's not eighteen by the time he comes out."

I can't even take in the fact that Rose White complimented me because reality falls on me like a cold shower. My brain just won't process that this is a likely possibility. I know she's already thought of it, but I ask anyway.

"It doesn't happen every time. He could get off with a warning or some community service maybe?"

"Sure," she nods, and I can sense the lie.

She's hiding something from me. I mean, she always hides things but this one looks like something I should know.

"Oh my Gosh, he's got previous convictions, doesn't he? He's had warnings already."

"Not my place to talk about," she says in a voice that doesn't leave any place for debate.

"The Murrays, they can help. Can't they? They'll at least pay for bail," I try.

She scratches the back of her head then eyes at the police officer again. "Yeah...let's hope."

Why? Why just hope? They've been taking care of them for three years. Why wouldn't they pay bail? It's not like they don't have the money.

She tells me I'm smart but clearly not enough for her to share everything she knows or why she's cutting the conversation short. She knows there's no hope she just can't be bothered to discuss the details with me.

I want to ask more questions but she's not acknowledging me anymore. She's watching Craig picking up his cell to type in a number.

"Fucking asshole," she mutters as she gets up. "Craig, hold on!"

This time I don't want to wait for her to explain. I follow her to the counter because I know she's too focused on him to worry if I'm overhearing her or not.

"Wait, please wait," she says, not meaning that 'please' one bit but knowing men in power do love girls begging them to listen.

She tries to grab the phone from him, but he takes a step back.

"I'm still waiting for our foster parents to get back to me. Just wait. They'll have the bail money for sure, there's no need to call him."

Craig looks at her with a sorry face, he doesn't look so happy himself. He stops dialing and puts the phone down. "I'll wait another thirty minutes."

"Really?" Her tone turns manipulative as I can see that look in her eyes. The same she uses to get out of trouble at school or when she tries to get out of a red card during a lacrosse game. "It's three am. Do you really want to wake him up at this time? It's a forty-minute drive from D.C. You wake him up now, that's his whole night ruined–"

"Rose, I'm going to have to call him for Nathan anyway," he cuts her off.

Her jaw ticks and the dead stare she throws his way is anything but reassuring.

"As I said, thirty minutes," he concludes.

She throws her head back in a groan before walking back to her seat.

I observe officer Miller for a few more seconds. He's young,

young enough that my dad would have never met him. His bushy black single brow raises in question as he looks at me. The uniform doesn't suit him, there's something not reassuring about him although he seemed to retreat when Samuel was talking to him. I turn around and walk back to my seat.

"What was that about?" I ask as soon as I've settled next to Rose again.

"Huh?" she looks at me like she completely forgot I was even in the room.

"You and this...this officer. Craig. Rose, give me something. What is all of this about?"

Her eyes lock with mine and the plethora of emotions is almost making me dizzy. There is a storm raging in her deep blue eyes. A fight of titans between fear and pride, confidence and uncertainty. She wants to win a battle she's doomed to lose and she's fighting herself to not ask for help. Why would she not? Is the Whites' pride really that damn stubborn?

"Why didn't you want to call the cops, Rose?"

For a second, I truly believe she's going to tell me. Here and now, she's going to open up to me so I can help, so we can sort this out together. So we can stay side by side, sharing our mutual love for Jake.

But she doesn't.

"I need a fucking smoke," she drops.

Of course she doesn't. Because why would she open up to her twin's brand-new girlfriend that insisted on hiding their relationship until tonight when she never even opened up to Rachel, whom she's presumably in love with.

She grabs a pack of cigarettes out of her purse, throws the bag back on her seat, and storms out of the station, her silk

269

dress wrapping around her long legs.

I look around in a sigh. My body is exhausted, but my mind is working overtime. What if Jake goes to juvie? His whole future will be compromised. He's smart enough to get into an Ivy League college, he codes better than a professional. The potential he has at finally getting the life he deserves could be destroyed by a stupid fight. Over what? Pride? Resentment for his brother? *Me?* I would never forgive myself. Why did I engage with Nathan? Why didn't I keep walking? I should have just kept walking.

Another half-hour of Rose fidgeting and checking her phone next to me, of me asking officer Craig Miller if there is any news and being told the same response: they're being interrogated. Another half-hour. 4 am. Both I and Rose have sunk deep into our seats. Craig looks at the time, shakes his head, and walks over to us. Well, to Rose exactly.

"Anything?" he asks.

"Yes, Craig, I got ahold of them an hour ago, but I just love spending my nights here, so I didn't say anything."

He shakes his head again. His hands are in his uniform pants, but I can still make out that he's moving his fingers in an anxious gesture.

"I waited a whole hour. I'm calling." He sounds like he would rather jump from the silver falls than make this call.

"Sam is right, you're so fucking weak," she seethes.

He doesn't say anything and just goes back behind his counter as Rose tries her best to kill him with her look. She doesn't insist though, resolved.

"Who is he calling?" I try again. Maybe after the tenth time she'll give in.

"No one," she growls.

"Would they be able to help?"

She watches Craig pick up his phone and disappear to the back where we can't see him anymore. She lets out a loud sarcastic cackle as she gets up from her seat.

"Yeah actually. They'll help." She grabs her pack of cigarettes again but this time her hands are shaking as she pulls out a cigarette and puts it in her mouth. She throws the empty pack on the seat. "No need for bail, no trial. The whole thing will just disappear," she continues as she grabs her lighter. "Poof, like that." She waves her hands in the air to imitate something disappearing by magic and a second later she's out again, this time slamming the door hard enough to make me jump in my seat.

I can't figure out if she was being sarcastic or not. Surely that's impossible. To make it all go away? Yet, I can't help but hope it's true.

When she comes back in, the anger seems to have passed. She's resigned but has a somber look on her face.

"How long ago did he make that call?" she asks me.

I check my watch for the millionth time tonight and look back up.

"About twenty minutes."

"You should go." I'm not quite sure I heard her right because surely, she can't be telling me to leave.

"What?" I have to ask.

She can't be serious. Does she not realize that I would wait a whole week if that's what it took to see Jake? I'd stop eating and drinking, I'd sleep on the floor of this station. I'd throw myself in this interrogation room if it meant he would be out.

"Jake will be fine. But you should really go, Jamie."

"I'm not going anywhere. If-*when* he gets out, I want to be here."

She thinks for a second and seems to think it's not worth the fight. "Whatever," she mutters as she sits back down, her spine straighter this time.

She's not even glancing at Craig anymore. She's just looking at her hands, pressing them together on her knees as if trying to stop them from trembling.

Every now and then she takes deep shaky breaths and the anxiety pouring out of her is telling me nothing good is about to come.

"How long now?" she asks in a quiet, quivering voice that's making everything in me tighten in fear.

"Fo-forty minutes or so," I stutter. I'm scared, I'm genuinely scared of what's about to happen because there is nothing but fright coming from her behavior.

"Right," she swallows thickly. "Right. Okay." She lets out a long breath as if trying to control her fear but it's not working. None of what she's doing is working. "You got a...um...a hair tie or something?" she asks, struggling to focus on her words.

I frown but quickly give her the hair tie around my wrist.

This is strange. Not the strangest thing that's happened tonight but I couldn't even count the times Rose and I fought on the field because she wouldn't tie her hair up when she played or trained. '*I fucking hate ponytails, don't make me punch you, Goody.*', '*If my hair is up my fan club will lose their shit*'. I can't count the excuses.

I have never seen her with her hair up. Even after all the times I've stayed over at her house.

Rose White.

She doesn't try to, but she's always perfect. Snap any

272

moment of her day and it could be the cover of a magazine, and her hair is part of that. Her long, thick, and curvy inky hair are part of who she is.

"Th-thanks," she mumbles as she grabs the hair tie from me. She scratches her throat, almost like she's embarrassed that I caught her stuttering on a word.

"Rose?" I make an attempt to check on her even if it might backfire. "Are you okay?"

She chuckles quietly and smiles at me. "'Course. I'm fine."

Her smile almost seems real, but I know it isn't. It isn't because she and Jake could be the same person. They have the same dimples on their cheeks. When they both show, in the middle of their cheeks, their smile is genuine. When there's only one, low, at the corner of their mouths, it's the fake bullshit they put on for everyone who doesn't know them.

Do I insist? Do I leave it? She doesn't owe me any explanations. She starts pulling all her hair up and ties it in a high ponytail. It's long and thick, like mine. She looks the same... but different. Everything right now about her is different. I see Rose and hear Rose but it's like another girl is moving her body and saying her words.

"Rose, you're being...weird?" Why am I asking her as if she would reply '*Yes Jamie, dead on. I am not acting like myself at all.*'

I don't have time to think of it anymore. The door to the station opens and two men in black suits come in. They look like some sort of celebrity bodyguard, with their black ties and serious faces.

One of them steps sideways from the door and the other holds it open for a third man coming in. He's wearing a grey fitted suit on an average body. Not too tall but not small, not big but just fit. He doesn't look old enough to be my dad but much older than me still. His skin is tanned like Rose and Jake. That golden Mediterranean tan. His hair is the same as them as well, jet black, only his are peppered with bits of grey hair just above the ears.

His eyes land on us and a satisfied smirk forms on his face. I'm the only one who sees it because Rose is still facing me. Her eyes squeeze shut at the sound of the door closing. Everything is complete silence except for his leather expensive-looking shoes now hitting the floor as he makes his way toward us. She reopens her eyes and is looking directly at me.

"Jamie," she whispers so quietly I'm not even sure I heard her. "Do me a favor. When Jake and Nate get out. Tell them I'm in Washington D.C. You got it?"

"Wh—"

"Keep that for me," she cuts me off as she hands me her phone.

She gives me a sad smile and for the first time ever it looks like the most honest smile in the world. There's no fake happiness in it, no fake innocence, no manipulation just... the truth.

A shape appears right behind Rose and I look up as the man in grey and one of the guards settle right behind her. The other one is still standing by the door, keeping an eye on the outside.

She slowly gets up, plasters a horrific artificial bright smile on her face, and turns around.

"Rose," the man says in a relieved sigh. "My beautiful flower."

He puts a hand on her waist and the other grabs the back of

her head, right above her neck, as he brings her into a hug, pushing her head against his shoulder. Her arms, however, stay straight by her side.

"*Mi sei mancato tanto.* So so much." His hand on the back of her head tightens and my eyes fall on a mark on her neck.

In thick letters, 'M.B.' are scarred just below her hairline, like it's been burnt into her skin. My whole body shivers and I can feel my brows furrowing as things start to add up in my head.

M. B.

M. B.

Like Mateo Bianco.

The realization creeps up on me and it takes me three attempts to swallow the knot in my throat.

"Me too," she replies when he lets her go. "Can we," she scratches her throat, "can we just get this over with? I've been here for hours, I'm exhausted."

"Of course, of course," he says waving a hand in the air. "We need to get you to bed."

The way he says this sends a chill down my spine. His voice is warm but there's an underlying tone hinting that it's all just fake. A tone saying the warmth in his voice instantly disappears if things don't go his way.

He didn't even notice me. I watch as they both walk to the counter, a hand still on the small of her back. Her posture is so stiff I'm surprised she hasn't snapped in two already. I can't take my eyes off that scar. Who would do that? Just *brand* someone like that? And why her? I know for certain that Jake's only mark on his skin is that tattoo he shares with Sam, Nathan, and Rose.

Talking about that stupid gang tattoo. The man I'm assuming is Mateo unconsciously plays with strands of Rose's ponytail as he signs some paperwork. On his right hand is that exact X tattoo they all have. That makes things pretty clear now.

He talks to Craig, who's trying to make himself small, and finally, he gestures at the man in a suit next to him. The man grabs something from the inside pocket of his jacket and throws a wad of bills on the counter.

All in all, it must have lasted five minutes. The longest minutes of my life. The five minutes that felt like hours as I slowly realized who the man was, as I watched his hands in Rose's hair and on her back, as I realized she was going to leave with him. Certainly not by choice, but she was leaving with him.

Five minutes where I re-ran the whole night in my head: her fear of someone calling the cops, her begging Craig not to call '*him*', her anger, her resignation, her terror. Five minutes where I recall Jake telling me how horrible it had been at Bianco's without ever getting into it. Five minutes of debating myself horribly: Do I do something? Say something? Will she let me? Will she be mad?

Five minutes where I remembered how this whole situation started and came to the same awful conclusion: it's my fault.

When they both turn around, he finally notices me. Grey, steel eyes run through my whole body, sending chills of disgust all over my skin. He locks his gaze with mine and I raise my chin, doing my best to throw him my darkest look. Only, I know that for someone my size and appearance, that does absolutely nothing.

He finally lets go of Rose and walks toward me. As he approaches, I stand up and cross my arms over my chest, grateful for the heels I'm still wearing that give me extra height. Rose's eyes widen behind Bianco and she shakes her head 'no' at me. As if warning me to not piss him off. Warning me to not go against him.

How? How can she be like this and just let this slide? She hurries to follow him and stands beside him.

"Now, who might be this little thing?" he asks.

Rose's face turns to stone. "I don't know, some bitch Jake is fucking at the moment," she says. "I can't remember her name."

My heart drops in my stomach as Bianco laughs at her cruel words.

What is she doing?

"Right. If that's it, then let's go."

Rose turns to him completely. "Are we not waiting for them? They'll be out in no time now, surely."

I can see she already knows the answer before she asks but she's throwing her last hopes into this. "*Per favore Mateo, cinque minuti.*"

Her Italian sounds so real my mouth drops open in shock. For a second I'm wondering if she's even American, if she was born in Italy maybe, before I remember that we don't know. Not even her.

The man that I now know for sure is Bianco simply smiles at her, his voice silky smooth. "Don't be ridiculous. They managed to get themselves in this mess on their own. They can find their way home on their own too."

"*Pero–*"

"Speaking Italian to please me won't bring out my good side, Rose," he grounds. "I know your little manipulative methods by now."

And there it is, the real voice. The coldness that just seeped from his mouth as he scolded her like a disobedient girl keeps both of us quiet.

"Now," he says in a mellow tone again. "I think I've been nice enough to get them out of trouble. Don't you think?"

She nods but I can see how tensed her jaw is, how her muscles tighten below her ears.

"Great. So, let's go then."

He smiles a goodbye at me and puts a hand on her neck, but she took her first step towards the door before he even touched her skin.

She's leaving. She's leaving with him like it was the plan all along. She didn't ask him, he didn't tell her to, she just knows. She said to not get the cops involved because she knew. She knew the minute we called them, one of the cops on Bianco's payroll would get him involved.

She walks out the door without even as much as a glance back and I fear for her life.

CHAPTER 16

Pray – jxdn

Jake

I squint my eyes at the two zipper bags in front of me struggling to find the one with *Jacob White* written on it in thick marker. I had to take my contacts out an hour ago when I couldn't hold the burn anymore. It smells like mold and piss in here. My head is pounding and the harsh white light from the police station isn't helping. Nothing ever fucking happens in Stoneview and they still manage to have a dirty, stinking station.

Nate grabs the other bag, his knuckles are colored with dried blood. His or mine, I don't even fucking know anymore.

The lady officer before us eyes at the last name on our bags, then us.

"Oh, boys," she smiles cheekily. "Brothers' quarrel?"

Neither of us acknowledges her as we grab our different items. My phone, watch, and wallet take me about three seconds to gather and I'm already on my way to the door,

Nate close behind, when the police officer calls again.

"Trust me, boys, she ain't worth it."

I don't even know if the grunt I hear is from me or him, I just keep going. I don't hold the door for him and as soon as I'm in the waiting room my eyes search for my sister, but she isn't there.

In fact, no one is here except a small-shaped form asleep on a seat. One that I'd recognize anywhere even without my glasses on. She waited for me. For hours. I hurry to the seat where she's sleeping and put a hand on her shoulder as I squat in front of her.

"Jamie, baby, wake up," I whisper.

She wakes with a start and looks around, confused. Her eyes stop on Nate, somewhere behind me, and my heart freezes. What if she didn't wait for me? What if she waited for *him*?

All those hours in the interrogation room, I didn't feel one hint of remorse. Nate had it coming. After everything he did, he deserved every single punch to his perfect face. I wish I could say I was so mad because of the years of bullying or because he got us in a gang. But I know I'd be lying to myself. The main reason I wanted to beat the shit out of him is sitting right in front of me and I just have to pray I didn't make the worst mistake of my life tonight, getting in a fight over her.

I used to get in stupid fights with weak assholes over Camila. She was the queen of making me jealous with other guys just for me to show I cared for her. She was thrilled when I would let my rage out on a poor bastard. But I didn't care for her, I was possessive because I've always been, it had nothing to do with Camila. Now, it has everything to do with Jamie.

"Oh my Gosh, are you okay?" She sits up straight and takes my head in her tiny hands, making me wince when her thumbs graze the countless bruises and cuts. "Jake," her voice tightens like she's about to burst out crying. "I was so worried about you." Her head drops on my shoulder. "I'm sorry. I'm so so sorry."

As soon as her warmth touches my skin, I know she's here for me. She sobs on my shoulder and I hold her tight enough that my bruised ribs beg at me to let her go but I can't. I can't let her go. Not now. Not ever.

"None of this is your fault," I reassure her.

How could it be her fault? Nate and I simply decided to add another element to our ongoing feud. I get up and help her up in the process.

"Where's Ozy?" Nate's cold voice makes me want to turn around and bust open his lip all over again, but Jamie's frightened eyes chill me.

"Jamie? What happened?" I ask, not even sure I want to know.

Something's wrong, I can see something's wrong. I can *feel* something is wrong from my heart beating against my chest hard enough to jump out. It's telling me there's a reason my sister isn't here. She would never leave me here on my own.

Jamie grabs something on her seat and turns around holding Ozy's phone.

"She said to keep this and tell you she was in D.C.," she tells me as my worst fear falls down on me.

I don't realize Nate is coming toward us until both his hands land on Jamie's narrow shoulders.

"'Me," he almost shakes her. "Was Bianco here? Was he here?"

I will my body to push him away from her, but my head is already running the worst scenarios on repeat. Everything

281

we've been avoiding, praying to escape forever, it's all here. One night, one mistake and it all came back.

The cold sweat suddenly covering my body makes me shiver. Was Bianco here? He must have been, otherwise, why would we be out?

"I–" she hesitates, her eyes darting to mine.

Nate is leaning towards her face, his eyes full of love for Jamie but his face filled with concern for our sister. He tries to soften his movements and his words but he's struggling because he's scared. He fucked up and he's worried about what Bianco's going to do for his slip up, not that he would ever admit it.

"This is very important, 'Me, we need to know," he insists.

My brain finally clicks. "She doesn't know what he looks like, asshole. Get off her," I push him away, ready to beat him up all over again. Adrenaline is controlling my mind and my body, so is panic.

"I think he was here," Jamie whispers to me like she doesn't really believe it herself.

As fucked up as it is, it means something to me that she says it to *me*. That she talks to me and not him.

"Are you sure?" I double-check, putting a hand on her cheek to selfishly keep her attention on me and block her view of Nate.

She nods. "With two other men, like...like guards or something. He gave a wad of cash to officer Miller and Rose left with him." She scratches her throat before saying something we both already know. "I think she was scared."

She *was* scared. He's her worst nightmare. He's everyone's worst nightmare. We've spent the last three years trying to stay off his radar and all it took was a stupid fucking fight with Nate.

Rose probably hates me right now. All the times we ended up at this police station before, knowing we took a risk of needing him to bail us out. We promised each other we would never do something bad enough to have anyone on his payroll call him on us. I broke that promise. Gun possession. After Jamie warned me I was putting us in danger by carrying. Maybe I should have just listened to her.

I should have just walked away. I should have just grabbed Jamie's hand and walked the fuck away. But I had to prove to him I was better, that she chose me. For someone addicted to control, the situation is well fucked and truly out of my hands.

Nate is already on his way to the officer at the counter.

"You called him?" I hear him say calmly.

I can imagine the look on the guy's face is probably giving Nate even more confidence. That officer knows the calmer Nate is, the more you should fear for your life. The hold he has on his anger puts my control to shame. It makes me truly jealous to know he has the kind of control over himself I'll never have. When he explodes though...apocalypse.

"Mr. White, I had to get you out."

I can't help but snort at hearing him call my brother Mr. White. What a fucking joke.

"Where's Chris?" I ask Jamie.

"Last time I checked he was at the ER with Luke."

I walk to Nate and settle next to him. "What the fuck are you doing talking to this guy? Ozy is with Bianco, and it's your fault," I seethe.

"My fault," he laughs sarcastically. "I'm not the one who stole my brother's girl. I was bound to split your head open with my fists at some point." His voice is low when he finishes his sentence, rage boiling low in his chest.

"I'm not the one who used his girl to spy on his siblings," I retort, feeling Jamie shift behind me.

Two officers notice our argument renewing.

"All of you, get out of here before the situation gets worse for you," one of them yells. Jamie takes hold of my hand, squeezing tight enough to let me know she's scared.

She wants to leave. Just like she wanted to leave Cal's house. I didn't listen then, and this is where it got me. I need to listen now. I should know by now that following Jamie's instinct only brings me good, so I head toward the door with her.

I look back at Nate again, he's standing still in front of the reception. "You," he points at the officer Jamie called Miller, "you're coming with me."

From here and without my glasses, they're both blurry shapes but I can imagine the look on my brother's face clearly. Jamie must see me squint my eyes and she quickly hands me the glasses I had put in her bag. It warms my heart to be with someone thoughtful and observant like her. Fuck, it's nice to see properly again.

"Thanks," I whisper to her as Miller walks around the counter to join my brother.

You'd think a police officer wouldn't listen to a twenty-one-year-old who just got released from custody. I guess that would be true if that cop had an ounce of courage in his body and he wasn't facing the new gang boss in town that has him by the balls.

"Let's go," I say, squeezing Jamie's hand.

I grab her golden purse and start walking, opening the door out of the station for her.

It's only once outside that I realize I don't have a ride or a working phone.

"My phone is dead, you?"

She only shakes her head no and hands me Rose's phone. Fear curls around my stomach and clutches too hard for me to ignore. I need to know she's okay. I need to know he's not hurting her. She's not okay though. The invisible bond we share between twins always tells me when she's not fine.

I unlock her phone quickly, typing the password she's convinced I don't know, and look at her recent calls. Chris is getting his tooth fixed. Luke is with him. Either way, I wouldn't want any of them to come with me to Bianco's house. I can't put them at risk.

There's only one person I know that will be here in a split second without hesitation and as I'm about to tap his number on the screen, his car pulls up in front of me. At the same second, Nate settles behind me, his hand on the shaking shoulder of the officer that called Bianco.

"I-I only did what you had told me, Mr. White," his shaking voice forces me to roll my eyes. What a fucking coward. "You said to always get you out."

Nate ignores him completely and walks to Jamie. I can't help sliding an arm around her shoulders.

"You need to go home. Can anyone pick you up?" he asks her.

Behind Nate, Sam has gotten out of his car and lights up a cigarette as he lays back on the driver's door.

"We'll drive her home," I reply before she can say anything.

Nate barely looks at me but gives Jamie a single nod.

"Where are you going?" she questions me.

Nate is already talking to Sam and the latter is looking right into the cop's eyes, a wicked grin slowly forming on his lips.

285

The fuckers are out for blood but they're only wasting time.

"You're not going to D.C., are you?" she insists.

How can I tell her no? Of course we are.

Rose is only surrounded by people who love and adore her. Some of them are even obsessed with her but out of all of them, only three would kill for her and that's us. As much as I want to keep Jamie close to me right now, I have to get my sister back from Bianco and it's too dangerous for her to come with us. Even Nate knows that.

"I am," I reply. "I have to."

What else can I say? 'Sorry to leave you after you waited all night for me, but I need to make sure my sister doesn't get molested by the guy who runs the gang I grew up in.' I shiver at the thought.

I try to be strong, I really do. But I can be the strongest man on earth, Nate and Sam can be the toughest, but in the end, your weaknesses always lay in the ones we love.

Thankfully Jamie doesn't ask for an explanation. If it's because she saw Bianco, if it's because she saw the fear in Rose when he showed up, then she can only understand.

"Please, be careful." That's the only thing she says. Her voice is a mix of pleading and understanding.

She doesn't say anything when I settle her in Sam's white SUV that he should have never been able to afford. She keeps her eyes fixed on the headrest in front of her when Sam knocks out that cop and we both put him in the trunk of his car. This is when I understand that Nate has a bigger hold on this city than I thought. He's not worried the slightest to kidnap a cop in the parking lot of a police station. He thinks he's invincible, like always.

Jamie still doesn't talk when I settle next to her and Sam

starts driving to her house or when that cop wakes up and starts screaming in the trunk of the car.

She lets me hold her hand when Nate calmly pulls out a gun from the glove compartment, Sam stops the car, and my brother opens the trunk to get Miller to keep quiet by knocking him out with the gun handle. I've seen these kinds of things countless times during my childhood, and it doesn't affect me anymore, not like it does to her right now. Her body is with me, but I think her mind has escaped. I think she doesn't want to be here with us because it's gone too far for her.

I leave her be, I stay quiet beside her, squeezing her hand to show that I'm here and she's safe but inside me, there's havoc. Is my life really going back to this? Three years of peace, that's all I got. All I was allowed.

I wouldn't be surprised if that was their plan, if they knew they were gonna get me and Ozy back all along. Mateo and Nate were counting the days until they were going to take over Stoneview and have us back on their side. Nate played dead for three years, getting his perfect plan ready.

My brother sits back in the car and turns to Sam. "Drop her home. Then I need to fix this shit with Mateo."

I hit my head against the headrest, praying that tonight can be it. I can drive to D.C., get Ozy, and go back to my normal life in Stoneview.

Who the fuck are you kidding?

Life won't go back to normal. The clock started ticking as soon as Sam showed up at our school and we had already lost when Nate magically reappeared. He might have come back from the dead, but he doomed us all when he came to get us.

I can drive to D.C. all I want, I can bring Ozy back, it won't stop Mateo. He knows where we are, and I've given him a chance to waltz back into our lives with a big smile on his face.

When we park at Jamie's, I plan to walk her to her front door. I need to make sure she's safe and locks herself in. It's not like she has the kind of typical Stoneview driveways that take you up to the front door. We have to park on the street because her house is a cottage up a flight of stairs. Now that Mateo's found us, I need to be extra careful with everyone I love.

I put one foot on the ground and Nate's voice cuts through the heavy silence.

"I don't have time for your teenage bullshit, Jake. You leave this car, you stay here."

I grind my teeth, my jaw already killing me and my whole body tense. I'm about to snap back but Jamie's hand comes to rest on my shoulder.

"It's fine. I'm fine, honestly. You go."

Before she opens the door, she grabs my face with both hands and puts her soft lips on mine. She kisses me long and deep and my heart swells with pride and love. I don't need to prove anything to Nate, she's doing all the work herself, and fuck if I don't fall deeper for her after this.

"Please be safe," she whispers in my ear before heading out.

Jamie has flaws, she's too shy sometimes, not very social, and stubbornly curious, but when it comes to her qualities, they shine over everything like a thousand stars. Right now, the fact that she's one of the bravest people I know and trusts me – even though there's so much we need to talk about – is reassuring me that I can go see Bianco without worrying about her.

Nate watches her walk to her house and as soon as she closes her front door behind her, he nods to his best friend. It kills me how much he cares for her. Sam abuses the gas pedal out of town and about twenty minutes later he stops at the edge of a forest.

"What the fuck are you doing?" I scold him.

He ignores me, being the usual quiet asshole, and gets out before leaning back on the car and lighting up a cigarette.

It's like he loves being a cliché of himself. The typical dark, brooding gangster. Always silent, sporting his tattoos like medals, proof of a tough life. Never seen anywhere without his black jeans and a tight black tee, tight enough to show that one of his punches knocks you out cold.

He keeps to himself but, really, he loves having to prove himself, to have an occasion to get in a fight and demonstrate he shouldn't have been provoked. He won't do anything without reason but when he does, he revels in it. Like stopping a fight between me and Nate. He wouldn't do it until Ozy begged him to but fuck if he wasn't delighted to put us both down in front of her. A fucking hero in her eyes.

Nate finishes typing something on his phone and opens his own door to come out of the car too. I follow, fuming, to see my brother is opening the trunk to let the half-conscious cop out of the car.

"Are you for fucking real?" I seethe as he drags Miller out and a few steps into the forest. "You just said we have no time to waste."

This fucker has always had every priority wrong. He's all about imposing fear and dominance, never about doing the right thing. He would rather prove this guy he should have never defied him than go get his sister out of trouble. Even when it has anything to do with caring for one of us, he'll make sure he goes about a psychotic way to do it.

Miller slowly comes back to reality as he watches Nate looming over him with his gun. Sam is still smoking his cigarette against the car and I slam the door before joining my brother.

"Nate, we have more pressing concerns if you don't fucking mind."

His face is bruised up from our fight and he hasn't had a chance to clean his cut lip. Just like I haven't had a chance to wipe my cheek from all the blood that splashed out when he got me right in the eyebrow. This one will leave a scar, for sure. It took hours to stop bleeding even with the tissues one of the officers gave me at the station. I might need a stitch but don't have the time nor do I care right now.

My brother smiles wickedly at the cop and tuts at him when he whimpers and tries to crawl away.

"If you try to run away, I'm going to kill you very slowly, Miller," he taunts.

I can't fucking watch this. This is exactly why I don't want to be part of this life. I don't have the guts it takes. I don't have Sam's composure or Nate's pleasure for torture. I don't want money and domination.

I want to go to college and have a normal life that I can control. I've had my share of fun and fucked up situations. Now I want nothing or no one else but Jamie. Go to college with her, settle down together. Far, far from Bianco and my brother. But that's not about to happen, is it? I'm a lightyear away from my dreams. I haven't been given this chance.

At birth, you either get the lucky side – you get ups and downs, but overall life isn't too bad – or you get the shit side.

Downs only. The few ups only give you false hope. I'm far deep into the shit side and the older I get, the more I realize there is no bridge between the two opposite sides.

I try to look away, but Nate's voice keeps bringing me back to the scene in front of me.

"You know what you did wrong here, my friend?" my brother asks like a teacher scolding his elementary student.

"I thought I was doing th-the right thing, sir. You said to get you out if you were ever in custody. I did...I did."

"Not by calling Bianco, you fucking idiot." I can hear the way he rolls his eyes from his tone. Like I or Rose would, thinking 'I'm surrounded by idiots.'

"Please don't kill me, Mr. White. I'll make it right. I will... I-I-"

"What you did wrong," Nate cuts him off, sick of the whining, "is that my sister begged you not to call Bianco and you decided her opinion wasn't worth listening to, didn't you?"

Nate has no proof but we both know this is what happened and for that reason, Nate wants to punish him. This is how different we are. I just want to get to my sister, he wants revenge. Always revenge on his mind. Don't get mad, get even.

"She's a White. That makes her more important than you or any of your pig friends. You work for *me* first, Bianco second. Do you get that? She gives you an order, you listen. She asks you not to call Bianco? You don't. Fuck, if she asks you to crawl on the floor, I want you on all fours licking it."

Nate squats down and puts his gun to the cop's head. He's gone into his rant. He's made himself angrier than he initially was, and he could snap any second from now. He starts talking through gritted teeth as if barely containing his rage anymore. He wants to pull the trigger so bad.

"Do. You. *Understand?*"

"Yes, Sir, yes! Please, p-p-please don't kill me."

I glance at Sam, he's stopped smoking and is just watching the scene, his arms crossed over his chest, casually. The calmness on his face brings a chill down my spine. Does this guy even feel anything? I wonder what he looks like in Ozy's eyes because he looks like a fucking sociopath in mine. For as long as I can remember, I've never seen him laugh.

The cries of mercy from Miller are starting to irritate me and I almost *want* Nate to shoot him already. Cut this short, I need to see my twin. Nate's words have made me angrier at this cop. I want to take out my rage on him too. Had he listened to Rose, I wouldn't be wondering if she's still alive or not. I know she's alive, Mateo would never kill her, I mean alive on the inside. Our ex foster parent has always made a point to kill the flame that burns so bright in her.

Nate straightens back up. "I'm gonna let you live, Miller." His voice is cold enough to freeze fire. "Because I need someone to tell everyone what happens when you put my little sister in danger. Or any member of my family for that matter. Don't. Piss. Me. *Off.*" As he says the last word, he shoots Miller in the calf.

The sound makes me jump. I didn't expect it and this kind of sound is not exactly part of my daily life anymore. The cop's strident scream pierces my ears and I look at Nate deadpan.

"You just said you wouldn't kill him."

He looks down at the mess of a guy crying on the floor. "Stoneview is about four miles that way," he points somewhere behind the trees. "You should hurry before you bleed out."

Miller struggles to get back up but manages and stumbles out of the way, hopping on one leg.

Once settled back in the car, I look at Nate through the rearview mirror.

"No time to walk Jamie home but enough time to shoot a cop to teach him a lesson, huh?" I point out.

He smiles at me with that wicked grin that shows he perfectly knows what he's doing.

"Maybe I had a problem with you walking my girl home." I see him shrug and I'm about ready to fuck him up all over again.

"Shut the fuck u−" I'm cut off when Sam accelerates suddenly, my back hitting the seat, then speeds up on the highway. His way of telling us to quiet down.

The sun is starting to rise by the time we get to the private drive of Bianco's house. A horrible feeling settles in my stomach as soon as we stop by the gate. I know exactly what stands after the long road that leads to him. A gigantic Mediterranean-style house that doesn't fit with the American architecture of this elite area of Washington.

A house that screams 'Look at me, I'm invincible!' to the cops and all his enemies. A house where it's difficult to pass security to get in and impossible to get out. A house I moved into when I was just an eight-year-old boy. When I had no idea what true monstrosities life could throw at you. This is where Nate lost his soul, this is where Rose suffered silently for five years. This is where my life was dictated, where I bled and cried, forced to do unthinkable things. Things I will never forgive myself for – where the beast inside me was born. The one that protects me from being hurt again.

I feel sick to my stomach, but I don't let anything show. Every single wall that the Murrays tried to break through, that my friends sometimes took down, that Jamie somehow absolutely destroyed, quickly come back up. Brick by cemented brick.

We're stopped at the gates by two guards armed to the teeth but as soon as Sam rolls down his window they step back and the gates open. As soon as he's parked, Sam holds his hand out behind him, toward me while Nate gets out of the car.

"It's dead," I simply say.

"You know the rules, mate. You can stay in the car if you want."

You can go fuck yourself, *mate.* His British accent makes me want to stab him in the throat every time he opens his mouth. It's a good thing he never talks.

Bianco and his stupid fucking no-phone rule. I put my iPhone and Rose's in Sam's hand. Every second that passes, I feel sicker. My heart gets heavier, and I have to dig out my old courage to open the door and get out.

The yellow villa stands tall, and I remember the number of times I wondered if I could hang myself with the ivy that hangs over the walls. We walk around the car and toward the front door. Guards nod at Nate and Sam but clearly don't recognize me.

I do. I recognize every single one of them that tried to stop me and my sister from leaving when we were just desperate kids that didn't want to be in pain anymore. Some are older, some are new, but I know exactly which ones are at the top of my list of people I wish I could kill.

Before Nate passes the front door, he turns to me and whispers in a warning, "Keep your pretty boy mouth shut and let me do the talking."

I don't bother replying. I don't want to talk to Bianco. I don't want to face him. Does that make me a coward? I don't give a shit. I just want to get my sister and leave.

I remember the first time Ozy and I walked through these doors. We looked at the twenty-five-foot-ceiling main entrance with big eyes and mouths hanging open. It was impossible to separate us back then, always holding hands, always reacting to everything the same way. My sister has always been boy-ish and before height and muscles separated us, we were just two little kids that looked exactly the same. People always thought we were identical twins, that's how similar we were. We were gobsmacked by the long gallery decorated with Italian paintings and marble floors. I'm not impressed now.

I started hating the floor the first time Bianco smashed my head against the marble. I couldn't look at the golden china vases when Nate threw one at Rose. His excuse was always the same: 'He hates it when there's a fuck up on her stupid, perfect face.'

Is it normal that it took me so long to get it? Was I too young? Too naïve? Too stupid? Maybe I just refused to understand. Nate believes he was doing the right thing, that's why he never felt bad about beating her up. That's why he feels so betrayed that she tried to get rid of him. As I said, his priorities were always fucked up.

If he really wanted to save her, he would have left with us or at least helped us leave. But he didn't, he helped Bianco keep us here for their own selfish benefits and he manages to sleep at night by telling himself he was saving his sister from being raped because he hit her every time we left the house. Fuck knows how Ozy's face stayed so perfect after the beatings she took.

We cross the gallery and head straight for the dining room. None of the rooms here actually give in to the front of the house. It's too risky, Bianco's got too many enemies for that. We have to walk deeper into the gallery to reach the bright dining room decorated in sharp reds, greens, and yellows.

My stomach drops when I see Bianco but as usual, nothing shows. I'm a block of stone. Control over myself is all I have right now.

There's a feast of breakfast on the table, made of pastries, fruits, and all sorts of eggs and bacon but there are only two people sitting. Bianco at the head, as always, and Ozy on his left. My throat dries up and I have to tighten my fists to stop myself from shaking.

I feel like I'm being thrown back into my childhood. Bianco in his white linen suit, my sister constantly within his reach. Always with her tight high ponytail so he can see the letters he branded on her neck when she was nine years old.

My hatred for him has never been so strong. It was easy to tame it when we were rid of him, when we thought Nate was dead and we wouldn't be found. It's impossible now. I hate him with my entire being.

He looks a little older but barely. A few extra wrinkles around his eyes and between his brows. He has some grey hair now, he never had grey hair before. He was young and handsome three years ago. The kind of charm that no one can resist. The kind that hides demons behind a beautiful face.

Rose is looking at her full plate in front of her, an arm

splayed on the table and the other with an elbow on the edge and holding her head by the temples. She tries to act like she's fine, but I can see her whole body tensed up. She looks like she hasn't slept, still wearing her dress from yesterday, now with a dark grey hoodie. She looks exhausted and I'm praying that it's only because she was waiting at the station all night for me to get out.

Bianco is beaming as if he's been hit by the light of a thousand gods. He's happy, truly happy because he's been reunited with his obsession. He's eating his breakfast talking to Ozy and making big gestures with his knife and fork, but she doesn't acknowledge him. Neither of them has noticed us yet but Nate quickly corrects that.

"Boss, how you doing?" he asks casually as if he is just meeting with an old friend, not with someone fifteen years his elder that groomed him into becoming a gangster.

When Bianco dies, Nate will take over his organization, his precious mafia family, and Sam will be his right-hand man. Where do Rose and I stand in all of this?

Ozy snaps out of wherever she went to escape reality and looks up at us. She was probably listing shit in her head. That's her thing, she remembers *everything*. Like the exact ingredients for the box of cereals in front of her. Or the names of every single previous owner of this house. Whatever she hears, sees, or reads she remembers. When she has nothing to focus on, she lists whatever comes to her head. People think it's a blessing and call her a genius, but it drives her mad because she can't stop it.

Nate walks over to sit on Bianco's right. His right-hand man is always on his right and Sam on Nate's right. Nothing has changed. Absolutely nothing. I should be on Ozy's left but I can't bring myself to do it. If I sit next to her, it'll be like it's always been, and I won't let that happen.

"I don't know, son, it seems you've been dying to waste my damn time lately." Bianco smiles at Nate.

Nate grabs a strip of bacon and pops all of it in his mouth, taking his time to chew. Sam is casually sitting at the table, he doesn't touch anything, doesn't move but his eyes are fixed on Ozy.

Nate shrugs as he swallows and lays back in his seat. "Jake and I got in a bit of a disagreement."

Bianco's steel grey eyes snap to me and his smile sharpens. That lying smile that he uses to lure everyone in. I slide my hands in my tux pocket, that I've been wearing since last night, to hide my tightened fists or he'll take it as a threat, and I don't want to start anything.

I just want to grab my sister and leave.

Mateo replies to Nate, but his gaze stays on me. "I thought you'd be busier than that. I did give you a whole town to take over. How's my old friend Volkov?"

Nate pulls the sleeves of his shirt up and grabs another piece of bacon. There's blood on his shirt but Bianco doesn't say anything. He just keeps staring at me. A housemaid walks by me and goes to Nate to pour him a cup of coffee.

"Thanks, sweetheart," he mumbles with a hand on her lower back. She blushes but he doesn't notice. "Hiding somewhere with his puppies, as usual. I haven't been to Stoneview much. Ask Sam."

So that's why we haven't seen him much since he turned back alive. He wasn't in Stoneview.

Bianco's gaze finally goes back to my brother and he raises an eyebrow. The first step into showing he disapproves. After

298

that, it goes straight to punishment. It's his only warning. Nate clicks straight away but he doesn't show any fear, his behavior stays relaxed, and he carries on explaining.

"I have other cities, Mateo, I can't be in Stoneview all the time."

Unsatisfied, Bianco puts his cutlery down and lays back in his chair. He crosses his legs, resting an ankle on his knee, and rests his arms on the armrests of his seat.

"Your other cities run themselves. I need all eyes on Stoneview, I need *you* on Volkov. He's the last big head of business that hasn't associated with our new alliance in this area." And by alliance, he means mafia, motherfucking mafia.

Ozy slightly turns to me and digs her gaze in mine. She wants to leave. She *needs* to leave.

"Do you know why my other cities run themselves?" Nate insists. "Because I know how to do my job. Let me handle this my way. Sam is doing fine. We've taken over all Volkov's sellers. They've sided with us, including the Diaz brothers. Volkov can produce all he wants, he's got no distributors to bring it to the city. He's got no link either. We cut all his transportation. All we've got left is his sex trafficking, and I need to get in with Stoneview's politicians for that. So, again, let me handle it."

Sam doesn't even move when his name is mentioned. He stays his stoic self.

Bianco laughs loudly and slaps a hand on the table playfully but hard, making Rose jump in her seat. "You fear nothing son, that's why I trust you."

I look at Rose again and that's when I see it. For a second I'm not sure if I made it up but when she readjusts her right hand holding her head, I see it clearly, the purple bruise on her wrist. Her oversized hoodie hides her arm, and I don't know how far it goes but what I've seen is enough. We're leaving, I'm done. I take a few steps further in the room and stand by the other end of the table.

"We're leaving," I say in a voice of steel.

Everyone suddenly turns my way, even Sam. I can hear Nate's thoughts in his eyes; 'I told you to let me do the talking'. I don't give a shit, I have no doubt he's seen the same bruise I have since he's sitting right opposite her. Fucking bastard. This time, Bianco raises a brow at me, and I stare back at him, giving him my strongest face. I'm not your foster kid anymore, you can't do shit. All he can do is kill me, which I know he won't because he knows Ozy would never forgive him, and he cares what she thinks of him.

"Nate, tell your brother to sit down," Bianco orders his right-hand man, his eyes piercing through me.

Nate insists with a look and I know I have to sit down but can't get myself to. I'm still weighing if I should listen to them and do this the peaceful way or if it's about time I fuck Bianco's face up.

I take too long to decide though, one look from Mateo behind me and I recognize the sound of guns cocking. I turn around and watch two guards settle by the door. *Fuck.* The bastard has no limits when it comes to keeping his favorite close to him.

I run a hand in my hair and take a seat. But I have to make a point, so I sit on the opposite end of the table, at the head, like him. A smile tugs at Bianco's lips and he turns to Nate again.

"Who's raising him now, huh? Where's the respect?"

Nate shakes his head, unimpressed.

"What's this?" I quip. "Big family reunion?"

My statement makes Bianco chuckle, and Nate throws me the darkest looks. He's hating that I'm not folding like all of them expect me to.

They don't know me anymore. Not even a little bit. That kid that used to do everything he was told because he was scared to death, he's gone. The teenager that followed every order thinking they would hurt him and his twin. Gone. The only one left is the cold-hearted bastard in control of every single thing in his life.

"How's life been treating you, Jake?" Bianco asks as if he is truly interested.

It's been good, Mateo. I have foster parents who love me. I've fucked countless girls. I'm on my way to an Ivy League college and, most of all, I've met Jamie.

Jamie.

I need to get back to her, like, last night.

"None of your business," I reply without an ounce of feeling in my voice.

I could use a cigarette right now. Or a joint. I don't smoke half as much as Ozy does, but I need something to take the edge off.

"Something's wrong with you, son." Hearing this word coming out of his mouth twists my stomach. I feel so fucking sick and I know my control is slipping, stirring burning rage inside me.

"Wrong?" I smile a wide grin. "I've never been better."

I lay back in my seat to act relaxed, but I need a fucking drink to stop my heart from hammering in my ears. I want to look at Ozy but I can't look away from him. I can't show weakness, he'll feed on it.

"You're not scared anymore. That's what's wrong with you. It's going to get you in trouble." He gives me a sardonic smirk and points at what I can only imagine is now a black eye on my face. "Seems it already has."

I chuckle to pretend he's wrong. "Like Nate said, disagreement."

Bianco nods slowly showing he understands. "That disagreement had anything to do with the gorgeous creature who was waiting for you two at the station?" He grins as he says this like he's got both of us all figured out.

He does have us figured out because he raised us, and there's nothing I can do about that.

"Did you have anything to talk about?" I ask, avoiding his last question. "I don't get what we're doing here. Don't get me wrong, I don't care, but I'd love it if you could get your bitches out of the way so I can go back to my parents."

I never call the Murrays my parents, they're not, but it's time to hit Bianco where it hurts. His face goes from mocking to a deep scowl, and I can't help thinking I've won this round.

"The Murray's aren't your parents, Jake. You're a White and you don't just get to leave because some lonely wealthy couple is guarding you. We're not some bullshit street gang, we're a family, there's no way out of that, and your *real* family needs you."

My family? Who the *fuck* does he think he is?

He thinks because he bribed some judge into giving me the last name he chose and because he kept me hostage here means he's my family?

I raise from my chair so hard it falls back in a heavy thud. When my fist hits the table to the point that I feel my bones rattle, I know I've lost my temper. But if Mateo *fucking* Bianco thinks he's still got a hold on me, I'll have to show him he's got no chance at getting us back.

"Don't call yourself my family, asshole. You've got your two sluts doing your dirty deeds, it's more than enough. Leave us out of this, let's not make reunions a weekly habit, or I'm sure the cops would love to hear about all your dirty secrets. You know what? Fuck the cops, they're all your dogs, I'll go straight to a judge. I'm tight with a few of them, trust me."

My whole body is dying to shake from anger, but I manage to keep it all under control. My teeth are taking the fall but who fucking cares right now.

Bianco explodes laughing, throwing his head back. Nate and Rose are looking at me like I've lost my fucking mind, but Sam is still looking at my sister like he can read her mind or something.

"Are you threatening me, son?" he keeps laughing. Fuck him.

Fuck.

Him.

"Interpret this as you fucking wish. Rose, let's go," I order.

I have to call his bluff that he would never kill me, but I might be in a body bag by the end of the day. You know, after he's taken a few hours to torture me. Let's hope I still know him well.

Ozy's gaze is following a tennis match between me and Bianco. She's scared to move but dying to. I nod slightly to encourage her. She takes a shaky breath as she stands up.

"Ozy," Nate tries.

He's not warning or threatening her, he's begging. It breaks his heart every single time she chooses me over him. I hope it's shattering into a million pieces right now.

303

She makes a move to get away, but she hasn't taken a second step before Bianco's hand clamps around her wrist. I see her face contorting as she winces, but she doesn't make a sound.

"*Un minuto, bellissima,*" he whispers low and angry.

"*Mateo,*" she growls through gritted teeth.

The way Sam's fists clench tight on the table, I really think he's going to intervene. But he doesn't move.

"*Sit* your ass back down. *Now,*" he orders Rose.

She looks at me, a million questions in her eyes and the main one being: *What do I do?* She's going to kill me when we get home. For playing a dangerous game and putting her in the middle of it. Hell, she's going to kill me for ordering her around when she's already sick of Mateo telling her what to do.

The staring contest between Bianco and I seems to last forever. It only stops when Rose makes the executive decision of following *his* order. She slowly sits back down and the smile growing on Mateo's face – telling me he's won this round – makes me want to scream and break everything.

"You too," he says when Rose is back in her initial position.

This time her bruised wrist is in Bianco's hold instead of holding her face. She's too exhausted to fight. Scratch that, she stopped fighting him a long time ago. She chose running away instead, we both did.

I sit back down, this time on the edge of my chair, ready to pounce if anything happens.

"What did you think was going to happen, Jake? Don't you know who makes the rules around here?" His steady voice shows he's back in complete control and I feel like a failure.

Something cracks inside me when I see him releasing Rose's wrist, satisfied that everything is going his way again. I'm suffocating from his authority and I wonder how long I can last before I turn to Nate for help, before I ask Sam to do something. That would be the ultimate defeat but if it means we're both going home safe, maybe I can put my pride aside?

"Our family is expanding, and you want to be with the winning team when shit goes down," Bianco explains, un-wavering. "I can give you a good life, both of you." His eyes dart to Rose and she squirms uncomfortably in her seat. "I've always given you a good life, you were just too young to understand back then. I'm hoping you've matured enough to agree with me."

I hate it when he talks to me like I'm a kid. He's far from stupid but I'm too smart myself to fall for his shit.

"What do you want, huh?" I ask. "You want me to fight for you? The money you get from those fights is spare change to you." He only nods in return, so I keep going. "What do you want Rose to do? Move packages? Fuck Bianco, do you realize the kind of potential you're wasting when you ask us to do that? A lot. I'd hope you've matured enough to agree with me." A smile tugs at my lips when I see his face harden but I shouldn't be happy to make him angry. He's dying to make me pay for my words.

"I don't make decisions for you and your sister, Jake." Liar. Fucking liar, you've dictated our whole lives. "I can only warn you: you're either with us or against us. There is no in-between. I raised you, that makes you Volkov's enemy. You don't want to be mine as well."

The threat in his grey eyes makes my skin prickle but I keep my face emotionless.

He continues, "I should've killed both of you for running away. I'm nice enough to offer you to pick up where you left off. You won't be fighting for me forever. I have big plans for you. It's your choice only, whether you accept my offer or not. If not, good luck."

And here we are ladies and gentlemen, Mateo Bianco's special offer. The *specialité du chef*: pretend it's your choice when he's backed you into a corner.

He gives me one last poisonous smile and lays back in his chair. I hadn't even realized he had moved forward to talk to me.

"Take your time to decide. No rush." He slowly extends his left arm from his chair and below the table until I know it's resting on Rose's leg from her eyes squeezing shut.

Nate frowns and scratches slowly behind his right ear, his head slightly to the side, like every single time he's trying to think fast.

"We're meeting with those kids from the North Shore of Silver Falls today. We shouldn't leave too late," my brother suggests to his boss.

That's his only way to get us out of here since he'll never actually stand up against Bianco. I guess that's his way of being nice to us.

Bianco nods at him and indicates behind me in a head gesture. He smiles at me politely.

"You can leave now."

I can't help the sardonic chuckle from escaping my lips. He was fine with us leaving all along, he just wanted it to be on his terms. He wanted to summon us and order us to leave at his will. He is so predictable.

I get up slowly, taking my time to walk around the table, and put a hand on my sister's shoulder. "Let's go, Ozy," I whisper.

She gets up in a rush, pushes my hand away, and hurries out of the room. I don't hesitate to follow her.

"I want to talk to you two," Bianco orders Nate and Sam but the latter shakes his head and gets up from his seat.

"Later," Sam growls at Mateo in his low voice before following me and Rose out of the room.

As soon as the door closes behind us, Ozy lets out a heavy breath. As if she had stopped breathing the whole time we were in there. She has to put a hand on the wall next to her to hold herself as her other palm rests on her heart to calm herself down.

"Fuck. Fuck, fuck, fuck. *Fuck,*" she keeps whispering in panic.

I take a step closer, but she looks up at me and her dark eyes stop me in my tracks. She straightens back up and takes a step toward me to push me with both hands.

"What the *fuck* is wrong with you?! What were you playing in there? This is no fucking joke, Jake." She pulls her hair with both her hands at the roots, messing up her ponytail. "Why are you trying to get us killed?" Her voice falters when she says her last word.

I take another step towards her, but she turns around and bumps right into the arms of Sam waiting behind her.

Her fucking knight in black armor. Black and covered in sins. He wraps his tattooed arms around her skinny frame and leans down to whisper something in her ear. I can't hear what he says but she nods, her head nestled on his shoulder. He pulls away and looks up.

"Get in the car, I'll be out in a minute. I'll drive you both home."

As soon as both car doors are closed, I turn to my sister.

"Let me see your wrist," I say in a soft voice.

She's already done being mad at me because she smiles at me and shakes her head.

"I'm fine Jake, honestly." She makes sure to keep the ends of the sweater sleeves over her wrists, holding them with her fingers.

I've never been the kind of person who shares their feelings. My sister is exactly the same. Rose is not one to open up. She never will. She never explicitly said what happened all those years at Bianco's house, only that he was obsessed with her. Nothing else.

She never told the police, never told the social workers, never told her best friends Chris and Luke, never told her precious girl Rachel. She never told me.

It hurts but that's how it is. Some things she can only survive if she pretends they didn't affect her, and I can respect that. But how can we keep going if what we ran away from catches up with us? Could she take it all again without saying anything? I sure as hell couldn't.

"Ozy," I start but the driver's door opens, and Sam sits behind the wheel.

He doesn't say anything, just gives us a look through the rearview mirror before starting the car. We drive in complete silence.

After a few minutes, Rose puts her head on my lap. Her ponytail is knotted, and she smells of alcohol and cigarettes. I probably smell the same on top of blood and sweat. We both haven't been home since we left for Stoneview Prep's winter ball.

There's nothing I can say or do right now, so I undo her hair because I know she hates it up and I keep quiet. I let my head fall back against the headrest and scratch her head like she expects me to. This is about the furthest she'll go in showing her vulnerability.

The whole ride, I hear her whisper the list that is going on repeat in her head. *Water, sodium laureth sulfate, citric acid, cocamidopropyl betaine, sodium hydroxide,* etc., etc. I think that's her shampoo bottle. Rachel tested her the other day. We were in our cozy living room, she was holding the bottle in her hands and giggling as my sister was repeating the chemicals to her in a bored voice. She hates doing it, but she did it for Rach because she loves her like that.

As soon as we park by the Murrays' gate, it opens as if Chris was monitoring our arrival. Sam drives all the way up the hill and stops by the front door. He hands me mine and Rose's phone and we both take them. Chris is waiting by the door, arms crossed over his chest and the darkest look on his face I've ever seen. He's got a light bruise on his left cheek, but I doubt he even feels it.

Sam gets out to open the door for Ozy but my friend is already on it.

Chris' gaze is not leaving Sam's and the latter doesn't move any closer. This is not about us right now. This is not about their hatred for each other. Rose heads to the front door, probably straight to Chris' room, her official safe haven.

Sam nods at us and leaves without a word. As soon as he's left, I reach under my glasses to rub my eyelids with my thumb and index finger. I've got another terrible headache coming my way.

"Jake..." Chris scolds.

"I know," I cut him off.

I respect the shit out of Chris. I don't think I've ever

309

respected someone as much as I do him. He's the big brother Nate never was. That's the only reason he's allowed to tell me off, to suggest, to scold and I let him. I try to listen to him as much as I can. I do my best to follow his path when it comes to keeping calm. But how could I when Nate tried to put himself between Jamie and I?

So yeah, I know. I know I fucked up. I know if I hadn't gotten in a fight with my brother over pride, none of this would have happened. I fucking know. And I know this is all far from over.

By the end of the day, my headache is absolutely killing me despite the pills I took. I fell asleep on my bed as soon as Chris came to tell me Ozy was asleep in his.

When I wake up, I head straight for the shower and scrub all of last night away. My ribs on my right side are deeply bruised and the knuckles of my right hand are cut. I look down at my stomach and I have another bruise from when Sam kneed me in the guts. Asshole.

I wipe the mist on the mirror and look at my bruised face. I'm glad my eyebrow has stopped bleeding hard because I don't have the strength to go to the hospital. I put a band-aid on it and head for the kitchen to grab ice from the freezer. My black eye definitely needs it.

Now that the adrenaline is gone, all my muscles are aching, especially my shoulders and back. I could sleep for three days, easy. I put the ice cubes in a towel and head for my phone in my room before realizing I forgot to charge it. I let out an annoyed groan and plug it in. This headache is going to be the end of me, I need fresh air.

I get out of the pool house to find Ozy leaning on the wall

next to the door, a cigarette in her mouth. Her hair is clean and down, her make-up from the night before all gone. She's wearing one of Chris' Stoneview Prep hoodies that are about five times her size. She looks up from her phone when I close the door and gives me one of her mocking grins.

"You look like shit," she chuckles.

I try to smile back at her, but I can't get myself to. It annoys me how normal she's acting after spending the whole night at Bianco's on her own.

"How are you feeling?" I ask.

I try to not sound too worried as I grab a cigarette from her pack, but I know she can read it in my eyes.

"Dude, I'm fine. Don't be a Chris." She holds my gaze and I know she means it. Leave it alone.

I hold the ice to my eye and grab a chair from the patio to sit in front of her. She lights my cigarette as I put it between my lips.

"Was Bianco for real? About offering us to pick up where we left off? Is that really what he and Nate want?" My voice trembles slightly at my questions.

"Fuck if I know," she exhales smoke as she lets her head fall backward.

She looks at the sky full of stars and goes silent for a minute or so. Does she really not know? Doesn't Bianco tell her anything when he spends time alone with her? My stomach clenches at the thought and I look at the sky too, trying to calm myself. I hate winter, it's nighttime at six pm and I slept all fucking day, so no sun for me.

"How does that even work in his mind? Surely, he knows that it's not that easy to get back foster kids that have asked countless times to leave your house. Especially since we're doing so well at the Murray's. Social services won't just send us back to him."

My sister laughs at my statement like she knows something I don't. Or like she's already figured something out that I haven't. Yeah, that's probably it.

"Alright, give it to me. Show me how stupid I am compared to you," I say as I run my hand through my hair.

"You really don't get it? Let's see." She pushes herself off the wall, leaving her cigarette between her lips, and rubs her legs with her palms.

How is she not freezing with just a sweater on? It barely reaches the top of her legs, she's too tall to wear guy's sweaters as dresses like Jamie does with mine.

Once she's warmed herself, she starts stretching her arms. She can't start explaining things without doing something else. She has to put her attention on something else.

"Is there anyone you can think of who is of age, wants us back in, *and* would be close enough to us that it would make sense for social services to move us with him? Wait. Let me give you another clue. He looks *a lot* like us, but a blond, fucked up version."

My heart practically stops. How could I not think of this before?

"Bianco is not rushing us to come back because he knows he doesn't need to. I'm sure pretty soon, we won't have a choice." She shrugs as she concludes her theory.

Theory that we both know is entirely true. She shrugs but I know deep down she's terrified. If Nate becomes our guardian, our lives are over. There's no way we can get out of that one. We can kiss goodbye to our best friends, Stoneview Prep, *Jamie.* We'll be back to being surrounded by gang members, some probably even younger than us but with a will to please Nate much stronger than ours.

"He can't do this to us," I whisper in disbelief. She gives me a sad smile as a response.

"Didn't Jamie tell you where he lives? He just bought a huge ass mansion in Stoneview, Jake. He's already planned it all." She looks back at her phone after it pings.

"Is that Rachel?" I ask, trying to change the subject.

What are we going to do about it anyway? I want to talk about her night at Bianco's but she's never going to tell me what happened, so I'm left with changing the topic.

"Nope. It's Sam."

I'm surprised she told me the truth. She usually hides when they're texting or seeing each other.

"Rach is over my shit for good. Trust me." She takes another drag and talks as she exhales the smoke. "Sam, however, is texting to tell me, to tell *you* to lay low for a few days. Unsurprisingly, Nate is pretty pissed about the whole situation."

"I don't fucking care what Nate thinks. I'm not scared of him," I snap.

Why are we still living our lives depending on what that fucker threatens to do?

"Jake," she sighs. "Nate isn't just your big brother that used to order you around. He leads gangs now. He's building a crime syndicate with Bianco. He's got people working for him, dangerous people, and he's pissed at you. You stole his girl. You, Chris, and Luke kicked his ass. And now you fight him in front of his distributors. Don't act so fucking stupid, you know he's gonna get back at you. Try to use that brain of yours and take Sam's advice for once."

"I didn't steal his girl," I growl. "She was already mine."

Rose raises an eyebrow at me, unimpressed. "Really? You gonna pull this shit on me? I'm glad you found a girl you fell in love with, but I was there, Jake. I saw it all. You can't bully a girl into being your girlfriend. Especially when she was holding back because she had a boyfriend. That boyfriend was Nate."

"Who's fucking side are you on, Ozy?" I shout uncontrollably.

It makes me lose my shit when she sides with him. Does she really believe I stole Jamie from him?

"Fucking hell, what is with the guys in this city and their obsessivity? Why do I always have to pick a side? You and Nate, Chris and Sam. Can't you get in your fucking heads that there's right and wrong in everything you do? I'm just stupid enough to forgive your shit."

She gives me a second to think but she's not done.

"Nobody's perfect. I'm not choosing sides, you're not a side to pick, Jake, you're my twin. You're part of me. But Nate is my brother too, and he's allowed my forgiveness. If not that, at least my understanding. You pushed him to his limits, and you know it. I'm just trying to protect you and him both."

I laugh. It's loud and cold. So. Fucking. Cold.

"Protect us both?" I slowly get up from my chair and lower the ice from my eye. It's crushed in my clenched fist now. "You shot him in the chest you fucking hypocrite," I fume before going back into the pool house.

I slam the door behind me. How can she talk about forgiveness after everything he did to us? That's Rose White for you ladies and gents.

I've met a lot of different girls in my life. I don't have a mentality of 'you're not like other girls' because everyone is so different and similar at the same time. Camila is a cold bitch, even to me. She likes to hide and manipulate her feelings and when she doesn't, she looks weak. Jamie is the opposite. She's whole. When she's mad or sad, it breaks her heart. She cries easily and laughs heartily. But when she loves, it's deep and warm like a summer afternoon.

Rose...her brain is wired differently. Her feelings for people change like her mood. Love them one day, hate them the other. She forgives people she shouldn't and breaks the hearts of those who would do anything for her.

Rachel has given her everything and my sister threw it away despite loving her with all her heart. Nate has betrayed her in ways I can't even describe, and she still desperately looks for his approval. Sometimes, I wonder if she truly believes she doesn't deserve love and happiness.

That's what abuse does to someone though, doesn't it?

I grab my phone and look at my texts. Luke is offering to spend time together this evening, '*just us four*'. He wants to make sure we're all okay, but I think he also wants to take his mind off Emily.

I ignore it and go straight to the number of the only person I know will make everything better. She sent me countless texts, but I wasn't exactly in a situation where I could reply.

I tap on her name and the only fact that her picture shows up on my screen takes a weight off my shoulders. Jamie Williams has some sort of power over me and right here, right now, she can make all the pain go away. I know she can.

CHAPTER 17

Chainsmoking – Jacob Banks

Jamie

I'm on the sidewalk before Jake even parks. As soon as he called me, I got ready to hop in his car. It's late by the time he gets here, and I've done nothing but worry today. After getting home, letting mom know I was okay, and showering, my day consisted of laying down on my bed, checking my phone every five minutes, texting Jake every ten, and trying to get as much sleep as possible, which turned out to be pretty much nothing.

He doesn't come out to open the door for me and my stomach twists. That means he's not well enough to get out of the car and walk easily. I sit down in the passenger seat and turn to him. I know he can read my concern. Since Jake found me and Nate talking at Cal's party, it has been tattooed on my face in permanent ink.

I open my mouth to say something, but he grabs the back of my neck and pulls me toward him so quickly all I can do is hitch a breath before his lips crash on mine. His tongue crosses my lips to find my desperate one before his teeth possess my lower lip. When we separate, I'm panting, and my stomach is twisted with pleasure.

"I missed you," he whispers. His lips are hovering over mine and his eyes staring at my mouth hungrily.

"How are you feeling?" I ask. His eye is puffy now. "You should put ice on this." I point at his face and he gives me a small smile.

"I did. I'm so sorry about yesterday. I'm sorry for the stress and worry but I'm okay. I promise."

I have a million questions for him. Did he go to Washington D.C.? Is Rose alright? Did he see a doctor? How did he get back to Stoneview? What's going to happen with Nate now? I want to ask so much, but I don't want to remind him this is all my fault.

I hold his hand over the gear stick and smile my most genuine smile. He starts the car and pulls away.

'I'm in love with you', my eyes say when he glances at me. I'm dying to tell him. Not because I want to hear it back but because I want him to know someone loves him unconditionally.

"What are your plans for Christmas?" I ask, trying to bring up a new topic. One that will have us looking forward to something rather than look back on the darkness that has started to creep into our lives. "I think mom wants me to go to Tennessee, she won't be able to come but we can't exactly afford a plane ticket at the moment."

"If you want to be with your mom for Christmas, I'll get you a ticket, Angel," he replies like this is nothing to him.

I choke on a laugh and stare at him with wide eyes.

"There's no way I'd ever let you buy something like that for me. I'll look at the busses."

317

It's his turn to laugh at my idea.

"Absolutely no fucking way. You think I'm going to let you take a ten-hour bus ride to another state on your own? Please."

My mouth falls open at his nerve. How many times must we have this conversation? How many times do I have to explain that this kind of behavior is not acceptable? I know how he is in the bedroom. I know he needs his shot of alpha bullshit every once in a while, but I've already told him bedroom is all he gets.

"Jake," I say calmly. "You don't *let* me do anything. Remember?"

I can see his hands gripping the wheel harder and I know it's not the moment to have this conversation. He's been through enough in the past twenty-four hours. We both have.

"It doesn't matter. You're not getting on such a long trip on your own. Anything could happen."

Anger bubbles in me when I see he's not letting go and I can't let this slip.

"I think I'm independent enough to decide what is safe for me or not."

"I think if you keep contradicting me with that pretty mouth of yours, you're going to choke on my dick before we get home."

I don't control the pleasure warming my lower belly at his crude words and the lopsided cocky smile on his face tells me he knows exactly what he's doing. My clit tingles and I squeeze my thighs together to find some release but there's no point.

"Does that make you wet, Angel? When I tell you you're gonna choke on my dick?"

I ignore his statement and turn my blushing face to the window.

"You love when I order you around *way* too much to say that I can't tell you what to do," he chuckles.

"Quiet," I mumble. "You're beaten up and we haven't slept much in the last twenty-four hours. We're going to yours and we're chilling, that's it."

He doesn't reply. He knows I'm bluffing. We both know after what happened, he *needs* to take back control over something. We both know that something is me.

As soon as Jake closes the door to the pool house behind us, he grabs me by the waist and pulls me up. I wrap my legs around him, and he walks us to the room, his lips never leaving mine.

Every single time I have sex with Jake, I can't believe he was my first time. Not because it was *him*. That's not that surprising, I was always attracted to Jake – who isn't? Just like any girl in Stoneview Prep, I had my eyes on him since he transferred to our school, even if I always kept my distance and pretended I wasn't interested.

No, the reason I can't believe it is because he was always rumored to be rough, controlling, and dominant. No love, just pure, raw fucking. He's definitely all these things with me but our first time...it was magical. It was everything I *didn't* expect from Jake. It was loving and comfortable and sexy. Everything I could have dreamed of but surely not something I would have ever thought Jake to be capable of.

Since then, he's shown me how much he loves me through sex. It's almost like I don't need him to say it because he's shown it through his kisses, the thrust of his hips, and his hands on my body. But tonight, Jake is not going to love me. I can feel the way his hands grip my hips. I can feel his teeth biting and sucking at my neck. Tonight, he wants to possess me, to own, to control. I can feel the way he wants to push us past limits we've put up before...and God am I ready for this.

He throws me on his bed and takes a step back. I wonder how he can handle me so easily. He doesn't even look slightly in pain. It's like now that he's horny, adrenaline is back, his strength overtaking his battered body.

Jake crosses his arms over his chest, he's wearing a tight white tee and dark blue jeans that hug his muscles perfectly. He looks like a Calvin Klein model.

"Clothes. Off," he orders as he takes another step back and observes me carefully. I slowly unzip my hoodie and take it off one arm at a time. I go straight for my top and jeans until I'm in underwear in front of him. I push myself on my elbows and look at him.

His face is hard, but his eyes are burning with desire. "All of it."

I unclasp my bra and throw it on the floor. In a few weeks, all my shyness has gone around Jake. He worships my body like I'm a Goddess and I've learned to listen when he wants to see it.

I get rid of the black lace G-string that I wore specifically for him and face him again. A satisfied growl bubbles in his chest and I can see the bulge forming in his jeans. Being stark naked when he's still wearing all his clothes is strange but seeing the reaction it gets out of him makes it all worth it.

"I want to try new things with you tonight, Angel. But before we get to it, I want to make sure you know you can stop it anytime. You just have to say so. Do you understand? Because I will not repeat myself."

My lower belly twists in pleasure and anticipation at his low voice. He's got big things planned for us and just imagining what it could be is getting me wet. I nod as my mouth salivates at the idea of Jake showing me how much pleasure we can both get out of what he likes.

"Good," he says in a wicked smile. "If you disobey tonight, you're going to get punished. Got it?"

I nod again, my pussy more than ready for what he has in store. I trust him. Trust him with all my being. I know he's got no other intention than to pleasure us both in the craziest ways.

"I'm glad we're on the same page. Now get on your knees and rest that cute ass of yours on your heels."

It takes me a second to register, but when his smile drops from his lips, I hurry into position.

"What have you got in mind exactly?" I ask in a wavering voice, half anxious, half yearning.

He slowly walks to me, puts a hand to the back of my neck, and leans down to put his lips against my ear.

"Complete. Control," he whispers in a gravelly voice, vibrating with eagerness.

He leans back as I shiver with desire and takes a step back again.

"Now be a good girl and keep quiet. And when I say quiet, I mean not a sound. Every sound you make, I'll punish you with a spank."

I gasp in shock. He's never done this with me before. I know he has with Camila, it's not like she didn't take pride in the rumors that were going around our school, which she probably started.

"One," he smiles.

"Wait, I wasn't read–"

"Two," he cuts me off and I clamp my mouth shut. I'm not very good at this.

When he's sure I'm not about to say anything else, he talks again. "Put your hands behind your back," he commands.

I look deep into his eyes one last time. I trust him but I need to make sure I can go ahead with this without being hurt. And I mean emotionally. I'm about to give myself to him completely, like never before, and this is the most vulnerable I'll ever be to him.

In the deep ocean of his eyes, I find lust and desire. I find a raging need for control and ownership. I find the demand for my submission, but mainly, I find the burning flame of his love for me. And that is the only thing I need, the rest I leave for him to handle.

I put my hands behind my back and hold them together like I assume he expects me too. The look of approval he gives me reassures me. It also makes me proud. I want to please him so badly it burns in me.

He walks out of view and the next thing I know the mattress dips behind me as I imagine he's putting a knee on it. I feel a silky material between my wrists and arms and my wetness doubles in anticipation.

Where did Jake learn to do this? And when did I start loving it so much? He jerks at the material in a tight, controlled movement and I feel my wrists clash together. I inhale sharply at the surprise, making a breathless sound. It doesn't hurt but it was so sudden, I didn't expect it.

"Three," he whispers in my ear and I bite my lip not to reply or make any more noise.

He steps away and comes into view. I test the knots he's

done behind my back but they're sturdy. I should feel trapped and scared, but I don't. I feel more liberated than ever because I've got total faith in Jake. He admires what he's done with a hand stroking his chin. My shoulders are slightly pulling but nothing that hurts.

"You look beautiful. I hope you're not too comfortable."

I open my mouth to say something, but his smirk reminds me I'm not supposed to. So I raise a brow in question instead.

"It's not supposed to be comfortable, Angel. I want you desperate for me to make it better."

I'm not sure I follow. I thought he wanted to pleasure me, *us*. Why does he want me uncomfortable? As he says this, I realize the silk around my wrists is tighter than I thought. Slight panic overtakes me, and I know my gaze must be sharper because his is daring me to say something.

"Jake," I whisper agitated. "Be considerate. I've never done this before." I squirm in my bonds and he chuckles slightly.

"Four."

I glare at him. "Just tell me why you want me to be uncomfortable."

"Five. Do you want to stop? If not, you're going to have to work harder at submitting, Jamie."

My name on his lips is like a spell. The level of desire in his voice makes me shiver and my thighs clench without control. I shake my head no. I don't want him to stop, I'm just struggling to give him *absolute* control. But I'll learn. I can do it, I think.

His smile screams satisfaction. "Five it is, then."

He grabs his desk chair and places it in front of the bed but doesn't sit. Instead, he comes close to me and without warning, he dips a finger between my folds and relishes in the wetness. I gasp but manage to keep it soundless. The pleasure that surges from my lower belly makes my heart beat too fast for me to handle.

He leaves his finger there but doesn't move it in the slightest. The pad of it is at my entrance and the rest touches me all the way to my clit. I can't control my body when it starts squirming and thrusting to get friction, desperate for more, desperate for him to slide deeper.

"Stop moving," he snaps, and I jump in surprise. "You get what I give you."

I will myself to stop moving and he keeps his finger still for another few seconds before adjusting. It's an insignificant gesture, barely anything, but it rips a moan from my throat. I'm craving for more. I feel trapped in the bonds and this is the release I need.

"Six," he whispers and slides in. He goes as deep as his finger allows and I barely refrain a sound. Instead, my breathing hitches and my chest rises and falls in pants.

"Tonight, if you want to come, you're going to have to beg so, so hard, Angel. And only I decide if I'm going to give it to you. Yes?"

I nod quickly, the more I agree, the more he'll be good to me. Give me what I want.

"Good girl," he comforts me.

I feel rewarded when he lifts his other hand and pinches my left nipple, rubbing, and tugging. Then my right. He brings his mouth to my neck, slowly descends, and makes sure to give both my peaks the attention they deserve.

His finger is still moving inside me and it's overwhelming, but not nearly enough. I writhe under his touch, but I know he won't give me what I need. I do my best to not say a word, not make a sound. I'm not exactly looking forward to six spanks but somehow, I know that Jake will make it pleasurable.

He retreats his hand and takes his top off, giving me hope that this little torture session is over. I smile at him, encouraging him to come close to me again but he sits on the chair he's put in front of the bed.

What is he doing? He can't just leave me like this after working me up. I'm panting and my mouth is desperate for his. I feel my brows furrowing as he undoes his jeans and his rock-hard cock springs free. My mouth salivates automatically. I have become a master at satisfying Jake's dick, and I know he loves when I suck him off. But tonight, I can feel he won't put himself in this position. He won't let me have any power over him.

He strokes himself, still sitting down, watching me intently, his eyes drinking every inch of my body. I struggle to swallow, my throat suddenly tight, my entire body thirsty for him. I want to feel him, drink him, touch him, become one with him. I wriggle in my bonds, so desperate to reach for him but he tuts me.

"Let's see how long you last," he taunts.

How long I last? Before what? Before I cry desperately for him?

He keeps stroking himself and my insides clench in need. *Fuck.* He knows exactly what he's doing. All I can do is watch him pleasuring himself and wish he will eventually come to pleasure me too. I'm left with nothing else to do but focus on him.

His messy inky hair, his dangerously deep ocean eyes. I drag my eyes to his hard jawline and his red lips. His square shoulders move to the rhythm of his slow strokes and I look down, dragging my gaze through his cut abs, they're clenching and covered in bruises, which makes him even hotter at this moment. One of his hands is resting on his thigh and the other clenching at his hard cock. I can't stop my mind from imagining and remembering all the things he can do with it.

I squirm, clench my thighs, move my hips, but nothing helps because it's not Jake. My clit is swollen and throbbing, my pussy tight and desperate to be filled. My gaze is glued to Jake's hand slowly moving up and down his shaft. He's getting turned on by seeing me struggle and crave him. I lick my dry lips as he spreads pre-cum over his tip.

"You're so beautiful." His voice is husky and filled with need.

He's torturing us both by staying where he is but he's loving it too much to do anything.

After another minute of desperately clenching my thighs and trying to rub against something, my head falls forward and my hair hangs in front of my face.

"Please," I whisper.

"Seven."

My heart is strumming from my pussy and all the way to my ears. It skips a beat when I finally realize what he's doing. He won't touch me until I've begged with all I have. But every time I open my mouth to beg, the number of spanks gets higher. I thought I was at least in control of how many of those I'll get but he knew what he was doing from the start. He'll touch me only when he's decided I've begged enough, when he's reached the number *he* wants to give.

I keep quiet for another minute but the need for release becomes unbearable. There's an ache deep in my body that only Jake can heal. My shoulders are in pain from the pull behind my back, my wrists are hurting, and my thighs are burning from holding the same position for so long.

I can feel pearls of sweat coming down my back and between my breasts. This is torture. Pure, pleasurable, torture. His words echo in my head; *'It's not supposed to be comfortable, Angel. I want you desperate for me to make it better.'* This is exactly what he wanted. I need him to make it better.

Jake finally gets up and takes his jeans and boxers off, throwing them on the floor, and the hope growing in my chest makes me want to cry tears of happiness. But when he sits back down and lazily grabs his dick back in his hand, I let out an uncontrollable whimper.

"Jake, please. I-I can't take this anymore. I need you to touch me." My chest is heaving.

He doesn't get it. I've never felt like this before. Or maybe he gets it *exactly.* I would do *anything* for his touch right now. I'll beg all he wants, I'll take as many spanks as he wants to give, I'll cry, I'll scream...I just need him to release the ache.

"Eight," he chuckles. "I think you're starting to understand the game, baby. How desperate are you now?"

"So much. Please..." I groan in need and pull at my binds again. I don't recognize my own voice. It's husky, gravelly, almost bestial.

"Nine."

He moves in the chair slightly and my heart speeds up. Is he coming? Is he having mercy on me? He catches my hope because he shakes his head, an evil smirk forming on his lips.

"Not yet. But you're being so good, I'm proud of you."

The wave of pride that washes through me tells me how deep I've fallen for his game. When did it happen? I was so

327

sure at the beginning I would struggle to give all of me. I was so afraid I wouldn't be able to do it. What now? He's got a hold on me that could ruin me completely. All I have left to hold on to is trust. *Trust and love.*

"How many spanks would you take for me to come over right now? Tell me how bad it is."

"However many you want," I blurt out with no control over my thoughts or my body anymore. I'm pretty sure I haven't had control over my heart for a while now. "I just need you. Please. Anything. I'll do anything." My voice dies down as my craving eats me up from the inside. I'm rubbing against nothing, thrusting my hips into the air shamelessly.

"Whichever number I want, huh? You know it'll hurt, right? You know I won't be gentle, my love?"

I nod. I can only nod, hard, and stiff. *Please. Please. Please.*

He finally gets up and walks over to me. He puts a finger under my chin to lift my head up. This touch only makes me exhale a loud, fiery breath. I try to swallow but I know I won't be able to function properly until he gives me what I need.

His thumb finds one of my nipples and grazes slightly. The simple gesture sends a ripple of pleasure through my body.

"Would you take twenty?"

I nod again. "Yes," I moan as his thumb grazes my other nipple. "Anything."

"Thirty?" My stomach twists at the number but I don't care. I'll take a hundred if that's what it takes. So, I nod again.

He smiles, a wicked grin, satisfied and full of pride. "You're such a good girl," he whispers. "But ten will do, trust me. Now say 'please'"

I exhale a breath of relief before I can talk again. "Please."

His smile is condescending and that's how I know he's not

done playing. "Again."

"Please...Jake."

"Again."

I repeat '*please*'. Over and over again, hoping it will satisfy him. I lose count; the word echoing in my head, not sure if I'm saying it out loud or thinking it really hard. Not sure if I'm shouting or whispering.

I'm so lost in the begging that I jump in a cry of pleasure when he suddenly pinches my clit hard with his thumb and forefinger. I don't care about making a sound anymore. This is too good, too much, too fulfilling.

His hand under my chin grabs my jaw tightly and he pushes me until my back hits the mattress. I whimper with need as he places his head between my legs and laps at my pussy. My cries of pleasure reverberate against the walls of his room. I'm so loud I'm surprised the walls don't tremble. My body, however, is trembling all right. I'm a second away from coming when he pulls away and the groan that leaves my throat is unrecognizable.

He flips me around in one movement and my cheek hits the mattress. I'm looking at his wall, my vision fuzzy from pleasure. I don't have time to think as he pulls me by the hips until my ass is up and he's got full access.

"Beautiful," he growls. "So fucking wet and beautiful, Angel."

"Fuck me," I order and, in return, I get a hard slap on my ass cheek.

It makes me jump in surprise. The erotism from a simple slap in this situation is through the roof. I would have never expected it to be like this. My cheek burns but he soothes it with his palm.

"One," his sultry breath penetrates the thick, sexual air.

He puts his dick at my entrance and I'm about to move back when another slap lands on my other cheek. This time I scream at how much harder it is from the first one.

He moves an extra inch, making me moan in pleasure. Another slap, another inch. Soon I don't know if I'm moaning at the spanks or him penetrating me further. Everything blurs into a big moment of ecstasy as it all accelerates and my first orgasm rips through me so hard and intense, I can feel tears prickling at my eyes and I see stars.

I'm so thankful for the pleasure he's allowing me to have that I whisper 'thank you' over and over again and I feel in his movements he's loving it.

"You're most welcome," he says, pulling out and flipping me around again before entering me without warning. This time he slows down, the difference is severe and intimate.

My second orgasm comes slowly as if it is still building as it releases and releasing as it builds more. He keeps going, steadily, and I already feel another ecstatic moment coming. It rolls over my whole body and this time, I can't stop the tears.

They fall down my cheeks as the strength of my third orgasm turns me into a puddle of pleasure beneath him. I don't even feel my shoulders or the binds anymore. All I feel is the love between me and Jake, the pleasure of our bodies becoming one. I know the moment he notices my tears because he freezes.

"Jamie," he asks calmly. "Are you okay?" He lifts up and is about to pull away when I smile and shake my head.

"Don't," I sob, my throat tight. "They're happy tears. Please, *God*, please don't stop."

He slithers his hands below me and grabs my joint wrists to use as a lever. He starts slow again but quickly picks up the pace. He kisses my tears away, my cheeks, devours my mouth. He swallows my moans as he pushes into me with unforgiving thrusts, and I come for a fourth time with his mouth on mine and his hands gripping my wrists.

As his mouth leaves mine and my cries get louder, he releases himself in me and I only realize now that we didn't bother using a condom. I thank Emily internally for helping me get on the pill a week ago. I will still have to discuss STDs with Jake but now is really not the time.

Jake lets his body fall on mine and I wince as the ache in my shoulders comes back. He quickly releases my wrists, and my arms are so stiff it hurts to bring them back into their natural positions. Jake doesn't say anything, but I read the satisfaction on this face.

We're tired but he still helps me stretch my arms to help the ache go away and massages my shoulders. He goes to the bathroom and brings me back a warm wet cloth. I clean myself and fall back on the mattress, but he quickly grabs my waist and helps me back up.

"You need to go pee, baby," he whispers before kissing my forehead.

I execute without question. UTI's are no joke. When I come back into the room, he's on his front, his whole naked body splayed over the bed. My eyes stop at his perfectly shaped bum and then his one and only tattoo between his shoulder blades.

I still haven't asked him the meaning of the X or the numbers and letters around it.

The pace at which his chest is rising tells me he's fallen

asleep, and I'm not surprised. This session drained me of energy. Add a fight, a night at the police station, worrying about your twin, confronting your old foster parent and I think Jake has more than earned a good night of sleep.

I slip into bed beside him. He shifts until he's on his side, grabs my waist, and tucks me against him. I'm fearful that my body so close to his is hurting his bruised ribs and stomach but I also remind myself that he just fucked me into oblivion and if that was fine for him, sleeping like this shouldn't be too painful. It's dark, but I still make out the black-and-white picture hanging on the wall next to me, of him in his lacrosse kit, holding his helmet and smiling his perfect teeth at the camera with Rose next to him in our Stoneview Prep kit too. I recall him saying Luke took the pictures he's put in his room. He looks so happy, his smiles genuine and forcing my own lips to curve. Maybe, when this whole Nate and Bianco thing is over, Jake will have that kind of smile on his face again. I want that for him, for us. Just pure happiness. I grin at the thought and let sleep overtake me.

I wake up to the sound of the front door slamming. Someone is angry and since I can still feel Jake's arm around my waist, it can only be Rose. I hear her footsteps in the hall and her husky voice easily infiltrates our room. Apparently, she 'can't fucking believe he actually did it' and for a few seconds, there's no response until Chris' voice asks her to calm down and not do anything irrational.

The walls in this house are very thin and I'm glad none of them were here yesterday. What an embarrassment that would have been. I shiver with pleasure at the reminder of what happened last night, and I can already feel wetness coating between my legs. I slide my hand lower but before I can reach my clit, Jake's hand clamps over mine.

"Are you out of your mind?" His sleepy voice enhances my desire for him, but I don't say anything. "Don't touch my pussy," he says before I feel him shift and his hand replaces mine.

There's a wonderful ache inside me from yesterday and when he starts stroking me it turns into full-blown ecstasy. He rubs two skilled fingers against my clit and goes lower to spread my wetness around as he puts his mouth on my shoulder, giving me light kisses.

I inhale a sharp breath and I feel his lips shape into a smile. Moans are forming in my throat when a knock on Jake's door makes us both jump.

"Wake up, Don Juan. We have a problem." Rose's hoarse voice behind the door forces me to put some space between myself and Jake.

"Someone's in a shit mood," he growls as he pushes the comforter off him.

There are things I wish I could have talked to Jake about this morning. Just the two of us in bed, calm and rested. Like, if I was safe from STDs after we didn't use protection for the first time. If last night was like he imagined. Maybe mention his night in custody, his brief trip to D.C.

I guess it doesn't work like that when your twin sister has the door across from yours and doesn't care about boundaries. Not that I would mention that it annoys me how comfortable Rose is to put herself between us during our most intimate moments. He's too close to her, too protective for me to mention anything without it turning into an argument.

He puts sweatpants on over his morning wood and runs

a hand through his hair before hurrying to the bathroom. I follow to brush my teeth and head back to the room before him. By the time he comes back, I'm dressed in yesterday's clothes and brushing my hair.

"What are you doing?" he asks surprised.

I put my hairbrush back in my bag and grab my lip balm. "I'm heading home? I thought you might want to deal with whatever you have to deal with with Rose? Just the two of you."

"Oh really," he marvels. "I think if you leave *you* are going to have to deal with a lot worse than a little spanking, Angel."

A shiver of pleasure runs through me. Pleasure? I never thought hearing about being spanked could make me feel pleasure.

"Let's see what she wants," he concludes before dropping a kiss on my forehead.

I follow him out and when we enter the living room. Rose is sitting on the kitchen bar, her long legs dangling in front of her. She's rolling a joint on her lap and putting her whole focus in the meticulous work. Chris is on his phone on the sofa, laying down, his head on one of the armrests. He's so tall that his feet are still far off the other edge.

"What brings me the pleasure of being woken up at," Jake looks at the clock on the kitchen wall and looks back at Rose, "ten am on a Saturday?"

"It's Sunday," Rose comments without looking up, spreading tobacco on the paper with the weed.

"Even worse. It's God's day."

A wave of anxiety squeezes through me. It is God's day, and since I've been seeing Jake, I have barely been to Church. Mom doesn't know, but I'm sure Pastor Gilligan will tell her soon and she will be disappointed about it. She won't be mad, but she'll be sad that our Sunday family trip with dad and Aaron has officially turned to nothing.

Jake walks around the bar and grabs two glasses to fill them with orange juice. His bruised ribs are a darker color than yesterday. I noticed that he never puts a shirt on in the morning. He always has breakfast in sweatpants and nothing else. Much to my liking.

Chris straightens up on the sofa, leaving space for me and Jake to sit. I settle next to Chris, mumbling a shy 'good morning'. I'll never forget that the first orgasm Jake ever gave me, Chris was holding me from the back, his thumb in my mouth. It's no big deal for them, but I don't usually play in their league and I'm not a girl who is used to those kinds of things.

It seems a lot of my fellow teenage girls at Stoneview Prep have experienced all sorts of crazy sex despite our age. A lot of it includes Chris and Jake and what they used to call their 'sexcapades'. This is what it's like to be amongst the rich and famous, everyone grows up too fast due to the lack of their parents being around and they do whatever they want, indulging in drugs and sex at an early age. I wonder what else hides behind Chris' sweetness. I wonder for whom he stopped playing with girls.

"How are you feeling?" he asks me. "I haven't seen you since the party at Cal's."

I shrug, not really knowing what to say since not much happened to me. "I'm not the one who lost a tooth. How are you?"

"Same tooth as usual?" Jake questions as he sits next to me and passes me a glass.

Chris chuckles and nods. "They put it back *again*, but they said I should get an implant next time."

"Always take care of your teeth, baby bear, it's important," Jake jokes. "So, what's up?"

I sip on my orange juice, waiting for Chris or Rose to announce whatever it is that's so bad and I know from the atmosphere that it really *is* bad.

Chris points towards the bar in a head gesture and only now do I notice the envelope sitting next to Rose on the bar. "That came in the mail this morning."

Jake gets up in a huff and opens the huge brown envelope. He only needs to glance at it for his face to fall.

"What is it?" I ask.

I see the anger creeping up on his beautiful traits and my heart picks up.

Jake doesn't reply to me though, he turns to his sister as she licks the paper of her joint to make it stick.

"Have you read all of it?" he asks her.

She simply nods and puts the joint between her lips.

"And so?" Jake insists.

I know Jake is smart. I'm pretty sure his IQ would qualify him as a genius. I mean, if elitist Stoneview Prep offered him to skip a year, he *has* to be. But if his twin is around, he always relies on her for brain usage. It's like he knows she'll understand quicker, analyze quicker, conclude quicker and he doesn't even bother wasting his time or energy if her computer-comparable brain is already working on it.

"Do you want the good news or the bad news first?" she mumbles with the joint between her lips as she hops off the bar and taps her jeans pockets to look for her lighter.

"You want the good news first," Chris suggests next to me

and Jake nods, encouraging her to go on.

"Good news is we're over sixteen and wherever we're being offered to go, we have to sign on it. If we don't want to go anywhere and the Murrays are happy to keep us, we don't have to. This is what this paper is, a suggestion with a dotted line. As long as we don't put any ink on it, it has no power in the eyes of the social system or in court."

I'm completely lost as to what she's talking about, but I really don't like it. I get up to join Jake and he easily lets me grab the paperwork from him. My heart drops in my stomach when I read the offer to change guardians and households.

But that's not the worst, the name under the new guardian and the address of the new household I both know too well. I have to squeeze my eyes closed and look again before the name 'Nathan Brian White' doesn't burn into them anymore.

Holy shit.

He's requesting to be their legal guardian.

"What's the bad news then," Jake demands in a voice of steel that makes me shiver but clearly has no effect on his sister.

"Well..." she goes behind the kitchen counter and opens drawers, still in search of a lighter. "First of all, he's got a fucking great lawyer behind him."

I look at the lawyer's name at the bottom of the cover letter. *Attorney Gloria Garcia-Diaz.*

"Diaz as in Camila Diaz?" I ask. I already know the answer, but I can't believe it.

Jake's eyes widen and he grabs the letter from my hands.

"Fuck," he huffs. "That's her mom. She's a court shark."

"And she hates your guts," Rose adds, finally taking a lighter out of a drawer.

"Yeah, thanks, I know that," he growls.

Jake puts the letter on top of the rest of the paperwork on the kitchen bar and Rose comes back around. She puts down her lighter and joint next to the pieces of paper and puts her coat on, grabbing it from the back of a highchair.

"What else?" Jake insists.

Rose shrugs. "It's Nate we're talking about. He doesn't shy away from pressuring someone into doing what he wants. Especially us. Cam's mom is the least of our worries in this situation."

"The fucker doesn't scare me, Ozy. Why is it impossible for you to stick that into your brain?" He runs a hand through his hair, messing it up more than it already was, and I look back at Rose as she chuckles mockingly at her twin.

"And you're such a brave boy, Jake. But I think we both know being scared or not won't stop him from doing whatever the fuck he wants. And if you think he won't go to the extent of threatening the people you love," her eyes flick to me and my heart flutters at the thought of her knowing Jake is in love with me, "then I'm sorry to say all that braveness made you a little bit naïve." She grabs the joint to put it in her mouth, then the lighter, and heads outside.

Jake turns to me, grabs my shoulders, and pulls me to him as if being in his arms would protect me from the rest of the world.

"I'm not scared of him," I whisper, my cheek against his chest, my ear against the crazy heartbeat wrecking his body.

"You should be." His voice wavers slightly when he replies so I wrap my arms around his waist, tightly, showing him I will always be there for him. "But I would never, *ever* let anything happen to you. I can promise you that."

338

When he lets me go, he looks toward the door before dropping a peck on my nose. "I'm going to smoke, do you want to come outside?"

I join him, but once in the yard, I decline the joint Rose is offering. They smoke while Chris and I chat about the upcoming lacrosse season. He doesn't play but he knows it's a big one for me as captain of the women's team.

We're cut off by Rose and Jake's sudden laughing fit.

"These two are up to no good, that's their stupid plan sort of laugh," Chris mutters to me.

"Come on," Rose giggles. "Do it, show him how unafraid of him you are."

"You do it," Jake laughs back as he plays with the lighter, rolling his thumb over the metal wheel and flickering the flame. He pauses, observing it. "Better yet. Let's burn the fucking thing."

Rose's eyes widen at the same time as her gorgeous smile spreads across her lips. "Fuck, yes."

Jake gives Rose the lighter, runs inside and comes back with the paperwork.

"I hope you know this is a really stupid thing to do," Chris scowls, mist clouding around his face from the cold winter day. The twins both nod.

"Just worry about clicking record," Jake smiles as he hands him his phone.

I hear the sound of the phone recording and Rose lights up the joint again between her lips as Jake rolls up the paperwork he's holding. He grabs the joint and lighter from Rose, puts it in his mouth, takes a long drag, and lights up the paperwork with the lighter. Rose starts laughing and grabs the joint back. She takes another long drag and talks as a cloud of smoke escapes her mouth.

"Go fuck yourself, *brother*," she says as she blows the rest of the smoke and Jake throws what's left of the burning paper on the floor. It all dies in a pile of ashes and Chris stops recording.

I can't say I agree with what they did, but I like how confident they feel that they're not going to move houses. Because I don't think I could handle it if they went to live at Nathan's.

CHAPTER 18

Infinity – Jaymes Young

Jamie

I knock three times on the front door and rearrange my deep red velvet skirt. I check the flowers I bought for Chris' parents to make sure not one of them is out of place and replace my bag that's falling off my shoulders. I'm pulling down on my tight Christmas sweater when the door opens to Jake and his smile brightens his face the second his eyes fall on me. His dimples pop out and I feel my entire self melting.

"Merry Christmas." His voice is merely more than a whisper as his gaze rakes all over my body.

"Merry Christmas to you too," I whisper back.

I'm just like him, full of unbelievable happiness. It feels so surreal, too good to be true. I get that sort of feeling every time I see him but today is extra special. We're spending Christmas together. My aunt's case has been deteriorating in the past weeks and my mom doesn't want to leave her alone for Christmas. Our savings are running low since my mom had to take time off work to be there and my part-time pay didn't allow me to take a plane ticket. Jake insisted on paying it, Chris joined him, but I refused to be a charity case. So, they invited me to spend Christmas day with them.

I used some of my savings to have a present delivered to my mom so she wouldn't feel alone or guilty for not being able to come back. It's strange spending Christmas without her. We went from a family of four to just the two of us and suddenly I'm celebrating without her.

I walk in with Jake, it's weird to be in the main house when we usually spend all our time in the pool house.

The whole place has been decorated from floor to ceiling in a red and golden Christmas theme. The Murrays are not often in Stoneview but when they are, it shows. We leave my bag and the flowers with their maid and keep going.

"You look gorgeous," Jake slips in my ear as we walk the dark wooden floor to what I know is their dining room.

I giggle because my sweater is sporting Olaf from Frozen, with his nose stuck in the snow and him trying to pull it out.

"Interesting sweater," he chuckles. We stop in front of a closed door and I pull my sweater to look down at it.

"Don't make fun of me," I pout. "My dad gave me this one Christmas when I was little, and I've been wearing it every Christmas since."

I remember begging my dad for a Frozen sweater for Christmas when the film came out. That year wasn't exactly good financially and I cried like a spoiled brat when I didn't get it. When the craziness of Frozen ran out he managed to get it on sale at Walmart. I would wear it everywhere. Camila and Beth were already making fun of me back then. We were just little girls, and they would mock me for having a Frozen sweater a year and a half after the hit film came out. I didn't care, it was a gift from my dad. Now, even more, I love wearing it.

He offers me his most genuine smile and cups my cheek with one hand. "I guess it's good you're still the same size as you were when you were a little kid then."

I laugh and hit his arm. I love that Jake can always take a situation that makes me sad and distract me with something that'll make me laugh.

"I'm a normal size." I cross my arms pretending to be upset and he slides both his arms around me.

"You are, Angel. If you consider bite-size normal." He gives me a lingering kiss and I completely melt in his arms, my heart beating out of my chest. "Let's eat," he says as he pulls away and opens the door to the dining room.

Nothing could have prepared me for the scene on the other side of that door. As soon as we walk in, the cinnamon smell of mulled wine tickles my nostrils. The decorations are the same as the rest of the house but everything else is messier. I would have bet my house that I would find a formal dining table with everyone sitting around in awkward silence. That's pretty much how I imagine every millionaire spending their Christmas. Clearly, not the Murrays.

The table is a mess from all the crackers they've already popped. They've opened two bottles of champagne. On my left, Thomas – that I remember vividly from my childhood as a warm man full of dad jokes – is holding his arm high above himself to try and take a selfie that would include himself and far behind him, his wife Hannah, and Chris and Rose.

Chris is holding Rose in a piggyback and she's wrapped both her arms around his neck as her long legs fall in front of him. Both are in tears from laughing, shouting indications at Thomas on how to hold his phone.

I can't help but smile at the sight. They truly are a happy family. I can't, for one second, imagine Nathan could separate them. I wait, retreat slightly as Jake runs toward them, and grabs Hannah to put her on his back too. She shrieks and, despite the fact that she's a tall, well-endowed woman, he easily holds her on his back. Thomas takes a picture and soon notices me.

"Jamie, sweetheart, my God! Join us!" His voice is merry from the champagne and family time.

I hesitantly walk toward the group and place myself on the side. That's until Hannah gets off Jake and he brings me in front of him before wrapping his arms around me.

"Say Merry Christmas!" Thomas shouts.

We all execute in a laugh, giving our best smiles. And just like that, I don't feel awkward anymore spending Christmas with my boyfriend's family. As soon as Thomas puts his phone back in his pocket, both he and Hannah come to talk to me. Chris and Rose ignore our conversation as they both sit down at the table watching videos on his phone. Jake stays with me. He keeps a gentle hand between my shoulders to show me he's with me as he introduces me to his foster parents.

It's not like I don't know them, Chris and I were friends as kids. Way before the twins came into his life. This time, however, not only have I not seen them in years but I'm also being introduced as *Jake's girlfriend.* I wonder if that ever happened before. Had they met Camila?

"You guys know Jamie," he simply says.

They both smile down at me with wide grins. Chris didn't get his height and mass out of nowhere. Both Hannah and

Thomas are extraordinarily tall and big. Especially Thomas.

"Jamie, we haven't seen you in years!" Hannah beams.

"I'd love to say 'you've grown so much' but I think you're about the same height as I last saw you. When you were thirteen," Thomas jokes.

I laugh heartily as Hannah gives him a light slap on the shoulder.

"Don't listen to him, sweetie. You're a gorgeous young woman. How are you? How's your mom?" she asks.

"Mom's good. She's in Tennessee, visiting her sister," I reply, staying as vague as possible. This is not the 'poor Jamie show'.

"Yes, Jake said your aunt wasn't well. I was sorry to hear. I wish her a good recovery."

I'm surprised Jake talked to them about me. I thought he was the kind of guy who wouldn't share girlfriend things with his 'parents'. Even if he was, I would have never imagined he was this close to Hannah and Thomas.

"Well, I'm glad you're here, we haven't seen you in so long," Thomas changes topics.

"And as Jake's guest," Hannah adds. "All those years we thought Chris would suddenly show up with you to family dinners and here you are...with our baby Jake! We thought he'd never introduce anyone to us."

"Hannah," Jake groans in a chuckle. "It's Christmas, do I have to put up with the whole 'parents embarrassing me in front of girlfriend' thing?"

"It's a rite of passage, son. We took out the childhood pictures when Rachel first came over. Didn't we, Rosie?" Thomas turns to Rose as he remembers. "Where's Rachel, by the way? We haven't seen her since we've been back."

Rose makes a face as she looks up from the video she's watching with Chris. "Far far away from me," she shrugs. It's forced and she's clearly pretending it's not affecting her, but Thomas just goes with it and nods.

I try to keep my eyes from widening at, not only the nickname that the Murrays use for Stoneview Prep's bad bitch, Rose White, not only that Rachel was actually introduced to their family as her girlfriend, but mainly that Thomas calls Jake 'son'.

It's always so strange to see people from school in their home, with parents. They're more vulnerable, truly themselves. They don't put up masks and fake attitudes. Seeing the twins, especially Jake, with their family brings me incomparable joy. He deserves the happiness the Murrays bring him.

"Here, here. Have a glass of champagne, Jamie," Thomas orders more than he suggests when he brings the glass over to me.

After countless pictures and games, we sit for a late lunch cooked by their chef. They seem like a normal family, but let's not forget they still are unbelievably rich. It would have surprised me more if they didn't have a chef bringing all the delicacies we currently have on the table.

I indulge in the delicious turkey and all the side dishes that come with it. We drink way too much wine, which doesn't seem to bother Chris' parents.

Jake and I can't get enough of each other and our hands keep meeting, under the table at first, until he brings them to rest on the silk tablecloth. I don't miss the look Hannah and Thomas give to each other when they notice their foster son running his thumb on my small hand, or when he smiles down at me and kisses my forehead. They're happy for him. For us. Jake and I have had so many people against us along the way that it feels reassuring to finally be able to be ourselves and still be supported by the people we love and that matters the most. It's the only thing that counts.

I enjoy the intellectual conversations with the Murrays, we get along even more now than we did in the past and there's no wondering where Chris got his knowledge. They're open to debate and doubt, to teaching and evolving and I see why their son is so kind-hearted.

As we're just finishing our desserts, pushing our stomachs past their limits, the staff comes to get our plates. The conversation slightly dies down and Chris suggests moving to the game room. His parents leave us for their own entertainment and the four of us end up playing old arcade games together.

A couple of hours later, I'm still supporting Jake playing an old version of Street Fighter with Chris, jumping on the spot next to him and clapping like a fangirl. Chris laughs at my encouragement and pouts.

"Come on, Jamie, I could use the support too!" he laughs.

"Oh, shit," Rose's voice cuts through our video game fun. She was lying on the red vinyl sofa on the far end of the room but suddenly sits up, looking at her phone.

"Did you see what happened to the Diaz brothers?"

Jake and Chris look up and I turn to her fully.

"What?" Jake queries. He's still toying with the remote in his hand but not looking at the screen anymore. Lately, anything related to Nathan has been getting him fidgety.

"They got jumped by some of Volkov's guys," Rose replies as she gets up to walk toward us.

347

She stands next to me, showing her phone to her brother and reminding me of the height difference between her model size and mine. I glance at the phone to see her conversation with Carlo, which includes a picture of his face and it's anything but a pretty sight right now. A few texts that explain how they were jumped on their way to delivering bags of weed accompany his beaten-up face on the screen.

"Why do you still talk to them," Jake snarls.

"Does your brain really not process danger *at all?*" Chris adds straight away.

I kind of feel bad for her. She was just trying to keep them in the loop, and it's being thrown back in her face. I can see why she sometimes withholds information.

"Man, I should have just kept this to myself," she mumbles. She snatches her phone back, runs a hand through her hair, and slumps back down on the sofa.

"Are they going to be ok?" I ask to take the topic away from Rose's lack of understanding danger.

She looks at me surprised but a small smirk appears on her face.

"Who fucking cares. We don't want to be involved with anything related to Nate anymore," Jake cuts off. He drops the controller completely and points at her in a warning. "Fuck, if I catch you buying from them, Ozy..." he threatens.

I nudge him in the ribs. He still has bruises from the fight with Nathan but he barely winces.

"Jake," I whisper in shock.

I hate it when he talks to her like that. We're all the same age, we're all equally responsible for ourselves and each other and it's not like she's stupid.

Rose rolls her eyes but doesn't retort anything. I notice

her pulling at the sleeves of her sweater before typing on her phone again. I feel like I haven't seen her tattoos in ages. Maybe she hides them when the Murrays are around.

"Hey, should we have a dip in the pool? It's heated right?" I insist on changing the topic.

"It's snowing," Jake chuckles.

"So what," I shrug, a smile tugging at my lips. "You said it was *heated.* You rich people don't know how to enjoy what you have."

My statement earns me a laugh from Chris and an agreement from Jake as he puts a hand on my shoulder and squeezes softly, almost massaging me.

"Let's do this," Chris exclaims.

Rose gets up from the sofa and heads straight for the door, ignoring our excitement.

"Are you not coming?" Jake questions, surprised.

She turns back to us, her eyebrows drawn together. "It's a pretty fucking stupid idea. I'll not be catching pneumonia in my room if you don't mind."

"What's pretty fucking stupid is you pretending you're fine when you're obviously not," he retorts. "Spend time with us instead of being a moody bitch."

He tries to get a reaction out of her but she's already on her way out of the door and the only thing we hear from the hall is a loud 'Fuck you, Jake'.

He lets out a frustrated groan and turns to Chris. "Tell me she talks to you about it." His voice is desperate.

Chris only shakes his head 'no' and I can sense both their frustrations. "She's been so hot and cold since D.C."

"I know," Jake concludes, his annoyance and anger palpable.

He still hasn't spoken to me about anything that happened in D.C. I tried mentioning it, but Jake being Jake refused to share anything that has to do with Mateo Bianco. I'm assuming for him it was a moment of weakness, he was out of control and he struggles too much with those to share them with me. We'll get there, I'm sure, but those things take time.

Out of all the questions I had running through my mind in the last week, the only thing we've talked about is the fact that we had sex without a condom. It was an argument since I learned that he hadn't been careful with many girls. Not only did I have to worry about catching something and he had to get tested but it also was a harsh reminder of the stupid number of girls he'd been with before me. All while he was with Camila.

It's hard to trust him when I'm reminded of him cheating on her over and over again. The only thing that comes as a slight reassurance is that the whole of Stoneview Prep was aware of him cheating, and I know the harpies at school would take great pleasure in telling me if he was doing this to me. He also came back all clean, which was a good thing, I guess.

"I'll talk to her," Chris sighs.

He heads out and it takes a minute of Jake running his hand through his hair and muttering how annoyed he is before we follow. When we walk past Chris' room, we see him stroking Rose's head as he talks to her. Her head is buried in the pillows, but I know for sure she's not crying because this bitch never cries.

* * *

"They're sleeping," Jake whispers as he swims closer to me. He just went inside to check on everyone.

We ended up spending the evening with Hannah and Thomas while Chris and Rose were chilling in his room. But now it's one am and everyone is asleep. I'm in the corner of the pool, both my arms spread on the edge, facing Jake. The warmth of the heated water compared to the outside temperature is magical. The only lights on are the pool lights and as Jake gets to me and puts his hands on my hips the whole atmosphere turns sexual.

"Did I ever tell you that you're the most beautiful girl in the world?" he asks in a gravelly voice.

His mouth goes to my neck and I giggle as I try to reply that yes, he told me countless times.

"I want to be inside you," he murmurs as one of his hands grabs my breast and he starts massaging my nipple through my bikini.

My brain starts screaming at me.

You're in the pool.

Anyone could see.

The lights are literally all on you!

And as usual around him, my body forgets my brain and instead, agrees to everything Jake says. My hand goes under his swim shorts on their own accord, and I grip his already steel-hard length.

"Fuck me," I groan as his fingers slip beneath my bikini bottom and between my folds.

I watch with half-closed eyes as he shakes his head no. He smirks when he sees my face.

"I'm making love to you tonight, Angel."

I gasp at his words mixed with his fingers entering me.

351

"Let me love you, please," he purrs in my ear and my heart melts.

Jake doesn't say please, he takes. Especially in a sexual situation, I'm the one usually doing the begging. The vulnerability in his voice is like I've never heard. We're both still waiting for the other to say the magic three words. I know he doesn't because he hates being vulnerable and he might lose control of the situation. I don't because I'm scared. I freeze every time I think I'm going to say it and open myself to being hurt.

Before I realize, he pushes my bikini to the side and enters me in one long stroke. He pauses as my mouth falls open and waits for my body to adjust. He then starts moving at a torturously slow pace, but the warm feeling that spreads to my chest is overwhelming.

He spends long minutes undulating his hips with my legs around his waist, my arms around his neck, and his hands gripping the edge of the pool behind me. It's slow and tender and it drives me to the edge of sanity. My orgasm comes so slowly, but the waves last for an eternity. They wash over me, over and over again as our breaths become one. I'm not screaming like when he pushes his anger into his strokes. No, I'm moaning long and slow as he keeps a steady rhythm. My whole body is relaxed even as it's reaching its highest high ever.

For the second time in a week, tears slip out of my eyes as Jake and I reach a climax together. My inner walls tighten around his cock and uncontrollable tears of happiness spill down my face. I let my legs float in the water as he pulls out but I keep my arms around his neck and he keeps me caged in between himself and the wall of the pool. He lets his forehead fall on mine, breathless. After a minute or so of calming down in the quiet night, he puts a strand of hair behind my ear and rests his hand back on the edge again.

"What's wrong, baby?" he asks quietly.

This is one of the most intimate moments we've ever had. It's restful and exciting at the same time. It gets my heart beating too fast but relaxes my muscles. It fills me with joy but still leaves me longing for more of him. I need all of him, his body, his love, his mind, his trust, his soul. All of it.

"Why are you crying, Angel," he repeats. "That's twice now and I'm worrying."

I let out a whispered chuckle and place both my palms on his cheeks, looking into the depth of his ocean eyes.

"I'm happy, Jake. I never thought it was possible to be loved entirely and unconditionally. Now I know it is."

He smiles at me but says nothing. He doesn't confirm 'I do love you'. I know he does. I just need him to say it.

Please say it.

He lifts up his head, reaches for something on the ground behind me, and brings his hand in front of me, between both our faces. He's holding something in his fist, but I can't see what it is.

"Merry Christmas," he breathes. He opens his hand and a small necklace falls in front of my eyes, hanging from his forefinger.

"Jake," I gasp. It's so gorgeous I have to refrain myself from crying again.

The gold chain is short and simple, the pendant is a flat heart made of gold. My stomach twists at the thought that I made him a calendar of us. It's not like I could have afforded something as nice as this necklace, so I went for sentimental.

"I want you to wear it this way around," he orders, showing me the front. On this side, there's a 'J' engraved elegantly on the heart and I can't help a laugh. There is no doubt he means Jake and not Jamie. It's so caveman, so Jake. He grabs my chin with his thumb and forefinger, keeping a firm grip on me.

"All day. Every. Single. Day." He kisses me and pulls away too quickly. "Read me the other side."

I frown at his request and especially because his face looks so serious. It makes me nervous, and I grab the necklace with trembling hands. Stress eats at me and I say the words engraved on the backside without registering them.

"I love you," I read with furrowed brows.

"I love you too." His gravelly voice makes me snap my eyes back up at him. I now see the cheeky smirk on his face and my brain finally processes what I just read.

"I..." I hesitate.

"I'm in love with you, Jamie. So fucking much it hurts. You make my heart go fucking crazy, you pull at its strings until it can only sing to the rhythm of yours. As long as your heart beats, mine will beat along with it." Hearing these words come out of his mouth takes a heaviness from my heart I didn't know existed. It squeezes my chest before releasing in a swarm of butterflies.

"Me too," I nod in a smile. "I love you." I never thought I would feel so free saying this. "I'm so in love I don't even remember how I lived my life before you in it."

He smiles at me, and our lips clash together in a heated kiss. "Fuck, I love you. Can I say it over and over again?" he asks, and I giggle on his lips.

"With pleasure," I reply.

I stand in front of Jake's mirror as he puts the necklace around my neck. He clips it at the back, and I realize how short it is.

"It's like a choker," I observe more for myself than him. It's definitely not as tight as a choker, but it's much shorter than a pendant.

He kisses my neck, making me squirm in pleasure. "I don't want it to hide behind your clothes. I want everyone to see it. Everyone to know who gave this to you."

I smile at him and reply in the most innocent voice possible. "Yes, everyone will finally know Jason and I are an item." I laugh, but his possessive growl is anything but amused.

Everyone already knows about us, there's no need for the 'J' but I like the intention behind it, and I like that it matches my name too.

"Keep going like this and I'll brand you," he chastises me. He kisses my neck. "Property." Another kiss on my neck, lower this time. "Of." A kiss on my shoulder. "Jake White." He nibbles at my shoulders.

A single shiver of tension mixed with yearning crosses my body. Why do I love it so much when he wants to own me?

He steps away and goes to sit at his desk while I keep looking at my gift in the mirror. I can't seem to take my eyes off it. It feels heavenly to finally have admitted that we are in love. It's a new chapter for us.

Full of confidence, I turn to him and watch him code something on his laptop for a few seconds before raising my question. "Jake?"

"Yes, Angel," he mumbles. The kind of mumbling he does when he's too busy to talk but doesn't want to ignore me.

"Can I ask you something?"

Tap, tap, tap, his fingers go rapidly on his keyboard. "Anything, baby." He doesn't turn around or stop, his focus entirely on the screen in front of him.

"Have you...um...before that night at the police station. Had you been arrested before?" I try to keep my voice as soft as possible when I carry on. I know this is touching on a topic he's never wanted to talk about. "Like, for something serious. When you were at Bianco's maybe?"

The tapping stops as he freezes, his spine going rigid. He slowly spins his desk chair around to face me, but he stays completely silent. He looks at me, his gaze darkened, his jaw ticking. He's in predator mode and I gulp at the realization.

I put my hands up in defense. "I don't mean to—"

"Now what could possibly make you ask this?" His top lip twitches slightly, almost like he's about to growl and I know this is a trick question, but I answer honestly anyway.

"That night you were being questioned at the police station with Nathan...Rose and I were waiting for you, we were so worried—"

"Get to the point, Angel," he insists impatiently.

"I was trying to say that there was a chance you would get off with a warning or community service but Rose, she wasn't convinced, and when I asked if you had previous convictions..." My flow of words per second accelerates as I see his face getting more serious by the minute. "I just thought I'd ask you, I guess I'm just being curious about your past, but you never want to talk about it—"

"Come here," he cuts me off. His voice is not reassuring, and I regret bringing up his past again.

I slowly pad over to him until I'm settled between his spread legs. He slides his arms around my hips and plays with the string of my bikini hanging down my back.

"You're asking questions about my past again, Angel. When you know I'm not going to answer them. But you're just being curious, huh?"

I nod, a pang of guilt going through my stomach. I know he doesn't want to talk about it, and it annoys him when I bring it up, but I just want to understand him.

He pulls at the string keeping my bikini in place, slightly uncovering my breasts. He softly grabs one of my wrists, then the other. His movements are so smooth, I only realize what he's doing when I feel the string sliding around my jointed wrists.

"What−"

"Do you know what happens to curious girls, my sweet Angel?"

I can only shake my head no. The gesture of him securing the string around my wrists is already making my thighs shake and my pussy tighten in anticipation. Once my wrists are completely secured behind my back, his hands slide down to my hips, my ass, and then along my thigh until they settle behind my knees.

"Curious girls who ask too many questions end up choking on cock." His voice is so low, husky from lust, I let it wrap around me and suffocate me with desire. "On your knees," he adds as he puts pressure behind them. I slowly slide to the floor, my mouth already watering.

"I see the anticipation in your beautiful eyes, baby. Don't get too excited, this is only going to be enjoyable for one of us."

He gets up from his chair, pushes his boxers down and his hard cock springs free.

He pushes his two thumbs in my mouth and pulls my jaw

wide open. He puts pressure on my tongue, playing with it, hurting me slightly, and then hooks his thumbs on either of my cheeks before spreading them wide. The stretch hurts and my arms jerk behind my back, desperately trying to reach his hands and push him away.

"Show me that pretty tongue of yours."

I stick my tongue out as far as I can and he slowly pushes his dick against it, sliding along until he settles in my mouth.

"Time to choke, my little Angel. Let's see how many questions you ask after that."

CHAPTER 19

Until We Bleed – Kleerup, Lykke Li

Jamie

"I think cotton candy wasn't such a good idea for you," Jake laughs as I jump on my seat. "Sugar rush."

He's driving next to me on our way back from the fair. We went to say goodbye to the Murrays at the airport and stopped at the fair on the way back. I hate rides so, really, we just stopped for cotton candy.

I'm overly excited because tomorrow is my birthday. I'm turning eighteen. It's also New Year's Day and I can't wait to celebrate with Jake.

Chris and Rose have headed to Camila's New Year's Eve party to celebrate at midnight. Jake didn't want to attend, and I couldn't agree more. The last thing I want is to turn eighteen at Camila Diaz's house so she can ruin my night.

Jake has a surprise for me tomorrow afternoon, but I'm guessing it'll include Emily and the rest of his gang and I'm looking forward to spending the night with just the two of us.

We're always surrounded by everyone, especially during the school break when the Murrays were here. Rose wasn't going out as much, Chris is always around except when he sneaks out to see his mysterious girlfriend, whom we're not totally sure exists anymore.

We know we've got the house to ourselves tonight, and for once we're actually going to stay inside the main house. Even the staff isn't there for New Year's Eve.

Jake throws the house keys on a side table as we get in and I shriek when my feet suddenly leave the ground. I laugh as he carries me up the stairs and throws me on the bed in one of the guest rooms.

We take a bath together, drink champagne and he cooks for me. Who knew Jake fucking White could cook?

"What about now?" I ask cheekily as I put another fork of delicious lasagna in my mouth.

He chuckles and puts his fork down to get more of the food from the dish. This guy eats so much.

"No, Jamie. You'll get your present at midnight, as I wish you a happy New Year. You'll have to give me a kiss first though."

I smile back at him, falling for him all over again when his dimples show on his beautiful face.

"But I can't wait," I fake pout. "Give me clues!"

"You'll see," he winks.

He clears both our plates when we're finished, and we settle on the sofa with ice cream. It quickly turns into tasting each other's ice creams then from each other's mouth. Jake grabs my waist, gets up, and lays us both down on the floor.

"I like how ice cream tastes in your mouth," he murmurs.

"Do you?" I giggle as he pulls my t-shirt up, exposing my

breasts.

"Yes. Let's see how it tastes from your gorgeous nipples."

He digs his spoon in the bowl of vanilla ice cream and spreads the frozen sweetness on both my nipples. I gasp at the cold, my buds tightening, the next second his warm lips and tongue overtake me, and I melt into him. He licks at both my nipples, grazing his teeth against them, making me writhe in pleasure.

"Jake," I gasp. "Shit, that feels so good. Fuck." The contrast between the frozen ice cream and the warmth of his body is driving me insane. The wetness spreading between my legs is becoming a desperate invitation,

"What are those filthy words coming out of your mouth, Angel? Swearing is not for you, I thought we established that."

He rids me of my jeans and soon enough my panties follow.

"Say 'I'm sorry for being a bad girl'," he growls as the spoon goes back into the vanilla.

"What?" I don't have time to wonder for more than a split second because the cold spoon is against my clit in the next, making my lungs beg for air as my mouth falls slack.

"You heard me. Say it." He rubs the freezing spoon against my clit and I moan desperately.

"I'm sorry," I mewl as he slows his movement and I rub myself against the spoon shamelessly.

He presses way too hard against my clit, making me scream in pleasure mixed with pain. "That's not what I said." This time, his voice is dark, anger rumbling in his chest at me refusing to give him complete control.

My heartbeat picks up, my wetness doubles. I didn't mean to get him angry, but I love it so much when he is.

He presses harder, and the words tumble out of my mouth.

"I'm sorry for being a bad girl." My voice is whiny, desperate for more of him.

"Atta girl, now wouldn't it be safer to prevent more of those curses from escaping your beautiful lips?"

The spoon retreats. My lips form a pout. It's back, colder, the rubbing torturously slow. I nod at Jake's statement. "Yes," I pant. "Yes, it would be."

"Ding, ding," he taunts. "Good answer."

It's when I feel fabric against my lips that I understand my eyes have closed. They snap open, just to watch him pushing against my lips and the smirk forming on his own. "Open like a good girl."

I do.

He pushes my pale pink lace panties far into my mouth, gagging me with them, and the next second, the spoon is gone again.

I protest, but only a muffled sound comes out.

"I'm sorry that wasn't quite clear," he mocks me. I go to grab the panties from my mouth, but his gaze darkens. "Do you have a death wish? Don't you fucking move."

I could take them out, my hands are free, and Jake would never truly hurt me. I simply don't want to.

I watch him bring the spoon to his lips, slide it into his mouth and moan in pleasure. "You taste way better than ice cream, my sweet Angel."

He doesn't take time for more teasing. I think licking the spoon tipped him over the edge. He grabs my hips to flip me around and pulls back, talking as I hear him take off his jeans. "Spread yourself for me."

Knowing exactly what he wants, I reach back with both hands and spread my ass cheeks for him, opening myself completely.

"Such a good girl," he breathes out. He rubs his dick between my lips, coating himself in my wetness and I moan into my panties.

He enters me in such a strong thrust, my cheek grazes against the living room carpet. I scream in pleasure, in surprise, in the delicious pain of being stretched and completely full.

He fucks me relentlessly, groaning how much he loves me. "I'm going to love you forever, you know that? I'll never let you go, you're mine. All." Thrust. "Fucking." Thrust. "Mine." Thrust. "Now come for me."

It's like my brain waits for Jake's authorization to release the chemicals that bring me a phenomenal orgasm. I scream into my panties as he unleashes mercilessly on my body. When one of my hands slips, he administers a hard slap on my cheek before spreading it himself. "Naughty girl can't keep her position," he growls. Another thrust, another scream, he's got my burning ass cheek in a bruising grip.

"Fuck!" he barks as he orgasms. "Fuck, Jamie." His voice breaks as he slows down and falls on top of me.

I lay there, completely high off him. Completely satisfied in our bubble of happiness, love, and orgasms.

For a long minute, we both lie there. It's not until Jake spins me back around and takes the panties out of my mouth that I realize I had just left them there.

"I should shower," I breathe out another ten minutes later. We're both still lying on the floor naked, next to the sofa where it all started. My body is covered in ice cream, stickiness making me feel dirty between my legs.

"Mm, can I join?" he smiles.

I laugh and give him a chaste kiss. "No, it's almost midnight. Next thing you're getting is your New Year's kiss."

I get up and head for the en suite bathroom inside a guest room. Jake joins me mid-shower because he doesn't care whether I told him he could or not. He realizes the time when we're both drying ourselves and practically jumps in his clothes.

"Shit! It's five to. I'll be back in one minute. You do *not* move from here."

I take time to get dressed, brush my hair, and lie down on the bed, daydreaming about the very same person that was here with me a minute ago. I check the time on my phone. It's 11:59 pm. I sigh, I can't believe he's going to miss the new year because he came to shower with me. I let my head fall on the pillow. All the sex tonight made me sleepy. I rest my eyes for a second and the next thing I know I jump up. I can't believe I fell asleep. I check the time again. Shit, I slept for ten minutes.

Wait.

Jake has been gone for more than ten minutes. That's a bit strange. Maybe he's setting something up downstairs? I should go check on him.

But he said not to leave the room. I don't want to ruin whatever he's got planned.

I settle on calling him to check on him. I grab my phone again and tap his name on my screen. The phone rings in the room straight away. I pick up his phone on the nightstand and watch my name and picture on the screen. I hang up and my face disappears. In no way do I mean to pry, but I notice a familiar name on the screen straight away.

Nate.

I can't help it. Curiosity eats at me and I unlock Jake's phone. We trust each other enough to know our passwords, and I sincerely hope he won't be mad that I'm checking. But I have to.

I go on the conversation with Nate straight away, trying not to look at anything and invade his privacy more than I already am.

"What the hell," I whisper in shock.

They've been talking for weeks. Part of the conversation is about me. Nate has been threatening his brother. In countless texts, he tells him he'll regret it if he doesn't break up with me. There are too many threats for me to count but they don't include only me. He also talks about the change of guardians. Jake replies once in a while. Mainly to stir the pot when it comes to me.

In other texts, Nate is saying Rose is with Sam and to pick her up because he doesn't want them hanging out. Since Jake sent a video of him and Rose burning *another* pile of paperwork from the lawyer there have been very few texts.

A dark feeling starts to creep up my stomach and I stand up from the bed.

Where is Jake?

I scroll to the latest message and my heart drops from my chest to crash in my stomach. In a split second, I feel sick and the need to sit down comes back. I drop on the bed again, looking down at Jake's phone.

Three days ago, Nate sent another text to reply to the video.

Nate: About time to stop fucking around. Sign. I know Mateo will ask me to make you sign if you don't do it on your own accord.

Nate's text isn't what makes me feel lightheaded, it's not what freezes my blood. No, the worst is Jake's response.

Jake: Try your best.

I know instantly that something is wrong. It's 12:27 am and Jake still hasn't come back up. I jump up from the bed, my heart beating so hard it resonates in my ears. I'm probably too late. Nathan did something. I don't know what, but Jake is not well. I can feel it in my bones, so deep in my body that I already ache for him.

CHAPTER 20

PARANOID – Chase Atlantic

Jake

I feel a presence behind me before I hear the click of the gun. I went to get Jamie's present from the pool house, and I knew I was done for. I walked out of the front door and I felt it as soon as I turned to round the house. Fuck knows why I went through the front door and not the back. I guess I was closer when I walked down the stairs. All I know is I should have gone the other way.

"Happy new year, brother." Nate's satisfied voice rings in my ears.

How the fuck did he get past the gate? I turn around to face him and his gun in my face. To my surprise, he didn't come alone. I mean, of course, Sam is behind him smoking a cigarette, they come as a pair. But I didn't expect Carlo Diaz to be there with him. This is serious shit and I know when a situation isn't going to end well for me. This is one of those. Nate alone I'd find it hard to take on. Nate armed and with two of his bitches isn't exactly going to go down nice and easy.

But I'm not worried about myself. All I'm worried about is that they don't get in and find Jamie. They came for me. Me and Rose more specifically. They want us to sign their fucking change of guardianship form. Jamie shouldn't be involved in this, especially not when Nate is obsessed with her.

I don't think I ever heard of a girl breaking up with my brother before. The hair, the eyes, the tattoos, the suits, they love it. He probably didn't take it too well when she blocked him after his countless texts.

"Let's talk in your house," he orders.

Fuck no. I'd rather go and be tortured at Bianco's house than for them to know Jamie is here.

"Let's make this quick, I'll come with you to Bianco's," I reply as casually as possible.

He chuckles and the sound makes me grind my teeth. "Bianco's got no time to waste on you. He's spending New Year's Eve with a few escorts and bottles of whiskey. Get in your house."

"It's not my fucking house. I know the psycho in you wants to drag this out, but I have other things to do. Let's go."

His smirk turns into a dark smile and I know I should have played this cooler. Now he knows I really don't want to get in.

"That's true. It's not your house," he quips. "It's the Murrays'. It wouldn't really play in your favor if something happened to it." He puts his gun in the back of his jeans and takes a step towards the front door, but I get in the way.

"This is only the start of the night, Jake. And it's going to be a very long night. I'd suggest you buy your time before it starts getting painful for you. And it will be painful."

I regret it as soon as I shove him back but what else was I

meant to do? I need to delay him getting into the house as much as possible and the situation is already slipping out of my control.

The first two punches hurt. So. Fucking. Bad. Especially because they come from Nate. They add to the bruises that hadn't faded from our fight at Cal's.

The adrenaline takes over when Carlo joins in and I fight back as much as I can. I practically black out when my brother lands a punch that knocks me to the floor. I can't feel much anymore, I think I'm passing out. The last thing I see is Sam calmly pushing the front door open and the last thing I feel is someone grabbing my shoulders and dragging me.

* * *

Jamie

My heart stops when I'm faced with the scene downstairs and I can't help the gasped whimper from leaving my lips.

All heads turn to me and the surprise in Nathan's eyes is not my imagination.

"What are you doing here?" he seethes.

I want to shout, cry, claw at him. I want to reply confidently 'I'm returning the fucking question, asshole'. But I do nothing, I'm frozen on the last step, watching as Carlo Diaz and Sam drag Jake's barely conscious body in the foyer.

Nathan clearly didn't expect me to be here and it's messing

up his plan. There's a sliver of hesitation in his eyes. For a split second, I see the Nathan I knew, the one that cared for me and protected me, but it disappears as fast as it came. His gaze turns dark, and I can sense the evil part of him winning over everything else.

He turns to Sam. "Go get the shit from your car," he says in a voice of steel.

The door opening and slamming shut finally allows me to move my body again. I run to Jake as he starts to come back to reality, but Nate stops me straight in my tracks. He grabs me by the back of the head, tangling my hair in his fist and I scream as I'm being pulled back with force.

Jake tries to stand up but as soon as he starts moving Carlo hits him with a kick in the ribs. Another.

"Stop! Stop hurting him," I scream but that only makes Carlo laugh. "Nathan, please make him stop."

"He's fine," he growls in my ear and the chill that runs down my spine is the exact opposite of how he used to make me feel.

I put a hand on his one in my hair to try and ease the pain coursing through my scalp, but he doesn't budge. Carlo finally stops hitting Jake and I wouldn't be surprised if his ribs were broken.

When Sam walks back in, my eyes are instantly brought to the rope he's holding.

"No. Nathan let go of me," my voice quivers as my whole body starts to tremble.

He sounds so cold when he talks to me, I barely recognize him. "Now, now. You haven't forgotten what I told you, 'Me, have you? I warned you if fell for him or let him touch you like I did I would raise hell. Jake should have said that I always serve my revenge very cold."

The burning pain on my scalp brings tears to my eyes, one slips when he drags me with him to the living room. I hear Carlo command Jake to get up and after a few seconds of struggle, they both join us, Carlo pointing a gun at Jake's head. Another whimper escapes my lips, squeezing desperately past my tight throat.

Nathan pushes me on the chair he's just pulled away from the table but as soon as he's not holding my hair anymore. I jump back up to go help Jake. I freeze at the click of a gun.

"You move, he's dead," Carlo sneers, making Nathan laugh.

"Fucking hell, I train them good, don't I?"

I don't know who he's talking to, me or Sam, but I'm too focused on the gun at the back of Jake's head and the way Carlo is holding him to care. He's holding him like Jake would fall if he let him go. His lip is bleeding, his eyes keep rolling to the back of his head, and the two big bruises forming on his left temple and jaw explain why.

He won't shoot him.

He will NOT shoot him. He needs him!

Rationality might be screaming at me but my body refuses to listen. All it knows is that danger is imminent and if I want to avoid it, I shouldn't move.

So I don't.

"Sit back down. I need you to be nice and quiet for me, baby," Nathan orders.

I want to find Jake's gaze. I want him to reassure me, to tell me it's all going to be okay. I want him to be his cocky self and threaten to snap Nathan's neck if he so much as touches me. But the more I look at him, the more dreadful I feel. His head is hanging in front of him, chin to chest and I'm dying to grab him in my arms. He's dripping blood on the carpet. I can't help but look at it. Nathan has officially decided to put action into his threats. The fight at Cal's was nothing to him. *This.* This is what he does.

I sit back in the chair, quiet, tears drying on my cheeks. I've already accepted that tonight is going to be the worst night of my life. Up until today, it was watching my dad and brother get shot. I've grieved them, accepted that none of them will ever come back in my life. I kept on living and I fell in love. Now I'm watching the love of my life suffer at the hands of someone else. The pattern repeats itself and I can feel something break inside me. Probably my heart.

I watch as Sam comes to me with the rope, but I don't say anything. I flinch when he ties my wrists and ankles to the chair, forcing myself to show nothing else. He's ever so quiet, I barely ever hear him say anything except to Nathan or Rose, so I didn't expect him to walk me through how to behave when you're being tied to a chair.

I keep my gaze on Jake, praying that he stays awake. His head is lolling back and forth as he tries to look at me and he uncontrollably spits blood on the floor. The ropes are digging deep in my skin and I suddenly wish I was wearing more than one of Jake's long tees.

When Sam is done, I can barely move anything. The asshole is good with this. He's tied my waist to the chair too. As if a 97-pound girl is going to cause mayhem to three gang members. As I look at them again, I do wonder where Roy is. It's rare to see Carlo without him. His face is still bruised from when Volkov's men jumped him.

I see from the corner of my eye that Sam quietly settles by the window giving into the backyard and lights up a cigarette.

The coffee table is the only thing separating me and the sofa Jake is sitting on, so when Nathan slams paperwork on the table I can recognize what it is straight away: the form to change guardians and household.

I remember thinking there weren't a lot of criminals that could get away with anything and that Volkov was one of them. He used to run the city of Stoneview with an iron fist. Since being part of Jake's life, I've realized that might be easier than I thought.

Nathan White can get away with anything.

Kidnapping.

Attacking a cop.

Home invasion.

Battery.

Hostage-taking.

Duress.

Anything.

He isn't scared because he knows he will get away with it.

He isn't scared of anything and that's the most terrifying thing about this situation.

Nathan walks to me and grabs my jaw with a strong hand, forcing me to look up at him. I pull at the rope, but I should know there's nothing to do.

"I'm going to handle him and then, I promise, I'm going to deal with you." His voice makes my whole body tremble.

"Let go of her." Jake's pained voice is nothing more than a whisper but we both hear him loud and clear.

It only makes Nathan chuckle. He turns around and walks to his brother, grabbing him by the hair and pulling him to the floor. Jake grunts in pain, he can only get back up on his knees, putting himself in a weak position. Nathan keeps a firm grip on his hair before he punches him in the face again.

"Stop, fucking stop!" I shriek as tears threaten to fall again.

I can't watch this. Jake being beaten up in front of me is worse than the day a bullet lodged itself in my shoulder. I can feel every hit, I can feel his heart breaking. My skin prickles every time I hear the sound of flesh beating flesh and disgust grows in my stomach. I have to swallow again and again to stop myself from being sick.

"Please, Nathan, stop," I cry.

Nathan laughs as he stops hitting. "You two are so fucking pathetic." He gives me a disappointed look. "Especially when you know how it all started."

I frown in confusion.

"What are you talking about?" I ask with a raw voice. Screaming and acids coming up my throat are weakening my vocal cords.

He doesn't reply to me, instead, he lets go of Jake and lets him crash on the floor.

"Jake," I heave desperately. "Please help him back on the sofa," I beg Nathan, but he walks to me and squats in front of my chair to look right into my eyes. His forearms are resting on my bare thighs.

"He made your life hell at school!" he shouts in anger. His eyes dart to the necklace Jake gave me and turn darker.

He gets up and storms back to Jake looking down on him as he hopelessly tries to get back on the sofa.

"She didn't want you, Jake. So you bullied her until she gave up. Fuck, who do you think you are, huh? You think you're all that to her, but who do you think she came back crying to? Who do you think she confessed to that someone at school was harassing her because he couldn't take that she was already seeing someone? Fucking. Pathetic."

He kicks him in the legs and Jake makes another desperate sound. I try to tell myself that as long as he makes noises, he's still conscious but his eyes are puffy and rarely open anymore. He tries to push himself into a sitting position, but Nathan kicks him down again, making Carlo laugh.

"Stay down," Nathan orders dangerously.

Jake doesn't listen. He tries to get up again, earning himself another kick, this time to his nose. Everyone can hear the crack it makes and my heart sinks in the darkest abysses.

"Oh my God," I whimper. "Please, Jake, stop fighting back."

"Mate, you're losing the point here." Sam's voice cuts the tension like a sharp knife and Nathan finally reacts.

He looks up at his friend by the window and nods.

"Right...right," he points at the paperwork. "I need you to sign this." He taps the paper on the coffee table with a finger.

Jake lets out a chuckle that turns into a cough. "Fuck you," he forces out. "Might as well kill me." He coughs again.

Nathan laughs and shakes his head. "Do you think I'm stupid? That I don't know you?" He sits down on the coffee table and rests his elbows on his knees. "See the thing with you is that you don't mind pain. I could never get you to do anything by hurting you physically. I can punch you all night, it would bring me great joy, but I know you won't sign that fucking thing. That's a great trait we have in common. Pain doesn't faze us."

He runs a hand through his hair, undoes his blond bun, and redoes it. He pulls up his shirt's sleeves that were already at his elbows anyway and settles back in his initial position.

"Your problem, however, is that you're so fucking weak

to the people you love. You and your useless twin care too much. And that's the difference between you and me. And look how lucky I am tonight. Not only is Jamie here," he takes his phone out, grabs Jake by the hair to pull his head up, and takes a picture of him, "but you know the second Ozy receives this picture of you she's going to come running. And, really, I only need one of you to sign. The other will follow."

I can't believe my eyes. The extent he is willing to go to to have them sign the form is terrifying. Are we even all going to last long enough to see tomorrow?

It takes less than a minute for Nathan's phone to ring. He chuckles to himself and mumbles a 'too easy' before picking up and putting it on speaker.

"Hi Ozy," he smiles.

"*Where are you, you fucking psychopath?*"

"At yours. Staining the Murrays' expensive carpet. Roy will pick you up. Come alone."

Jake makes a few moans and I think he means to tell her not to come but he doesn't make much sense.

"*I hate you.*" The line goes dead, and Nathan puts the phone away, a satisfied grin glued to his face.

We hear the tires screeching in the driveway and the front door slamming before we see Rose storming in the living room. She's out of breath and her eyes widen when she sees me on the chair and Nathan standing right behind me.

"Better late than never, Ozy."

He's spent the last ten minutes right there, listing me the mistakes I've made by choosing Jake, describing what he'll do to him if I keep seeing him. I stopped disputing his words when I couldn't take the pull on my scalp every time

I disagreed. I've just been listening, trying to block out his words but it's impossible. Every single threat is defined too clearly for me to shut it down. When he recalled everything we've done, everything he wants to do to me again, I struggled to keep my calm. I've just been staring at the floor. I can't look at Jake anymore, but I try to listen to his unsteady breathing, praying he'll make it until we can call an ambulance.

Roy bursts into the room a minute after Rose with a bloody lip.

I hear Nathan laughing. "What the fuck, Roy."

"I tried to get her in my car, she's got a good punch."

Rose ignores their conversation, her eyes look for her twin in the room. As soon as she finds him lying between the coffee table and the sofa, she runs to him.

"Jake," she shakes him slightly but he only groans in return. "Jake, talk to me," she panics.

His words are too slurred for any of us to make out what he's saying. She gets back up, walking to me and Nathan. I can feel him shift behind me and I jump in fear when I feel both his hands on my shoulders.

"You've officially lost it, you know that, right?" she growls at him.

Her voice is raspier than usual, and her words sound like they're being forced out of her throat. She's not shaking though. Her whole body looks perfectly fine apart from her ticking jaw. Her hair is wild, and she smells of weed and sex mixed with her usual flowery perfume. There's no wondering what she was up to at Camila's before she came, because for once, she wasn't with Sam.

"What are you gonna do?" Nathan asks, mocking her. "Call the cops? So you can pay Bianco another visit?"

377

I don't miss the tremble that crosses Rose's body at the mention of Bianco.

"I think someone should call an ambulance for Jake," Nathan jests. My eyes automatically dart to Jake's unmoving form on the floor and the fear gripping my gut is lethal.

"Yeah, what a great fucking idea. Are you gonna let me?" she snarls as she takes her phone out, probably already knowing he won't let her.

Before she can even unlock it, Roy grabs her wrist and wrestles her phone out of her hand. It lasts a second before he manages to violently snatch it from her. Sam is on them in a few sleek steps, he grabs Roy by the back of his neck and pushes him away quietly.

"I'll take it from here," he says calmly, making sure Roy isn't anywhere near touching Rose anymore.

"I'll be the one calling," Nathan drawls. "As soon as you sign the change of guardianship."

Rose scoffs but her eyes darken as rage overtakes her. "How could I miss?" she sneers. "I wanted you dead so badly, how could I miss your fucking heart?"

It's like a cold shower, being reminded that Rose shot Nathan in an attempt to kill him. It's hard to think she would be capable of pulling the trigger on her own brother. When I think of who Nathan really is, I shouldn't be surprised.

Nathan walks in front of me and I can see her flinch in the slightest but she's a master at controlling her body's reactions.

"You wanna know why you missed, Ozy?" he asks as he plants himself in front of her. "Because there was no heart to shoot," he continues without waiting for her reply.

"I'm not signing, Nate," she insists but her voice is growing quieter.

"Jake needs help," he insists.

Rose runs a hand through her hair in a sad sigh before shaking her head. She looks at Jake and I notice her hands trembling as they fall back beside her hips. Her eyes lock with mine for a split second.

"Why is she here? This has nothing to do with her." She sniffles and only now do I see the size of her pupils. She runs a hand on her nose and lifts an eyebrow at Nathan.

The fact that she wants me out of here warms my heart, but I wouldn't want to be anywhere else. I need to be close to Jake, I need to help him get out of this situation.

"I have my own problems to solve with Jamie, this is not exactly your concern." His eyes dart to Jake again and hers follow.

"Why are you doing this?" she pleads. "We were just fine being out of your way. We didn't cause trouble. We didn't mention you or Bianco. We just wanted to be left alone."

"You were fine because you thought I was dead, you stupid bitch," he rages as he grabs her by the hair.

She winces but doesn't say anything until he pulls her to the floor, slamming the side of her face on top of the coffee table. Her grunt makes Sam flinch and I look at him with wide eyes, silently begging him to do something but he doesn't move. I quickly turn back to Nathan as he keeps Rose's cheek on the flat surface, right next to the paperwork.

"Look at him!" Nathan barks, and I know he's talking about Jake.

His body looks lifeless on the floor and I can't help the tears that are pooling in my eyes.

Please be alive. Please be alive.

"Nate...don't do this to us." Rose's voice is strained with pain and I grimace for her.

"Do you think he's still breathing?" Nathan seethes, his hand pushing Rose's face further into the table. "Sign, Rose. Sign or I swear to God someone is dying tonight."

"Nate, too far," Sam growls but it seems this time it's not enough. Nathan is lost in his fury and none of us can get him out of there.

"I said *sign*!" he screams the last word, and no one misses the whimper that escapes her mouth.

Sam strides toward them. Nathan stops him with a look, asserting a hierarchy I hadn't seen between them before. He suddenly looks young in my eyes, much younger than Nathan. I had never wondered how old he is. He's tall and big and it never occurred to me that he wasn't the same age as Nathan. Sam runs a hand through his hair, his body emanating anxiety like I've never seen on him before. He whispers a 'fuck' and turns around to face the wall as he paces the room. I wish I could do the same. The scene in front of me will haunt me forever.

Rose taps the table blindly with a trembling hand, looking for the pen not far from her head.

"I-I can't see," she squeaks in pain and fear as her hand wraps around the pen.

He pulls at her head, straightening her on her knees and she grabs the paperwork, shaking.

I want to scream at her to not do it because that's what Jake would do, but just like her I want this to be over, and if signing is what it'll take then so be it.

She signs as quickly as possible and he lets go of her, patting the top of her head.

"Good choice," he taunts.

She gets back up, raging. "I hate you," she spits at him. "Enjoy this, because next time, I won't miss."

He smiles at her in all his power. "I'm shaking with fear," he says calmly.

He grabs his phone and asks for an ambulance to the house. He mentions a home invasion and hangs up after giving the address.

"Fuck everything up," he orders Carlo and Roy and they both go out, coming back with a bat each.

"Nathan! You've done enough," I fume. I pull at the ropes with rage but none of them move in the slightest. He comes back to me and tips my head up with a strong hand.

"I want to take you upstairs and fuck you, can we keep the ropes?"

The mixed reactions in my body make me sick. I hate him, I've never hated someone as much as I do now. My boyfriend, the love of my life, is lying unconscious on the floor and that's because of him. He's dangerous, his moral compass is broken, *he's* broken. And he breaks everyone around him for fun.

But my muscle memory doesn't care about all of this. It remembers the way he made my body feel and squirm under him before. I shudder at his words. No, I don't want to be fucked by Nathan upstairs while downstairs, Jake is beaten up to an inch of his life and Rose was just coerced into signing her life away.

He leans down to put his mouth to my ear so that only I can hear him. "I'm taking your silence as a yes, beautiful."

"It's not," I groan, pulling harder at the ropes. "Untie me," I order.

"And then I can take you upstairs?"

"And then leave!" I shout with enough anger to make him retreat slightly.

"But then how am I meant to show you that you've made a huge mistake?" He rests a hand on my naked thigh, too close to my core. "You know when you give yourself to me, I'll make you feel so good, Jake will be a distant memory. It's only a matter of time." I tremble at his words.

"Get the fuck out of my house, fucking creep," Rose's cold voice breaks the eye contact between me and Nathan.

He straightens up and looks down at me with a knowing smile. When he turns to Roy and Carlo, they start executing his orders. One breaks a lamp with the bat while the other starts hitting the TV.

"What the fuck," Rose shrieks. "Nate!" She goes to grab Carlo's arm, but Sam grabs her by the waist and lifts her up easily. He pulls her away, caging her with his massive form.

"Leave it," he orders.

"Stop! Let go. This has nothing to do with us!"

The panic in her stare as she turns her eyes to her older brother breaks my heart.

"You already got what you wanted," she protests in a broken voice. Her eyes fill with tears but as usual, none of them fall. "Nate, please," she whispers in defeat. "They only wanted to take care of us. They're good people."

His smirk is bright as he walks to Sam and her, putting a hand on her cheek. "And we're not, Ozy. You got a taste of the good life, but it's not for us. Time to get back to reality."

By the time the ambulance siren rings down the street, the Diaz brothers are finished with the whole ground floor of the house, Rose is sitting on the floor in a corner of the room, Sam standing in front of her, so she doesn't even think of making a move. My eyes are strained, trying to look for the uneven rise and fall of Jake's chest. The four men make their way out calmly, not without Nate telling Rose to bring the signed papers to Bianco by the end of tomorrow.

"Make sure he doesn't put blood on them," he chuckles. "Oh, and you know the names to give for the home invasion."

She nods in response and they all leave without looking back.

Rose unties me before the ambulance comes in and I jump up, ready to run to Jake but I fall suddenly, and she catches me just before I hit the ground.

"My legs are dead." I look up at her in panic.

"You'll be fine," she whispers back to me, running a hand up and down my back.

I think this is her attempt at being reassuring. I sit back down on the chair and try to wiggle my legs as much as possible until they feel like I can stand again.

There are multiple knocks on the door until we overhear the police forcing their way in. Rose is on Jake, trying to talk to him and making sure he is still responding. He's talking to her, but I can't discern his words. All I hear is her broken voice.

"I'm so sorry, I had to," she repeats for the second time. "I had to sign."

A police officer shouts to put her hands up when they barge into the living room. First responders are following closely. Rose slowly gets up, but she doesn't put her hands up. "I live here, asshole."

I can understand the confusion. She's hunched over a beaten body, wearing tight black jeans and a tight black turtleneck. She has the typical burglar look on her right now.

383

Jake is put on a stretcher and they take him away. I will my legs to work and I start running after them while another police officer talks to Rose. I can hear her insults and overhear him ask if she's inebriated or under the influence.

I run into the cold night in Jake's t-shirt and reach the ambulance just before they close the door.

"I'm coming," I shout. The condensation from my breath in the night air makes me realize I'm shivering, bare legs, only wearing Jake's large tee and nothing else. I extend a shaking hand to hold onto something and get in, but the medic gets in the way.

"This is an emergency, miss, and we can't take minors in here with us. We're going to the Silver Falls ER, you can meet him there."

"I-but...I need to be with him." My bottom lip trembles at the thought of being separated when he's in this state.

Another medic comes forward. "Miss, I'm gonna need you to step back so we can leave. This is for his safety."

I take a step back automatically and watch as the ambulance drives away, the flashing light and siren making it look surreal. I take another step back when it hits me that I'm not actually a minor. Tonight, I'm eighteen.

Happy Birthday to me.

CHAPTER 21

The One – Chainsmokers

Jamie

"They wouldn't let me in," I exclaim as Rose comes out of the front door. The police have just left warning her to not drive in her condition – Drunk? High? In shock? – and she's hurrying to her car in the garage.

"I know," she says almost out of breath. "I'm going now." She opens the door to her Bentley.

"Great, I'm coming with you."

She freezes and turns to me, a hand on top of the car door. "You should stay here," she declares.

She throws something on the passenger seat and gets in the car. As she goes to close the door, I put a hand on it.

"Are you joking? I'm coming!"

She sighs and runs a hand through her hair. "Jamie, this... " She looks around and back at me. "You need to give us a minute. Stay here."

I'm gobsmacked by her reaction. "Rose, surely you can't

expect me to…" My gaze wanders and stops on whatever she threw on the passenger seat. "Is that the form? You're bringing it to him? Are you expecting him to sign because you have?"

"What?" She turns around and realizes what I'm talking about.

I can see she's refraining herself from rolling her eyes at me. I'm not following fast enough and it's pissing her off. How can I understand what's going on? I'm in way over my head.

"I'm just not leaving them for anyone to find. This is pure gold to Bianco, and I can't trust anyone with it."

"Not even me?" I ask, incredulous.

There's a long pause but she finally admits, "You're his girlfriend, not mine, and no, you're not on my list of people I trust."

"What the hell is your goal here? You don't want to let me see him, you don't want to leave the paperwork with me. You know perfectly well if this ends up in the same room as Jake he will sign them. He would never let you move to Nathan's on your own."

"My *goal* is checking that my brother is alive and not leave my fucking life on a paper with the girl that used to date the *other* brother, who just coerced me into making him my legal guardian. Maybe that makes a little more sense to you now?"

I let out a shocked scoff. "You don't trust me because I dated Nathan? That was before I knew of any of this mess, surely you can't still hold me accountable for this!"

"That would be easier to do if you didn't get all wet and bothered when Nate's around. Now get your hand off my car." Her tone doesn't leave me a choice. It's dark and deep. Like the growl from a guard dog protecting its property.

I retrieve my hand, shocked at what she said. I've spent the last few weeks trying to figure out what she thought of me. If the little comments here and there were really aimed at me or if that's just who she is. Now I know; she doesn't like me. She doesn't like that I went from Nathan to Jake and worse, she caught on to my shame from earlier.

I run back inside the house to find my phone. It's a mess. Not only the situation, the house as well. Roy and Carlo have turned the beautiful mansion into a slum. Mirrors are broken, furniture destroyed, floors soiled.

I find my phone on the bed in the guest room and look at the Ubers. I don't care if Rose doesn't want me there, she has no right to put herself between Jake and me. As soon as I open the app, I understand how naïve I am. It's New Year's Eve and there are no cars available. Usually there are not many cars. Stoneview is small and people rarely need taxis or Ubers since they all have their own drivers.

I let myself fall on the bed and dial the only person I know will help me no matter what. Again, my hopes fall to nothing when Emily's voicemail talks back to me.

"Fuck!" I rage, hating my mom for never teaching me to drive and myself for not being able to afford a driving test.

In the following hour, I try Chris and Luke but none of them pick up. The lines are crowded with everyone calling each other for the new year. I text Rose countless times, call her but all I get in reply is a text: 'he's fine'. That was ten minutes ago. I try Uber again but there's nothing.

Another hour passes by of me pacing the room. I tried the only cab company in Stoneview. They laughed in my face. I want to clean the house for them, but I don't know where to start. I settle on the kitchen because I can't put a foot in the living room without seeing Jake on the floor.

I sweep broken glass, clean up the floor, and wash the walls where they threw food. I do my best but it's still clear that the room has been messed up. I check my phone and sigh. Another night I'm going to spend wide awake waiting for Jake to show up. The night at the police station and the whole day waiting for him to come back from D.C. was a nightmare. It was something I thought we'd never have to go through again.

I was wrong, it was only the beginning.

I go back up to the bedroom and lay down on the bed. There is nothing to do but wait and it's the worst part. I grab Jake's phone on the nightstand and look at it again. There are countless texts and DMs from people wishing him a happy new year, but one catches my eyes particularly.

Cam: Happy New Year, baby

Cam: You're missing a great party...

The second text has a picture attached and I want to smash the phone against the wall. How can she still send nudes to him after everything he said to her?

Should I reply to her? Should I send back a picture of me? Or even better, a picture of Jake and me?

No, Jamie.

Jake is at the ER and I'm thinking of his ex. What is wrong with me tonight?

I'm about to put the phone down next to me when it starts vibrating in my hand. The name 'Rachel' appears on the screen and I look at it in confusion before picking up. I don't have time to say hello when Rachel's panicked voice reaches through the phone.

"*J–Jake, she did it again,*" she says in a tight voice. "*Oh my God, you need to pick her up, I can't take her to mine like this.*"

"Rachel, it's Jamie, Jake isn't here."

There's a pause before I hear Rachel whisper 'shit'.

"*Are you at theirs?*"

I nod before saying yes.

"*I'm on my way. I'll go straight to the pool house.*"

I'm about to reply but she's already talking to someone else.

"*Baby...I'm here. Please stay with me. We're going home,*" Rachel sobs on the other end of the phone. I want to assume she's talking to Rose. It has to be or why would she call this number. But Rose was meant to be at the hospital with her brother. Why isn't she?

"Is everything okay?" I ask.

"*Run a cold bath. I'll be there in five.*"

She hangs up and I jump out of bed to run to the pool house. I start filling up the tub with cold water. It's barely halfway when I hear the door open. I run to the doorway and watch in shock as Rachel passes the door, struggling to hold Rose up.

"What happened?" I gasp. Images of Nathan hitting her run through my head, but she doesn't look like anyone touched her.

Rose's head is hanging in front of her and she's mumbling incoherent words.

"Help me take her to the bathroom," Rachel hurries me, her voice drowning in concern.

I grab Rose's other arm even if my height makes it that I'm barely any help for her. We take her to the bathroom and

Rachel doesn't hesitate one second, she helps her in the cold bath with her clothes on.

"What's wrong? What happened to her?"

Rachel takes the shower jet and makes sure the water is freezing cold before running it over Rose's head. She's barely conscious and Rachel has to hold her head.

"She-she took too many pills. She drank too much. Who knows what other shit she ingested this time."

"This time?" I choke.

"Here, hold this," she says as she gives me the shower jet. She pushes strands of her blond hair away from the face. Her pale blue eyes keep drifting back to Rose as she talks to me.

"Me? Why?" I panic.

"Because I have to leave. My little sister's babysitter was meant to leave two hours ago, and my parents aren't home."

"Can't she take care of herself," I insist, not wanting to end up with this responsibility.

"She's one!" Rachel fumes.

"Right, okay. I didn't know, I'm sorry." I hold Rose's head and keep showering her hair with freezing water.

"She'll be fine. Keep doing this for another two minutes. Take her clothes off but don't dry her, just put her to bed. Stay with her, she might vomit more. She'll be fine in the morning, she already puked most of what she took."

"How many times has this happened before?" I ask as Rose moans a complaint under my hands. I pull away the jet to listen, but she doesn't say anything else, so I put it back.

"This is the third time. Jake usually takes care of her. I have no idea where he is. She left the party and came back more upset than I've ever seen. She drank, took pills with Ciara, and disappeared. I don't know what happened after that. She's going to be fine though. Right, baby?" Rachel coaxes as she leans down to brush Rose's hair behind her ears. "Promise me you'll be fine."

Rose nods but she's not in control of her movements. The only whispers that come out of her mouth are 'I'm sorry' and 'I love you' on repeat.

Rachel lets her forehead fall on Rose's. "I love you too," she whispers. "I'll see you tomorrow."

"Thank you, Jamie," she admits before leaving. "I owe you one."

She disappears and I turn back to the mess in my hands. How could tonight get even worse?

When I feel like Rose is slightly coming back, I stop the water.

"Are you alright?" I ask quietly. She doesn't reply. "Let's get you out of the bath, you'll freeze."

I put both my arms under her armpits and help her up. I pull to get her out but she's too tall and we both fall to the bathroom floor. My head hits the tiles, and I stay there for a beat before I come back to reality.

"Shit," Rose mumbles as she rolls to the side.

"You're heavier than you look," I rasp as I go back to a standing position to help her up. I help her walk to her room and she falls on her bed.

"You need to get out of these clothes," I huff as she curls into a ball.

She lets out an annoyed groan and twists and turns until she's out of her jeans. There's a tattoo on her left hip that I'd never seen before. A small heart with an even smaller 'S' in it. It's so miniature, I have to look at it twice to discern what it is.

"I can't get this off," she blurts as she fights with her wet, tight turtleneck.

I help her out of it not without having to fight her to get it off her head. I take a step back, my breaths short from the exercise, and when my gaze grazes over her body my heart stops.

"Rose," I squeak in complete disbelief.

Her belly, her torso, her arms, they're covered in bruises and welts. All the way to her wrists. Her forearm tattoos look strange with the yellow-ish bruises fading on them. I can clearly see they stop above her black, lace shorties and they don't go under her lace bra. She's got some other tattoos on her ribs, but they all look distorted with the different colors of her battered skin.

"What happened?" I panic.

She groans a 'shut up' and turns to her side, grabbing a pillow to hug it. Her back is just as bad as the front. Some bruises have already faded but some others are still purple.

"Rose," I shake her shoulder. "Who did this to you? Was it Nathan? Samuel?"

She laughs and lays on her back again.

"What do you know about them, Goody? Except that Nate makes you feel all sorts of things. You don't know shit." She huffs and runs a hand on her face. "Ugh, I feel sick as fuck."

"Do you need to throw up?"

"No," she growls. "I just want to sleep. No more questions." Her words are slurred, and I don't want to push it.

"Rachel said not to leave you alone," I hesitate, shifting on my feet.

"Then get into bed and let me sleep," she says tartly.

I wait a few seconds, checking if she's for real and when she turns around, hugging her pillow, I understand she doesn't care if I stay or leave. I get under the covers with her and stay far from her.

After a whole minute of silence, I finally ask what I've been dying to know. "I need to ask you if Jake is okay."

She moves and I think she's about to reply but she suddenly sits up, grabs the vase on her nightstand, and pukes into it. I shoot up, shift over to her side, and hold her hair back, patting the top of her head.

"It's okay," I murmur. "Rachel said it might happen."

When she finally stops, I run to the bathroom to get her a cloth and I grab a bottle of water from the fridge.

"Here," I say softly as I hand her the bottle. She struggles to grab it from my hands, so I tilt it to her mouth and help her drink. She mumbles something but I don't get it. I feel like she's worse than when she went to bed.

"Are you okay?" I quiz. She tries to lift her head to talk to me, but her chin falls back to her chest straight away.

She mumbles something and I lean down to listen. "I didn't hear you," I admit.

"What would you do to gain back control over your body?" she asks, and I frown in confusion.

"What do you mean?" I put the bottle of water on her nightstand.

"Nothin'," she slurs. She lets herself fall back on the mattress but she either said too much or not enough.

I escape to the bathroom for barely a minute to clean the vase. I don't want to leave her alone too long.

When I walk back in she's in the exact same position.

"Rose...you can talk to me. What did you mean exactly?"

She opens and closes her eyes multiple times, looking at

393

the ceiling.

"I've got no control over my life, Goody. I never did. But the worst is not having control over my body. It hurts. And I don't want to hurt. So I'm left with trying not to feel anything."

This is the clearest sentence she's managed to form until now.

I sit on the bed next to her and put a gentle hand on her forearm. "Who did this to you?"

She snorts sarcastically and eyes me before looking back at the ceiling.

"Mateo," she attests, her eyes fixed on an imaginary spot above us.

There is no hesitation, no lie. Just the cold, hard truth. I grimace at the revelation and my eyes uncontrollably fill with tears.

"He did it for five years," she keeps going. "Every time we were alone. But it was worse this time because I ran away." She explains this like it's logical. A worse punishment for running away from abuse.

I'm lost for words. My hand slides down from her arm to her hand and I squeeze it like my life depends on it.

"Why?" I manage to push out of my tight throat. I'm willing my tears not to fall. This is not about me, this is her pain.

"He wants to marry me one day. But..." she scratches her throat, and I can hear that she struggles with the rest. It's like her tough act has gone, her defenses have fallen. "He has ways he prefers, with everything." Another pause. "He likes to inflict pain."

I feel sick to my stomach at her words. She doesn't need to explain. I understand in which ways he likes to inflict pain.

"And he wants his wife to like his ways," she adds. She

starts laughing but it's a crazy one. "I don't." She scratches her throat again and the next words come out so pained, I don't think I've ever heard this kind of pain in my life. Her gaze doesn't leave the ceiling. "So he teaches me," she whispers like it's a secret no one should know. "But I don't want to. I don't want to be his wife and I don't want to enjoy pain." She takes a deep, shaky breath. "It's agony," she chokes on her words and I can't stop my tears from falling.

This is a horror story. This is the most awful thing I've ever heard in my life. I can't help a sob as I fall back on the bed. She's squeezing my hand back so hard it hurts but I want it all. All her pain, all the bruises, and the things she keeps inside. We're now both looking at the ceiling, the only light in the room is the one coming from the bulb in the hallway.

"Rose...you can't go back," I plead.

"How?" she sniffles. "He really thinks he's going to marry me. He believes it so *so* deeply. He's *obsessed*, Jamie."

I feel cold sweats breaking out all over my body as I'm about to ask the worst question I could think of.

"Has he ever..." I have to pause, not finding the courage to say it out loud.

"No. Only bruises. Always my arms and my stomach or my back. The rest has only ever been promises and threats." She laughs again. "The fucker actually believes that it's fine if he waits for marriage. He's forcing himself to wait until I'm eighteen."

I choke on air as I try to take a deep breath. This can't be possible. Not here, not in this day and age. I feel like I've lived in a fairytale my whole life and Rose's experience is shattering it all.

I think she hears me sob because she squeezes my hand

again. I can't believe what I'm hearing.

"It won't happen though," she reassures me. She must sense my confusion and she keeps going after a brief pause. "I'll be gone before he can put his plan in action."

"Gone?" I ask. "What do you mean?"

She ignores my question and I feel her shifting until her head rests on my chest.

"You smell like Jake," she giggles like a little girl and it sounds nothing like her. She never sounds like a little girl because she never got to be one. Bianco stole her childhood from her.

I understand that this topic is over and when she says Jake's name, my heart picks up. I wonder if she can hear it with an ear so close to it.

"Jamie, what I just told you," she shifts in awkwardness, "I've never told anyone."

"No one? Not even Chris?"

"No one. Not Chris, not even Jake. If you say anything, I'll deny it." Her words sadden me even deeper. She's never shared her pain with anyone.

"We'll find a way. I won't let you go through this," I promise her.

She chuckles and I know she doesn't believe me, but I do.

"He's fine by the way," she admits. I can't help the sigh that leaves me. "He was already awake when I arrived. He broke a finger. Out of everything, all he had was a minor concussion, a broken thumb, and a couple of fractured ribs. Can you fucking believe it? His nose is bad, but not broken. He'll be out before the morning."

"Is that why you left? Because he was fine?" I know that's not why, but I would like to hear the real reason.

She grabs my hand and puts it on her head, making me understand she wants me to stroke her hair. I do so before she starts talking again.

"He was so mad because I signed. He didn't want to see me. He asked me to leave the papers with him and leave him alone."

"What is he going to do?"

I feel her shoulders shrugging close to my ribs and I don't ask for more. Jake is fine. I can talk to him tomorrow.

Tomorrow, I'm going to see Jake, we're going to destroy the paperwork, burn Rose's signature. We're going to talk to someone about this, maybe not the police but at least the Murrays. Rose might not want to talk to anyone about what Mateo does to her, but I can still try to help in other ways. Tomorrow, we'll find a solution to all of this. For now, we need rest and Rose's even breathing on my body is lulling me to sleep.

I startle awake at the sound of the pool house door closing. Rose wakes up slowly as we hear Chris and Luke's voices in the living room.

"Shit," she mumbles.

She gets up in a rush and grabs an oversized sweater from a chair. I had completely forgotten I fell asleep with her half-naked body on mine. She groans when she opens the curtains and the light hits. "Fucking...fuck."

"Are you okay?" I ask. I can't help my gaze from going to her bruises again.

"I'm fine," she huffs as she puts the sweater on. She catches me watching. "As long as you don't repeat whatever bullshit I said to you yesterday. It's blurry but it was probably a lie, I do that a lot."

I nod to reassure her. It almost makes me smile to hear Rose being back to her rude self. I will never forget what she told me yesterday and I know it was the truth no matter what she says now. Her opening up to me was the first step toward getting both her and Jake out of trouble.

She heads out of the room and I follow. When I walk into the living room, she's already explaining what happened to Chris and Luke.

"Jake called me from the hospital," Chris explains. "He said he was on his way back and to not worry about him, but that was two hours ago."

"He'll be fine," Rose says as she grabs a cigarette from her pack. "I need to show you something," she grimaces.

I can't describe the pain on Chris' face when he sees the state of his house. Rose keeps repeating that she's sorry, but he knows it's not hers or Jake's fault. When we walk out of the main house and back to the pool house, I realize the time.

"It's eleven, where's Jake?" I ask.

We all walk back into the pool house and I almost faint in relief. My heart picks up, I feel lightheaded, and a small giggle leaves my mouth.

"Jake," I sigh in relief as I run to him.

He's standing by the kitchen counter. His nose is swollen, both his eyes sporting black bruises below them, his forehead has a big, inflamed bump on it. I stop dead in my tracks, right in front of him, by fear of hurting him. He's got a cast around his left thumb and leading to his wrist. I don't want to make anything worse.

"How are you feeling? Is your head okay?"

He simply nods at me but doesn't make any effort to kiss

me or touch me.

He just got out of the hospital. He was beaten up.

I shake any wrong ideas out of my head, especially the red flag reminding me of Camila's text yesterday, but something feels off.

He keeps his right hand in his jeans pocket and keeps his back against the counter, his head held high.

"I'm fine," he mumbles dismissively.

I feel Rose settling behind me. "Where is it?" she asks in her gravelly voice.

His jaw ticks. "Where do you think?" he replies coldly. "In Mateo's hands. With both our signatures on it."

My mouth falls slack. "Y-you signed?" I question, puzzled.

"Ozy signs. I sign," he shrugs. "He knew it would only take one of us." He looks at me and back at Rose. "Thanks, by the way."

"What did you expect me to do?" she growls. "You were dying on the floor, he wouldn't call an ambulance unless I did it."

"It doesn't matter. What's done is done. We have to move in before school starts again."

"What?" Rose chokes. "That's like, less than two weeks!"

Jake shrugs, he walks past me and his sister and into the hall before disappearing in his room.

Rose turns to Chris in complete disbelief. "What are we gonna tell your parents?" she asks.

Chris shakes his head in defeat, lost for words. The pain in his eyes is breaking my heart. That's his siblings, leaving him for another household.

"We'll figure something out," Luke jumps in. "For now, you guys should rest."

Both Chris and Luke leave the pool house and Rose turns to me. "He's being stubborn. You should talk to him. I'll be in the main house." She leaves and I turn to the hallway.

Something doesn't feel right, and I'm scared to talk to Jake.

My stomach churns as I walk into his room and find him standing by his closet, topless. He doesn't turn around or acknowledge me, so I walk to him and put a hand on his shoulder.

"Jake," I whisper. "Are you okay?"

He dismisses my hand in a shoulder movement and pauses before turning around. I can see in his eyes that he's not the Jake who's desperately in love with me. The blue is dark, dangerous and his irises are hiding demons I'm not sure I want him to let out.

"Talk to me," I insist. "I love you, please talk to me."

He doesn't say it back. Instead, he takes a dangerous step forward, forcing me to take one backward. The toxic energy emanating from him is pushing me to put distance between us.

"You do love me, don't you?" he grunts.

"Of course I do. I thought that much was obvious."

The evil smirk that slowly displays on his lips sends a shiver down my back.

"Turn around and put your hands behind your back."

"Jake," I huff as my stomach twists in anticipation. "I know how you must be feeling right now but I don't think this is the solution. Control is not everything."

"Do it for me, Angel. I need this."

I swallow the lump in my throat, taking a minute or so to think about it. Slowly, I turn around and put my hands behind my back. It's not like this doesn't get me wet. I just wish he also learned to deal with problems another way.

I hear him unbuckling his belt and feel the leather slithering and wrapping around my wrists. It's all fairly loose until one last tug brings everything crashing together in tightness.

"Bend over," he whispers in my ear. His breath on my skin brings pleasure tingling all the way down.

I start leaning over, but his patience runs short, and he pushes a strong hand on my back until my cheek hits the mattress.

"I'd love for you to choke on my cock right now, but I don't think I can wait to bury myself inside you."

His crude words have my panties dampened before the end of the sentence. Said panties disappear in a split second as he slides them down to my knees. Two fingers slide between my folds and a moan escapes my lips.

"This one is for me. Don't come."

He enters me in one hard stroke, and I gasp in shock. I'm stretched beyond limits and the sting lasts slightly longer than usual.

"I wasn't ready," I whimper, but everything turns into pleasure as he starts moving, and my heavy breaths quickly stop me from talking.

Jake grabs his belt by my wrists and uses the pull to slam harder inside me. The scream that leaves my throat is a mix of pure bliss and pain.

"Calm down," I pant as he pushes harder and deeper.

"Shut up," he orders. Another wave of pleasure surrounds me as he pulls away slightly to avoid being too deep or hurting me. I'm reassured to see he still listened to me. "Why can't you just take it like a good girl, huh?"

I feel myself tightening at his words and the mix of tingles and shivers brewing in my lower belly is ready to ignite me any second. I'm a second away from exploding when I suddenly feel him tighten his hold in a loud grunt and slam one last time. He slows down until he freezes and suddenly pulls out.

"What the-Jake!" I complain.

This is the worst teasing he's ever done to me. I have never been so ready to come and have it pulled away. Not when he's already inside me.

He pats my back condescendingly and I hear his zipper. "I told you that one was for me."

He releases my wrists and I turn around, flushed and embarrassed.

"I thought you meant it as a joke or some sort of game," I say as I cross my arms over my chest.

He didn't even bother taking my top off. I feel his cum running down my legs and I'm surprised he still hasn't gone to get me something to clean myself up. I realize it's not in his plans when he goes back to his closet to pick a t-shirt. I grab a towel hanging from his desk chair and clean myself in a hurry. Anger is boiling inside me no matter how calm and understanding I'm trying to be.

"Jake," I snap as I pull my underwear back up. "Can you stop pretending like I'm not here? What the hell is going on?"

He turns to me, his face stoic and his eyes emotionless. "Have you got any clothes here?"

"Probably," I reply confused. "They're in my bag in the main house." I shake my head to refocus. "Can we sit down for a second and think about what's important here?" I insist. "You're acting weird."

"Yeah, you're right. We should talk."

My heart skips a beat before going into a frenzy. "We should talk?" I repeat in a shaky voice. "Why do you sound like you're breaking up with me?" I mock, half-joking, half-anxious.

"Because I am." His voice is cold, heartless. It's not sad or angry. It holds no regret or apologies. It's a matter of fact.

"What?" I scoff. An anxious chuckle escapes my mouth and this time I'm the one walking toward him. "What are you saying?"

"I'm saying that I'm fucking bored." The words stab me like a sharp knife and my chest constricts uncontrollably.

"Don't lie," I fume. "You love me."

He laughs and it freezes my blood. "I *said* I loved you, Goody. I was feeling charitable, it doesn't mean I'm actually in love with you. How many times do you think I told Camila I loved her? Get real for a second, will you?"

My jaw drops and tears prickle at my eyes. That fucking nickname is back on his lips and I know he's lying. He couldn't possibly have lied for weeks and played me. Something happened between yesterday and now and he won't tell me what.

"You're lying," I force the words out. "What did Nathan say? Or was it Bianco? You're pushing me away, Jake, but you don't have to. You don't have to protect me, you don't have to keep me away from this."

I take another step towards him, but his hard stare stops me in my tracks.

"Listen, I don't need to lie. You were a cute little virgin and I needed something to distract myself. Thanks for your services but let's both go back to our own lives now. Honestly, I had fun, but you and I can't really be a long-term thing. We both knew that when it started."

"Jake," a single tear falls down and I quickly wipe it away.

"You're hurting me. If you keep pushing, you'll lose me. I'm not joking around."

He laughs again. "You're hurting? It's a breakup, Goody. It's not exactly meant to be all fun and games."

"Why are you doing this? Please, talk to me," I implore.

He starts walking around in the room and grabs my phone and coat. "Look, you're embarrassing yourself. I really think you should leave. I want to say sorry but then again, you should have known what you were getting yourself into. Maybe next time, don't be so naïve when it comes to boys." He passes me my stuff and looks around the room. "Take your time to get your stuff, I'll be in the living room."

I put on a pair of leggings and wait a few moments, gathering my thoughts before I walk into the living room. I thought I'd take the time to calm down, but the rage is getting worse.

"So is this how it goes with you? You fuck me one last time before telling me to get my shit and go?" I seethe.

He gets up from the sofa and chuckles. "I wasn't exactly gonna say 'bend over for your last fuck' was I?"

The slap that lands on his cheek is so powerful that I wonder for a second if it was actually from me but the sting in my palm doesn't leave any doubt. He winces, probably because he's already covered in bruises.

"Fuck you," I spit at him.

I didn't hear the door open, but I hear Rose's hoarse voice loud and clear. "What the actual fuck is going on in here?"

"What is going on?" I fume. "Your asshole of a brother is too much of a coward to tell me why he's pushing me away. He'd rather act like the fuckboy he truly is and break-up. What a fucking solution."

"You're breaking-up?" she asks him in disbelief. "What's

wrong with you?"

"I don't have to justify myself to either of you. You should leave, Jamie. And please delete my number."

"Whoa, did I just open the door to asshole-town? What are you doing, Jake?"

I can feel Rose's anger and I appreciate it, but all I want to do is leave. If Jake wants us to be over, so be it. I'll cut it short. I try to walk past Rose, but she keeps a hand on the door handle and doesn't move out of the doorway.

"Jake, seriously, what is this?" she asks again.

"Fuck, Ozy. I don't intervene every time you change guys, do I? You want her so bad, you have her then. She can go through the whole family for all I care but I want her out of my house."

His words make me feel sick to my stomach. My chest is so tight I feel like I'm choking, and I can't control the tears. I give Jake another look, trying to find any sign that he doesn't mean what he's saying, any sign that he's about to tell me that he can't do it, he can't break up with me.

But there's nothing.

There's no love and there's no hatred.

There's no desire and no disgust.

His eyes have lost the spark they used to shine with when I was around. Now, there's only indifference. And that's the worst of them all.

Jake takes three big steps towards me and Rose. He grabs his sister by the arm and pulls her out of the way. He has no idea he's pinching already existing bruises that Bianco put there. "Do you have to get in the way of everything?" he growls at her.

"You're hurting me, asshole," she snarls.

405

"Yeah, well I'm trying to get her to leave and you're in the way. Now, Jamie, if you don't mind."

I realize this is it and I look at him one last time. "This is not how it was meant to be, Jake. I love you," I try in a desperate last attempt.

I might look ridiculous, and this might be the most humiliating moment of my entire life, but it turns out, I can't let this go. The moment I close this door, it's over and I'm not ready for that. I can't let him go. I can't live without our moments together, without his smile and kisses. I've given him my whole heart and my life is nothing without him. I shouldn't have, but I did. He became my entire life and I have nothing if not for him.

"It wasn't meant to be any sort of way, Jamie. You were just another name on the list."

I can't take any more. I put one foot outside and as soon as I pass the door, I run. I run so fast my heart is begging to be let out of my rib cage and my lungs are on fire, filled with thick smoke. I run until my feet hurt and my eyes stop crying. I run so much that my shoes feel useless, and my knees are ready to shatter. I know I've run more than four miles when I recognize my street.

I push one last time and reach my door. I feel like I haven't been here in ages.

I have no idea how long ago I last saw Jake, but it already feels like an eternity. I find my keys and take my time to open the door. Everything is going to feel so lonely. It already does.

Once inside, I close the front door and lean my back on it. I'm about to break down in cries again when a small noise makes me aware that I'm not alone in the house.

"Hello?" I say in a shaky voice. I take one step towards the kitchen.

I take another step toward the kitchen, my instincts warning me of imminent danger.

"Surprise!" Mom and Emily jump out from behind the counter as my heart almost stops in my chest. "Happy Birthday!" They both scream again.

"Mom?" I say as I struggle to comprehend what's happening.

"Jamie, sweetie, are you okay?" My mom asks as she rounds the counter to join me.

I can only shake my head 'no' as everything overwhelms me. She takes me in her arms, and I feel the weight of the last few months suffocating me.

"Where's everyone else?" I hear Emily behind my mom.

"Baby, what's wrong?" mom asks, her voice filled with concern.

But I can't reply. I'm crying so hard my sobs are choking me. She's here, with me, at the moment I need her the most and my heart swells with relief despite the sadness that's overtaken me.

My mom is back. That was my big surprise. She's back, I'm safe and Jake White broke my heart on my eighteenth birthday.

CHAPTER 22

Scars − Boy Epic

Five hours earlier . . .

Jake

"You made the right choice, brother," Nate murmurs as we wait to be invited into Bianco's office.

I didn't have much of a choice, I want to retort but I keep my mouth shut.

We're sitting on the two red velvet armchairs right outside his door, facing the opposite wall of the hallway. Nate went in a half an hour ago to give him the paperwork Rose and I signed, then came back out.

I'm fuming, fucking raging. There's havoc exploding in my head and my heart, but I keep still. The migraine beating against my skull is threatening to make me throw up every minute or so. My thumb is still sore despite the painkillers, my chest feels so fucking tight, and I can feel every single one of my ribs every time I take a breath. I can't even breathe through my swollen nose courtesy of my own flesh and blood.

And yet, that's not why I'm so angry.

Of course I'm angry at Nate. That's not news though, I've always hated him. I've hated him for so long it's like a dull ache in my heart that never ceases to exist.

But right now, I want to break every single one of Rose's bones. That's how angry I am at her. How could she do this to me? How could she sign? We expected Nate to threaten us. We expected him to bully us into signing and we both promised we wouldn't give in.

I have vague memories of last night. I remember Nate finding Jamie in the house and I remember her cries when they tied her up and she watched me get beaten up. Guilt twists in my guts for putting her through this. That's not how her senior year was meant to go. I burst into her life and fucked her tranquility. Tranquility she more than deserved after what she'd been through with her dad and brother.

Rose was there when I came back to reality, and I wish I never did. I couldn't face her, I couldn't talk to her, I couldn't tell her it was okay because it really wasn't. The way she apologized broke my heart. I know she was scared for my life, but I was still too mad to forgive her. It'll come. Just not now. Because of her, the first thing I did after being released from the hospital was come here. So here I am, 7:30 am, waiting for Bianco to let us into his office.

"Stop making this face, Jake. You would have done the same in her situation."

Can the fucker read my mind or something? I glance at Sam walking in circles, his phone to his ear. I can't see him properly because of my swollen eyelids and I can't hear what he's mumbling because of the ringing in my ears. I'm running purely on adrenaline right now and I could shut down any minute.

"That bastard isn't letting go, you know that?" Nate grumbles in the seat next to mine.

I'm not sure what he means but I know I'm about to understand when he gets up, annoyed. He walks to Sam and snatches the phone from his hand.

"I think you need to start taking my advice more seriously, *mate*. You and my sister are not a thing. You're never gonna be a thing so stop feeding her hope by checking on her every time you do something wrong," Nate says, exasperated.

"I just want to know she's alright," Sam growls after Nate gives him the phone back.

"I'll save you time. After what we did last night? Probably not."

There's only one thing Nate and I will ever agree on and that's that Sam is not an option for our sister. Not now, not ever. I don't even care how it sounds. It's not fucking happening. Nate is about to sit back down next to me when the door to Bianco's office opens to a petite blonde with big brown eyes.

"Boys, please come in," she tells us.

I walk in and Nathan follows.

"Anne," he purrs as he brushes her arm walking past her.

"Nathan," she replies in a sweet voice.

I roll my eyes as much as I can in my state. He fucks everything with legs and then dares trying to break me and Jamie up.

"Jake," Bianco chuckles, sitting on his pine green leather

chair. "You're a sight for sore eyes," he smiles, his voice dripping sarcasm.

I'm only capable of offering a chesty grunt in response. I prefer not to engage with him, he would love that too much. Nate takes a seat opposite his boss, but I can't sit down, it makes it too real.

"You should sit, son. This could take a while. Unless you're feeling extra compliant today?"

I take the seat next to Nate and wait in silence. I remember spending time here after the fights. If I won, he would open a bottle of champagne and incite me to drink. It didn't matter that I was thirteen. He would celebrate until the bottle was finished and I remember blacking out on the Persian rug covering the old parquet. If I lost...

I swallow the lump forming in my throat at the thought of how Bianco used to hit my already beaten body when I didn't bring the money from the fight back to him.

"Thank you for signing, Jake," he smirks then turns to Nate. "I just hung up with Gloria, she said she would go over the paperwork and send it to Judge Joly tomorrow. She is going to be busy with her family today. It is the new year after all."

The new year. Jamie's birthday. I didn't even get to wish her a happy eighteenth birthday, let alone give her a present.

"What was her daughter's name again?" Bianco asks.

"Emily," Nate replies straight away, and it brings my focus back onto the conversation.

"Right, don't let her forget that we know where *Emily* takes her precious dancing classes."

"What the hell could you possibly want with her?" I growl. I don't care for Emily like Luke does, but she is a close friend. She's Jamie's best friend and I wouldn't forgive myself if anything happened to her.

"That judge needs to know we don't forgive mistakes. Hopefully, she won't make any when she approves Nathan being your new legal guardian."

I shake my head slowly. Nate has been spying on us for months. He and Sam made sure to find out who our close friends are just so they could use everything and everyone against us.

"Onto important things, for both of you," Bianco says more seriously. He grabs something in the mahogany desk's drawer, opens a file, and slams it on the desk. "Do you know who this is?"

Nate barely glances down but I have to lean closer to see. No glasses, no contacts, swollen eyes. I still manage to see a CCTV picture of a man. His head is turned slightly to the side, looking somewhere on his right, but I can still see his face and it's familiar, though I couldn't place who he is if my life depended on it. He must be around the same age as Nate, barely twenty probably. The main element I'm guessing Bianco wants us to see is the tattoo on the side of his neck. The seven moons showing the phases of the satellite.

"Quite obviously a Wolf, but I'm guessing you figured that one out yourself," Nate smiles.

Bianco smiles back but he doesn't lose his focus. "This Wolf, boys," his finger jabs the picture, "is Aaron Williams." His smile turns smug when he adds, "I heard you both fucked his little sister, Jamie."

To be continued...

AFTERWORD

To be continued! Yes, I know…another cliffhanger. But this one isn't as bad as the first one, is it?

If you made it to the end, thank you from the bottom of my heart for sticking with me. If you've followed this series since the start, thank you for your continuous support and I hope you enjoyed the second book, the third one will be coming soon. If you've just entered the world of Stoneview, welcome to our crazy gang and thank you for taking a chance on me.

If you enjoyed the book please do rate it and leave a comment on Amazon and Goodreads. As an independent author, this means the world to me and they're the best support I could ask for. Your reviews can be one word, they're everything to an author!

Please, let's stay in touch! I love talking to you guys!

Instagram: @lolaking_author

Facebook Readers group: Lola's Kings

ACKNOWLEDGEMENT

It always makes me a bit emotional to think of all the people who support me and help me through the process of writing a book.

Maman, you will always be the first one I thank. You're my pillar, you're my first call when I break down, you're the reason I am me (the good and bad I'm afraid). I love you and I hope you will like your shoutout - if you know you know.

Maman, tu seras toujours celle que je remercie en premier. Tu es mon pillier, tu es mon premier appel quand je vais mal, c'est grace à toi que je suis qui je suis (le bon et le mauvais). Je t'aime et j'espère que tu apprecieras mon clin d'oeil – si tu sais tu sais.

Papa, thank you for your encouraging talks. I hope you know every time we have a call and you give me life lessons, they turn into quotes I keep close to me. I know you want me to be more confident with myself and I promise I'm trying, thanks to you. Every time we talk, I am reminded a little more that success is seeing pride in the eyes of the people we love.

Papa, merci pour tes encouragements. J'espère que tu sais que à chaque fois qu'on a une conversation et que tu me donnes des leçons de vie, je les transforme en citations que je garde près de moi. Je sais que tu veux que j'ai confiance en moi et je te promets que j'essaye grace à toi. A chaque fois qu'on parle je me rappelle que la réussite c'est de voir la fierté dans les yeux des gens qu'on aime.

Thank you, J. You're my biggest fan, my hype man, my everything. Thank you for bringing my confidence back up every time it crashes (so like every ten minutes). Thank you for helping me focus on myself rather than comparing myself to the rest of the world. Thank you for reminding me that as long as I write, everything else will be fine. I love you, you're my King, always and forever.

Estellou, thank you for always sharing the hype and for being a fan despite not even liking the books.

Thank you to Lauren, my alpha/editor. You know these books wouldn't be the same without you. You are an amazing alpha and person!

Gabby and Laura, you girls know I would not survive this community, or simply survive writing, without you. The way you help me and force me outside of my comfort zone is exactly what I need. Even if I complain about it.

Brittany, Katjana, Zoe, thank you queens for your invaluable help and support. I know I can always turn to you whenever I need and your kind words honestly mean everything to me.

Thank you to my AMAZING street team, who put up with my disappearances from social media, who are always there no matter what, ready to share and hype me up. Who are always there for a chat in our group. I just want us to have a big party together so I can love you in real life rather than through my phone!

Thank you Julia for your help and just taking over everything when the world scares me too much.

And I keep the best for last. Thank you to my readers. To every single person who gave this book a chance. This is all for you!

Made in United States
North Haven, CT
27 July 2022